喚醒你的英文語感 ！

Get a Feel for English !

喚醒你的英文語感！

Get a Feel for English !

雅思單字背完也沒多幾分？原因在於實際產出應用的字太少！

IELTS 高點

雅思制霸 7·0⁺字彙通

Meaning

Vocabulary for production

Context

Chunk

Spelling

Pronunciation

豐富例句用聽的！ MP3線上下載

作者 高點登峰 雅思教父
Quentin Brand (張昆廷)

Score higher than 7·0

閱讀主題文章　內化語境常用語

精熟字詞搭配　擴充各類應用字

理解常用語塊　確保語句正確性

釐清易混淆字　提升用字精準度

前言

本書的目標有三個：

① 教你一些字彙
② 教你學習字彙
③ 教你學會運用所學的字彙

也許你會覺得對一本字彙學習書來說，這三個目標不是理所當然的嗎？請仔細回想你所用過或翻閱過的一些字彙書，在收錄了成千上萬個單字及例句的情況下，當然可能達到 ① ② 兩個目標（如果你都背得起來的話），但坊間有多少字彙書能真正幫助你達成目標 ③ ？本書將跳脫傳統只羅列單字例句而不解說的學習方式，逐步帶領各位從閱讀雅思測驗高頻議題的文章開始，先掌握你已經會的精熟單字，再藉由字詞搭配擴充主題相關字彙量，最終目標是幫助大家除了在閱讀時能辨識字彙外，還能確實將所學字彙運用於口說或寫作中！

準備好要開始了嗎？

CONTENTS 目錄

PART 1
社會相關議題 Social Issues

PART 2
哲學相關議題 Philosophical Issues

淺談學習英文字彙

　　許多人在學習英文字彙時最大的難題不外乎「要學、要記的字實在太多了！哪裡學得完？」其實，換著角度看待學習字彙這件事，或許可帶給你不同的啓發。

　　基本上，每個人腦中的英語字彙都可區分成兩個群組。一組是認識並能夠在必須說話或書寫的時候產出，也就是能加以應用的單字；一組則是認識，並且在閱讀的文本中出現時可以辨識其含義的單字。一般來說，第一個群組的字約莫比第二個群組少三分之二。這是由於在大部分情況下，我們從事日常活動之際，通常會使用相同的字彙，因為我們會討論相同的話題，有相同類型的日常遭遇，以及每天使用相同的語言來與世界互動。而在閱讀文章或收聽播客 (podcast) 時，我們所遇到的單字和主題通常會比在日常生活中實際產出的要多得多。第一個群組的字可稱爲 **vocabulary for production**「產出字彙」，第二個群組的字可稱爲 **vocabulary for recognition**「辨認字彙」（見下圖）。

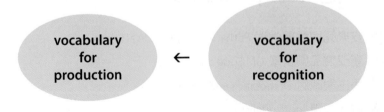

　　對 IELTS 考生或其他基於任何原因而想要提升字彙能力的人來說，最大的挑戰在於增進這兩個群組字之間的重疊，學習該如何「產出」原本只

能辨認的字彙，亦即學會如何運用更多的單字。

　　大多數人在學習字彙時，基本的方法就是把字彙表背起來。這對學習「辨認單字」非常有用，可是當想要把花了這麼多時間和努力所背起來的單字實際「產出」時，幫助就不大了。原因在於，這樣的單字表通常是聚焦於單一的字彙，然而使用字彙的重大原則是「單字從來都不是單獨運用」，此即 leximodel 背後的基本觀念，我們在下一節會作解釋。這也是本書背後的基本觀念，除了帶領讀者學習全新的單字，也要學會怎麼把單字從辨認組移到產出組，最終的目的就是讓每個認真學習這本書的人都能夠提升可運用的字彙量。

　　在學習新單字時，當然主要會聚焦在「意思」上：這個字在我的語言中是什麼意思？我能怎麼翻譯它？一般會認為，能翻譯單字也就能運用單字，這是人們會犯的第一個大錯誤！其實英文的字詞在華文中有直接對應的比各位所想的要少得多，只有像 dog 或 green 這樣非常基本表示物件的單字，在兩種語言中有直接的對應。但要是單字是關於感受或概念，或是更複雜的物件、感受和概念組合呢？類似的單字通常沒有跨語言直接對應的意思和用法，認為它們有便是個錯誤。

　　所以學習新單字意味著什麼？從以下圖示各位就能看出，知道如何運用一個單字所會牽涉到的一些元素。

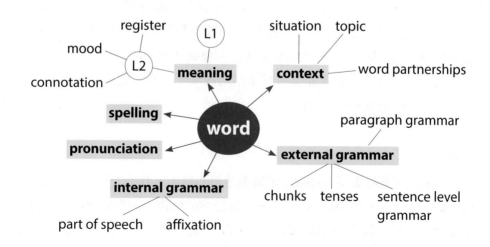

接下來，我們就逐一詳細地來看這些元素。

❏ Pronunciation 讀音

學單字當然需要知道單字的發音，尤其是想要在口說上運用的話。

❏ Spelling 拼寫

單字的拼法也是很重要的，尤其是想要在寫作上運用的話。

❏ Meaning 意思

學到一個新字當然會想要知道在華文 (L1) 中有沒有直接對應的字詞，以及那是什麼。大部分的人（和大部分的字典）都會就此打住。但是知道這個字詞在它本身的語言 (L2) 中是什麼意思是很重要的。我們必須學習它的 **connotation**「隱含義」──它有什麼情緒，它是肯定字、否定字還是中性字？以及 **register**「語域」──它是在學術或技術語境中使用的正式單字，還是在日常溝通中使用的非正式單字？

❏ Internal Grammar 內部文法

接下來是單字的內部文法。我們需要知道單字的詞性──它是名詞還是動詞、形容詞還是副詞、連接詞還是介系詞？這關係到單字的 **affixation**「詞綴」。所謂詞綴就是指為單字加上片段來改變詞性，例如加上 -ly 來把它變成副詞，或是加上 -tion 或 -ment 來把它變成名詞，加上 un- 或 im- 來把它變成否定。有時透過詞綴來改變單字的內部文法時，也會從根本上改變其字義，因此也改變了其用法。

❏ External Grammar 外部文法

外部文法意指緊接在關鍵字前後所使用的單字。我們則稱之為 **chunks**「語塊」。在下一節中將會對 chunks 做更詳盡的解釋。如果關鍵字是動詞，必須知道如何根據動詞屬於規則或不規則，來形成不同的時態。另外，我

們想學會單字或語塊是如何使用於句子中，所以需要知道句子的語法，在英文中就是主動賓 (SVO)。由於句子從來不會是單獨出現，而是會連同其他句子一起呈現，所以對於段落是怎麼運作也必須有一些概念。假如一個單字在段落中重複出現，則可以選擇使用同義字。

❏ Context 語境（即上下文脈絡）

單字不能脫離上下文語境而單獨使用。語境有兩種：當下的語言脈絡，例如單字所在的 chunk、句子、段落或文本，以及該文本或會話的主題。第二種語境是情境，尤其是在對話中。**word partnerships「字詞搭配」**在此變得很重要。同一個單字在不同主題中的字詞搭配會有所不同，例如在談論醫院和醫療話題時，我們或許會使用 emergency room，但若主題是法律和政治，我們則可能會使用 emergency law。一般來說，主題決定了字詞搭配，亦即字詞搭配取決於主題。在下一節中同樣會對 word partnerships 做更詳盡的解釋。

若想讓所學到的單字從只能「辨認」進階到能夠「產出」，就必須充分掌握以上元素。本書的目標就是要幫助各位做到這點。

📖 語言是由字串所構成 (the Leximodel)

在這個部分，我要向大家介紹 leximodel。leximodel 是我看待語言的方式，它是以一個很簡單的概念為基礎：

> **Language consists of words which are used with other words.**
> 語言是由字串所構成的。

這個看法非常簡單易懂。它的意思是：與其把語言看成文法和單字，與其學習個別的單字，然後再學習句型，我們認為語言是一群字或是字的組合，即語言是由字串所構成。

也就是說，有些字的組合比其他字的組合更容易預測。例如，我們可以預測到 listen 的後面永遠都會跟著 to，而不是 at 或 under 之類的其他字，所以我們可以說這個組合是完全固定的 (fixed)。另一方面，English 這個單字後面可接很多字，例如 gentleman、test、tea，所以很難預測接下來是哪一個字。我們可以說，這種組合是不固定的，它是流動的 (fluid)。

我們可以根據可預測度，把這些字串組合沿著以下的光譜來擺放：

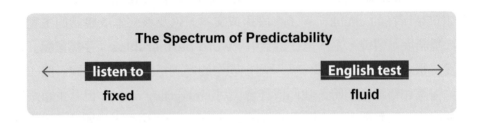

知道哪些字串組合是固定的，哪些是不固定的，可以讓你更快學習和使用英文。如果你學習的是一群字，而不是單一一個字，你的學習速度會更快，也會知道如何使用它們，因為這些字從來都不是單獨使用的。

我們可以把所有字串（稱之為 MWIs = multi word items）分為三類：chunks、set-phrases 和 word partnerships。由於中文裡沒有和這些詞相對應的概念，所以請直接記住它們的英文。讓我們更仔細看這三類字串，你很快就會知道，它們其實很容易理解和使用。

☑ Chunks

chunks 通常被我們當成文法的部分。chunks 通常很短，並且由 meaning words（有意義的字，如 listen、depend）和 function words（功能性的字，如 to、on）所組成。chunks 包含了不固定元素和固定元素。例如，我們可以改變動詞時態 (was listening to / have not been listening to)，但不能改變後面的 to 這個字。

你知道的 chunks 可能已經很多，卻不知道自己知道！我們來進行一個

任務，看看你是否明白我的意思。進行這個任務時，很重要的是不要先看答案，所以，請不要作弊！

Task 1 請閱讀這篇短文，把你找到的 chunks 畫上底線。

A chunk is a combination of words which is more or less fixed. Every time a word in the chunk is used, it must be used with its partner(s). Chunks combine fixed and fluid elements of language. When you learn a new word, you should learn the chunk. There are thousands of chunks in English. One way you can help yourself to improve your English is by noticing and keeping a database of the chunks you find as you read. You should also try to memorize as many as possible.

現在，請把你的答案和下列語庫做比較。如果你沒有找到那麼多的 chunks，請再看看你能不能找到語庫裡所有的 chunks。

… a combination of n.p. …	… thousands of n.p. …
… more or less …	… in English …
… every time v.p. …	… help yourself to V …
… be used with n.p. …	… keep a database of n.p. …
… combine s/th and s/th. …	… try to V …
… elements of n.p. …	… as many as possible …

- 注意，語庫中的 chunks 是用原形 be 來表示 be 動詞，而不是 is 或 are。
- 記錄 chunks 時，會在 chunks 的前後都加上 …（刪節號）。
- 注意，有些 chunks 的後面會接著 V、Ving、n.p.（noun phrase，名詞片語）或 v.p.（verb phrase，動詞片語）。關於這部分，你很快就會學到更多。
- 學習大量的 chunks 可以提升在寫作上的文法精準度。你將在這本書學到很多 chunks。

☑ Set-phrases

set-phrases 通常被當成組織或互動的部分。我們用 set-phrases 來完成工作,例如在餐廳點餐、在文章裡組織訊息。因為我們平常都用一樣的用語來做這些常見的事,所以 set-phrases 是更固定的 chunks。它們通常比較長,而且可能包含好幾個 chunks。chunks 通常是沒頭沒尾的片斷文字組合;set-phrases 則通常有個開頭或結尾,或是兩者都有,這表示有時候一個完整的句子也可能是一組 set-phrase。現在請看看下面的語庫並進行任務。

Task 2 請想想以下的 **set-phrases** 你是否曾在哪裡見過?把認識的打勾。

- ☐ I disagree with the view that v.p. …
- ☐ There are many reasons why I think so.
- ☐ I do not believe that v.p. …
- ☐ It's my opinion that v.p. …
- ☐ There are many ways to solve this problem.
- ☐ I (dis)agree with this, and think that v.p. …
- ☐ This essay will look at some of the common problems and will then suggest two solutions.
- ☐ I can think of two solutions to this problem.
- ☐ There are two/three main reasons.
- ☐ I firmly believe that v.p. …
- ☐ There's no doubt in my mind that v.p. …

- 注意,set-phrases 通常以大寫字母開頭,或用句點結束。這三個點 (...) 表示句子裡不固定的部分要開始了。
- 你可能已經在 IELTS 文章中看過這些 set-phrases。它們通常用來表達對一個議題的看法。
- 由於 set-phrases 是三類字串中最固定的一種,所以在學習時,必須非常仔細留意每個 set-phrases 的細節。稍後對此會有更詳細的說明。

- 有些 set-phrases 以 n.p. 結尾，有些以 v.p. 結尾。
- 學習大量的 set-phrases 可以彰顯你在寫作上組織想法的能力。在本書中將可學到很多 set-phrases。

☑ Word partnerships

　　word partnerships 是三類字串中最不固定，也就是流動性最高的一類。它是由兩個或更多的意義字（不同於 chunks 結合了意義字和功能字）所組成，通常是「動詞 + 形容詞 + 名詞」或是「名詞 + 名詞」的組合。word partnerships 會根據你寫的主題而改變，而 chunks 和 set-phrases 則可用於任何主題。現在，請進行下一個任務，藉此更清楚了解我的意思。

Task 3 請看下列各組 **word partnerships**，並判斷它們來自於哪一種主題內容。請從主題列表中選擇。

主題
A. acting and theatre　　　B. psychological experiments
C. the environment　　　　D. the history of cities
E. the law　　　　　　　　F. the life of whales
G. social media

word partnerships ①

natural resources / environmental pollution
global warming / carbon dioxide emissions
主題是（　　）

....

word partnerships ②

personal responsibility / conduct experiments / analyze results / collect data
主題是（　　）

....

word partnerships ③

social networks / social withdrawal / virtual reality game / addictive behavior

主題是（　　　）

··

• 請注意，word partnerships 包含意義，由兩個字組合而成，有時候甚至由三個或四個字組合而成。
• 學習大量 word partnerships 可以讓你精確使用字彙和表達你的想法。

➲ Task 3 答案：① C　② B　③ G

因此，我們最終版的 leximodel，現在看起來是這樣：

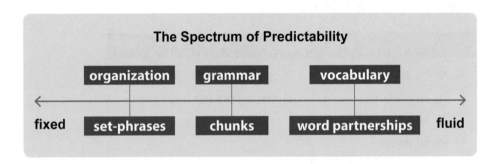

The Spectrum of Predictability

organization　grammar　vocabulary

fixed　set-phrases　chunks　word partnerships　fluid

　　這樣更接近語言在人腦中記憶和使用的習慣。如果你把重點放在學習 chunks，你的文法能力會提升，因為大多數的文法錯誤實際上是誤用了 chunks；如果你把重點放在學習 set-phrases，組織文章的能力會提升；而若是把重點放在 word partnerships，則使用詞彙的精準度會更高。

📖 如何使用這本書

　　本書由「社會」及「哲學」兩大範疇中，精選出十個重要議題作為單元主題。每個單元之學習內容規劃為七個部分：

❶ 閱讀文章

　　首先是主題式閱讀文章。Unit 1 到 Unit 5 是雅思必考之問題／解決方案 (problem/solution) 形式的文章，Unit 6 到 Unit 10 則是論證／意見 (argument/opinion) 形式的文章。再強調一次，字彙向來都是在一個主題的上下文脈絡中使用。本書閱讀文章除了是雅思測驗和其他測驗的常見主題外，Task 的設計也是為了培養讀者對英語文本組織的覺察力，尤其是每個段落是如何圍繞著主題句來組織。在此部分的練習會要求各位選出段落的主題句，接著除了提供中文翻譯供對照外，另提點段落構成的摘要，以凸顯「問題／解決方案」或「論證／意見」文章的組織。

　　閱讀文章中包含了每個主題相關的重要語彙，所以各位可以看到字彙是如何被使用在不同的語境當中。而藉由從文章中去找到所學習的語言項目，可以更加熟悉在該語境中所使用的語言，這種練習對學習非常重要，請不要跳過。

　　另外，閱讀文章是從最簡單的等級 (A2) 開始，逐步進階至最難的主題和文章 (C1) 上。若能按書中規劃的學習內容從第一單元開始仔細研讀到最後，各位將從 A2 進到 C1，約莫是雅思級數的 8 ～ 8.5。

❷ 字詞搭配

　　每個主題將精選 15 個關鍵名詞，並連同每個字的 word partnerships 和例句一起學習。這 15 個關鍵名詞是依單字在該主題中使用的頻率，以及在雅思測驗中出現的頻率所篩選出來的。藉由學會與每個關鍵名詞最常搭配使用的動詞、形容詞，將有助於擴充字彙量。「字詞搭配表」是一種非常簡單而有效的方式，可以將你已經知道的字彙清楚建構起來，以下將示範要

怎麼運用：

Task 4

請研讀這個字詞搭配表、例句和底下的說明。

〈範例 1〉

搭配在前的動詞	搭配的形容詞	關鍵字	搭配在後的動詞
switch on turn on switch off turn off	household domestic electrical faulty	**appliance**	work run function break down

字詞搭配使用範例

- It's impossible to **turn off** many **electrical appliances**.
- The **appliance broke down**, but now it is **functioning** smoothly.
- Some **appliances** cannot **be turned off**.

説明 「字詞搭配表」要從左讀到右，它會列出最常搭配使用的動詞，然後是形容詞。在以上這個字詞搭配表範例中可以看到兩欄的動詞，這意味著關鍵名詞是第一個動詞的受詞：It's impossible to **turn off** many **electrical appliances**，或是第二個動詞的主詞：The **appliance broke down**, but now it is **functioning** smoothly。若是想要把關鍵名詞當成第一個動詞的主詞，那麼有時則可使用第一個動詞的被動語態：Some **appliances** cannot **be turned off**。請仔細研讀例句即可看出我所要表達的意思。

〈範例 2〉

搭配在前面的動詞	搭配的形容詞		關鍵字
practise enter go into join	chosen	medical nursing healthcare legal teaching accountancy auditing	**profession**
搭配在前面的片語			
be a disgrace to their ~ be at the top of s/o's ~ be by ~			

字詞搭配使用範例

- She **was** originally a nurse **by profession**, but she studied hard and **entered** the **legal profession**.
- Doctors who assist patients in dying are often regarded as **being a disgrace to their profession**.

說明 在形容詞的第二欄（以實線隔開的欄位）中，各位常會看到不同類型關鍵字的列表，在此例中就是不同類型的 professions。另外有些「字詞搭配表」中包含了能連同關鍵字來使用的慣用片語，其在句子中通常是用於關鍵字之前。而在每一個「字詞搭配表」底下的例句將示範如何將表格中的字詞運用於單元主題中。由例句中即可看出，只要從表格左欄到右欄，非常容易就能造出高級的句子。

❸ 常用語塊

　　在每個單元都會列出該主題相關的 chunks，並以深入的注解來說明這些 chunks 要怎麼用。由於 chunks 通常是代表語言的文法部分，因此注解將強調要在什麼時候使用 v.p.、V 或 Ving，並聚焦於是否有任何受詞，以

及受詞的類型是人物 (s/o) 或事物 (s/th)。

❹ 可作動詞或名詞的單字

英文中有非常大一類的單字是既可當動詞，也可當名詞，而且形式不變。這類單字運用起來格外困難，因為根據單字是名詞或動詞，其 chunks 或許會相當不同，有時甚至連意思也會改變。以筆者多年的教學經驗，學生在文法上所犯的錯誤很多都是來自這類的單字。而此部分彙整的 chunks 也是慣用於該單元主題的常用語塊。

❺ 談論或寫作該相關主題常用的「片語動詞」

片語動詞是英文中非常重要的部分，無論在口說和寫作時都經常需要使用，但學生通常並不會察覺到片語動詞在談論各主題中使用的頻率有多高。片語動詞有四種類型，請看以下解說：

Type 1 這類片語動詞沒有受詞。例如 take off，意指「起飛」：The flight took off at 21:00。

Type 2 這類片語動詞有受詞，但受詞總是接在片語動詞的後面，這意味著片語動詞的兩個部分——動詞和介系詞——是不能分開的。一般將這類片語動詞稱為 inseparable phrasal verb「不可分開的片語動詞」。例如 get over s/th，意指「從病中復原」：She soon got over the flu.。句中 s/th（受詞）的位置是在片語動詞的後面，由此可知其為不可分開的片語動詞。

Type 3 這類片語動詞也有受詞。受詞有名詞或代名詞（it、them 等等）兩類。名詞受詞可以置於片語動詞的後面，或是片語動詞中的動詞和介系詞之間。代名詞受詞則只能置於片語動詞中的動詞和介系詞之間。這類片語動詞稱為 separable phrasal verb「可分開的片語動詞」。例如 rule s/th out，意指「去除某事的可能性」：The government have ruled out any further progress. / The government have ruled any further progress out. / The government have ruled it out.。以上句子中 s/th（受詞）的位置都是在動詞和介系詞之間。

Type 4 這類片語動詞有兩個介系詞，而且都是 inseparable 不可分的，這意味著名詞和代名詞這兩類受詞都必須接在片語動詞的末尾。例如 run up against s/th，意指「遇到意料之外的困難」：The plan ran up against opposition from the public。

在本書各單元中將會把每個片語動詞的文法和意思講得非常清楚。為確保各位了解片語動詞的四個類型，我們先來做個小練習：

Task 5

請看以下片語動詞，並寫出它是什麼類型。

① **phase s/th in**　　　　　type _____
② **come out**　　　　　　type _____
③ **hack into s/th**　　　　type _____
④ **come up with s/th**　　type _____

Task 5 答案：① type 3　② type 1　③ type 2　④ type 4

❻ **談論或寫作該相關主題常用的「慣用語」**

慣用語也是英文的一個重要組成部分，本書特別規劃慣用語的學習內容是因為，將其運用在各種主題當中，可以使英文表達更有趣、更有韻味。由於慣用語是完全固定的語言單位，所以它們事實上是 set-phrases，在使用時必須百分之百完全精確。我們在各單元的慣用語部分也將幫助各位聚焦於把慣用語運用得完全正確。

❼ 易搞混的字詞

在每個主題中都有許多組單字會讓學習者容易產生混淆。混淆的原因主要有三個：(1) 單字的讀音聽起來非常類似；(2) 單字在華文中的意思相同，但在英文中的意思卻完全不同；(3) 單字在英文中的意思非常類似，但文法和用法卻非常不同。在本書各單元中的「易混淆的字詞」部分，將針對每一組可能會搞混的單字進行詳盡的解說，幫助各位釐清混淆點，學會正確使用這些字彙。

在研讀本書時，各位可以按部就班地完整學習各單元的內容，也可以只聚焦於掌握每個主題的關鍵名詞、字詞搭配，或是所有的 chunks。選擇最符合自身需求的學習方式才能事半功倍。

每個單元中的七個學習部分都附有練習任務，目的是讓各位實際運用所學到的字彙項目。請務必按照書中的指示確實做練習，並在完成後詳讀解答和解說。記住，本書的目標之一是要讓各位真正學會運用所學到的字彙，而不僅僅為了可以辨認字彙而把它背下來。在達成這個學習目標的過程中，練習題便是很重要的一環。要認識字彙就意味著要使用它；而要使用字彙就意味著要先理解它。

希望各位覺得本書有趣又有用。

PART 1
社會相關議題
Social Issues

Unit 1

環境
The Environment

閱讀文章 Reading

　　在學習單字時，我們將從閱讀一篇主題文章開始，因為理解這些字彙向來是運用在文章的上下文脈絡中是很重要的。在運用字彙時，要考慮到的文章脈絡有兩種。第一是文章或會話的概括主題，第二則是可連同主題關鍵字、搭配詞或字詞組合來運用的其他單字。

Task 1

閱讀文章並盡可能地理解文章內容。請先不要使用字典。

---

(1) _____ All other issues, such as the current pandemic which has broken out, or racial inequality, no matter how important they might seem at this time, are simply not as urgent as the climate crisis, which threatens the long-term survival of our species. We are all a part of the same ecology, a system of delicate balance that allows all the species of flora and fauna on our planet to live together. Everything we do now effects everyone and everything else.

(2) _____ Scenery which used to be lush and beautiful with forests and wetlands is now a scene of utter destruction caused by logging and rampant deforestation. Ecosystems which are millions of years old have been destroyed in just a few months. Complex systems of biodiversity have been trashed as a result of global corporations' search for more profits. Extreme drought effects 370 million worldwide. This has resulted in the mass movement of people and caused problems of refugees. Conservation efforts have been small and virtually ineffective – a drop in the ocean of the massive efforts we need to make.

---

(3) _____ The solution also lies in us. There is no help coming from outside, and journeying to another planet when we have thoroughly trashed this one is a stupid dream which simply is not suitable for our current needs. If we are to continue living on the earth, we will need to work together to solve this problem of our own making.

(4) _____ Climate scientists agree in general that we need to light a fire under governments and corporations to get them to act now before it is too late. They all agree that this is something that we all need to be concerned about, and which we all need to pay attention to, and we need to do so soon, before time runs out. However, one of the main problems is that many scientists do not agree on the way to move forward, and the methods we need to use to reverse the damage.

(5) _____ "We are caught between a rock and a hard place," he says, "because although our energy needs are becoming greater and greater, the natural resources we need to create that energy are fast running out, and the carbon pollution which is a by-product of that energy is slowly killing us. We are drowning in waste, and mother nature cannot cope."

(6) _____ "This is not something that each individual can take responsibility for," he says, "although we can all do our little bit to help to reduce waste and change our behaviour. It needs a concerted, international, multi-governmental effort." He is very clear that what is needed is radical, comprehensive change. "In the future it will be necessary to cut down on our consumption. We need to move to an economy in which we do more waste recycling, reusing and less chucking things out when they are broken or no longer new. At the moment we are

throwing away around 73 percent of all plastic that we produce, for example, and this figure needs to come down. We need to cut down on our production of plastics and change over to recyclable materials. Current efforts to slow down plastic production cut no ice because they are simply not enough."

(7) _____ "The current methods of dealing with solid waste include landfill, burn offs, and dumping at sea. The aim of these methods is simply to remove the problem. But that doesn't mean the problem goes away. It just means it becomes someone else's problem, somewhere else. We are looking at the problem from the wrong end. We need to aim to reduce the production of waste to begin with, not only think about waste disposal. We need to stamp out polluters and those who deliberately break the law by releasing emissions into nature."

(8) _____ Activists have been making waves about it for a few years now, and most people are eager to see some tangible improvement. "I'm encouraged by what we are seeing. There is much greater awareness now," says Dr Wassaruputon. "But what we want to see is less talk, and more action. We urgently need to make this problem the focus of all our efforts. We now have an opportunity to start again. We should not waste it." The question remains are we able to change, or are we too stuck in our ways? We all know that it is very hard to ask people to change their habits, but this is a problem we can hardly ignore. It will not go away.

Task 2

請從下列句子選出適當的主題句以完成 Task 1 每個段落的填空。

A All across the globe, the natural environment has been the victim of man's activity.

B Dr Roger McGilles, a researcher at the University of Somewhere, says that governments and corporations need to be responsible for this.

C Dr Sanjay Wassaruputon, a scientist at the UN, is concerned about our energy needs as the world becomes more digitized.

D Professor Susan Wilson, a colleague of Dr McGilles, says we need to find ways to curb waste.

E So what can we do to save the planet, and is it not too late?

F The biggest challenge facing humanity as we go into the future is climate change.

G The cause of all these problems is our short-term greed and our long term lack of vision.

H It is encouraging that everyone is focussing on this issue.

✅ 答案・中譯・說明

(1) F (2) A (3) G (4) E (5) C (6) B (7) D (8) H

譯文

在走向未來之際，人類所面臨的最大挑戰就是氣候變遷。其他所有的課題，例如目前所爆發的疫情或是種族不平等問題，無論它們在此時看起來多麼重要，都不如氣候危機威脅到我們這個物種的長期存續要來得迫切。我們全都是同一個生態系的一部分，靠著這個微妙的平衡系統，使我們星球上的所有動植物物種能夠一起生活。我們現在所做的每件事都會影響到其他人和其他事物。

在全球各地，自然環境一直都是人類活動的受害者。過去茂密而美麗的森林和濕地風光，如今已是由於伐木和濫墾濫伐所造成的徹底破壞景象。數百萬年之久的生態系在短短幾個月內就被摧毀。全球企業追尋更多利潤的結果，就是複雜的生物多樣性體系遭到了破壞。極端乾旱影響了全球 3.7 億人。這導致了人員大舉遷移，並造成了難民問題。保育工作的力度小到近乎無效——與我們需要付出的巨大努力相比根本微不足道。

所有這些問題的成因在於我們短期的貪婪和長期的缺乏遠見。解決之道也在我們身上。外來的幫助不會有，而且壓根不適合當前需求的愚蠢夢想是，等我們徹底摧毀了這個星球，就跑去另一個。如果我們要繼續生活在地球上，就需要共同努力來解決這個我們自行造成的問題。

所以我們能做些什麼來拯救地球且又不會為時已晚？氣候科學家們普遍認為，我們需

要去鞭策政府和企業，使它們現在就採取行動，以免為時已晚。他們全都認同，這是我們所有人都需要關切的事，我們全都需要予以關注，而且必須在時間耗盡前趕緊這麼做。不過，一個主要的問題在於，對於前進之道和我們需要用來扭轉損害的方法，很多科學家並不認同。

在世界變得更加數位化之際，聯合國的科學家 Sanjay Wassaruputon 博士關切起了我們的能源需求。「我們左右為難，」他說。「因為儘管我們的能源需求變得愈來愈大，但創造那些能源所需要的天然資源正快速耗盡，而且那些能源的副產品碳污染正慢慢扼殺我們。我們正遭到廢棄物淹沒，而大自然無力應付。」

某地大學的研究員 Roger McGilles 博士說，政府和企業需要為此負責。「這不是個人能各自負起責任的事，」他說，「儘管我們全都能為幫忙減少廢棄物和改變我們的行為盡一點力。它需要協調一致的、國際性的、跨政府的努力。」他非常清楚，現在需要的是徹底的、全面的變革。「在將來，減少我們的消費是必要的。我們需要走向的經濟模式是，做更多的廢棄物回收、重複使用，而不是在東西壞了或不再新穎的時候扔掉它。例如就眼前來說，在我們生產的所有塑膠裡，我們丟掉了約 73%，這個數字需要降下來才行。我們需要削減塑膠的生產，並改用可回收使用的材料。當前減緩塑膠生產的努力起不了作用，是因為它壓根就不夠。」

McGilles 博士的同事 Susan Wilson 教授說，我們需要找到遏止浪費的方法。「目前處理固體廢棄物的方法包括掩埋、焚化和傾倒在海裡。這些方法的目的僅僅是把問題給撇開。但這並不意味著問題就沒了，它只是變成了別人在別個地方的問題。我們是從錯誤的角度在看問題。我們首先應以減少廢棄物的產生為目標，而不是只想到廢棄物的處理。我們需要杜絕污染源和那些蓄意違法把排放物釋入大自然的人。」

令人鼓舞的是，人人都在關注這個課題。行動主義者們已經為此掀起了幾年的波瀾，而且大部分的人亟欲看到一些確切的改善。「我對於我們所看到的事感到鼓舞。現在人們已有了更大的覺醒，」Wassaruputon 博士說。「但我們想要看到的是少空談、多行動。我們迫切需要使這個問題成為我們所有努力的重點。我們現在有機會重新開始，不該把它浪費掉。」問題仍然在於我們是否能夠改變，或者我們是不是過於墨守成規？我們全都知道，要人們把習慣改掉是非常困難的，但這是我們幾乎無法忽視的問題。它並不會就此消失。

....

☆ 請注意本文是如何以描述一個問題開始，然後提出解決方案。這是典型的問題／解決方案 (problem/solution) 的文章。

☆ 請留意主題句 (topic sentence) 總是段落中最概括的句子，以及段落中的其他部分是如何以特定的例子或理由來申論主題句的論點。

字詞搭配 Word Partnerships

我們現在將學習「環境」這個主題的 15 個關鍵字，以及可搭配這些關鍵字使用的 word partnerships「字詞搭配表」。首先，請看關鍵字語庫。在開始前，各位或許可先回顧「導讀」中談論字詞搭配的部分，以檢視自己的概括理解程度。

Task 3

請仔細研讀這些主題字彙和下方的說明。

關鍵語庫 ❶　⊙ Track 1.1

名詞	動詞	形容詞	字義
biodiversity Ⓤ	-	-	生物多樣性
climate Ⓤ	-	-	氣候
conservation Ⓤ	conserve	conservative	保育、保持
consumption Ⓤ	consume	-	消費、消耗
deforestation Ⓤ	deforest	-	砍伐森林
destruction Ⓤ	destroy	destructive	毀滅、破壞、摧毀
drought Ⓒ	-	-	乾旱
ecosystem Ⓒ	-	-	生態系（統）
emissions Ⓒ	emit	-	排放
environment Ⓤ	-	environmental	環境
nature Ⓤ	-	natural	大自然
pollution Ⓤ	pollute	polluted	污染
recycling Ⓤ	recycle	recycled	回收

resource ©C	-	-	資源
waste ©U	waste	wasted	廢棄物

☆ 需留意哪些名詞是可數，哪些是不可數。

☆ 有時候一個名詞是可數或不可數，須視主題而定。例如，在指一般的 situation 時，你可以把 environment 當作可數名詞來使用，但當主題是「環境」時，就像 Task 1 的文章一樣，environment 向來都是不可數。

☆ 一定要用可數名詞的複數來表示一般概括的事物。例如 Resources are scarce 是指總體上的所有資源缺乏，Resource is scarce 則沒有意義。

☆ 要在「環境」這個主題中用到 emissions 時，必須使用複數形。

☆ 請注意，在使用 environment 時，必須在其前加上定冠詞 the。但是 nature 指大自然時則不可加 the。

☆ 留意單字的其他詞性形式，如動詞和形容詞。

　　接下來，我們將以 5 個關鍵字為一組，深入地學習與這些字最頻繁搭配的字詞組合及正確用法。

Task 4

請研讀這個字詞搭配表、例句和底下的說明。

搭配在前的名詞 + of	搭配的形容詞	關鍵字
the preservation of the conservation of the protection of	soil agricultural	
systems of	marine	
the loss of	freshwater	
搭配在前的動詞		**biodiversity**
save		
sustain		
protect		
lose		

字詞搭配使用範例　　🎧 **Track 1.2**（收錄本單元 Task 4~Task 20 字詞搭配使用範例）

- We are **losing agricultural diversity** due to over-farming (over-cultivation).
  我們正因為過度耕種而失去農業的多樣性。

- The **preservation of biodiversity** should be our priority.
  維護生物多樣性應該是我們的首要之務。

- If we don't try to **protect soil biodiversity**, we will have terrible problems in
  the future. 假如我們不設法去保護土壤中的生物多樣性，未來將會遇到可怕的問題。

☆ 在這個字詞搭配表和各位在本書中將學習到的所有字詞搭配表當中，動詞和形容詞都是將意思相似的字詞歸類成一組。例如在上表 (Task 4) 中，the preservation of、the conservation of、the protection of 便可當成同義來使用。

☆ 同樣地，當 soil 和 agricultural 是跟 biodiversity 一起使用時，這兩個單字也是同義詞。

☆ 當主題是「環境」，而且是跟 biodiversity 一起使用時，sustain 和 protect 也能當成同義詞來使用。

☆ 請記得，同義詞向來都是 topic and collocation specific「特定主題和搭配」。例如 soil 和 agricultural、sustain 和 protect 並非向來都是同義詞，只有在主題是「環境」並連同 biodiversity 來使用時，才可將它們視為同義詞來使用。

Task 5

請研讀這個字詞搭配表和例句。

關鍵字	搭配的名詞
climate	change crisis scientist science policy

字詞搭配使用範例

- The **climate crisis** is the most urgent problem of our age.
  氣候危機是當代最迫切的問題。

- Governments need to have a clear **climate policy**.
  政府需要制訂明確的氣候政策。

Task 6

請研讀這個字詞搭配表、例句和底下的說明。

搭配在前面的動詞	搭配的形容詞	關鍵字	搭配在後面的名詞
promote encourage prioritize	energy resource biodiversity	**conservation**	efforts measures action

- We need to **encourage energy conservation**. 我們需要鼓勵節能。
- Current **conservation measures** are not enough. 當前的保育措施並不夠。

···

☆ 請注意 efforts 和 measures 必須使用複數形。

☆ action 必須使用單數，因為在這個主題和搭配詞表中，它是不可數名詞。

Task 7

請研讀這個字詞搭配表和例句。

搭配在前面的動詞	搭配的形容詞	關鍵字
cut down on limit reduce	energy electricity power	**consumption (of s/th)**

字詞搭配使用範例

- We urgently need to **reduce** our **consumption of** energy
  我們迫切需要減少能源的消耗。
- We need to **limit** our **power consumption**. 我們需要限制電力的耗費。

Task 8

請研讀這個字詞搭配表和例句。

搭配在前面的動詞	搭配的形容詞	關鍵字
halt curb slow	rampant	**deforestation**

• We need to **curb rampant deforestation**. 我們必須遏止森林的濫墾濫伐。

現在，我們來看看各位是否能用一些字詞搭配來擴大對字彙的運用。

Task 9

請從 Task 4 到 Task 8 中選出正確形式的字詞，完成以下段落填空。

The most important thing we need to do now is (1) _____
biodiversity, especially (2) _____ biodiversity. If we (3) _____
(4) _____ biodiversity, we will not be able to grow enough food. We
also need to (5) _____ conservation (6) _____, especially by
(7) _____ (8) _____ deforestation and by (9) _____
consumption (10) _____ energy.

範例答案

1. protect/save
2. soil/agricultural
3. lose
4. agricultural/soil
5. encourage/promote/prioritize

6. measures/action/efforts
7. halting/curbing/slowing
8. rampant
9. limiting/cutting down on/reducing
10. of

....

☆ 請留意各組同義字詞，空格中選填同一組內不同的字也是可以的。例如以 (1)
來說，填入 protect 和 save 都是正確的。

☆ 須確認所選用的單字都是正確的形式。請檢查單數或複數，以及動詞的正確形
式。例如在空格 (7) 和 (9) 當中，不管選用哪一個動詞，都必須用 Ving，因為
它是接在 by 後面。

現在來學習另外 5 個單字。

Task 10

請研讀這個字詞搭配表和例句。

搭配在前面的動詞	搭配的形容詞	關鍵字
cause inflict halt stop prevent	utter wholesale massive environmental	**destruction (of s/th)**

字詞搭配使用範例

- Our greed has **caused** the **wholesale destruction of** our environment.
  我們的貪婪造成了環境大肆毀滅。

- We need to **stop** this **massive environmental destruction**.
  我們需要阻止這種大舉的環境毀滅。

Task 11

請研讀這個字詞搭配表和例句。

搭配在前面的動詞	搭配的形容詞	關鍵字	搭配在後面的形容詞
endure suffer end	extreme severe recurrent prolonged	**drought**	resistant

字詞搭配使用範例

- Many parts of the world **are suffering prolonged drought**.
  世界上很多地方正遭逢長期的乾旱。

• We will need to develop **drought resistant** crops. 我們會需要培育抗旱作物。

Task 12

請研讀這個字詞搭配表和例句。

搭配在前面的動詞		搭配的形容詞	關鍵字
restore	threaten	fragile	
conserve	disrupt	marine	
	damage	coastal	**ecosystem**
	destroy	forest	

字詞搭配使用範例

• We **have destroyed** many **fragile ecosystems**. 我們破壞了許多脆弱的生態系。
• **Marine ecosystems are being threatened** by offshore drilling for oil.
  海洋生態系正受到海上石油鑽探的威脅。

Task 13

請研讀這個字詞搭配表、例句和底下的說明。

搭配在前面的動詞	搭配的形容詞	關鍵字
reduce	greenhouse gas	
cut	carbon	
lower	fossil fuel	
curb	harmful	**emissions**
limit		
regulate	vehicle	
	exhaust	
release		

- We need to **reduce greenhouse gas emissions**.
  我們需要減少溫室氣體排放。

- We need to **regulate** and **limit vehicle emissions**.
  我們需要規範和限制車輛的排放。

- We are **releasing** too many **harmful emissions**.
  我們釋放了太多的有害氣體。

....

☆ 請記得,在書寫或講述「環境」這個主題時,emissions 通常必須使用複數
  形。例如,We need to limit harmful emission. 是錯的,正確應為 We need to
  limit harmful emissions.。

Task 14

請研讀這個字詞搭配表、例句和底下的說明。

搭配在前面的「名詞 + of」		搭配的形容詞	關鍵字
the preservation of	the destruction of		
the conservation of	the damage to		
the protection of	the harm to		
	the pollution of		
搭配在前面的動詞		the natural	**environment**
protect	destroy		
preserve	damage		
conserve	harm		
	pollute		

字詞搭配使用範例

- **The damage to** the **environment** must stop. 對環境的破壞必須停止。
- We need to **protect the natural environment**. 我們必須保護自然環境。

• Corporations **are** slowly **destroying** the **environment**. 企業正慢慢地破壞環境。

....

☆ 注意，在用 environment 這個字時，前面應該加上定冠詞 the。例如，The preservation of the natural environment is very important. 是正確的，而 The preservation of natural environment 則是錯的。

　　就像前面所做過的，我們再來練習這第二組 5 個單字的字詞搭配應用。

Task 15

請從 Task 10 到 Task 14 中選出正確形式的字詞，完成以下段落填空。

The (1) ＿＿＿＿＿＿ destruction (2) ＿＿＿＿＿＿ the (3) ＿＿＿＿＿＿ environment cannot go on without serious damage to all species on the planet. We have already (4) ＿＿＿＿＿＿ enough destruction, and it must stop now.

Millions of people are (5) ＿＿＿＿＿＿ (6) ＿＿＿＿＿＿ drought as a result of environmental damage, and many (7) ＿＿＿＿＿＿ ecosystems in many parts of the world have already been (8) ＿＿＿＿＿＿.

Another problem is (9) ＿＿＿＿＿＿ emissions, which are (10) ＿＿＿＿＿＿ to our children's lungs. Governments need to (11) ＿＿＿＿＿＿ (12) ＿＿＿＿＿＿ emissions if we are going to continue building and selling cars.

範例答案

1. utter/wholesale/massive

2. of

3. natural

4. inflicted/caused

5. suffering/enduring

6. extreme/severe

7. fragile

8. destroyed/damaged

036

9. greenhouse gas/carbon/fossil fuel

10. harmful

11. regulate/curb/limit

12. vehicle

....

☆ 再次提醒，請留意各組同義字詞。空格中選填同一組內不同的字也是可以的，例如以 (1) 來說，utter、wholesale 和 massive 全都正確，因為它們在此是同義詞。

☆ 務必確認所選用的單字都是正確的形式。檢查單數或複數，以及動詞的正確形式，例如空格 (4) 不管是用哪個動詞，都必須使用 past participle「過去分詞」，因為該句中的動詞時態是 present perfect「現在完成式」(have + p.p.)。而空格 (5) 不管是用哪個動詞，都必須使用 Ving，因為該句的動詞時態是 present continuous「現在進行式」(be + Ving)。

現在我們來學習最後一組的 5 個單字。

Task 16

請研讀這個字詞搭配表、例句和底下的說明。

搭配在前面的「名詞 + of」		搭配的形容詞	關鍵字
the preservation of the conservation of the protection of	the destruction of the damage to the harm to the pollution of		
搭配在前面的動詞		mother	**nature**
protect preserve conserve	destroy damage harm pollute		

- We need to work harder to **protect mother nature**.
  我們必須更加努力地保護大自然。

- **The destruction of nature** is one of the worst things our species has done.
  破壞大自然是我們這個物種所做過最糟糕的事之一。

☆ 注意在使用 nature 這個字時，前面不可以加 the。例如，The destruction of mother nature 是正確的，而 The destruction of the mother nature 則是錯的。

Task 17

請研讀這個字詞搭配表、例句和底下的說明。

搭配在前面的動詞		搭配的形容詞		關鍵字
emit	curb	air	industrial	**pollution (of s/th)**
produce	limit		carbon	
	cut	water		
cause			plastic	
	prevent	noise		
reduce			particulate	
tackle		light		

字詞搭配使用範例

- The modern industrial economy **causes** all kinds of **pollution**.
  現代工業經濟造成了各種污染。

- We need to **curb light pollution** to preserve the biodiversity of insect life.
  我們需要抑制光污染，以維護昆蟲界的生物多樣性。

- This factory **has been emitting pollution** for years.
  這家工廠長年在排放污染物。

- The **pollution of** the environment **must be tackled** now.
  環境污染必須現在就應對。

☆ 請留意不同類型污染的說法。

Task 18

請研讀這個字詞搭配表、例句和底下的說明。

搭配在前面的動詞	搭配的形容詞	關鍵字	搭配在後面的名詞
do	water		bin
maximise	waste		centre
boost			facility
promote	electronics	**recycling**	plant
encourage	plastics		
	garbage		
	trash		

字詞搭配使用範例

- There are many **recycling facilities** in Taiwan, but we still need to **promote electronics recycling**.
  台灣有很多回收設施,但我們還是需要推廣電子(廢棄物)回收。

- We are **doing** more **water recycling**, but it's still not enough.
  我們正在做更多的水循環利用,但還是不夠。

··

☆ 請注意 recycling 可形成複合名詞。

Task 19

請研讀這個字詞搭配表、例句和底下的說明。

搭配在前面的動詞		搭配的形容詞		關鍵字
allocate	manage	limited	water	
share	protect	scarce		
pool	conserve		mineral	**resource**
		natural		
	waste		renewable	
	exhaust			

- We need to **pool** our **natural resources** and not **waste** them.
  我們需要匯集天然資源並且不浪費。

- We are trying to **protect** our **water resources**. 我們正試著去保護水資源。

☆ 請留意不同資源類型的說法。

Task 20

請研讀這個字詞搭配表、例句和底下的說明。

搭配在前面的動詞		搭配的形容詞		關鍵字	搭配在後面的名詞
create cause generate deal with dump dispose of	reduce cut down on curb minimise eliminate prevent prohibit	hazardous toxic radioactive	solid food electronic	**waste**	disposal management reduction

- Most industrial processes **create** too much **hazardous waste**.
  大部分的工業製程都會創造出太多的有害廢棄物。

- Most factories **dump** their **waste** right into the sea.
  大部分的工廠都直接把廢棄物傾倒進海裡。

- The problem of **waste disposal** is becoming very urgent.
  廢棄物處理的問題變得非常迫切。

☆ 當然，waste 也能當動詞來用。它也能用在很多慣用語中，諸如 waste of time、waste not, want not 等等。但在這裡，當主題是「環境」時，waste 則必須當成不可數名詞來用，此即我在前面一直提到的「單字的用法須視主題和

搭配詞而定」。

接下來，我們來練習這最後一組 5 個單字的字詞搭配應用。

Task 21

請從 Task 16 到 Task 20 中選出正確形式的字詞，完成以下段落填空。

(1) _____ nature is not going to happen as long as we continue to allow factories to (2) _____ their waste into rivers, (3) _____ the pollution of the sea. We seriously need to (4) _____ the amount of waste we (5) _____. For example, (6) _____ pollution (7) _____ the oceans is now a serious problem, with plastic washing up on beaches all over the world. We must (8) _____ recycling, and set up more recycling (9) _____. We also need to make sure we (10) _____ (11) _____ resources and not keep them for ourselves: (12) _____ nature is there for everyone, not just rich countries.

範例答案

1. The preservation of/The conservation of/The protection of
2. dump/dispose of
3. causing
4. reduce/cut down on/curb/minimise
5. create/cause/generate
6. plastics
7. of
8. maximise/boost/promote/encourage
9. centres/facilities/plants
10. allocate/share/pool

11. natural

12. mother

....

☆ 再提醒一次，務必留意各組同義字詞。空格中選填同一組內不同的字也是可以
的，例如以空格 (1) 來說，the preservation of、the conservation of 和 the
protection of 全都正確，因為它們在此是同義詞。

☆ 請確認所選用的單字都是正確的形式。檢查單數或複數，以及動詞的正確形
式，例如空格 (3) 中的 cause 必須是 Ving，因為它是在描述前述子句的結果。

    最後，我們要進行這個部分的最後一個練習，這對於各位記憶 15 個關
鍵單字和它們的字詞搭配將有非常大的幫助。記住，多閱讀有助於擴充字
彙量，而在文章上下文脈絡中查看大量例子則能幫助你記憶新的用語。

Task 22

請從 Task 1 和 Task 2 的閱讀文章中找出關鍵語庫 ❶ 所列的 15 個關鍵字，
並留意這些字在文章中是如何使用的。

常用語塊 Chunks

　　前面學過了字詞搭配的用法，我們現在要來學一些可用在寫作或談論環境問題的 chunks「語塊」。本書的「導讀」中有提到，使用語塊的主要困難點在於所需要的精準度。換言之，學習和使用語塊時，對用語的小細節極度準確是非常重要的。在接下來的一些練習裡，我會說明一些大家在使用語塊時最常犯的錯誤。而在開始前，各位或許可先回顧「導讀」中的相關內容，以檢視自己對語塊的概括理解程度。

Task 23
研讀這些語塊和底下的說明。

關鍵語庫 2

Chunk
❏ be a part of n.p./Ving　是 n.p./Ving 的一部分
❏ be capable of n.p./Ving　能夠 n.p./Ving
❏ be concerned about n.p./Ving　關切 n.p./Ving
❏ be eager to V　亟欲 V
❏ be necessary to V　V 是必要的
❏ be responsible for n.p./Ving　對 n.p./Ving 負責
❏ be suitable for n.p./Ving　適合 n.p./Ving
❏ have an opportunity to V/for n.p.　有機會 V/n.p.
❏ pay attention to n.p./Ving　對 n.p./Ving 加以關注
❏ take responsibility for n.p./Ving　對 n.p./Ving 負起責任

☆ 別忘了在使用這些語塊時需要改變動詞的時態。

☆ be responsible for n.p./Ving 是用於描述狀態時，若是要描述行動則應使用 take responsibility for n.p./Ving。

☆ 請務必記得，在學習和使用語塊時要完全準確。須特別注意小詞、字尾和語塊的結尾，以判斷需要的是 n.p.、v.p.、Ving 還是 V。

下一個 Task 將聚焦於大家在使用這些語塊時經常會犯的錯誤。

Task 24

請改正這些句子中使用語塊的常見錯誤。

① Polluting companies are only a part from the problem.

_____

② Most people are not capable to change their behaviour.

_____

③ Some people very concern about the environment.

_____

④ They are eager to looking for solutions.

_____

⑤ It will be necessary for changing our habits.

_____

⑥ The government should be responsibility for this problem.

_____

⑦ This area of land is not suitable to build on.

_____

⑧ We have a small opportunity to solving the problem.

⑨ If we pay attention on this problem, we can solve it together.

⑩ I hope they will take responsible for their mistakes.

✓ 答案・中譯・說明　**◎ Track 1.3**

① Polluting companies <u>are only a part **of**</u> the problem.
　污染企業只是問題的一環。

② Most people are not capable **of changing** their behaviour.
　大部分的人並不能改變自己的行為。

③ Some people **are** very **concerned** about the environment.
　有些人非常關切環境問題。

④ They are eager to **look** for solutions.
　他們亟欲尋找解方。

⑤ It will be necessary **to change** our habits.
　改變我們的習慣是必要的。

⑥ The government should be **responsible** for this problem.
　政府應該要為這個問題負責。

⑦ This area of land is not suitable **for building** on.
　這樣的土地面積不適合興建。

⑧ We have a small opportunity to **solve** the problem.
　我們有一個小小的機會來解決問題。

⑨ If we pay attention **to** this problem, we can solve it together.
　假如我們對這個問題加以關注，就能一起來解決它。

⑩ I hope they will take **responsibility** for their mistakes.
　希望他們會對自己的錯誤負起責任。

☆ 我已經把錯誤的部分標示出來，所以各位可以清楚看出哪裡用錯了。

☆ 請將 Task 24 的句子與關鍵語庫 ❷ 的語塊做比較，以確保能清楚看出句中哪裡用錯了。

☆ 請將正確句子中的完整語塊畫上底線（參照第 1 句的示範），這能幫助你完整而正確地記住語塊。

下一個練習對於記憶語塊將有非常大的幫助。請記住，多閱讀有助於擴充字彙量，而在文章的上下文脈絡中查看大量語塊則能幫助你記憶新的用語。

Task 25

請從 Task 1 和 Task 2 的閱讀文章中找出關鍵語庫 ❷ 列出的所有語塊，並留意這些語塊在文章中是如何使用的。

Task 26

現在請嘗試用前面學過的語塊來寫出你自己的句子。

關鍵字語塊	造句
be a part of n.p./Ving	
be capable of n.p./Ving	
be concerned about n.p./Ving	
be eager to V	
be necessary to V	

be responsible for n.p./Ving	
be suitable for n.p./Ving	
have an opportunity to V/for n.p.	
pay attention to n.p./Ving	
take responsibility for n.p./Ving	

範例答案

☆ 我顯然無法在此改正你的句子，但你可以透過確認語塊所有的小細節，自行改正。再次提醒在寫作中運用語塊時，須特別注意小詞、字尾和語塊的結尾，無論所需要的是 n.p.、v.p.、Ving 還是 V，並且確保你所使用的語塊是完整的。

5 個可作動詞或名詞的單字
5 words which can be verbs or nouns

　　在接下來這個部分，我們將要學習如何使用一組非常棘手的單字，亦即名詞和動詞是相同形式的單字。各位或許會以爲動、名詞同形，所以用起來應該更容易，但情況並非如此。因爲語塊通常會視關鍵字是名詞或動詞而有所不同，這將造成這些單字使用上的困難。

Task 27

看以下幾個名詞和動詞同形的單字。

關鍵語庫 ❸

關鍵字	名詞字義	動詞字義
aim	瞄準的方向；目標，目的	將……針對；意欲，旨在
cause	原因；理由；目標	導致，使發生，引起
focus	焦點；聚焦	使聚焦；聚焦
help	幫助；有益的東西	幫助；促進
result	成果；效果；戰績	產生；結果；導致

Task 28

閱讀句子並判斷關鍵字是動詞或名詞，填入 V 或 N。

① _____ The program **aims** to clean up the lake in five years.

② _____ The **aim** of the program is to clean it up in five years.

③ _____ No one knows what the **cause** of the problem is.

④ _____ No one knows what might **cause** the problem.

⑤ _____ If we **focus** on this problem, we might be able to solve it.

⑥ ＿＿ This problem should be the **focus** of our efforts.

⑦ ＿＿ The government was not willing to **help**.

⑧ ＿＿ There was no **help** from the government.

⑨ ＿＿ The **result** of the experiment was interesting.

⑩ ＿＿ We hope the experiment will **result** in a new understanding of the problem.

◆ 答案・中譯・說明

① V 這個計畫旨在五年內把湖泊清乾淨。

② N 該計畫的目標是在五年內把它清理乾淨。

③ N 沒人知道問題的成因是什麼。

④ V 沒人知道問題可能是由什麼所造成。

⑤ V 如果我們聚焦於這個問題，或許就能把它解決。

⑥ N 這個問題應該是我們努力的重點。

⑦ V 政府不願意幫忙。

⑧ N 沒有來自於政府的幫忙。

⑨ N 實驗的結果很有趣。

⑩ V 我們希望這個實驗能讓我們對問題有新的了解。

☆ 有時候你會發現還蠻難判斷的，這意味著你必須去看關鍵字周圍的其他單字。例如 cause 在第 3 句中顯然是名詞，因為它接在 the 之後；而在第 4 句中則是動詞，因為接在情態助動詞 might 之後。

☆ 在第 5 句中，focus 是動詞，所以要注意後面需接 on，亦即動詞的語塊是 focus on。但在第 6 句中 focus 的語塊則是 the focus of，因而是當名詞使用。

☆ 能夠掌握這些字在動詞語塊和名詞語塊上的差別是非常重要的。接下來的練習將幫助各位更加熟悉相關用法。

Task 29

請看以下所彙整的語塊及用法說明。

關鍵語庫 ④ 🎧 **Track 1.4**

關鍵字語塊	關鍵字詞性	例句＆翻譯
the aim of X	*nc*	The aim of the program is to prevent more destruction. 該計畫的目的是防止更多的破壞。
aim to V	*v*	The program aims to prevent more destruction. 該計畫旨在防止更多的破壞。
the cause of X	*nc*	No one knows what the cause of the problem is. 沒人知道問題的成因是什麼。
X cause Y (to V)	*v*	No one knows what causes the problem (to happen). 沒人知道問題（發生）是由什麼所造成。
Y is caused by X	*v*	The problem is caused by too much waste. 問題是由太多的廢棄物所造成。
the focus of X	*nu*	We need to make this the focus of our efforts. 我們需要把這當成我們努力的重點。
focus on X	*v*	We need to focus on this. 我們需要聚焦於此。
help	*nu*	There is no help. 沒有幫助。
help (s/o) to V	*v*	The government is helping people to reduce waste. 政府正幫助民眾減少廢棄物。
the result of X	*nc*	It's the result of years of destruction. 這是長年破壞的結果。
X result in Y	*v*	Years of destruction have resds in this situation. 長年破壞導致了這樣的場面。

☆ 須留意哪些名詞是可數，哪些是不可數。

☆ 請注意，cause 當動詞時，使用主動語態 X causes Y (to V) 或被動語態 X is caused by Y 都可以。

☆ focus 當動詞時需特別留意，不可以用 be 動詞：be focus on，例如 We need to be focus on 是錯的。

☆ 當 help 作動詞用時，若想要特定指出受到幫助的是誰，便可加上受詞 (s/o)。

☆ 在使用動詞形式時，若是要表達不分時間的事實，而且主詞是第三人稱，請務必確保動詞加上了 s。例如：Pollution causes problems.、Plastic results in waste.。

☆ 請仔細學習這些語塊，並把重點放在諸如介系詞和冠詞這些細節。

好的，現在讓我們來嘗試正確使用這些語塊。

Task 30

請選用正確形式的單字或語塊，完成下列各句。

① **caused/the cause of**

No one knew what _____ the problem.

② **We aim/The aim of**

_____ the program is to plant 1000 trees.

③ **Resulted in/The result of**

_____ the oil spill was the deaths of hundreds of birds.

④ **focus on/the focus of**

We need to make solving this problem _____ our efforts.

⑤ **help/helps**

They were not able to give us any _____.

⑥ **The cause of/Causing**

_____ the problem is our greed, which is destroying the environment.

⑦ **helps/help us to**

They were not able to _____ reduce our waste.

⑧ **aim to/the aim of**

We _____ plant 1000 trees.

⑨ **be focus on/focus on**

Governments need to _____ this before the situation is too late.

⑩ **the result of/resulted in**

The oil spill _____ the deaths of hundreds of birds.

答案・中譯・說明　 **Track 1.5**

① No one knew what caused the problem.
沒人知道問題是由什麼所造成。

② <u>The aim of</u> the program is to plant 1000 trees.
這個計畫的目標是種植一千棵樹。

③ The result of the oil spill was the deaths of hundreds of birds.
漏油的結果是數百隻鳥死亡了。

④ We need to make solving this problem the focus of our efforts.
我們需要把解決這個問題當成我們努力的重點。

⑤ They were not able to give us any help.
他們給不了我們任何幫助。

⑥ The cause of the problem is our greed, which is destroying the environment.
問題的起因是我們的貪婪，它正在破壞環境。

⑦ They were not able to help us to reduce our waste.
他們無法幫助我們把廢棄物減少。

⑧ We aim to plant 1000 trees.
　我們的目標是要種一千棵樹。

⑨ Governments need to focus on this before the situation is too late.
　各國政府必須在形勢變得太遲之前就聚焦於此。

⑩ The oil spill resulted in the deaths of hundreds of birds.
　漏油導致數百隻鳥死亡。

☆ 請拿正確的句子來與關鍵語庫 ❹ 的語塊做比較，確保名詞或動詞語塊都用得正確。

☆ 請確認動詞的時態都正確無誤。

☆ 請將正確句子中的完整語塊畫上底線（參照第 2 句的示範）。這將有助於各位把語塊完整而正確地記起來。

PART
1

　　接下來，我們要再重複一次前面做過的練習。請詳讀本單元開頭的閱讀文章，並從中把這 5 個動詞和名詞同形的關鍵字語塊全部找到。再次提醒，盡可能地多閱讀有助於擴充字彙量，而在文章上下文脈絡中查看大量語塊則能幫助你記憶新的用語。

Task 31

請從 Task 1 和 Task 2 的閱讀文章中找出關鍵語庫 ❹ 列出的所有語塊，並留意這些語塊在文章中是當動詞還是名詞使用？

Task 32

請練習用關鍵語庫 ❹ 的語塊來造句。

關鍵字語塊	造句
the aim of X	
aim to V	

the cause of X	
X cause Y (to V)	
Y is caused by X	
the focus of X	
focus on X	
help	
help (s/o) to V	
the result of X	
X result in Y	

範例答案

☆ 我顯然無法在此來改正你的句子，但你可以透過確認語塊所有的小細節，自行改正。再次提醒在寫作中運用語塊時，須特別注意小詞、字尾和語塊的結尾，無論所需要的是 n.p.、v.p.、Ving 還是 V，並且確保你所使用的語塊是完整的。

5 個談論或寫作環境相關主題常用的片語動詞 5 phrasal verbs for talking or writing about the environment

現在我們要繼續學習另一種語塊：phrasal verbs「片語動詞」。片語動詞在英文裡非常常見，而且為了在寫作和口說上拿到高分，考生必須展現出這部分的運用能力。在開始學習前，各位或許可先回顧「導讀」中談到片語動詞的部分，以檢視自己對它的概括了解。

Task 33

研讀語庫中的片語動詞、例句和其下的說明。

關鍵語庫 ❺ 🎧 Track 1.6

片語動詞	例句
cut down on s/th 減少	• We need to cut down on our use of plastics. 我們需要減少塑膠的使用量。 • We need to cut down on our dependency on fossil fuels. 我們需要減少對化石燃料的依賴。
break out 出乎意料的事自行發生，諸如火災或流行病	• A fire broke out on the mountain. No one knows how it started. 山區發生了火災。沒人知道它是怎麼開始的。 • A pandemic has broken out in China. 中國爆發了一場大流行病。
stamp s/th out	• Governments across the world are trying to stamp the epidemic out. 世界各地的政府正試著把這種流行病杜絕掉。

stamp s/th out 以強大的努力來阻止某事繼續下去，即消滅、鎮壓、杜絕	• Governments across the world are trying to stamp out the epidemic. 世界各地的政府正試著杜絕這種流行病。 • Governments across the world are trying to stamp it out. 世界各地的政府正試著把它杜絕掉。 • It was stamped out very quickly. 它非常迅速就被杜絕掉了。
throw s/th away 丟棄、去除	• Don't throw your phone away. It can easily be repaired. 不要把你的手機丟掉。它很容易就能修好。 • Don't throw away your phone. It can easily be repaired. 不要丟掉你的手機。它很容易就能修好。 • Don't throw it away. It can easily be repaired. 不要把它丟掉。它很容易就能修好。 • It was thrown away yesterday. 它昨天就被丟掉了。
chuck s/th out 驅逐（某人）、丟棄	• We need to stop chucking things out and start recycling more. 我們需要停止把東西扔掉，並開始多多回收利用。 • It was chucked out with the trash. 它被當垃圾扔掉了。

☆ 在學習和使用片語動詞時，你必須非常留意動詞有沒有受詞 (s/th)，以及這個受詞是擺在哪個位置。請仔細確認上方語庫中的片語動詞及其受詞的位置。

☆ 請注意 cut down on s/th 有兩個介系詞，而且不能用受詞隔開來。這個片語動詞千萬不能以被動式來使用。

☆ break out 這個片語動詞沒有受詞，而且也不能以被動式來使用。

☆ stamp s/th out、throw s/th away 和 chuck s/th out 都有受詞。若受詞是個名詞，你可以把它放在動詞和介系詞之間，或者放在介系詞之後。但若受詞是 it，則只能擺在動詞和介系詞之間。請看上放語庫中的例句。Don't throw your phone away.、Don't throw away your phone.、Don't throw it away. 全都正確。Don't throw away it. 則是錯的。

☆ 注意，若以受詞來當作主詞，stamp s/th out、throw s/th away 和 chuck s/th out 就能使用被動語態。意即，We throw most plastic bottles away. 是主動。Most plastic bottles are thrown away. 則是被動。

☆ throw s/th away 和 chuck s/th out 是近義詞，但 chuck s/th out 是非正式用法。

☆ 另外，非常重要的是，請記得片語動詞是動詞，所以還必須考慮動詞要用什麼時態。

下一個練習將有助於各位聚焦於受詞的正確擺放位置這些細節上。

Task 34

下列各句中的第一個字是正確的，請按照順序將其後的字詞重組成正確的句子。

EX. **We to cut of on need fuels consumption our fossil down**

We need to cut down on our consumption of fossil fuels.

① This south summer have forest a lot of fires across broken out the

_____

② The factories is government polluting trying stamp to out

_____

③ We stop to need away so much throwing stuff

_____

④ People a out chuck lot stuff of

_____

⑤ They are being on number cutting the of factories down built

_____

① This summer a lot of forest fires <u>have broken out</u> across the south.
今年夏天，南方各地發生了很多森林火災。

② The government is trying to stamp out polluting factories.
政府正試圖杜絕污染的工廠。

The government is trying to stamp polluting factories out.
政府正試著把污染的工廠杜絕掉。

③ We need to stop throwing away so much stuff.
我們需要停止丟棄這麼多東西。

We need to stop throwing so much stuff away.
我們需要停止把這麼多東西給丟掉。

④ People chuck out a lot of stuff.
人們會扔掉很多東西。

People chuck a lot of stuff out.
人們會把很多東西給扔掉。

⑤ They are cutting down on the number of factories being built.
他們正在削減興建工廠的數量。

∙∙

☆ 將正確的句子與關鍵語庫 ❺ 中的片語動詞做比較，確認你的用法都正確。

☆ 請將正確句子中的片語動詞畫上底線。（參照第 1 句的示範）

☆ 須特別留意受詞的位置。

☆ 這將幫助你完整而正確地把語塊記起來。

　　來看看這些片語動詞是如何運用在文章脈絡中。

Task 35

請從 Task 1 和 Task 2 的閱讀文章中找出關鍵語庫 ❺ 列出的所有片語動詞，
並留意它們在文章中是如何使用的。

Task 36

請練習用關鍵語庫 ❺ 的片語動詞來造句。

片語動詞	造句練習
cut down on s/th	
break out	
stamp s/th out	
throw s/th away	
chuck s/th out	

☆ 再次提醒在寫作時，若運用到這些片語動詞，要特別留意動詞的時態和受詞的位置。

5 個談論或寫作環境相關主題常用的慣用語 5 idioms for talking or writing about the environment

現在各位要學習的是在寫作或談論「環境」這個主題時，所能運用的一些慣用語。慣用語的關鍵在於它是全然固定的，千萬不能用任何方式加以更動。在慣用語中只有一件事能改變，那就是動詞時態——假如這個慣用語包含動詞的話。你不能做其他任何的改變，例如從肯定變否定，從主動變被動，這些都不能變動！

Task 37

研讀語庫中的慣用語、例句和其下的說明。

關鍵語庫 6 🎧 Track 1.8

慣用語	例句
be caught between a rock and a hard place 進退兩難、左右為難	• We are caught between a rock and a hard place: on the one hand we need more energy, on the other, we are running out of fossil fuels. 我們左右為難：一方面，我們需要更多的能源，另一方面，我們正在耗盡化石燃料。
cut no ice (with s/o) 起不了作用、沒有意義、無效	• This argument cuts no ice with scientists. 這項論點對科學家們起不了作用。
a drop in the ocean 微不足道	• The new laws are simply a drop in the ocean of what we really need. 以我們真正需要的來說，新法壓根就微不足道。

light a fire under s/o 鞭策	• We need to light a fire under governments all around the world, otherwise they will be too slow to take action. 我們必須去鞭策全世界的政府，否則它們會太慢才採取行動。
make waves 掀起波瀾、興風作浪	• Environmental activists have started making waves. People are beginning to wake up. 環保人士已經開始掀起波瀾。大家正開始覺醒。

☆ 為了讓慣用語有意義，它必須完全準確才行，這意味著你必須將慣用語的所有細節都使用正確。

☆ 使用慣用語時唯一能更動的是動詞時態。

☆ 使用 be caught between a rock and a hard place 這句慣用語時，向來都是用在被動語態。你不能說 it caught me between a rock and a hard place，這是錯的。

☆ 一定要確實記住哪些慣用語有受詞 (s/o)、哪些沒有。

　　下一個練習將有助於各位聚焦於使用這些慣用語時，經常會犯的錯誤。

Task 38
改正這些句子中的常見錯誤。

① I was caught between some rocks and a hard place.

_____

② Her argument didn't cut any ice with me.

_____

③ The small amount of pollution this factory produces is just some drops in the sea.

_____

④ We need to light fire under politicians to make them see how urgent this is.

_____

⑤ Government scientists don't want to make some waves.

_____

① I was <u>caught between a rock and a hard place</u>.
我現在進退兩難。

② Her argument cut no ice with me.
她的主張對我起不了作用。

③ The small amount of pollution this factory produces is just a drop in the ocean.
這座工廠所產生的小量污染根本微不足道。

④ We need to light a fire under politicians to make them see how urgent this is.
我們必須鞭策政治人物，讓他們明白這有多迫切。

⑤ Government scientists don't want to make waves.
政府的科學家們並不想要掀起波瀾。

⋯⋯

☆ 請仔細比較錯誤句子和正確解答，務必確實掌握錯在哪以及為什麼是錯的。

☆ 這些錯誤通常是漏掉了小詞、改變了小詞或單字結尾、慣用語不完整，或者在
　 一個不該有受詞的地方加上了受詞。

☆ 請將正確句子中的慣用語畫上底線。（參照第 1 句的示範）

　　現在我們要練習的是，在文章上下文中找出慣用語。

Task 39

請從 Task 1 和 Task 2 的閱讀文章中找出關鍵語庫 ❻ 列出的所有慣用語，
並留意它們在文章中是如何使用的。

Task 40

請練習用關鍵語庫 ❻ 的慣用語來造句。

慣用語	造句練習
be caught between a rock and a hard place	
cut no ice (with s/o)	
a drop in the ocean	
light a fire under s/o	
make waves	

☆ 再次提醒在寫作時若運用到這些慣用語，要特別留意動詞的時態和完整的慣用語包含哪些細節。

易混淆的字詞 easily confused words

在本單元的最後一部分，我們將聚焦於幾組使用時很容易混淆的字詞。會造成混淆的原因可能有以下幾點：

☐ 該組字的意思只有些微的差異。

☐ 該組字的用法或許有所不同。例如有些單字只能用在特定的主題上，用在別的主題則不適當，或者只能與某些詞搭配使用，而不能與其他詞搭配使用。

☐ 該組字可能在文法上有非常大的差異，但是意思卻只有些微不同。

☐ 你在過去壓根就把單字用錯了，而這個錯誤一直沒改正。

☐ 你所用的華文字典給錯了意思，漢英字典中就有很多像這樣的情況。

接下來，請各位務必好好釐清這些字詞的意思、文法和用法。

Task 41

請仔細研讀各組易混淆的字詞、例句和其下的說明。

關鍵語庫 7 🎧 **Track 1.10**

易混淆字詞		例句
1	**scenery** (*nu*) 風景、景色	• The scenery from the mountain top is very beautiful. 山頂的景色非常美。 • If they build that hotel, it will spoil the scenery. 假如他們蓋了那家飯店，它將會破壞景色。
	scene (*nc*) 場景、情節、現場	• The scene was of utter destruction. 現場被完全破壞了。 • I need a change of scene. 我需要改變局面。

2	**hard** (*adj./adv.*) 困難的、堅硬的	• It's a very hard question. 這是個非常難的問題。 • It's very hard to solve this problem. 這個問題很難解決。
	hardly (*adv.*) 幾乎不、簡直不	• I could hardly see the trees in the distance because the rain was so heavy. 因為雨勢太大，我幾乎看不見遠處的樹木。 • We are hardly aware of how serious this problem is. 我們幾乎沒有意識到這個問題有多嚴重。
3	**less** (uncountable determiner) 較少的、更少的	• We need less pollution. 我們需要更少的污染。 • Less emphasis on this problem will be harmful. 少強調這個問題將會有害。
	few (countable determiner) 很少的	• A few people understand it. 少數人了解它。 • There are a few things we need to do. 有少數事情我們必須去做。
4	**method** (of Ving) (*nc*) 方法	• This method isn't working. 這個方法行不通。 • We need to find another method of getting this working. 我們需要找到別的方法來讓這管用。
	way (to V) (*nc*) 辦法、方式、途徑	• There must be another way. 一定有別的辦法。 • It's that way. 就是這樣。 • There's no way to stop it now. 現在沒辦法阻止它了。

5	_____ing (adj.)	• It's very interesting! 它非常有趣。 • What a disappointing meeting! 多麼讓人失望的會議！
	_____ed (adj.)	• She's very interested in new solutions. 她對新的解決方案非常感興趣。 • He was rather disappointed. 他相當失望。

☆ scene 和 scenery 在語法上有相似之處，但意思卻大不相同。scenery 專指風景，而風景向來都是不可數。scene 則用於泛指一個場面或情節，它也可以有比喻的意思。

☆ hard 和 hardly 看起來非常相似，實際上意思和用法皆不同。不過，它們非常容易被搞混。hard 意指「困難」，它向來都必須連同 it is 或 it was 來使用，例如：It was hard to follow her reasoning.。但是 I was hard to follow her reasoning. 的說法是錯誤的，因為 hard 不能用任何其他的主詞。

☆ hardly 意指「幾乎不」，我們可以把這個字視為用來使其後動詞幾近否定的一小部分語法，而不是用來表達困難的單字。例如：I could hardly understand what he said. 意指 I almost could not understand.，而 I hardly know what to think. 意指 I almost don't know what to think.。在語意中是有隱含困難之意，但實際上並沒有載明在用語中。在使用時應把 hardly 擺在主詞和動詞之間。

☆ less 和 few 的意思、用法皆相同，都是用於名詞之前表示名詞的少量。差別在於 less 是用來形容不可數名詞，而 a few 則用來形容可數名詞。a few 意指「一些」，few 若沒加 a 則意指「鮮少」。

☆ method 和 way 的文法相同，但意思稍有不同。method 是專指做事情的方法，牽涉到程序中的步驟，重點在於達成這個結果所需的步驟。例如 This method doesn't work. 意指程序中有事搞錯了。method 的語塊是 a method of Ving。

☆ way 可用來指代更廣泛的「方法」，也可以隱喻地用它來指代通往目標的途徑、概括的方向或習慣。way 有兩個語塊：the way to V 和 a way of Ving。它

們的意思相同。

☆ 表達感受的形容詞以 ＿ing 結尾時，通常是聚焦於產生這種感受的「外在成因」，其主詞通常是 it 或事物。而表達感受的形容詞以 ＿ed 結尾時，則是聚焦於「內在的感受」，主詞通常是 I 或體驗到感受的人。

　　在做下一個練習時，請仔細思考句意、文法和用法來選出正確的單字。

Task 42

請選出正確的單字來填入下列各句。

① **depressing/depressed**

Bad leadership can be very ＿＿＿＿＿＿.

② **Few/Less**

＿＿＿＿＿＿ wild animals are left in these woods. They've all gone.

③ **hard/hardly**

I can ＿＿＿＿＿＿ understand what is going on.

④ **depressed/depressing**

It is a very ＿＿＿＿＿＿ situation.

⑤ **hardly/hard**

It's ＿＿＿＿＿＿ for people to change their habits.

⑥ **method/way**

It's hard to get people to change their ＿＿＿＿＿＿ of thinking.

⑦ **hard/hardly**

It's ＿＿＿＿＿＿ to understand people who do not see this.

⑧ **depressing/depressed**

Many people are _____ by the amount of plastic in the oceans.

⑨ **scenery/scene**

The music _____ has been killed by the pandemic.

⑩ **scene/scenery**

The _____ was majestic and beautiful, with mountains and forests spread out.

⑪ **less/a few**

There are _____ things we can already start doing.

⑫ **scenery/scene**

They were one of the first teams to arrive on the _____.

⑬ **less/few**

We need _____ focus on profits, and more on resources.

⑭ **way/method**

We've developed a cheap and efficient _____ of purifying waste water.

⑮ **method/way**

Which _____ did they go?

✓ 答案・中譯・說明　　◎ **Track 1.11**

① Bad leadership can be very <u>depressing</u>.
差勁的領導會令人沮喪。

② Few wild animals are left in these woods. They've all gone.
這些樹林裡所剩的野生動物很少。牠們全都不見了。

③ I can hardly understand what is going on.

我幾乎無法理解是怎麼回事。

④ It is a very depressing situation.

這是一個非常令人沮喪的情況。

⑤ It's hard for people to change their habits.

人要改變習慣很難。

⑥ It's hard to get people to change their way of thinking.

要人改變想法很難。

⑦ It's hard to understand people who do not see this.

要理解看不見這點的人很難。

⑧ Many people are depressed by the amount of plastic in the oceans.

許多人對海洋中的塑膠數量感到沮喪。

⑨ The music scene has been killed by the pandemic.

音樂界被這波疫情扼殺了。

⑩ The scenery was majestic and beautiful, with mountains and forests spread out.

景色壯闊而美麗，山脈和森林綿延。

⑪ There are a few things we can already start doing.

有幾件事是我們已經可以開始去做了。

⑫ They were one of the first teams to arrive on the scene.

他們是首批抵達現場的團隊之一。

⑬ We need less focus on profits, and more on resources.

我們應該少關注利潤，多關注在資源。

⑭ We've developed a cheap and efficient method of purifying waste water.

我們已經開發出一種便宜而有效率的廢水淨化方法。

⑮ Which way did they go?

他們走的是哪條路？

....

☆ 第 1 句和第 4 句是在描述產生感受的外在原因，而不是感受本身。Bad leadership 是 it，而不是 I。第 8 句則是在描述人的內在感受。

☆ 在第 2 句中，animals 是可數，所以應該用 few；在第 11 句中，things 是可數，所以要用 a few；在第 13 句中，focus 是不可數，所以必須用 less。

☆ 第 3 句是在表示「幾乎不理解」。而第 5 句和第 7 句則是在表示「困難」，請注意這些句子中的主詞都是 it。

☆ 第 6 句中有一個可以學習的語塊：way of thinking。在第 14 句中，選用 method 是因為 cheap and efficient 暗示了程序中的步驟，而且語塊是 Ving。而在第 15 句中，必須選擇 way 則是因為意思是關於方向的問題。

　　最後我們還是要來練習從閱讀文章中找出這些容易搞混的單字。當你在文章中每找到一個單字，都必須停下來思考它是意指什麼、它的文法是什麼，以及它是如何使用的。

Task 43

請從 Task 1 和 Task 2 的閱讀文章中找出關鍵語庫 ❼ 列出的所有易混淆字詞，並留意它們在文章中是如何使用的。

Task 44

請練習用關鍵語庫　　的易混淆字詞來造句。

易混淆字詞	造句練習
scenery	
scene	
hard	
hardly	
less	
few	

070

method (of Ving)	
way (to V)	
_____ing	
_____ed	

☆ 在寫作中運用這些易混淆的字詞時，記得把重點放在文法、句意和用法上，而不是只注意單字的意思。

　　在你結束這個單元之前，請將下列清單看過，確定你能將所有要點都勾選起來。如果有一些要點你還搞不清楚，請回頭再次研讀本單元的相關部分。

☐ 我確實閱讀並理解了關於「環境」的長篇文章。

☐ 我完全知道字彙在文章中是如何使用，並更加了解到要怎麼用單字來表達特定的主題。

☐ 我已經學會 15 個關於「環境」主題的關鍵字，以及可與其搭配使用的動詞和形容詞。

☐ 我已經練習使用這些搭配詞來描寫「環境」。

☐ 我已經學到了一些同義詞，也了解在運用時需要注意的一些問題。

☐ 我學到了很多關於這個主題可以運用的語塊，包括片語動詞以及名詞或動詞為同形的單字。

☐ 我已經練習使用這些語塊。

☐ 我學到了 5 個關於這個主題的慣用語，且知道如何運用。

☐ 我已經理解在運用慣用語時需要特別注意的一些問題。

☐ 關於這個主題，我已經能確實掌握一些易混淆字詞的用法。

Unit 2

科技
Technology

閱讀文章 Reading

　　在前一個單元裡，各位學到了單字的用法要視主題和上下文而定。在本單元裡，主題則是科技以及我們與它在整個歷史上不斷變化的關係。

Task 1

閱讀文章並盡可能地理解文章內容。請先不要使用字典。

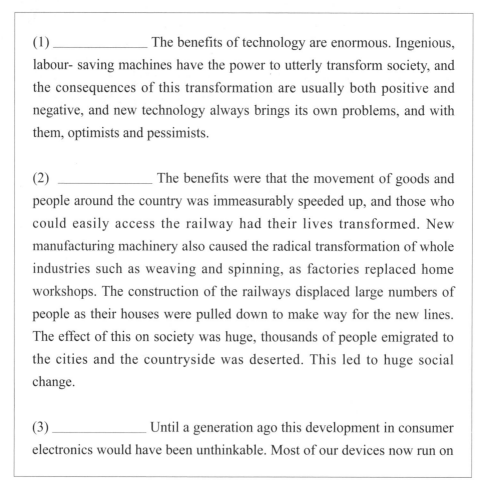

(1) _____ The benefits of technology are enormous. Ingenious, labour- saving machines have the power to utterly transform society, and the consequences of this transformation are usually both positive and negative, and new technology always brings its own problems, and with them, optimists and pessimists.

(2) _____ The benefits were that the movement of goods and people around the country was immeasurably speeded up, and those who could easily access the railway had their lives transformed. New manufacturing machinery also caused the radical transformation of whole industries such as weaving and spinning, as factories replaced home workshops. The construction of the railways displaced large numbers of people as their houses were pulled down to make way for the new lines. The effect of this on society was huge, thousands of people emigrated to the cities and the countryside was deserted. This led to huge social change.

(3) _____ Until a generation ago this development in consumer electronics would have been unthinkable. Most of our devices now run on

rechargeable lithium batteries which are capable of storing electricity for long times, and they can easily be charged up within a matter of hours. Many new devices are impossible to turn off: that little red light is always on. They also include all kinds of bells and whistles which a few years ago people didn't even know they lacked. Now, for example, your all singing, all dancing cell phone can make movies, take professional quality pictures, remind you when to exercise, play you music, in short do everything except wash the dishes. Some people feel this is excessive and they say that all these new functions are merely a fifth wheel: I don't need my washing machine to play music, they say. The trouble is once one company introduces an innovation, all the other companies in the same industry climb on the bandwagon and produce the same kind of device until there is actually very little to choose between them. Another disadvantage of this advanced functionality is that once our domestic appliances and ingenious, hand held devices break down it is not easy to get them repaired, they need to be discarded and replaced with new ones. This of course has a negative impact on the environment. However, the supply of lithium and other precious metals needed to produce these miraculous batteries is rapidly running out and mining companies say they can no longer supply the same large amounts as before. Electronics engineers fear that unless we can get access to new supplies of raw materials, this shortage will mean that continuous innovation will be possible in the future, and a lack of innovation means the progress of technology will effectively cease.

(4) _____ This new machinery will have a massive impact on our lives in the future. Proponents say the advantages of the new technology are that it will provide us with all kinds of benefits and freedoms that we can only now imagine. Humanoid, intelligent robots will be helping us at home, in schools and hospitals, and industrial robots

will be deployed in factories, allowing us more leisure time and freedom from work. And these benefits will only increase. Opponents say the problem with this is that there will be a massive increase in the number of serious traffic accidents as the technology is not yet ready to deal with the uncertainties of real-world traffic conditions. They fear the risks of allowing driverless cars on the roads. Designers of autonomous cars say the solutions to these problems are already being sorted out and they are optimistic about the technology, saying that the number of accidents will decrease as AI includes a technique for learning about real road conditions through experience. Eventually this decrease in accidents will result in zero road deaths.

(5) _____ Pessimists say our overdependence on it could likely kill us all and destroy the planet. They have made resolutions not to use the new technologies. Optimists say only a deficiency of imagination can prevent our progress, and that it's not a question of where our physical limits are, but of what our vision of the future is.

Task 2

請從下列句子選出適當的主題句以完成 Task 1 每個段落的填空。

A From the earliest days of the Industrial Revolution, the invention of the railways impacted society.

B The next technological wave of the future is the development of AI, especially in the area of autonomous cars and industrial robotics.

C Technology has always brought about unimaginable changes to human society, and the relationship between technology and society throughout history is complex.

D We are currently standing at the crossroads in our relationship with technology.

$\boxed{\text{E}}$ The biggest technological breakthrough of our time is in the remarkable extension of battery life.

◆ 答案・中譯・說明

(1) C   (2) A   (3) E   (4) B   (5) D

譯文

　　科技總是會對人類社會帶來難以想像的改變，而綜觀歷史，科技與社會之間的關係是很複雜的。科技所帶來的好處巨大。巧妙的、節省勞力的機器有本事全面地轉變社會，而這種轉變的結局通常是正負面兼具，新科技總是會帶來自身的問題，以及隨之而來的樂觀派和悲觀派。

　　從工業革命初期開始，鐵路的發明就衝擊了社會。好處是貨物與人員在國內的移動大為加速，使得那些能輕易運用到鐵路的人，生活發生了轉變。新的製造機具也造成了全體產業劇烈轉變，諸如紡織，因為工廠取代了家庭工坊。興建鐵路使得許多人流離失所，因為他們的房子遭到了拆除，以讓路給新的路線。這對社會的影響重大，成千上萬的人移居到城市，而農村則荒廢了。這導致了重大的社會變遷。

　　我們這時代最大的科技突破就是電池壽命大幅延長。直到一個世代之前，消費電子領域的這種發展是無法想像的。現在大部分的裝置都使用可充電的鋰電池，這種電池能長時間儲存電力，並能在若干小時內就輕易把電充好。很多新裝置都不可能關掉：那個小紅燈總是都亮著。它還包括了大家在幾年前甚至不知道自己缺少的各種鈴聲。例如現在無所不能的手機可以拍電影、拍出專業品質的照片、提醒你什麼時候去練身體、播音樂，總之就是除了洗碗，什麼事都做。有些人覺得這過頭了，並說這些新功能全都只是畫蛇添足：他們說，我並不需要洗衣機會播音樂。問題是，一旦有一家公司推出了一項創新，同行的其他公司全都會一窩蜂來生產同一種裝置，直到彼此間實際上有得選擇的非常少為止。這種先進功能的另一個缺點是，家用器具和精巧的手持裝置一旦故障，要把它修好並不容易，便必須加以丟棄並換成新機。這對環境當然會有負面的衝擊。不過在生產這些神奇的電池時，所需要的鋰和其他貴金屬在供應上正迅速耗盡，而且礦業公司表示，它們再也無法供應跟以前一樣大的量了。電子工程師怕的是，除非我們能在原料上獲得新的供應源，否則這樣的缺短就意味著，未來將不可能持續創新，而缺乏創新則意味著，科技的進步將會畫下句點。

　　未來的下一波科技浪潮是人工智慧的發展，尤其是在自駕車和工業機器人領域。這樣的新機具將對未來的生活產生巨大的影響。支持者說新科技的優點是，它會為我們提供現在只能靠想像的各種好處和自由。人形的智能機器人會在家裡、學校和醫院幫我們的忙，

工業機器人則會部署在工廠裡，這讓我們在工作以外有更多的閒暇時間與自由。而且這些好處只會增加。反對者表示，與此有關的問題是，嚴重交通事故的件數將會大幅度的增加，因為科技還沒準備好來應付現實世界交通狀況的不確定性。他們害怕允許無人駕駛車上路的風險。自動駕駛車的設計人員表示，這些問題的解決方案已經找到，而且對這項科技持樂觀態度的他們說，隨著人工智慧納入技術，以透過經驗來學習現實中的路況，事故的件數就會減少。這樣的事故減少最終則會使交通死亡為零。

在與科技的關係上，我們目前正站在十字路口。悲觀派說，對它過度依賴很可能會害死所有的人並毀滅掉地球。他們下定了決心不使用新科技。樂觀派說，只有想像力不足才能阻止我們進步，而且它的問題不在於我們的身體極限在哪，而在於我們對未來的願景是什麼。

....

☆ 請留意主題句 (topic sentence) 總是段落中最概括的句子，以及段落中的其他部分是如何以特定的例子或理由來申論主題句的論點。

☆ 在這篇文章裡，problem/solution「問題／解決方案」的結構出現在各主體段落中，第二段是關於過去，第三段是關於當前，第四段則是關於未來。

字詞搭配 Word Partnerships

我們現在要來學習「科技」這個主題的 15 個關鍵字，以及可搭配這些關鍵字使用的 word partnerships「字詞搭配表」。首先，請看關鍵字語庫。

Task 3

請仔細研讀這些主題字彙和下方的說明。

關鍵語庫 ❶　　⊚ **Track 2.1**

名詞	動詞	形容詞	字義
accident Ⓒ	-	accidental	事故、意外
appliance Ⓒ	-	-	器具、裝置、設備
battery Ⓒ	-	-	電池
breakthrough Ⓒ	-	-	突破、突破性進展
device Ⓒ	-	-	裝置、設備
electricity Ⓤ	-	electrical	電力
electronics Ⓤ	-	electronic	電子
engineer Ⓒ	engineer	engineered	工程師
functionality Ⓤ	function	functional	機能、功能
innovation Ⓒ	innovate	innovative	創新、改革
machine Ⓒ	-	mechanical	機器、機械
machinery Ⓤ	-	-	機具
robot Ⓒ	-	robotic	機器人
robotics Ⓤ	-	-	機器人學
transformation Ⓒ	transform	transformed	轉變、變革

☆ 需留意哪些名詞是可數，哪些是不可數。

☆ 要記得，名詞是可數或不可數，有時候須視主題而定。

☆ 注意單字的其他詞性形式，包含動詞和形容詞。

☆ electronics 在當名詞時，結尾必須要有 s。假如漏掉這個 s，你用的就是形容詞！由於這個名詞是不可數，所以動詞必須使用單數形，例如 Electronics is interesting. 是正確的，而 Electronics are interesting. 則是錯誤的。請特別留心這些細節！

☆ 注意，engineer 的名詞和動詞是相同的形式。當它是動詞時，意指製造某物，通常是一台機器。

☆ functionality 與動詞 function、形容詞 functional 的意思略有不同。function/functional 是指起作用的，或者某物可以正常運作，而 functionality 則是專指可以在一台設備上進行的所有不同操作。

☆ 當你想表達 innovation 的想法或過程時，請使用不可數單數形式：Innovation is very important in this industry.。若是要表示一種新裝置時，則可以用複數形式：New innovations are coming onto the market now.。

☆ a machine 是指一台機器，machinery 則是許多機器一起運作的系統。

☆ 注意，robotics 在當名詞時，結尾必須要有 s。假如漏掉這個 s，你用的就是形容詞！robotic 意指舉止像機器人，沒有感情或主動性。由於這個名詞是不可數，所以動詞必須使用單數形，例如 Robotics is interesting. 是正確的，而 Robotics are interesting. 則是錯誤的。請務必留意這些使用細節！

　　接下來，我們將以 5 個關鍵字為一組，深入地學習與這些字最頻繁搭配的字詞組合及正確用法。

Task 4

請研讀這個字詞搭配表、例句和底下的說明。

搭配在前面的動詞	搭配的形容詞	關鍵字	搭配在後面的動詞
have be involved in meet with cause reduce prevent	traffic car industrial work serious terrible	**accident**	happen occur take place

字詞搭配使用範例　(🎧) **Track 2.2**（收錄本單元 Task 4~Task 20 字詞搭配使用範例）

- She **had** a **terrible traffic accident**. 她出了可怕的交通事故。
- Fatigue **causes** a lot of **industrial accidents**. 疲勞會造成很多工業事故。
- AI will **reduce** the number of **accidents**. 人工智慧將減少事故的件數。
- **Serious accidents happen** when people are not concentrating.
  嚴重的事故往往發生在人們注意力不集中的時候。

☆ 搭配表中的動詞和形容詞是將意思相似的字詞歸類成一組。不過請記得，同義詞向來都是 topic and collocation specific「特定主題和搭配」。

Task 5

請研讀這個字詞搭配表、例句和底下的說明。

搭配在前面的動詞	搭配的形容詞	關鍵字	搭配在後面的動詞
switch on turn on switch off turn off	household domestic electrical faulty	**appliance**	work run function break down

- The **appliance broke down**, but now it is **functioning** smoothly.
  該器具故障過，但現在它運轉順暢。

- It's impossible to **turn off** many **electrical appliances**.
  不可能把很多電器都關掉。

- Some **appliances** cannot **be turned off**. 有些電器無法關閉。

☆ 注意，turn off/turn on 和它們的同義詞能使用於被動語態。

Task 6

請研讀這個字詞搭配表和例句。

搭配在前面的動詞	搭配的形容詞	關鍵字	搭配在後面的動詞
charge	dead		run out
recharge	flat		
charge up			
	rechargeable	**battery**	
replace	lithium		
connect			

- I think my **battery** is going to **run out**. I need to **recharge** it.
  我想我的電池快要沒電了。我需要充電。

- Your **battery** is **dead**. We need to **replace** it.
  你的電池沒電了。我們需要更換它。

Task 7

請研讀這個字詞搭配表和例句。

搭配在前面的動詞	搭配的形容詞	關鍵字
be make achieve represent	major big important significant historic scientific technological	**breakthrough**

字詞搭配使用範例

- AI **represents** the **biggest scientific breakthrough** in the last 20 years.
  人工智慧代表了過去 20 年來最大的科學突破。

- The team **achieved** their **historic breakthrough** by working together.
  這個團隊一起攜手合作達成了歷史性的突破。

Task 8

請研讀這個字詞搭配表、例句和底下的說明。

搭配在前面的動詞	搭配的形容詞	關鍵字	搭配在後面的動詞
design develop make use	clever ingenious electronic hi tech portable hand held	**device**	work run function be designed to V break down

- Samsung have **developed** an **ingenious portable device**.
  三星開發了一款精巧的可攜式裝置。

- The **device is designed to stop working** if someone tries to steal it.
  該裝置是設計來在有人嘗試竊取時停止運作。

☆ 請注意 device 能當作動詞的主詞來使用。

現在，我們來看看各位是否能用一些字詞搭配來擴大對字彙的運用。

Task 9

請從 Task 4 到 Task 8 中選出正確形式的字詞，完成以下段落填空。

> The (1) _____ (2) _____ battery (3) _____ the most (4) _____ (5) _____ breakthrough this century. It has allowed us to (6) _____ (7) _____ devices which we can carry around in our pocket. There are dangers, though, because (8) _____ (9) _____ accidents can (10) _____ if people are looking at their devices while driving. However, many (11) _____ appliances cannot (12) _____, which means increased power consumption.

範例答案

1. rechargeable
2. lithium
3. represents/is
4. important/significant
5. scientific/technological
6. design/develop

7. ingenious/clever
8. serious/terrible
9. traffic/car
10. happen/occur/take place
11. household/domestic
12. be turned off/be switched off

☆ 請留意各組同義字詞，空格中選填同一組內不同的字也是可以的。

☆ 須確認所選用的單字都是正確的形式。請檢查單數或複數，以及動詞的正確形式。例如在空格 (12) 中不管選用哪個動詞，都必須是被動式。

　　現在來學習另外 5 個單字。

Task 10

請研讀這個字詞搭配表和例句。

搭配在前面的動詞	搭配的形容詞	關鍵字
generate produce use supply store	high voltage low voltage static cheap expensive	**electricity**

字詞搭配使用範例

• The device **uses** very little **electricity**.
該裝置用電非常少。

• The invention is helping us to **generate cheaper electricity**.
這項發明有助於我們生產較便宜的電力。

• **Static electricity** can cause sparks. Be careful!
靜電可以引起火花。要小心！

Task 11

請研讀這個字詞搭配表和例句。

搭配在前的名詞 + prep.	搭配的形容詞	關鍵字
the development of the study of new developments in	consumer hi-tech state-of-the-art	
搭配在前的動詞		**electronics**
develop study work in		

字詞搭配使用範例

- **The development of consumer electronics** has made great progress this century. 消費性電子產品的發展在本世紀有長足的進展。

- **New developments in hi-tech electronics** have made many things possible. 高科技電子技術的新發展把許多事情化為了可能。

- More people now **work in electronics** than any other industry. 現在從事電子業的人比其他任何行業都要多。

Task 12

請研讀這個字詞搭配表、例句和底下的說明。

搭配在前面的動詞	搭配在前面的形容詞	搭配的形容詞	關鍵字
be train as	chief qualified skilled	aeronautical agricultural chemical civil electrical mechanical recording software	**engineer**

- Martin **is** the **chief engineer** on the project.　馬丁是該專案的首席工程師。
- He **trained as** a **civil engineer**.　他受過土木工程師的訓練。

....

☆ 請留意許多不同類型工程師的說法。

Task 13

請研讀這個字詞搭配表和例句。

搭配在前面的動詞	搭配的形容詞	關鍵字
have extend enhance add combine	basic core increased added advanced built-in	**functionality (of s/th)**

- Over the years, manufacturing companies **have enhanced** the **core functionality of** their products.
  多年來，製造業的公司已經增強了產品的核心機能。

- This product **has advanced built-in functionality**, so you don't need to add any apps.　這項產品有先進的內建功能，所以你不需要添加任何應用程式。

Task 14

請研讀這個字詞搭配表和例句。

搭配在前面的動詞	搭配的形容詞	關鍵字
encourage	constant	
facilitate	continuous	
stimulate		**innovation**
	scientific	**(in s/th)**
stifle	technical	
limit	technological	

字詞搭配使用範例

- We need to **stimulate continuous innovation in** this field.
  我們需要刺激這個領域的持續創新。

- The government is **stifling innovation** in the field of electronics.
  政府在扼殺電子領域的創新。

就像前面所做過的，我們再來練習這第二組 5 個單字的字詞搭配應用。

Task 15

請從 Task 10 到 Task 14 中選出正確形式的字詞，完成以下段落填空。

The (1) _____ engineers in modern factories are all highly (2) _____, and have all (3) _____ electronics, so they all have a lot of experience. (4) _____ innovation (5) _____, so that software products are always excellent and up to date. Modern products are designed to (6) _____ very little electricity, especially when one considers their (7) _____ functionality. In the past, previous products only had very (8) _____ functionality, but contemporary products can do a whole range of tasks.

1. software/electrical	5. is encouraged/is stimulated/is facilitated
2. skilled/qualified	6. use
3. studied/worked in	7. advanced
4. constant/continuous	8. basic

☆ 再次提醒，請留意各組同義字詞。空格中選填同一組內不同的字也是可以的。

☆ 務必確認所選用的單字都是正確的形式。檢查單數或複數，以及動詞的正確形式。例如空格 (5) 不管選用哪個動詞，都必須是被動式。

現在我們來學習最後一組的 5 個單字。

Task 16

請研讀這個字詞搭配表和例句。

搭配在前面的動詞	搭配的形容詞	關鍵字
design	huge	
	large	
build		
make	powerful	
install	labour-saving	**machine (for Ving)**
operate	ingenious	
use	versatile	
repair	reliable	
service		

字詞搭配使用範例

• They **designed** and **built** this **powerful machine** in record time.
  他們於破紀錄的時間內設計並建造了這台強大的機器。

- The **machine** is quite difficult to **operate**, so operators need training.
  該機器相當難操作，所以操作員需要受訓。

- It's an **ingenious machine for** washing clothes.
  它是一種巧妙的洗衣服的機器。

Task 17

請研讀這個字詞搭配表、例句和底下的說明。

搭配在前面的動詞	搭配在前面的形容詞	搭配的形容詞	關鍵字
replace update install set up operate maintain service	heavy complex complicated sophisticated	agricultural construction farm industrial manufacturing office	**machinery (for Ving)**

字詞搭配使用範例

- They are currently **replacing** all **manufacturing machinery** and **updating** it.
  他們目前正在更換所有的製造機具並進行更新。

- **Complex machinery** takes a great deal of power to **operate**.
  複雜的機具要花大量的動力才能運行。

- With **machinery** this **sophisticated**, you need to constantly **maintain** it,
  otherwise it can break down.
  使用這麼精密的機具，你需要經常保養它，否則它可能會故障。

☆ 請注意不同類型機具的說法。

Task 18

請研讀這個字詞搭配表、例句和底下的說明。

搭配在前面的動詞	搭配的形容詞	關鍵字	搭配在後面的動詞
design	humanoid		perform
build	autonomous		do
program	intelligent	**robot**	
control	mobile		
deploy	giant		
	industrial		

字詞搭配使用範例

- **Intelligent robots have been designed** to help us with all sorts of tasks.
  智能機器人是設計來幫助我們完成各種工作任務。

- An army of **giant robots was deployed** to construct a damn over the river, the first time robots have been used in this way.
  一支巨形機器人大軍被部署在河上興建一座水壩，這是機器人首次以這種方式來使用。

- The **robots are programmed** never to harm humans.
  這些機器人被設定為絕不會去危害人類。

....

☆ 注意，這些動詞中有很多可以使用於被動語態。

Task 19

請研讀這個字詞搭配表、例句和底下的說明。

搭配在前的名詞 + of	搭配的形容詞	關鍵字
the development of the study of	hi-tech state-of-the-art	
搭配在前的動詞	industrial	
develop apply study work in		**robotics**

字詞搭配使用範例

- All our engineers **have worked in robotics**. 我們的工程師全都鑽研過機器人學。
- **The development of hi-tech robotics** is the next technological wave of the future. 高科技機器人學的發展是未來下一波的科技潮。
- **Robotics** can **be applied to** almost every human activity.
  機器人學可應用到幾乎是每一項人類活動上。

☆ 注意，這些動詞中有很多可以使用於被動語態。

Task 20

請研讀這個字詞搭配表、例句和底下的說明。

搭配在前的動詞	搭配在前的形容詞	搭配的形容詞	關鍵字
undergo make achieve cause lead to	complete amazing dramatic profound radical fundamental rapid sudden	cultural economic historical industrial intellectual political social	**transformation (of s/th)**

- Society **underwent** a **transformation** during the Industrial Revolution.
  在工業革命的期間，社會經歷了一場變革。

- Technology has always **caused fundamental historical transformations**.
  科技總是會造成根本性的歷史變革。

- There will be a **profound transformation of** the social structure.
  社會結構將發生深刻的變化。

☆ 請留意不同類型的「轉變」說法。

接下來，我們來練習這最後一組 5 個單字的字詞搭配應用。

Task 21

請從 Task 16 到 Task 20 中選出正確形式的字詞，完成以下段落填空。

> (1) _____ robotics will (2) _____ a (3) _____ (4)
> _____ transformation. Society will never be the same again, as (5)
> _____ robots will (6) _____ tasks previously done by
> surgeons, nurses and teachers. In the field of industry, (7) _____
> machines are already (8) _____ to move enormous amounts of earth
> or material in mining or construction, for example. (9) _____ this (10)
> _____ machinery will require a large army of qualified engineers.

範例答案

1. the development of	6. perform/do
2. cause/lead to	7. huge/large
3. profound/radical/fundamental	8. being used/being operated
4. social	9. maintaining/servicing
5. intelligent/autonomous	10. sophisticated/complex/complicated

☆ 同樣的，還是要留意各組的同義字詞。

☆ 請確認所選用的單字都是正確的形式。檢查單數或複數，以及動詞的正確形式，例如在空格 (8) 中，因為前面有 already 的關係，use 或 operate 必須使用現在進行被動式。另外，在空格 (9) 中，你必須使用 Ving，因為這個單字是動詞 require 的主詞，而且主詞需要用 Ving 或 n.p.。

　　記住，多閱讀有助於擴充字彙量，而在文章上下文脈絡中查看大量例子則能幫助你記憶新的用語。下一個練習對於各位記憶 15 個關鍵單字和它們的字詞搭配將有非常大的幫助。

Task 22

請從 Task 1 和 Task 2 的閱讀文章中找出關鍵語庫 ❶ 所列的 15 個關鍵字，並留意這些字在文章中是如何使用的。

常用語塊 Chunks

前面學過了字詞搭配的用法，我們現在要來學一些可用在寫作或談論科技問題的 chunks「語塊」。

Task 23

研讀這些語塊和底下的說明。

關鍵語庫 ②

Chunk
❑ be capable of n.p./Ving　能夠 n.p./Ving
❑ be optimistic about n.p./Ving　對 n.p./Ving 持樂觀態度
❑ the advantage of n.p./Ving　n.p./Ving 的優點
❑ the benefit of n.p./Ving　n.p./Ving 的好處
❑ the consequence of n.p./Ving　n.p./Ving 的結果
❑ the disadvantage of n.p./Ving　n.p./Ving 的缺點
❑ the effect (of X) (on Y)　X 對 Y 的效應
❑ the problem with n.p./Ving　n.p./Ving 的問題
❑ the risk of n.p./Ving　n.p./Ving 的風險
❑ the solution to n.p./Ving　n.p./Ving 的解決方法

☆ 別忘了使用這些語塊時需要去改變動詞的時態。

☆ 這些語塊全都必須用 n.p. 或 Ving。

☆ 請注意在 The effect of X on Y 這個語塊中，所聚焦的可以是只有 X 或只有 Y，或者是都有。X 和 Y 要用 n.p. 或 Ving。

☆ advantage、benefit、consequence、disadvantage 和 risk 這些字指廣泛的層面時，要用複數 s 來表示；假如是意指專門的層面時，則要用單數。例如，

The benefits of technology are huge. ，這是從廣泛的層面來說明科技的好處，而 The benefit of this technology is that people can find out where they are. 則是專指一項好處。

☆ 請務必記得，在學習和使用語塊時須特別注意小詞、字尾和語塊的結尾這些細節，確保使用上完全準確。

　　下一個 Task 將聚焦於大家在使用這些語塊時經常會犯的錯誤。

Task 24

請改正這些句子中使用語塊的常見錯誤。

① Autonomous cars are not yet capable to understand all road conditions.

_____

② Most people not optimistic about the future.

_____

③ The advantages to having a phone are that you can always get in touch with people.

_____

④ The benefits to technology outweigh the advantage.

_____

⑤ The consequences for AI are not yet well understood.

_____

⑥ The disadvantages about robots are unemployment and high development costs.

_____

⑦ The effect on technology of the user are well known.

_____

⑧ The problem about this is that many people want it.

_____

⑨ The risks for having this technology are very high.

_____

⑩ The solution of the problem is very expensive.

_____

☑ 答案・中譯・說明　◉ Track 2.3

① Autonomous cars <u>are</u> not yet <u>capable **of**</u> understanding all road conditions.
自駕車還不能理解所有的路況。

② Most people **are** not optimistic about the future.
大部分的人對未來並不樂觀。

③ The advantages **of** having a phone are that you can always get in touch with people.
有手機的優點是，你隨時都能跟人聯絡。

④ The benefits **of** technology outweigh the advantage**s**.
科技的好處重於優點。

⑤ The consequences **of** AI are not yet well understood.
人工智慧的影響還沒有受到妥善了解。

⑥ The disadvantages **of** robots are unemployment and high development costs.
機器人的缺點是失業率和高昂的開發成本。

⑦ The effect **of** technology **on** the user are well known.
科技對使用者的影響是眾所周知的。

⑧ The problem **with** this is that many people want it.
問題在於很多人都想要它。

⑨ The risks **of** having this technology are very high.
使用這項技術的風險非常高。

⑩ The solution **to** the problem is very expensive.

這個問題的解決方案非常貴。

....

☆ 我已經把錯誤的部分標示出來，各位可以清楚看出哪裡用錯了。

☆ 請注意，在第 1 句和第 2 句裡，必須使用 be 動詞。

☆ 請將 Task 24 的句子與關鍵語庫 ❷ 的語塊做比較，以確保能清楚看出句中哪裡用錯了。

☆ 請將正確句子中的完整語塊畫上底線（參照第 1 句的示範），這能幫助你完整而正確地記住語塊。

　　下一個練習對於記憶語塊將有非常大的幫助。記住，多閱讀有助於擴充字彙量，而在文章上下文脈絡中查看大量語塊則能幫助你記憶新的用語。

Task 25

請從 Task 1 和 Task 2 的閱讀文章中找出關鍵語庫 ❷ 列出的所有語塊，並留意這些語塊在文章中是如何使用的。

Task 26

現在請嘗試用前面學過的語塊來寫出你自己的句子。

關鍵字語塊	造句
be capable of n.p./Ving	
be optimistic about n.p./Ving	
the advantage of n.p./Ving	
the benefit of n.p./Ving	

the consequence of n.p./Ving	
the disadvantage of n.p./Ving	
the effect (of X) (on Y)	
the problem with n.p./Ving	
the risk of n.p./Ving	
the solution to n.p./Ving	

☆ 我顯然無法在此改正你的句子,但你可以透過確認語塊所有的小細節,自行改正。再次提醒在寫作中運用語塊時,須特別注意小詞、字尾和語塊的結尾,無論所需要的是 n.p.、v.p.、Ving 還是 V,並且確保你所使用的語塊是完整的。

5 個可作動詞或名詞的單字
5 words which can be verbs or nouns

　　語塊通常會視關鍵字是名詞或動詞而有所不同，現在我們要來看 5 個動詞和名詞同形的單字，並學習使用正確的語塊。

Task 27

請看以下幾個名詞和動詞同形的單字。

關鍵語庫 ❸

關鍵字	名詞字義	動詞字義
decrease	減少量；減小	減少；減小；降低
increase	增加；增多；增長	增加；提高；增強
impact	影響；效果；碰撞；衝擊力	對……產生影響；衝擊；撞擊
access	接近；進入；接近的機會；進入的權利；使用	【電腦】存取（資料）；使用；接近
lack	欠缺（的東西）；不足	缺少；不足；沒有

Task 28

閱讀句子並判斷關鍵字是動詞或名詞，填入 V 或 N。

① ＿＿＿ The number of accidents has **decreased**.

② ＿＿＿ There has been a **decrease** in the number of accidents.

③ ＿＿＿ The program gets more accurate when there is an **increase** in the number of users.

④ ＿＿＿ If we **increase** the number of users, the program gets more accurate.

⑤ ＿＿＿ The **impact** of the technology on the local community was high.

⑥ _____ The technology **impacted** the local community in a big way.

⑦ _____ No one can gain **access** to the technology.

⑧ _____ The technology cannot be **accessed** easily.

⑨ _____ The population **lacks** technological knowledge.

⑩ _____ There is a **lack** of technological knowledge in the population.

✅ 答案・中譯・說明

① V 事故的件數減少了。

② N 事故的件數已經有所減少。

③ N 當使用者的人數增加時，該程式就會變得更加準確。

④ V 假如我們把使用者的人數增加，程式就會變得更準確。

⑤ N 科技對地方社區的衝擊很大。

⑥ V 科技大幅衝擊到地方社區。

⑦ N 沒人能接觸到該項技術。

⑧ V 該項技術無法輕易被獲取。

⑨ V 人們缺乏科技知識。

⑩ N 人們對科技知識有所缺乏。

☆ 當 increase 和 decrease 作動詞時，不可使用 be 動詞。這些動詞不會以被動語態來使用，The number of accidents was decreased.、The capability was increased. 都是錯的，The number of accidents decreased.、The capability increased. 才正確。

☆ access 當名詞時，要連同動詞 have、get、give、gain 或 receive 來使用。例如，I cannot get access to it.、It's impossible to gain access to it.。若要聚焦於受詞，可以把 access 當動詞以被動語態來使用。例如，Anyone can access the technology.（主動語態）；The technology can be accessed by anyone.（被動語態）。

☆ lack 這個字非常微妙，而且在台灣經常被用錯。請注意，lack 在當名詞時，要連同 there is（或相關時態）或者 have 來使用。例如，There is a lack of technology.。They currently have a lack of qualified people to work on the project. 。比起當動詞，lack 在英文裡當名詞來用要自然得多。

☆ 記住，在使用這些單字的動詞語塊時，務必要確保所使用的動詞時態正確。

☆ 能夠掌握這些字在動詞語塊和名詞語塊上的差別是非常重要的。接下來的練習將幫助各位更加熟悉相關用法

Task 29

請看以下所彙整的語塊及用法說明。

關鍵語庫 ❹ ◎ Track 2.4

關鍵字語塊	關鍵字詞性	例句＆翻譯
a decrease (of X) (in Y)	*nc*	There was a decrease of 2% in the number of failures. 失敗數有 2% 的減少。
decrease	*vi*	The number of failures decreased. 失敗數減少了。
an increase (of X) (in Y)	*nc*	There was an increase of 8% in the success rate. 成功率有 8% 的增加。
increase	*vi*	The success rate increased. 成功率增加了。
the impact (of X) (on Y)	*nc*	They studied the impact of the new technology on users. 他們研究了新技術對使用者的衝擊。
impact s/th	*vt*	The new technology impacted users in various ways. 這項新技術以種種的方式衝擊了使用者。
V access to	*nu*	Unqualified people do not have access to the technology. 不合格的人無法使用該項技術。
access s/th	*vt*	No one can access it. 沒有人能使用它。
V a lack of	*nu*	Robots still have a lack of accuracy. 機器人在準確度上還是有所缺乏。

lack s/th	*vt*	Robots still lack accuracy. 機器人還是缺乏準確度。

☆ 須留意哪些名詞是可數，哪些是不可數。

☆ 請注意，decrease 和 increase 當名詞用時，of 之後是接數目，in 之後則是接主題。

☆ 另外，decrease 和 increase 當動詞時都是不及物動詞，所以不能加受詞。例如，They increased the success rate.、They decreased the number of people. 的用法都是錯的，正確應為 The success rate increased.、The number of people decreased.。請仔細看語庫中的例句。

PART
1

☆ impact 當名詞用時，可以有兩個受詞。兩個受詞都必須是 n.p. 或 Ving。

☆ access 當動詞用時，不可使用 to。只有在當名詞時，access 才能使用 to。

☆ lack 當動詞用時，不可使用 of。只有在當名詞時，lack 才能使用 of。

☆ 請仔細學習這些語塊，並把重點放在諸如介系詞和冠詞這些細節。

好的，現在讓我們來嘗試正確使用這些語塊。

Task 30

請選用正確形式的單字或語塊，完成下列各句。

① **decrease/a decrease of**

Costs generally ＿＿＿＿＿＿ when robots are used.

② **access to/access**

Hackers might be able to ＿＿＿＿＿＿ the technology.

③ **gain access /access**

No one should be able to ＿＿＿＿＿＿ to the technology without permission.

④ **been increased/increased**

The number of technological breakthroughs has ——————.

⑤ **increased/an increase in**

There has been —————— battery life.

⑥ **lack/a lack**

There is —————— of innovation in the field.

⑦ **a decrease in/a decrease of**

There was —————— production.

⑧ **impacted on/impacted**

This invention has —————— our quality of life.

⑨ **the impact on/the impact of**

We have yet to fully understand —————— technology on society.

⑩ **are in lack of/lack**

We —————— the resources to develop more technology.

✔ 答案・中譯・說明　🔊 **Track 2.5**

① Costs generally <u>decrease</u> when robots are used.
使用機器人時，成本通常會降低。

② Hackers might be able to access the technology.
駭客或許能動用到該技術。

③ No one should be able to gain access to the technology without permission.
在未經允許下，任何人都不能接觸這項技術。

④ The number of technological breakthroughs has increased.
科技突破的數量增加了。

⑤ There has been an increase in battery life. 電池的壽命已有所增加。

⑥ There is a lack of innovation in the field. 這個領域缺乏創新。

⑦ There was a decrease in production. 生產有所減少。

⑧ This invention has impacted our quality of life.
這項發明影響了我們的生活品質。

⑨ We have yet to fully understand the impact of technology on society.
我們還沒有完全了解到科技對社會的衝擊。

⑩ We lack the resources to develop more technology.
我們缺乏發展更多科技的資源。

☆ 請拿正確的句子來與關鍵語庫 ❹ 的語塊做比較，確保名詞或動詞語塊都用得正確。

☆ 請將正確句子中的完整語塊畫上底線（參照第 1 句的示範）。這將有助於各位把語塊完整而正確地記起來。

　　請詳讀本單元開頭的閱讀文章，並從中把這 5 個動詞和名詞同形的關鍵字語塊全部找到。再次提醒，盡可能地多閱讀有助於擴充字彙量，而在文章上下文脈絡中查看大量語塊則能幫助你記憶新的用語。

Task 31

請從 Task 1 和 Task 2 的閱讀文章中找出關鍵語庫 ❹ 列出的所有語塊，並留意這些語塊在文章中是當動詞還是名詞使用？

Task 32

請練習用關鍵語庫 ❹ 的語塊來造句。

關鍵字語塊	造句
a decrease (of X) (in Y)	

decrease	
an increase (of X) (in Y)	
increase	
the impact (of X) (on Y)	
impact s/th	
V access to	
access s/th	
V a lack of	
lack s/th	

☆ 我顯然無法在此來改正你的句子，但你可以透過確認語塊所有的小細節，自行改正。再次提醒在寫作中運用語塊時，須特別注意小詞、字尾和語塊的結尾，無論所需要的是 n.p.、v.p.、Ving 還是 V，並且確保你所使用的語塊是完整的。

5 個談論或寫作科技相關主題常用的 片語動詞 5 phrasal verbs for talking or writing about technology

我們現在要來看一些在寫作或談論科技相關主題時，常會用到的片語動詞。

Task 33

研讀語庫中的片語動詞、例句和其下的說明。

關鍵語庫 ⑤　 Track 2.6

片語動詞	例句
break down 發生故障、失敗	• The technology has never broken down. 這項技術從來沒有發生故障過。 • If it breaks down, we will be in a lot of trouble. 假如它故障了，我們會遇到很多麻煩。
turn s/th off 關掉、關閉	• It's impossible to turn off this function. 這個功能不可能關掉。 • It's impossible to turn this function off. 要關掉這個功能是不可能的。 • It's impossible to turn it off. 要關掉它是不可能的。
charge s/th up 把空的電池完全 填滿電力	• It takes about 2 hours to fully charge up the battery. 電池充飽電大概需要兩小時。 • It takes about 2 hours to fully charge the battery up. 把電池充飽電大概需要兩小時。 • It takes about 2 hours to fully charge it up. 它充飽電大概需要兩小時。 • It can be fully charged up in about 2 hours. 它大概兩小時就能充飽電。

sort s/th out 挑選出、解決 （問題等）、分類	• We need to sort out these problems first. 我們需要先找出這些問題。 • We need to sort these problems out first. 我們需要先把這些問題找出來。 • We need to sort them out first. 我們需要先把它找出來。 • Has it been sorted out yet? 它被分類好了嗎？
bring about s/th 造成事物發生	• Technology has brought about huge changes to our lifestyle. 科技對我們的生活方式造成了巨大的改變。

☆ 在學習和使用片語動詞時，你必須非常留意動詞有沒有受詞 (s/th)，以及這個受詞是擺在哪個位置。請仔細確認上方語庫中的片語動詞及其受詞的位置。

☆ 請注意，break down 沒有受詞，而其他的片語動詞全都有受詞。假如受詞是 n.p. 的話，可以擺在動詞和介系詞之間或介系詞之後；假如受詞是代名詞，則只能擺在動詞和介系詞之間。

☆ bring about s/th 有點特別。在使用這個片語動詞時，名詞受詞向來應擺在介系詞之後，而不是動詞和介系詞之間。這是常見的用法。

☆ 請仔細看例句，以確保自己了解正確的受詞擺放位置。

☆ 注意，charge s/th up 和 sort s/th out 能以被動式來使用。請看例句。

☆ 另外，非常重要的是，請記得片語動詞是動詞，所以還必須考慮動詞要用什麼時態。

　　下一個練習將有助於各位聚焦於受詞的正確擺放位置這些細節上。

Task 34

下列各句中的第一個字是正確的，請按照順序將其後的字詞重組成正確的句子。

EX. **It's off to turn difficult it.**

　　It's difficult to turn it off.

① The of revolution will about robotics a development bring

_____

② If these can't sort we proceed problems out, we able be will not to

_____

③ You now charge can easily batteries quickly up and

_____

④ Most devices turn never their off people

_____

⑤ Sometimes down machines the break

_____

✔ 答案・中譯・說明　🔊 **Track 2.7**

① The development of robotics will <u>bring about a revolution</u>.
機器人學的發展將引起一場革命。

② If we can't sort these problems out, we will not be able to proceed.

= If we can't sort out these problems, we will not be able to proceed.
假如不能把這些問題找出來，我們就無法繼續下去。

③ You can now charge up batteries quickly and easily.

= You can now charge batteries up quickly and easily.
現在可以迅速又容易地替電池充電。

④ Most people never turn off their devices.　大多數人從不關掉他們的裝置。

= Most people never turn their devices off.　大多數人從不把他們的裝置關掉。

⑤ Sometimes the machines break down.　有時候機器會故障。

☆ 請注意，2、3、4 句有兩種解答，就看受詞是擺在哪個位置。

☆ 將正確的句子與關鍵語庫 ❺ 中的片語動詞做比較，確認你的用法都正確。

☆ 請將正確句子中的片語動詞畫上底線，這將幫助你完整而正確地把語塊記起來。（參照第 1 句的示範）

現在來看看這些片語動詞是如何運用在文章脈絡中。

Task 35

請從 Task 1 和 Task 2 的閱讀文章中找出關鍵語庫 ❺ 列出的所有片語動詞，並留意它們在文章中是如何使用的。

Task 36

請練習用關鍵語庫 ❺ 的片語動詞來造句。

片語動詞	造句練習
break down	
turn s/th off	
charge s/th up	
sort s/th out	
bring about s/th	

☆ 再次提醒在寫作時若運用到這些片語動詞時，要特別留意動詞的時態和受詞的位置。

5 個談論或寫作科技相關主題常用的慣用語 5 idioms for talking or writing about technology

現在來看看在寫作或談論這個主題時，所能運用的一些慣用語。請記得，在慣用語中只有一件事能改變，那就是動詞時態──假如這個慣用語包含動詞的話。

Task 37

研讀語庫中的慣用語、例句和其下的說明。

關鍵語庫 ❻　◉ Track 2.8

慣用語	例句
bells and whistles 眾多機能，非常花俏的東西	• This new phone has all the bells and whistles you could ever want. 對於你可能曾想要的花樣，這款新手機全都有。
all singing, all dancing 說明科技產品功能齊全，現代而先進	• Apple's new device is an all singing, all dancing marvel of technology. 蘋果的新裝置是功能齊全、無所不能的科技奇蹟。
at the crossroads 歷史的轉折點，重要的改變	• We find ourselves at the crossroads in our relationship with technology. 在與科技的關係上，我們發現自己面臨重大抉擇。
climb on the bandwagon 加入來讓某事蔚為流行，參與風潮	• Tech companies are climbing on the bandwagon to produce similar products. 科技公司正一窩蜂生產類似的產品。

| fifth wheel
無用之物 | • Some people think this function is a bit of a fifth wheel. Why would you need it?
有些人認為，這項功能有點畫蛇添足。你為什麼會需要？ |

☆ 使用慣用語時唯一能更動的是動詞時態。

☆ 為了讓慣用語有意義，它必須完全準確才行，這意味著你必須將慣用語的所有細節都使用正確。

☆ bells and whistles 和 all singing, all dancing 或多或少具有相同的意思。

☆ 請注意這幾個慣用語都沒有受詞，不要連同受詞來使用。

　　下一個練習將有助於各位聚焦於使用這些慣用語時，經常會犯的錯誤。

Task 38

改正這些句子中的常見錯誤。

① My new phone has a bell and a whistle.

_____

② Their new all dancing all singing product is amazing.

_____

③ We are standing at a crossroad.

_____

④ These things become popular when everyone gets on the wagon.

_____

⑤ Having four cameras on my phone is a bit like having an extra wheel.

_____

① My new phone has lots of <u>bells and whistles</u>.

我的新手機有很多花俏的功能。

② Their new all singing, all dancing product is amazing.

他們功能齊全、無所不能的新產品令人驚嘆。

③ We are standing at the crossroads. 我們正處於重大的轉折點。

④ These things become popular when everyone climbs on the bandwagon.

當每個人都一窩蜂時，這些東西就變得蔚為流行。

⑤ Having four cameras on my phone is a bit like having a fifth wheel.

手機上有四個鏡頭，有點像是畫蛇添足。

....

☆ 這些錯誤通常是漏掉了小詞、改變了小詞或單字結尾、慣用語不完整，或者在一個不該有受詞的地方加上了受詞。

☆ 請仔細比較錯誤句子和正確解答，務必確實掌握錯在哪以及為什麼是錯的。

☆ 請將正確句子中的慣用語畫上底線。（參照第 1 句的示範）

　　現在我們要練習在文章上下文中找出慣用語。

Task 39

請從 Task 1 和 Task 2 的閱讀文章中找出關鍵語庫 ❻ 列出的所有慣用語，並留意它們在文章中是如何使用的。

Task 40

請練習用關鍵語庫 ❻ 的慣用語來造句。

慣用語	造句練習
bells and whistles	

all singing, all dancing	
at the crossroads	
climb on the bandwagon	
fifth wheel	

☆ 再次提醒在寫作時若運用到這些慣用語，要特別留意動詞的時態和完整的慣用語包含哪些細節。

易混淆的字詞 easily confused words

- 在上個單元中，各位學到了在試著針對容易搞混的單字去了解差別時，需要思考的不僅是意思上的差異，還有文法和用法。
- 要記得，有些單字只能用在特定的主題上，用在別的主題則不適當。
- 另外要記得，容易搞混的單字，其差別常常是在搭配詞的使用上有所不同。

在做接下來幾個練習時，務必記得這些重點。

Task 41

請仔細研讀各組易混淆的字詞、例句和其下的說明。

關鍵語庫 ⑦ 🎧 **Track 2.10**

	易混淆字詞	例句
1	**technique** (*nc*) 方法、技巧	• Her piano playing technique is amazing. 她彈鋼琴的技巧令人驚嘆。 • It's a very useful technique, but it's hard to learn. 這是一個非常有用的技術，但是很難學。
	technology (*nc*) 科技	• Technology is man's greatest achievement. 科技是人類最偉大的成就。 • Some technologies are quite dangerous. 有些科技相當危險。

2	**supply s/o with s/th** (*vt*) 給予、提供、供應	• They are supplying us with all the materials we need. 他們供應我們所需要的一切材料。 • They will only supply us with four machines. 他們只會提供我們四台機器。
	provide s/o with s/th (*vt*) 供給、為某人提供某物	• Can you provide an explanation? 你能提供一個解釋嗎？ • They provided us with a few choices. 他們為我們提供了幾個選擇。
3	**shortage** (*nc*) 短缺、不足	• There is a shortage of rare metals needed to make batteries. 製造電池所需要的稀有金屬有所短缺。 • There is currently a water shortage. 目前缺水。
	deficiency (*nc*) 不足、缺陷	• We have a budget deficiency. 我們的預算不足。 • There is often a deficiency in understanding. 理解上往往有所不足。
4	**resolution** (*nc*) 堅實而持久的決定、決議、決心	• I have made a resolution to stop looking at my phone all the time. 我已經下定決心不再一直看手機了。 • I've broken all my New Year's resolutions. 我的新年決心全都破功了。
	solution (*nc*) 解決方案、解答	• The solution to this problem lies in us. 這個問題的解方就在我們身上。 • We need to find a solution soon. 我們必須趕緊找到解決辦法。
5	**question about** (*nc*) 懷疑、疑問	• There are many questions concerning the reliability of the technology. When can we talk about them? 關於該項技術的可靠性有很多疑問。我們什麼時候能談一談？
	problem with (*nc*) 問題	• There are too many problems with the equipment. We need to solve them soon. 該設備有太多的問題。我們必須趕緊解決。

☆ technique 和 technology 看起來字形相近,似乎是有關聯的,但事實上,它們的意思和用法截然不同。當要指稱的是技巧、才華或方法時,應使用 technique,這個單字不限於科技的主題,也可運用在其他許多的主題上。只有在談及科技的主題時,才使用 technology,當要指稱很多不同類型的科技時,可以使用複數形,否則就該用單數形。

☆ supply 和 provide 有相同的文法和類似的意思,但用法稍有不同。只有在指稱實體物件時,才使用 supply,但不能用 supply 來指稱概念或抽象事件,諸如 solutions、choices、explanations 等等。而 provide 則能用來指稱實體物件,也能用來指稱概念或抽象事件,諸如 solutions、choices、explanations 等等。

☆ shortage 和 deficiency 有相同的文法和類似的意思,但用法稍有不同。shortage 只能用來指稱可以量化的實體物件,但不能用來指稱概念或抽象事件。而 deficiency 則用來指稱概念或抽象事件,諸如 solutions、choices、explanations 等等,這個單字並不常用。

☆ resolution 和 solution 的字形也非常相近,似乎它們在某方面相關,然而實際上,這兩個字在意思和用法上非常不同。resolution 是改變人生的決定,常伴隨著誓言,例如我們會在除夕時下定決心說:I have made a resolution to quit smoking.。而 solution 則意指終結問題,你通常會在文章中一起找到 solution 和 problem 這兩個字。注意,在寫 problem/solution「問題 / 解決方案」的文章時,要使用 solution,千萬不可以用 resolution。

☆ question 和 problem 常會搞混,因為這兩個概念在中文裡所用的字詞相同,然而在英文裡則相當不同。A question about 是必須以 information「資訊」來回應的問題。資訊通常是以解答的形式出現,也就是說,若要聚焦在「資訊」上即需使用 question;而 A problem with 則是必須以 action「行動」來回應的問題。行動通常是以問題之解決方案的形式出現,若想要聚焦在解決方案或解決問題的行動上時,就應使用 problem。

在做下一個練習時,請仔細思考句意、文法和用法來選出正確的單字。

Task 42

請選出正確的單字來填入下列各句。

① **deficiency/shortage**

Income _____ means most of the world suffers in poverty.

② **technology/technique**

Over the years he has worked hard on improving his _____.

③ **Providing/Supplying**

_____ water to the factories is now our main task.

④ **provide/supply**

Technology allows companies to _____ a better service for their customers.

⑤ **provide/supply**

Technology companies _____ employment for millions of people.

⑥ **resolutions/solutions**

Technology has helped us find _____ to many of the world's problems.

⑦ **Technology/Technique**

_____ has many uses for mankind.

⑧ **solution/resolution**

The congress passed a _____ to limit the power of tech companies.

⑨ **supplies/provides**

The developing world _____ the raw materials for the developed world.

⑩ **shortage/deficiency**

The global _____ of lithium means batteries are becoming more expensive.

⑪ **question/problem**

The _____ is not easy to solve and will take all our efforts.

⑫ **problem with/question about**

The _____ security was soon solved.

⑬ **question/problem**

The _____ is how can we make the technology more cheaply?

⑭ **problems with/questions about**

There are always _____ security. But so far no one has come up with any answers.

⑮ **shortage/deficiency**

There is a serious _____ in our education system.

✅ 答案・中譯・說明　　🎧 **Track 2.11**

① Income <u>deficiency</u> means most of the world suffers in poverty.
所得不足意味著世界上大部分地區都處於貧困之中。

② Over the years he has worked hard on improving his technique.
長年以來，他都致力於改善自己的技術。

③ Supplying water to the factories is now our main task.
對工廠供水是我們現在的主要任務。

④ Technology allows companies to provide a better service for their customers.
科技使公司能夠為顧客提供更好的服務。

⑤ Technology companies provide employment for millions of people.
科技公司為數百萬人提供了就業機會。

⑥ Technology has helped us find solutions to many of the world's problems.
科技幫助我們為世界上的許多問題找到了解決辦法。

⑦ Technology has many uses for mankind. 科技對人類有許多用處。

⑧ The congress passed a resolution to limit the power of tech companies.
國會通過了一項限制科技公司權力的決議。

⑨ The developing world supplies the raw materials for the developed world.
開發中國家為已開發國家供應原物料。

⑩ The global shortage of lithium means batteries are becoming more expensive.
全球的鋰短缺意味著電池正變得越來越貴。

⑪ The problem is not easy to solve and will take all our efforts.
這個問題不容易解決,要靠我們全力以赴。

⑫ The problem with security was soon solved. 安全上的問題很快就解決了。

⑬ The question is how can we make the technology more cheaply?
問題在於,我們要如何使這項技術變得比較便宜?

⑭ There are always questions about security. But so far no one has come up with any
answers.
安全問題向來都存在。但到目前為止,還沒有人給出過任何解答。

⑮ There is a serious deficiency in our education system.
我們的教育制度存在著嚴重的缺陷。

....

☆ 第 10 句選擇 shortage 是因為描述的是實體物件或材料:lithium;而第 1 和
15 句用 deficiency 則是因為描述的是比較抽象的事件:income、education。

☆ 第 3 和 9 句需要用 supply 是因為描述對象為實體物件或物質:water、raw
materials;而第 4、5 兩句使用 provide 則是因為描述對象為比較抽象的事件:
service、employment。

☆ 請注意第 6 句中 solution 和 problem 是如何一起出現;另外,第 8 句中
resolution 又是如何用來描述政治決定。

☆ 第 13 和 14 句選用 question 是因為聚焦在資訊上,而第 11、12 句用
problem 則是聚焦在需要採取的行動上。另外請留意到語塊 question about、
problems with。

☆ 請將正確答案畫上底線。(參照第 1 句的示範)

最後我們還是要來練習從閱讀文章中找出這些容易搞混的單字。當你在文章中每找到一個單字，都必須停下來思考它是意指什麼、它的文法是什麼，以及它是如何使用的。

Task 43

請從 Task 1 和 Task 2 的閱讀文章中找出關鍵語庫 ❼ 列出的所有易混淆字詞，並留意它們在文章中是如何使用的。

Task 44

請練習用關鍵語庫 ❼ 的易混淆字詞來造句。

易混淆字詞	造句練習
technique	
technology	
supply s/o with s/th	
provide s/o with s/th	
shortage	
deficiency	
resolution	
solution	
question about	

problem with	

☆ 在寫作中運用這些易混淆的字詞時，記得把重點放在文法、句意和用法上，而不是只注意單字的意思。

　　在你結束這個單元之前，請將下列清單看過，確定你能將所有要點都勾選起來。如果有一些要點你還搞不清楚，請回頭再次研讀本單元的相關部分。

☐ 我確實閱讀並理解了關於「科技」的長篇文章。

☐ 我完全知道字彙在文章中是如何使用，並更加了解到要怎麼用單字來表達特定的主題。

☐ 我已經學會 15 個關於「科技」主題的關鍵字，以及可與其搭配使用的動詞和形容詞。

☐ 我已經練習使用這些搭配詞來描寫「科技」。

☐ 我已經學到了一些同義詞，也了解在運用時需要注意的一些問題。

☐ 我學到了很多關於這個主題可以運用的語塊，包括片語動詞以及名詞或動詞為同形的單字。

☐ 我已經練習使用這些語塊。

☐ 我學到了 5 個關於這個主題的慣用語，且知道如何運用。

☐ 我已經理解在運用慣用語時需要特別注意的一些問題。

☐ 關於這個主題，我已經能確實掌握一些易混淆字詞的用法。

Unit 3

新媒體
New Media

在本單元裡，我們所要探究的主題是新媒體和它為社會所帶來的危險。

閱讀文章並盡可能地理解文章內容。請先不要使用字典。

(1) _____ Cutting edge technology which allows videos and music to be shared instantly means that now it's difficult to see people who are not scrolling up or scrolling down on their phones, trying to see who has visited their page. There is hardly anyone on the planet now who hasn't applied for a social media account and set up a detailed profile promoting themselves, their family and their lifestyle to the world. Anyone can create a popular hashtag, and if you have enough visits to your blog or Instagram page, your page can generate money for you. This creates the illusion that you are important. In this modern world, anyone can become a celebrity.

(2) _____ First, when social media account owners put something up on a social media site and receive likes for it, they experience a rush of pleasure. It is very easy to become addicted to this. Posting opinions, livestreaming private family events and sharing lifestyle pictures with total strangers becomes a way to validate your own life, and not getting this validation makes many people feel that their lives are not worthwhile. There are very few people who have raised the question of whether it's actually worth spending time posting or blogging about the

triviality of everyday life. Competition to post the most exciting content and to move up a gear and become a social media influencer is intense, especially amongst young people. The pressure to be light years ahead of your peers is great, and it takes time to carefully curate a photogenic lifestyle. It's no coincidence that the suicide rate among young people has been rising since the explosion of new media. Those who blame the competitive nature of new media for this are right on the button.

(3) _____ This keeps happening, despite attempts of governments and parent organisations to block sites which do not prevent this. Young people, who already feel that the adult world is too busy to listen to them, are particularly vulnerable here. Hackers can hack into an account very easily and steal private pictures or access personal information and threaten to release it to the world if a payment is not made, usually in bitcoin.

(4) _____ This lets people express uninformed opinions, which eventually become worth more than hard facts. Truth is measured by the number of devoted followers one has, and the visibility of posts on your newsfeed is determined by how many lurkers – people who read but never comment, so that you don't know who they are - liked them, rather than whether the post has anything useful or true to say. Accurate information about current events can be drowned out by trolls - people who like to start fights and arguments for no other reason than that they enjoy it - and tweets. Fake news is hard to avoid, and this makes people suspicious about anything they read on the internet, even if it comes from respectable and trustworthy news sources. Another problem is that intellectual debate has become limited to or even replaced by infographics such as gifs, memes or emojis.

(5) _____ Or, do we need to apply more rules and regulations to the new media, in effect, ask netizens to police it better? Should we take down content which is deemed to be illegal, immoral or false? Ought we to forbid livestreams which do not serve some greater purpose? Who knows where it will all end?

Task 2

請從下列句子選出適當的主題句以完成 Task 1 每個段落的填空。

A Another, related, problem, is online bullying or grooming.

B But there are many dangers and problems with this.

C Perhaps things will hit a roadblock as the available bandwidth reaches a limit, and the flow of data will finally slow to a halt.

D The internet has exploded in the last 10 years with a mass of new social media sites.

E The second problem is that good investigative journalism has been replaced by fake news, and crazy conspiracy theories have permeated the blogosphere.

✓ 答案・中譯・說明

(1) D   (2) B   (3) A   (4) E   (5) C

譯文

　　網際網路在過去十年中有了爆炸性的發展，湧現出大量新的社群媒體網站。尖端的技術可以立即共享視頻和音樂，這意味著現在很難看到人沒有拿手機在往上或往下滑，以試著看看誰點閱了自己的頁面。現在地球上幾乎沒有任何人沒申請社群媒體帳戶，並建立詳細的簡介來向世人宣傳自己、家人和生活方式。任何人都能創造流行的主題標籤，而且假如部落格或 Instagram 頁面的點閱數夠多，你的頁面就能為你賺錢。這會給人一種你很重要的錯覺。在這個現代世界中，任何人都能成為名人。

　　但是，這樣有許多的危險和問題。首先，當社群媒體帳戶的擁有者把東西放上社群媒

體網站，並以此得到了讚，他們就會體驗到一種快感。這非常容易變得上癮。張貼意見、直播私人家庭活動並與陌生人分享生活照片成了驗證自己生活的一種方式，沒有以此來驗證就會使很多人覺得生活沒價值。非常少有人點出的疑問是，花時間來張貼日常生活的瑣事或寫在部落格上究竟值不值得。在發布最挑動人心的內容、加速提升自己成為社群媒體上有影響力之人的競爭非常激烈，尤其是在年輕人當中。要比同齡人領先好幾光年的壓力是很大的，而要精心策劃一種上鏡的生活方式需要花費時間。自從新媒體一飛沖天以來，年輕人的自殺率便在上升，這一切並非巧合。那些將此歸咎於新媒體競爭本質的人其實是一針見血。

另一個相關的問題是網路霸凌或誘騙。這種情況一直在發生，儘管政府和上級組織試圖去封鎖對此不加以防止的網站。覺得成人世界已經太忙而無法對自己加以傾聽的年輕人，在此格外容易受到動搖。駭客非常輕易就能駭入一個帳戶來竊取私人照片或動用個資，並威脅假如不付錢，通常是用比特幣，就要對外界散布。

第二個問題是，好的調查式新聞報導遭到了假新聞取代，瘋狂的陰謀論則瀰漫了部落格圈。這讓人可以表達無見識的見解，而這些見解最終會變得比鑿鑿的事實還有價值。真相是由人所擁有的死忠追蹤者數量來衡量，而在你的動態消息中，貼文的能見度則是取決於有多少潛水者——閱讀但從不留言的人，使你不知道他們是誰——為它點讚，而不是貼文有沒有任何有用或真實的話要說。準確的時事資訊可以被酸民——喜歡開戰和爭論的人，而原因不過就是要取樂——和推文所淹沒。假新聞難以避免，這便會使人去質疑在網際網路上所讀到的任何事，即使它是來自正派和值得信賴的新聞來源。另一個問題是，智識上的辯論已遭到諸如動態圖片、迷因或表情符號的資訊圖表所限制，甚或是取代。

事情或許會隨著可用頻寬達到極限而受阻，使資料流動最後慢到停滯下來。或者我們需不需要對新媒體施行更多的規則和監管，等於是要網友把它看管得更好？我們該不該把被視為非法、不道德或虛假的內容給撤掉？我們應不應當把不符合某種較優良目的的直播給禁絕掉？誰知道一切會在哪裡畫下句點？

....

☆ 在這篇文章裡，請留意第一段是如何概括介紹新媒體這個主題是什麼，以及它是如何運作的。第二、三、四段是在描述新媒體的好幾個問題，第五段則是在說明解決方法或許會來自哪，但實際上並沒有任何對解決方法的具體建議。這是另外一類的 problem/solution「問題／解決方案」論說文。

☆ 請留意主題句 (topic sentence) 總是段落中最概括的句子，以及段落中的其他部分是如何以特定的例子或理由來申論主題句的論點。

字詞搭配 Word Partnerships

　　我們現在將學習「新媒體」這個主題的 15 個關鍵字，以及可搭配這些關鍵字使用的 word partnerships「字詞搭配表」。首先，請看關鍵字語庫。

Task 3

請仔細研讀這些主題字彙和下方的說明。

關鍵語庫 ❶　　🎧 Track 3.1

名詞	動詞	形容詞	字義
account Ⓒ	-	-	帳戶、帳號
bandwidth Ⓤ	-	-	頻寬
blogosphere Ⓤ	-	-	部落格圈
content Ⓤ	-	-	內容、目錄
debate Ⓒ	debate	debatable	辯論、爭論
follower Ⓒ	follow s/o	followed	追蹤者、追隨者
hashtag Ⓒ	-	-	主題標籤、標籤
influencer Ⓒ	influence s/o or s/th	influenced	有影響力的人、紅人
information Ⓤ	inform	informed	資訊、信息、情報
journalism Ⓤ	-	-	新聞報導、新聞工作
media Ⓤ	-	-	媒體、媒介
news Ⓤ	-	-	新聞、消息、資訊
opinion ⒸⓊ	-	opinionated	意見、觀點

profile Ⓒ	profile s/o	profiled	簡介、形象
site Ⓒ	-	-	網站

☆ 需留意哪些名詞是可數，哪些是不可數。

☆ 要記得，名詞是可數還是不可數，有時候要視主題而定。

☆ 留意單字的其他詞性形式，如動詞和形容詞。

☆ 這些單字的動詞形都是 *vt*，這意味著你必須給它們受詞。注意不同的受詞：(s/o) 或 (s/th)。

☆ 請注意 information 向來都是不可數，你必須使用單數形動詞。例如 This information is correct. 是正確的；These informations are correct. 則是錯的。

☆ media 這個字的用法很微妙，它必須與單數形動詞連用。例如 The media is controlled by the state. 是正確的；The media are controlled by the state. 則是錯的。

☆ news 也是很微妙的單字，請留意它是不可數，必須使用單數形動詞。例如 The news is wrong. 是正確的；The news are wrong. 則是錯的。

☆ opinion 這個字可以是可數或不可數。欲表示某人的個人意見時，應用 opinion (*nc*)，例如 I have so many opinions I want to share with you.。若要表示每個人的概括意見時，諸如民意，則應該用 opinion (*nu*)，例如 Public opinion is usually wrong on this issue.。

☆ opinionated 意指有強烈的意見並一直加以表達。

☆ profile s/o 當動詞時意指寫出對人的描述，通常是依據訪談。這個動詞通常使用被動式，例如 She was recently profiled in a national newspaper.。

☆ 請注意這些單字的形容詞形式通常都是 ＿＿＿ed。

接下來，我們將以 5 個關鍵字為一組，深入地學習與這些字最頻繁搭配的字詞組合及正確用法。

請研讀這個字詞搭配表、例句和底下的說明。

搭配在前面的動詞	搭配的名詞	關鍵字
set up apply for open have hold close	bank customer Facebook Google Instagram social media	**account**

字詞搭配使用範例　　◎ **Track 3.2**（收錄本單元 Task 4~Task 20 字詞搭配使用範例）

• She **has** three **Instagram accounts**.　她有三個 Instagram 帳號。

• I **closed** my **Facebook account**.　我關閉了我的 Facebook 帳號。

• I'm **applying for** another **social media account**.　我要申請另一個社群媒體帳號。

☆ 搭配表中的動詞是將意思相似歸類成一組。不過，請記得同義詞向來都是特定於主題和搭配詞。

☆ 請留意不同類型 account 的說法。這是名詞當形容詞來用。

☆ 須留意有些類型的 account 字首需要大寫字母，因為它們是品牌名稱。

Task 5

請研讀這個字詞搭配表和例句。

搭配在前面的動詞	搭配的形容詞	關鍵字
consume waste hog conserve	unlimited limited available	**bandwidth**

- Some websites **consume** far more **bandwidth** than others.
  有些網站所耗費的頻寬遠大於其他網站。

- Advertising actually **wastes limited bandwidth**.
  廣告實際上會浪費有限的頻寬。

- This application **is hogging** all the **available bandwidth**, which is why your
  download speed is so slow.
  這項應用程式占掉了所有可用的頻寬，這就是為什麼你的下載速度這麼慢。

Task 6

請研讀這個字詞搭配表、例句和底下的說明。

搭配在前面的動詞	搭配的形容詞	關鍵字
surf	left wing	
scour	right wing	
enrage	foodie	**blogosphere**
troll		
	pro-migrant	
permeate	anti-migrant	

字詞搭配使用範例

- If you **surf** the **right-wing blogosphere**, you will find some very mad theories.
  假如上網瀏覽右派的部落格，你會找到一些非常扯的理論。

- I **scoured** the foodie **blogosphere** for a recipe.
  我為了食譜而尋遍了美食部落格圈。

- This is just the kind of thing which **enrages** the **anti-migrant blogosphere**.
  這就是那種會激怒反移民部落格圈的事。

- The **blogosphere was enraged** by the news. 部落格圈被這個新聞激怒了。

....

☆ 注意，enrage 能使用在被動語態。

請研讀這個字詞搭配表、例句和底下的說明。

搭配在前面的動詞	搭配的形容詞	關鍵字
generate post remove contain	interesting user generated intellectual exciting video audio banned illegal political	**content**

字詞搭配使用範例

• The site's success comes from the fact that it lets users **generate** their own **video and audio content**.
該網站的成功來自於一個事實——它讓使用者可以自製視頻和音訊內容。

• **Illegal** or **political content will be removed**.
非法或政治性的內容會遭到移除。

• The site **contains** very **interesting**, **user generated content**.
該網站含有非常有趣的、由使用者自製的內容。

☆ 注意，remove 能使用在被動語態。

請研讀這個字詞搭配表、例句和底下的說明。

搭配在前的動詞	搭配的形容詞	關鍵字	搭配在後的動詞
stimulate provoke spark trigger frame inform	heated lively vigorous intellectual political online	**debate (about s/th)**	be/become limited to concern shift

字詞搭配使用範例

- The issue **provoked vigorous debate** on the internet.
  該議題在網路上掀起了激烈的辯論。

- The **intellectual debate is framed by** the organisers, who determine content.
  此番智識辯論是由決定內容的主辦單位所框定。

- Much **online debate is informed by** right wing politics.
  很多網路辯論是受到右派政見所助長。

- The **debate has now shifted** online. 這項辯論現在已經轉向網上了。

- The **debate concerns** everyone. 該辯論事關每個人。

☆ 請注意，frame 和 inform 可以用於被動語態。

　　現在，我們來看看各位是否能用一些字詞搭配來擴大對字彙的運用。這篇文章描述了一場關於移民問題的激烈網路辯論，請詳讀內容並完成填空練習。

請從 Task 4 到 Task 8 中選出正確形式的字詞，完成以下段落填空。

The issue (1) _____ (2) _____ debate on the (3) _____ blogosphere, and also on the (4) _____ blogosphere, where those who were for or against allowing migrants into the country argued fiercely. In fact, the whole blogosphere (5) _____ by the news, and some news-sites even let their viewers (6) _____ more (7) _____ accounts and join in. These new users (8) _____ their own content, some of which was (9) _____ and afterwards (10) _____. The discussion eventually (11) _____ so much bandwidth, that soon the internet crashed.

範例答案

1. stimulated/provoked/sparked/triggered
2. lively/heated/vigorous
3. pro-migrant/anti-migrant
4. pro-migrant/anti-migrant
5. was enraged
6. set up/open/apply for

7. social media
8. generated/posted
9. illegal
10. removed/banned
11. consumed

....

☆ 請留意各組同義字詞，空格中選填同一組內不同的字也是可以的。

☆ 須確認所選用的單字都是正確的形式。請檢查單數或複數，以及動詞的正確形式。例如在空格 (5) 中的 enrage 必須是過去簡單式：was enraged。

☆ 另外，要非常留心所用的時態。由文章裡的其他動詞看出這起事件是發生在過去，所以在 (1)、(8)、(10) 和 (11) 裡，動詞必須用過去簡單式。

現在來學習另外 5 個單字。

Task 10

請研讀這個字詞搭配表、例句和底下的說明。

搭配在前的動詞	搭配在前的形容詞	搭配的形容詞	關鍵字
have attract keep retain urge incite	loyal devoted faithful avid	Twitter Instagram Facebook	**follower (of s/th)**

字詞搭配使用範例

- She **urged her followers** to buy this product. 她鼓勵她的粉絲去買這樣產品。
- We need to **attract** more **loyal followers**. 我們需要吸引更多忠實的追隨者。
- Their page was so boring they were not able to **retain** the same number of **faithful followers** as their competitors.
  他們的頁面乏味到無法留住跟競爭對手相同數量的追隨者。
- I'm an **avid follower of** your page. 對於你的頁面，我是熱切的追蹤者。

☆ 請注意，有關追蹤者類型的專有名詞字首必須使用大寫字母。

Task 11

請研讀這個字詞搭配表、例句和底下的說明。

搭配在前的動詞	搭配的形容詞	關鍵字	搭配在後的動詞
create use follow	Twitter Instagram popular	**hashtag**	trend

- I **created** a **popular hashtag** for this post.
  我為這則貼文創建了流行的主題標籤。

- I **followed** the **hashtag** for a while.
  我關注這個主題標籤一陣子了。

- The blacklivesmatter **hashtag is trending** on Twitter right now.
  「黑人的命也是命」的主題標籤現在在推特上是熱門話題。

☆ 說明主題標籤類型的專有名詞字首必須使用大寫字母。

Task 12

請研讀這個字詞搭配表、例句和底下的說明。

搭配在前面的動詞	搭配的形容詞	關鍵字
be/become target	Twitter Instagram social media key industry	**influencer**

字詞搭配使用範例

- Their marketing strategy is to **target industry influencers**, and let them do their marketing for them.
  他們的行銷策略是鎖定在業界中有影響力的人，讓他們來為自己做行銷。

- She **became** a **key influencer** very quickly, with thousands of followers.
  她很快就成為了關鍵的影響者，擁有成千上萬的粉絲。

- If you **are** a **social media influencer**, you can make a lot of money.
  假如你是社群媒體的紅人，你就能賺到很多錢。

☆ 注意，提到主題標籤類型的專有名詞必須使用大寫字母。

Task 13

請研讀這個字詞搭配表和例句。

搭配在前面的動詞		搭配的形容詞		關鍵字
have	get	accurate	background	
contain	access	correct	detailed	
retain	download	factual		
store	retrieve		general	
	exchange	false	basic	**information (about s/th)**
dig up	circulate	relevant	personal	
find	release	useful	private	
gather		latest		
look for		up-to-date		
obtain				
seek				

字詞搭配使用範例

- They **have** all my **personal information** and are threatening to **release** it to the world!　他們有我全部的個資，並威脅要對外界散布！
- It's easy to **dig up basic information about** almost anyone in the world.　世界上幾乎任何人的基本資訊都很容易找得到。
- They are **circulating** a lot of false **information about** her on the internet.　他們在網路上散播了很多關於她的虛假資訊。

Task 14

請研讀這個字詞搭配表和例句。

搭配在前面的動詞	搭配的形容詞	關鍵字
do study work in	investigative good professional tabloid print TV	**journalism**

字詞搭配使用範例

- He **studied journalism** but was not able to find a job as a journalist.
  他念的是新聞，但找不到記者的工作。

- Very few newspapers now **do investigative journalism**.
  現在鮮少報紙在做調查式新聞報導。

就像前面所做過的，我們再來練習這一組 5 個單字的字詞搭配應用。

Task 15

請從 Task 10 到 Task 14 中選出正確形式的字詞，完成以下段落填空。

The number of (1) _____ followers you (2) _____ can
determine how much money you can make as a (3) _____ influencer.
(4) _____ influencers can (5) _____ (6) _____ hashtags
which (7) _____ for a long time. Often it doesn't matter if the
information influencers (8) _____ is (9) _____ – it's more
important to be entertaining than truthful. This has important consequences
for those people who (10) _____ journalism and are concerned that
journalism should be (11) _____.

---

1. loyal/devoted/faithful/avid
2. have/attract/keep/retain
3. social media/Twitter/Instagram
4. Key
5. create/use
6. popular

7. trend
8. circulate/release
9. accurate/correct/factual
10. work in/study
11. good/professional

☆ 請留意各組同義字詞，空格中選填同一組內不同的字也是可以的。

☆ 須確認選用的單字都是正確的形式。請檢查單數或複數，以及動詞的正確形式。

　　現在我們來學習最後一組的 5 個單字。

Task 16

請研讀這個字詞搭配表和例句。

搭配的片語	搭配的形容詞	關鍵字	搭配在後的名詞
have access to ~ the role of ~ the explosion of ~	state controlled mass electronic mainstream new social	**media**	coverage attention bias censorship freedom empire

字詞搭配使用範例

• Most people on the planet now have **access to social media**.
　地球上大部分的人現在都會使用到社群媒體。

- His **media empire** is huge and has enormous influence.
  他的媒體帝國規模龐大，有廣大的影響力。

- There is no **media freedom** in that country.
  那個國家沒有媒體自由。

- The **mainstream media** is no longer trusted in many parts of the country.
  在這個國家的許多地方，主流媒體不再受到信賴。

Task 17

請研讀這個字詞搭配表和例句。

搭配在前面的動詞	搭配的形容詞	關鍵字
hear s/th on listen to see watch read turn on broadcast spread	radio television TV morning evening lunchtime fake	**news (about s/th)**

字詞搭配使用範例

- It's true, I **heard it on** the **news**.
  是真的，我在新聞裡聽說了。

- I never **listen to** the **radio news**, but I **watch** the **TV lunchtime news**.
  我從來不聽廣播電台的新聞，但會看電視的午間新聞。

- This channel only **broadcasts fake news**.
  這台只播假新聞。

Task 18

請研讀這個字詞搭配表和例句。

搭配在前面的動詞	搭配的形容詞	關鍵字
have	honest	
hold		
	expert	
express	informed	
voice	professional	
give	considered	
offer		opinion
state	uninformed	(about s/th)
form	popular	
	general	
change	public	
ask s/o for ~		
shape		

字詞搭配使用範例

- Media companies can use social media to **shape public opinion**.
  媒體公司可以用社群媒體來塑造公眾輿論。

- Most people love to **voice** their **opinions about** all kinds of stuff.
  大部分的人都愛抒發對各種事物的意見。

- I'm **asking you for** your **expert opinion**.
  我是在徵詢你的專業意見。

Task 19

請研讀這個字詞搭配表和例句。

搭配在前面的動詞	搭配的形容詞	關鍵字
have	public	
set up	internet	
create	personal	
develop	fake	**profile**
build up	detailed	
raise	career	
	company	

字詞搭配使用範例

- We **have been developing** our **company profile** for many years.
  我們多年來都在發展公司的簡介。

- I **created** a really **detailed profile** for my social media page.
  我為我的社群媒體頁面創建了十分詳細的簡介。

- Don't you **have** a **career profile** you can put up on the site?
  你沒有能放到網站上的職涯簡介嗎？

Task 20

請研讀這個字詞搭配表和例句。

搭配在前面的動詞		搭配的形容詞	關鍵字
access	put s/th up on	web	
browse	build	internet	
visit	create	e-commerce	
	design	social media	**site**
search for	set up		
	host	free	
	own	official	

- I **visited** your **site** yesterday and spent a long time **browsing the site**.
  我昨天造訪了你的網站，並花了很長的時間瀏覽網站。

- I tried to **put something up on the site**, but it didn't work.
  我試著在網站上放一些東西，但是沒有成功。

- We **are creating** a new **web site** at the moment.
  我們正在建立一個新網站。

- This company **owns** the biggest **e-commerce site** on the internet.
  這家公司擁有網際網路上最大的電子商務站。

接下來，我們來練習這最後一組 5 個單字的字詞搭配應用。

Task 21

請從 Task 16 到 Task 20 中選出正確形式的字詞，完成以下段落填空。

Media (1) _____ is of course desirable. Government censorship is always wrong.

(2) _____ (3) _____ media is not without danger to our society. (4) _____ sites allow anyone to (5) _____ their opinions, no matter how ignorant they are about the topic, and no matter how (6) _____ those opinions are. Other (7) _____ sites allow people to (8) _____ anything _____ the site without checking first whether it's illegal or offensive. People can even (9) _____ many different (10) _____ profiles under false names. In this way they can (11) _____ (12) _____ news – what used to be called lies – and thus (13) _____ (14) _____ opinion.

1. freedom
2. The explosion of
3. new/social/electronic
4. Social media/Internet/Web/Free
5. express/voice/give/offer/state
6. uninformed
7. social media/internet/web/free

8. put ~ up on
9. set up/create
10. fake/personal/detailed
11. spread
12. fake
13. shape
14. public/general/popular

☆ 再提醒一次，務必留意各組同義字詞。請確認所選用的單字都是正確的形式。
　　檢查單數或複數，以及動詞的正確形式。

☆ 空格 (5) 和 (6) 之後的 opinion 是可數，所以這意指「個人意見」。而在空格
　　(14) 之後，它是不可數，所以意指「民意」。

　　最後，我們要進行這個部分的最後一個練習，這對於各位記憶 15 個關
鍵單字和它們的字詞搭配將有非常大的幫助。記住，多閱讀有助於擴充字
彙量，而在文章上下文脈絡中查看大量例子則能幫助你記憶新的用語。

Task 22

請從 Task 1 和 Task 2 的閱讀文章中找出關鍵語庫 ❶ 所列的 15 個關鍵字，
並留意這些字在文章中是如何使用的。

常用語塊 Chunks

看過了 word partnerships，我們現在要來聚焦於這個主題所能運用的 chunks。

Task 23

研讀這些語塊和底下的說明。

關鍵語庫 ❷

Chunk
❏ make s/o *adj.*　使事物 adj.
❏ make s/o V　使事物 V
❏ let s/o V　讓事物 V
❏ keep Ving　一直 Ving
❏ be difficult/easy/hard(for s/o) to V　（事物）難以／容易／很難 V
❏ listen to n.p./Ving　聽 n.p./Ving
❏ information about/on n.p./Ving　關於 n.p./Ving 的資訊
❏ share s/th with s/o　對某人分享某事
❏ be/become addicted to n.p./Ving　對 n.p./Ving 變得上癮
❏ block s/o　封鎖事物

☆ 別忘了在使用這些語塊時需要改變動詞的時態。

☆ 須留意這些語塊是否全都必須用 n.p.、Ving 或 V。

☆ 注意受詞，尤其是需要使用人物受詞 (s/o) 或事物受詞 (s/th) 時。

☆ 在使用 make s/o adj. 時，不可同時使用動詞。例如 This makes them happy. 是正確的。而 This makes them be happy. 則是錯的。

☆ make s/o V 和 let s/o V 很容易搞混，因為它們在中文裡似乎沒有多大的差別，

但在英文裡卻非常不同。make s/o V 意指強制或規定某人去做某事；let s/o V 則意指假如他們想要的話，便容許他們去做。常見的錯誤是把 to 用到這兩個語塊上。例如 My boss lets me to use Facebook at work. 是錯誤的，應該說 My boss lets me use Facebook at work. 才正確。

☆ 各位或許記得在 Unit 1 裡，我們學過 hard 要怎麼用，easy 和 difficult 的用法也相同，它們必須連同 it is 來用。例如 It is easy for people to understand this. 是正確的。People are easy to understand this. 則是錯的。

☆ be addicted to 意指一種狀態，become addicted to 則指陷入那個狀態的過程、行動。

☆ 在使用 chunk 時，務必確認所有的細節、仔細檢查不同的介系詞，並確保把它們都用對了。

下一個 Task 將聚焦於大家在使用這些語塊時經常會犯的錯誤。

Task 24

請改正這些句子中使用語塊的常見錯誤。

① Do you have any information for this?

_____

② I like to listen music on my phone.

_____

③ I love to share pictures of my life to my friends on Instagram.

_____

④ I think I am becoming addict to this game.

_____

⑤ If you say that to me again, I will block.

_____

⑥ It's very difficult to let people stop playing games.

_____

⑦ It's very difficult to make people to stop playing games.

_____

⑧ Many players are addicted for this.

_____

⑨ People are easy to play the games.

_____

⑩ Playing online computer games makes me to be happy.

_____

⑪ They keep to bring out new editions of the game.

_____

⑫ We should not let our children to become addicted.

_____

✅ 答案・中譯・說明   🎧 Track 3.3

① Do you have any <u>information **on/about**</u> this?
你有沒有任何關於這件事的消息？

② I like to listen **to** music on my phone. 我喜歡用手機聽音樂。

③ I love to share pictures of my life **with** my friends on Instagram.
我喜歡在 Instagram 上和朋友分享生活照。

④ I think I am becoming addict**ed** to this game.
我想我開始對這款遊戲上癮了。

⑤ If you say that to me again, I will block **you**.
假如你再對我這麼說，我就封鎖你。

⑥ It's very difficult to **make** people stop playing games.
要使人停止玩遊戲非常難。

⑦ It's very difficult to make **people stop** playing games.
要使人停止玩遊戲非常難。

⑧ Many players are addicted **to** this. 很多玩家都沉迷於此。

⑨ **It's easy to play** the games. 要玩遊戲很容易。

⑩ Playing online computer games **makes me happy**.
玩線上電腦遊戲讓我感到開心。

⑪ They keep bring**ing** out new editions of the game.
他們不斷推出新版的遊戲。

⑫ We should not let our **children become** addicted.
我們不該使我們的孩子成癮。

···

☆ 我已經把錯誤的部分標示出來，各位可以清楚看出哪裡用錯了。

☆ 請將 Task 24 的句子與關鍵語庫 ❷ 的語塊做比較，以確保能清楚看出句中哪
裡用錯了。

☆ 請將正確句子中的完整語塊畫上底線（參照第 1 句的示範），這能幫助你完整
而正確地記住語塊。

　　下一個練習對於記憶語塊將有非常大的幫助。記住，多閱讀有助於擴
充字彙量，而在文章上下文脈絡中查看大量語塊則能幫助你記憶新的用語。

Task 25

請從 Task 1 和 Task 2 的閱讀文章中找出關鍵語庫 ❷ 列出的所有語塊，並
留意這些語塊在文章中是如何使用的。

Task 26

現在請嘗試用前面學過的語塊來寫出你自己的句子。

關鍵字語塊	造句
make s/o adj.	
make s/o V	
let s/o V	
keep Ving	
be difficult/easy/hard(for s/o) to V	
listen to n.p./Ving	
information about/on n.p./Ving	
share s/th with s/o	
be/become addicted to n.p./Ving	
block s/o	

☆ 我顯然無法在此改正你的句子，但你可以透過確認語塊所有的小細節，自行改正。再次提醒在寫作中運用語塊時，須特別注意小詞、字尾和語塊的結尾，無論所需要的是 n.p.、v.p.、Ving 還是 V，並且確保你所使用的語塊是完整的。

5 個可作動詞或名詞的單字
5 words which can be verbs or nouns

接下來我們要來看的這些單字，根據它們是名詞還是動詞，有非常不同的語塊。

Task 27

請看以下幾個名詞和動詞同形的單字。

關鍵語庫 ❸

關鍵字	名詞字義	動詞字義
post	崗位；郵政；貼文	貼出（布告等）；發布；郵寄
blog	部落格；網誌	（在網路上）記錄
like	同樣（或同類）的人（或事物）	喜歡；願意；希望
livestream	直播	現場直播
visit	參觀；訪問；視察	參觀；拜訪；訪問

Task 28

閱讀句子並判斷關鍵字是動詞或名詞，填入 V 或 N。

① _____ 80 people **liked** my post.

② _____ Her **blog** is very popular.

③ _____ How many people have **visited** your page today?

④ _____ I **blogged** about this topic last month.

⑤ _____ I only got 1300 **likes** for that post.

⑥ _____ I **posted** the pictures of our trip onto my profile.

⑦ _____ I will **livestream** our discussion at 21:00 p.m.

⑧ _____ I've only had 72 **visits** this week.

⑨ _____ This is an excellent **post**!

⑩ _____ You can join her **livestream** every Thursday morning.

☑ 答案・中譯・說明

① V 有 80 個人為我的貼文點了讚。

② N 她的部落格非常受歡迎。

③ V 你的網頁今天有多少人點閱？

④ V 我上個月在部落格上寫過這個主題。

⑤ N 我那則貼文只得到了 1300 個讚。

⑥ V 我把我們的出遊照貼在了我的簡介裡。

⑦ V 我會在晚上九點直播我們的討論。

⑧ N 我這星期只有 72 筆點閱。

⑨ N 這是一則很棒的貼文！

⑩ N 你每星期四早上都能加入她的直播。

··

☆ 這些單字是動詞時，全都是規則變化，所以在寫到或談到過去時，記得要加上 _____ed。

☆ 能夠掌握這些字在動詞語塊和名詞語塊上的差別是非常重要的。接下來的練習將幫助各位更加熟悉相關用法

Task 29

請看以下所彙整的語塊及用法說明。

關鍵語庫 ❹　◎ Track 3.4

關鍵字語塊	關鍵字詞性	例句 & 翻譯
post about s/th	*nc*	I wrote a post about that very issue! 我針對這個議題寫了一篇貼文！

post s/th	vt	I posted that picture yesterday. 我昨天發布了那張照片。
post (about s/th)	vi	I posted (about it) yesterday. 我昨天（針對它）發了貼文。
blog about s/th	nc	I have two blogs, one about my dogs, the other about my cats. 我有兩個部落格，一個是關於我的狗，另一個是關於我的貓。
blog (about s/th)	vi	I blog every day. I usually blog about my reading. 我天天都寫部落格。我通常是針對閱讀來寫部落格。
like	nc	Can you give me a like for my post? I haven't got any yet. 你能為我的貼文點個讚嗎？我還沒得到半個。
like s/th	vt	Not enough people are liking my posts. 為我的貼文點讚的人不夠多。
livestream	nc	I'm watching two livestreams at the same time. 我同時在看兩個直播。
livestream s/th	vt	They're livestreaming the concert right now. 他們現在在直播演唱會。
livestream (about s/th)	vi	She livestreams a lot, especially about food. 她經常直播，尤其是關於食物的。
visit to s/o	nc	I paid several visits to her site. 我造訪過她的網站好幾次。
visit s/o	vt	I visited your site yesterday. 我昨天造訪了你的網站。

☆ 須留意哪些名詞是可數，哪些是不可數。

☆ post 在當名詞來用時，可以連同這些動詞來使用：write、update、publish 或 edit。

☆ post 在當動詞來用時，可以有兩種用法。你可以給它受詞，在此情況下意指「發布」，例如 I posted my picture on my profile.。或者你可以與 about 連用，

此時便是想要聚焦於貼文中所寫內容的主題，例如 I haven't posted about this yet.。

☆ blog 當動詞時沒有受詞，所以若是想要指明部落格的內容，就需要使用 about，例如 I blog about the books I read.。

☆ like 在當名詞時，可以連同這些動詞來使用：have、give 或 have got。

☆ livestream 在當動詞來用時，可以有兩種用法。你可以給它受詞，在此情況下意指「播出正在發生的事件」，例如 I'm livestreaming my birthday party.。或者你可以與 about 連用，此時便是想要聚焦於所呈現內容的主題，例如 She livestreams about gaming addiction.。

☆ visit 在當名詞時，可以連同這些動詞來使用：make 或 pay。

☆ 請注意 visit 在當動詞用時，不可加 to，例如 I visited to her site. 是錯誤的；I visited her site. 才正確。

☆ 請仔細學習這些語塊，並聚焦於諸如介系詞這些細節。

　　好的，現在讓我們來嘗試正確使用這些語塊。

Task 30

請選用正確形式的單字或語塊，完成下列各句。

① **visited/visited to**

300 people _____ my blog last week.

② **likes/liked**

I have 700 _____ for this post, but it's still not enough.

③ **like/liked**

I _____ your post. Did you see?

④ **visited/visit to**

I paid a _____ her site last night, it's not very good.

⑤ **posted about/a post about**

I _____ our trip yesterday, but so far no one has seen it.

⑥ **posted about/posted**

I _____ it yesterday. It's a great picture!

⑦ **have a blog/blogged**

I used to _____ about my favourite movies, but I got bored with it.

⑧ **livestream about/livestreamed**

It's a _____ foreign travel.

⑨ **livestream it/livestream about it**

It's such an interesting topic I'm going to _____ tomorrow.

⑩ **blogs/blogs about**

She always _____ the same stuff, it's rather boring actually.

⑪ **post/posted**

That _____ I wrote about our trip got 700 likes!

⑫ **livestreaming about/livestreaming**

They are _____ the game here, so you can watch it online.

✅ 答案・中譯・說明　🎧 Track 3.5

① 300 people <u>visited my blog</u> last week. 有 300 人上星期點閱了我的部落格。

② I have 700 likes for this post, but it's still not enough.
我這則貼文有七百個讚，但還是不夠。

③ I liked your post. Did you see? 我為你的貼文點了讚。你看到了嗎？

④ I paid a visit to her site last night, it's not very good.
我昨天晚上造訪了她的站，它並沒有非常好。

⑤ I posted about our trip yesterday, but so far no one has seen it.
　我昨天針對我們的出遊貼了文，但到目前為止都沒有人看到。

⑥ I posted it yesterday. It's a great picture! 我昨天發布的。它是很棒的照片！

⑦ I used to have a blog about my favourite movies, but I got bored with it.
　我以往是有一個部落格來談關於我最愛的電影，但我對它感到厭倦了。

⑧ It's a livestream about foreign travel. 這是一個關於國外旅遊的直播。

⑨ It's such an interesting topic I'm going to livestream about it tomorrow.
　這是一個頗有趣的主題，我明天會直播來談它。

⑩ She always blogs about the same stuff, it's rather boring actually.
　她總是針對相同的事來寫部落格，其實還挺無聊的。

⑪ That post I wrote about our trip got 700 likes!
　我針對我們的出遊所寫的那則貼文得到了 700 個讚！

⑫ They are livestreaming the game here, so you can watch it online.
　他們正在這裡直播遊戲，所以你可以上網去看。

☆ 記得確認所使用的動詞時態都正確。

☆ 請拿正確的句子來與關鍵語庫 ❹ 的語塊做比較，確保名詞或動詞語塊都用得
　正確。

☆ 請將正確句子中的完整語塊畫上底線（參照第 1 句的示範）。這將有助於各位
　把語塊完整而正確地記起來。

　　接下來，我們要再重複一次前面做過的練習。請詳讀本單元開頭的閱
讀文章，並從中把這 5 個動詞和名詞同形的關鍵字語塊全部找到。再次提
醒，盡可能地多閱讀有助於擴充字彙量，而在文章上下文脈絡中查看大量
語塊則能幫助你記憶新的用語。

Task 31

請從 Task 1 和 Task 2 的閱讀文章中找出關鍵語庫 ❹ 列出的所有語塊，並
留意這些語塊在文章中是當動詞還是名詞使用？

請練習用關鍵語庫 ❹ 的語塊來造句。

關鍵字語塊	造句
post about s/th	
post s/th	
post (about s/th)	
blog about s/th	
blog (about s/th)	
like	
like s/th	
livestream	
livestream s/th	
livestream (about s/th)	
visit to s/o	
visit s/o	

☆ 我顯然無法在此來改正你的句子，但你可以透過確認語塊所有的小細節，自行
改正。再次提醒在寫作中運用語塊時，須特別注意小詞、字尾和語塊的結尾，
無論所需要的是 n.p.、v.p.、Ving 還是 V，並且確保你所使用的語塊是完整的。

5 個談論或寫作新媒體相關主題常用的 片語動詞 5 phrasal verbs for talking or writing about new media

　　我們現在要來看看一些在談論或寫作新媒體相關話題時可以用到的片語動詞。

Task 33

研讀語庫中的片語動詞、例句和其下的說明。

關鍵語庫 ⑤　 Track 3.6

片語動詞	例句
put s/th up **(on s/w)** 把東西發布到網際網路上	• I've put up three pictures on my site. 我放了三張照片到我的站上。 • I've put three pictures up on my site. 我把三張照片放到了我的站上。 • I've put them up on my site. 我把它們放到了我的站上。
take s/th down 把東西從網際網路上移除	• They've taken the offensive post down. 他們把冒犯性的貼文撤掉了。 • They've taken down the offensive post. 他們撤掉了冒犯性的貼文。 • They've taken it down. 他們把它撤掉了。
scroll up 向上滾動、往上滑	• If you scroll up to the top of the page, you can find the link. 假如你往上滑到頁頂，就能找到鏈結。
scroll down 向下滾動、往下滑	• You need to scroll down. Then you can find my comment. 你需要往下滑。然後你就能找到我的留言。
hack into s/th 對某人的電腦或網路加以非法動用	• They hacked into my computer and deleted all my contacts! 他們駭入我的電腦，把我的聯絡人全刪了！

☆ 在學習和使用片語動詞時，你必須非常留意動詞有沒有受詞 (s/th)，以及這個受詞是擺在哪個位置。請仔細確認上方語庫中的片語動詞及其受詞的位置。

☆ put s/th up 和 take s/th down 有受詞。若受詞是 n.p.，可以擺在動詞和介系詞之間或介系詞之後；若受詞是代名詞則只能擺在動詞和介系詞之間。請仔細察看例句。

☆ 請注意 scroll up 和 scroll down 沒有受詞。

☆ hack into 有受詞 (s/th)，但不可用受詞把動詞和介系詞隔開來。請仔細看例句。

☆ 請記得片語動詞是動詞，所以還必須考慮動詞要用什麼時態。

下一個練習將有助於各位聚焦於受詞的正確擺放位置這些細節上。

Task 34

下列各句中的第一個字是正確的，請按照順序將其後的字詞重組成正確的句子。

EX. I put information the up will tomorrow.

I will put the information up tomorrow.

① I work up the link but it put doesn't

_____

② Can down my please you picture take

_____

③ You see the picture scroll to up to need

_____

④ Scroll the page down to bottom of the

_____

⑤ Thieves stole dollars into the network and hacked millions of

_____

✔ 答案‧中譯‧說明 🎧 **Track 3.7**

① I <u>put up</u> the link but it doesn't work.
我放上了鏈結，但並不管用。

I put the link up but it doesn't work.
我把鏈結放了上去，但並不管用。

② Can you please take my picture down?
能不能麻煩你把我的照片撤掉？

Can you please take down my picture?
能不能麻煩你撤掉我的照片？

③ You need to scroll up to see the picture.
你需要往上滑才會看到照片。

④ Scroll down to the bottom of the page.
往下滑到頁底。

⑤ Thieves hacked into the network and stole millions of dollars.
竊賊駭入網路偷走了數百萬美元。

....

☆ 請留意第 1 句和第 2 句可以有兩種不同的解答，就看受詞是擺在哪。

☆ 須特別留意受詞的位置。

☆ 將正確的句子與關鍵語庫 ❺ 中的片語動詞做比較，確認你的用法都正確。

☆ 請將正確句子中的片語動詞畫上底線。（參照第 1 句的示範）這將幫助你完整
而正確地把語塊記起來。

　　來看看這些片語動詞是如何運用在文章脈絡中。

Task 35

請從 Task 1 和 Task 2 的閱讀文章中找出關鍵語庫 ❺ 列出的所有片語動詞，
並留意它們在文章中是如何使用的。

請練習用關鍵語庫 ❺ 的片語動詞來造句。

片語動詞	造句練習
put s/th up (on s/w)	
take s/th down	
scroll up	
scroll down	
hack into s/th	

☆ 再次提醒在寫作時若運用到這些片語動詞時，要特別留意動詞的時態和受詞的位置。

5 個談論或寫作新媒體相關主題常用的慣用語 5 idioms for talking or writing about new media

現在來看看在寫作或談論到這個主題時，所能運用的一些慣用語。記得，在慣用語中只有一件事能改變，那就是動詞時態——假如這個慣用語包含動詞的話。

Task 37

研讀語庫中的慣用語、例句和其下的說明。

關鍵語庫 6   ◎ Track 3.8

慣用語	例句
be cutting edge 非常新進的科技發展	• The website is cutting edge. It has videos, music and graphics, it's amazing. 該網站很先進。它有視訊、音樂和圖像，太棒了！
be light years ahead of s/th 遠優於競爭對手	• The device is light years ahead of anything we've seen yet. There's nothing else like it. 這款裝置比我們所看過的任何東西都要超前好幾年。沒有別的比它更好的了。
be right on the button (about s/th) 假定正確	• That is right on the button. You're totally correct. 這一針見血。你完全正確。
hit a roadblock 在進程中遇到某種阻礙	• Our development efforts have hit a roadblock. We can't go on. 我們在開發上的努力遇到了阻礙。我們無法繼續下去了。
move up a gear 增進速度、力道或衝擊力	• In order to stay popular, we need to move up a gear. 為了保持長紅，我們需要加足馬力。

☆ 使用慣用語時唯一能更動的是動詞時態。

☆ 為了讓慣用語有意義，它必須完全準確才行，這意味著你必須將慣用語的所有細節都使用正確。

☆ 一定要確實記住哪些慣用語有受詞 (s/th)、哪些沒有。

　　下一個練習將有助於各位聚焦於使用這些慣用語時，經常會犯的錯誤。

Task 38

改正這些句子中的常見錯誤。

① Her video was a light year's ahead of anyone else's.

_____

② If we move up the gear, we can beat the competition.

_____

③ The technology has a sharp edge.

_____

④ We hit some roadblocks.

_____

⑤ You are on the buttons about that!

_____

◆ 答案・中譯・說明　　◎ Track 3.9

① Her video <u>was light years ahead of</u> anyone else's.
　她的視頻遠遠領先了其他任何人。

② If we move up <u>a</u> gear, we can beat the competition.
　假如我們加足馬力，就能打敗競爭對手。

③ The technology is cutting edge. 這項科技很尖端。

④ We hit a roadblock. 我們遇到了阻礙。

⑤ You are right on the button about that! 關於那件事你是一針見血、完全正確的！

....

☆ 這些錯誤通常是漏掉了小詞、改變了小詞或單字結尾、慣用語不完整，或者在一個不該有受詞的地方加上了受詞。

☆ 請仔細比較錯誤句子和正確解答，務必確實掌握錯在哪以及為什麼是錯的。

☆ 請將正確句子中的慣用語畫上底線。（參照第 1 句的示範）

　　現在我們要練習的是，在文章上下文中找出慣用語。

Task 39

請從 Task 1 和 Task 2 的閱讀文章中找出關鍵語庫 ❻ 列出的所有慣用語，並留意它們在文章中是如何使用的。

Task 40

請練習用關鍵語庫 ❻ 的慣用語來造句。

慣用語	造句練習
be cutting edge	
be light years ahead of s/th	
be right on the button (about s/th)	
hit a roadblock	
move up a gear	

....

☆ 再次提醒在寫作時若運用到這些慣用語，要特別留意動詞的時態和完整的慣用語包含哪些細節。

易混淆的字詞 easily confused words

- 在試著針對容易搞混的單字去了解差別時，需要思考的不僅是意思上的差異，還有文法和用法。
- 要記得，有些單字只能用在特定的主題上，用在別的主題則不適當。
- 另外要記得，容易搞混的單字，其差別常常是在搭配詞的使用上有所不同。

在做接下來幾個練習時，務必記得這些重點。

Task 41

請仔細研讀各組易混淆的字詞、例句和其下的說明。

關鍵語庫 ⑦ 🎧 **Track 3.10**

	易混淆字詞	例句
1	**apply for s/th** 應徵；申請	• I'm applying for a job at that internet company. 我正在應徵那家網際網路公司的工作。
	apply s/th (to s/th) 應用	• Users are applying the new technology in interesting ways. 使用者正以有趣的方式在應用新科技。 • If we apply this idea to the internet, we can see the result. 假如把這個構想應用到網際網路上，我們就能看到結果。
2	**prevent (s/o from) s/th** (*vt*) 預防、防止某事 發生	• We need to prevent online bullying. It's not acceptable and must stop. 我們需要防止網路霸凌。這是不可接受的，必須停止。
	avoid s/th (*vt*) 避免、降低事物 的衝擊	• The only way to avoid online bullying is to stay away from those sites. 要避免網路霸凌，唯一的辦法就是遠離那些網站。

3	**spend s/th Ving** (*vt*) **spend s/th on s/th** (*vt*) 花費	• I spent a long time learning how to code. 我花了很長的時間學習要怎麼編碼。 • I spent a long time and a lot of money on the site. 我花了很長的時間和很多錢在該網站上。
	take (s/o) s/th to V (*vt*) 花費；耗費	• It took (me) a long time to learn how to code. 學習要怎麼編碼花了（我）很長的時間。
4	**worth s/th** (*adj.*) 值得（做……）； 價值……	• My Youtube channel is now worth millions. 我的 Youtube 頻道現在價值數百萬。 • It's not worth my time. 它不值得我花費時間。 • It's worth doing well. 這件事值得做好。
	worthwhile (*adj.*) 有價值的	• It's a worthwhile activity. 它是有價值的活動。 • It's not worthwhile. 它沒有價值。
5	**raise s/th** (*vt*) 點出；引起	• This raises the issue of bullying. 這點出了霸凌的議題。 • This raises the question: are we too obsessed? 這所點出的問題是：我們是不是太沉迷了？
	rise (*vi*) 上升	• The number of people who have experienced online bullying is rising. 經歷過網路霸凌的人數正在上升。

☆ apply for s/th 和 apply s/th (to s/th) 在文法和意思上都非常不同，在台灣經常被用錯。

☆ 意指「應徵、申請」時要用 apply for s/th，但別忘了加 for。例如 I applied a job. 是錯誤的；I applied for a job. 才正確。

☆ 而當意思是指「應用」時要用 apply s/th (to s/th)，但想要指明是應用到什麼上面時，別忘了介系詞。例如 I applied my site. 是錯誤的；I applied this idea (to my site). 才正確。

☆ prevent 和 avoid 在文法、意思及用法上稍有不同。

☆ 若要表達的是「你想要阻止或預防某事發生」時，應使用 prevent。請留意可以用兩個受詞，且這兩個受詞都必須是 n.p. 或 Ving。例如你可以防止別人做某事：I prevented her from accessing that site.。

☆ 想要表達的是「無法阻止某事發生，因為它總之就是會發生，但你可以減低它對你的衝擊」時，則要使用 avoid。注意，avoid 不能用來描述這個過程發生在別人身上。例如 We should avoid trouble. 正確，而 We should avoid people from trouble. 則是錯的。

☆ spend 和 take 的意思相同，它們都是在指稱時間。不過 spend 也能指稱錢，take 卻不能指稱錢，因此這兩個單字的文法和用法非常不同。

☆ 在使用 spend 時，受詞向來必須是時間或數目。假如想要指明活動，就必須使用沒有 on 的 Ving。例如 I spent twenty minutes doing this task. 正確；I spent twenty minutes on doing this task. 則是錯的。不過若是寫到錢並想要指明所買的物件，就必須使用 on。例如 I spent 200NT$ on lunch.。

☆ 在使用 take 時，主詞向來都是 it，而且必須使用 to V 來指明活動。例如 It took (me) twenty minutes to do this task. 正確；I took twenty minutes to do this task. 則是錯的，在此情況下應該要寫成 I spent twenty minutes doing this task.。

☆ worth 和 worthwhile 的意思非常類似，但文法和用法稍有不同。

☆ worth 可以專門用來表示某事物的金錢價值，例如 My laptop is worth 40,000NTD.。此外，worth 也能用於較為廣泛的層面來指事物本身有用或重要，但使用時記得要與 it is 連用，並在其後接上 n.p. 或 Ving。例如 If it's worth doing, it's worth doing well.。

☆ worthwhile 不能用來表示金錢價值，它只能用於非常廣泛的層面來表示活動有用或重要。而在用來表達這個意思時，它可以擺在名詞前面：Blogging is a worthwhile activity.。或者擺在片語或句子的結尾：Blogging is worthwhile.。但不可將它擺在 Ving 的前面，在此情況下應該用 worth。

☆ raise 和 rise 雖然字形相似，但意思、文法和用法其實非常不同。

☆ 想要導入議題、新主題、疑問或問題時，應使用 raise，例如 She raised the issue of addiction.。注意，raise 為及物動詞，必須要有受詞。此外，raise 是規則變化的動詞，所以過去簡單式記得加上 _____ed。

☆ 意指增加、上升的 rise 為不及物動詞，不可有受詞。此外，rise 是不規則變化

的動詞：rise、rose、risen，例如 A new dawn has risen.。

　　在做下一個練習時，請仔細思考句意、文法和用法來選出正確的單字。

Task 42

請選出正確的單字來填入下列各句。

① **applied/applied for**

I ＿＿＿＿＿＿＿＿ the job, but I didn't get it.

② **took/spent**

I ＿＿＿＿＿＿＿＿ $200 on a new mouse.

③ **spent/took**

I ＿＿＿＿＿＿＿＿ a long time googling this information.

④ **apply for this idea to/appply this idea to**

If we ＿＿＿＿＿＿＿＿＿＿ the real world, we can see what's wrong with it.

⑤ **It took/I took**

＿＿＿＿＿＿＿＿ me 20 minutes to remember my password.

⑥ **prevent/avoid**

It's hard to ＿＿＿＿＿＿＿＿ children from seeing unsuitable materials online.

⑦ **worthwhile/worth**

It's not ＿＿＿＿＿＿＿＿ learning how to code when you can employ someone to do it for you.

⑧ **worth/worthwhile**

My Instagram account is ＿＿＿＿＿＿＿＿ 2000 dollars a month.

⑨ **raising/rising**

Online bullying is _____.

⑩ **worth/worthwhile**

Playing the whole game from beginning to end is not _____.

⑪ **has risen/has raised**

The number of gambling sites _____ 200% in the last 6 months.

⑫ **rises/raises**

This _____ the issue of addiction to online gambling.

⑬ **prevent/avoid**

Although we can't stop it, we need to _____ excessive exposure to social media. Too much can be addictive.

✅ 答案・中譯・說明　🎧 **Track 3.11**

① I <u>applied for</u> the job, but I didn't get it. 我應徵了這個工作，但沒有錄取。

② I spent $200 on a new mouse. 我花了 200 元買一個新滑鼠。

③ I spent a long time googling this information.
我花了很長的時間在谷歌上搜尋這則資訊。

④ If we apply this idea to the real world, we can see what's wrong with it.
假如把這個構想應用到實現世界中，我們就能看出它有什麼問題了。

⑤ It took me 20 minutes to remember my password.
我花了 20 分鐘才想起來我的密碼。

⑥ It's hard to prevent children from seeing unsuitable materials online.
要防止孩童在網路上看到不恰當的內容是很難的。

⑦ It's not worth learning how to code when you can employ someone to do it for you.
當你能雇人來幫你做到時，就不值得去學要怎麼編碼。

⑧ My Instagram account is worth 2000 dollars a month.
我的 Instagram 帳戶一個月值 2000 美元。

⑨ Online bullying is rising. 網路霸凌問題上升了。

⑩ Playing the whole game from beginning to end is not worthwhile.
把整個遊戲從頭玩到尾並沒有價值。

⑪ The number of gambling sites has risen 200% in the last 6 months.
賭博網站的數目在過去六個月上升了 200%。

⑫ This raises the issue of addiction to online gambling.
這引發了在網路賭博成癮的議題。

⑬ Although we can't stop it, we need to avoid excessive exposure to social media. Too much can be addictive.
雖然阻止不了，但我們需要避免去過度接觸社群媒體。太多可能會上癮。

☆ 請仔細思考第 1 句和第 4 句在意思上的差別。

☆ 需特別留意第 2、3、5 句的文法問題，尤其是句子的主題。

☆ 第 6 句的行動是針對別人 (children)，因此要用 prevent；第 13 句使用 avoid 則是因為行動並不是針對別人，而是總之就是會發生。

☆ 第 7 句選用 worth 是因為主詞是 it，而受詞是 Ving；第 10 句選用 worthwhile 則是因為它是句子裡的最後一個字；第 8 句的意思顯然是關於錢，所以不能用 worthwhile。

☆ 請注意，第 9 句和第 11 句的 rise 需要用正確的動詞形式，因為意思是「增加」。而第 12 句需要用 raise 則是因為 issue。

☆ 為正確的解答畫上底線。

　　最後我們還是要來練習從閱讀文章中找出這些容易搞混的單字。當你在文章中每找到一個單字，都必須停下來思考它是意指什麼、它的文法是什麼，以及它是如何使用的。

Task 43

請從 Task 1 和 Task 2 的閱讀文章中找出關鍵語庫 ❼ 列出的所有易混淆字詞，並留意它們在文章中是如何使用的。

Task 44

請練習用關鍵語庫 ❼ 的易混淆字詞來造句。

易混淆字詞	造句練習
apply for s/th	
apply s/th (to s/th)	
prevent (s/o from) s/th	
avoid s/th	
spend s/th Ving spend s/th on s/th	
take (s/o) s/th to V	
worth s/th	
worthwhile	
raise s/th	
rise	

☆ 在寫作中運用這些易混淆的字詞時，記得把重點放在文法、句意和用法上，而不是只注意單字的意思。

在你結束這個單元之前，請將下列清單看過，確定你能將所有要點都勾選起來。如果有一些要點你還搞不清楚，請回頭再次研讀本單元的相關部分。

PART

1

☐ 我確實閱讀並理解了關於「新媒體」的長篇文章。

☐ 我完全知道字彙在文章中是如何使用，並更加了解到要怎麼用單字來表達特定的主題。

☐ 我已經學會 15 個關於「新媒體」主題的關鍵字，以及可與其搭配使用的動詞和形容詞。

☐ 我已經練習使用這些搭配詞來描寫「新媒體」。

☐ 我已經學到了一些同義詞，也了解在運用時需要注意的一些問題。

☐ 我學到了很多關於這個主題可以運用的語塊，包括片語動詞以及名詞或動詞為同形的單字。

☐ 我已經練習使用這些語塊。

☐ 我學到了 5 個關於這個主題的慣用語，且知道如何運用。

☐ 我已經理解在運用慣用語時需要特別注意的一些問題。

☐ 關於這個主題，我已經能確實掌握一些易混淆字詞的用法。

Unit 4

不平等
Inequality

閱讀文章 Reading

　　在本單元，我們將針對「不平等」這個主題來探討它的歷史和理論起源，以及我們能對它做什麼。

Task 1

閱讀文章並盡可能地理解文章內容。請先不要使用字典。

(1) _____ The top 1% of people have managed to accumulate vast and untold wealth. While the great majority of the world's people can hardly earn a living, a very few people are making very big bucks indeed. This situation puts most of the people in the world at a huge disadvantage. It means they don't have access to basic education, higher education and employment opportunities, not to mention basic healthcare. In fact, most people in the world live in extreme poverty and earn less than $10 a day. It is grossly unfair that such a small number of people hold most of the money in the world.

(2) _____ Instead they came up with the policy of austerity, which in practice meant cutting back on basic services such as education and healthcare. Local and regional governments were told to toe the line and stop providing basic services such as free meals for kids in school, free libraries, and help for the elderly; they cut unemployment benefits and reduced public welfare for the poor. They cut inward investment in new industries and training for the young. Governments no longer had enough money, so they said, for these things. They were being economical with the truth. Instead, they focussed on giving banks money

that they had lost in the crisis. The fact is, there has always been enough money to go around, but our ideas about what money is and how it works have lead to economic catastrophe, and our body politic has become sick as a result.

(3) _____ The idea is that as companies get rich, wealth will slowly trickle down to the rest of society as workers get higher wages and staff get higher salaries, allowing them to buy more goods and services, which in turn will bring about more wealth for companies, and so the cycle continues. The trouble is that this trickle-down model of economics is fundamentally flawed. Money does not behave like water, as economists think. Rather, it behaves like smoke, and constantly rises upwards. The price of goods and services does not go down, but is constantly increasing. The development of new labor-saving technologies means that there is less need for people to do unpleasant manual labor, which means less work and fewer jobs, and thus, more poverty.

(4) _____ We need radical changes to our economic system, they say, otherwise the open, democratic society that we live in will not be able to sustain the costs of this injustice. Protests have already started in major cities around the world. Law and order is slowly breaking down. Instead of listening to protestors' concerns, governments are sending in the police and enacting further legislation against protests and which helps to protect the interests of the privileged and the well-off.

(5) _____ Governments around the world need to draw up new plans which will change society and make it fairer. Instead of valuing the people at the very top of the pile who simply collect wealth, we should place more value in the people who actually do the work of creating the

wealth at the bottom of the pile. Governments need to increase large-scale investment in infrastructure and training. The way to pay for this is by increasing redistributive taxation. It is unfair to ask the world's poor to pay so much income and sales tax, when the world's rich are not even paying inheritance or wealth tax, and multinational corporations can easily find ways to avoid corporation tax, and are given tax break after tax break. It would be better for the rich to start paying their way as well. After all, it's also they who benefit from the infrastructure we all use in our daily life. Why shouldn't they also start to help pay for it instead of hiding their wealth away in secret bank accounts? It would be better if they were made to distribute their wealth instead of being allowed to hoard it. This won't solve all the problems of inequality, but at least it's a start.

Complete financial and economic equality will never be achieved unless we change the way we think about economics. It's simply a question of will.

Task 2

請從下列句子選出適當的主題句以完成 Task 1 每個段落的填空。

A After the financial crash in 2008, national governments missed the opportunity to restructure the global economy and make it fairer.

B But the question remains: what can we do about it?

C However, many people are now starting to question the justice of this situation.

D The main idea in free-market economics as we practice it and understand it today is that the financial markets in general and stock markets specifically are the most powerful instruments there are for creating and distributing wealth.

E The unequal distribution of wealth is the burning, central, political and social issue of our time.

✅ 答案·中譯·說明

(1) E　(2) A　(3) D　(4) C　(5) B

譯文

　　財富分配不均是當代最緊迫、最核心的政治和社會議題。頂端 1% 的人已經積累了龐大而數不清的財富。雖然世界上絕大多數的人幾近無法謀生，但極少數的人確實是賺了很多錢。這樣的情況使得世上大部分的人都處於巨大的劣勢中。這意味著他們無法獲得基本教育、高等教育和就業機會，更不用說是基本的醫療照護。事實上，世界上大多數人都活在極度貧窮中，一天賺不到十美元。這麼少數的人卻握有世界上大部分的錢是極其不公平之事。

　　在 2008 年金融危機後，各國政府錯失了重組全球經濟結構，使其更加公平的機會。相反地，他們提出了財政緊縮政策，這實際上是意味著削減諸如教育和醫療照護等基本服務。地方和區域政府奉命要嚴守規定，並停止提供基本服務，諸如對學童免費供餐、免費的圖書館和幫助長者；他們削減了失業救濟金，並降低了窮人的公共福利。他們削減了對新產業的投資和對年輕人的培訓。政府不再有足夠的錢來做這些事，他們是這麼說的。他們對實情避重就輕，反而是聚焦於把在危機時所賠掉的錢補給銀行。事實是，總是有足夠的錢可供支應，但我們對於錢是什麼和它是怎麼運作的想法導致了經濟災難，結果使得我們的國家生病了。

　　我們現今所實踐和理解的自由市場經濟學主要觀念是，在創造和分配財富上，廣泛的金融市場和專門的股票市場是最強大的既有手段。觀念在於隨著公司變有錢，財富就會慢慢下滴到社會的其他地方，使職工拿到較高的工資，職員拿到較高的薪水就得以購買更多的商品和服務，繼而就會為公司造就更多的財富，於是循環便繼續下去。麻煩的是，這種下滴的經濟學模型從根本上是有缺陷的。錢並不會如經濟學家所想表現得像水，它反倒是表現得像煙，不斷往上升。商品與服務的價格不會走低，而是會不斷上漲。節省勞動力的新科技發展意味著，人必須去從事討厭的體力勞動的需求變少了，而這意味著工作變少和職務減少，因而使得貧窮加大。

　　不過，很多人現在都開始質疑這個局面的公平正義。他們說，我們的經濟體系需要徹底的改變，否則我們所生活的開放、民主社會將無法承受這種不公不義的代價。抗議活動已經在世界各地的主要城市開始了。法律與秩序正在慢慢崩壞。政府沒有去傾聽抗議人士的疑慮，而是派出警察並頒布進一步的法規來反制抗議，所幫忙保護的則是特權階級和富人的利益。

　　但問題依舊是：對此我們能做些什麼？世界各國的政府需要擬訂新的計畫來改變社會，使其更加公平。與其重視頂層那些純粹在獲取財富的人，我們應該要賦予更多價值的是在底層實際從事工作來創造財富的人。政府需要增加在基礎建設和培訓上的大規模投

資。為此買單的辦法則是增加再分配課稅。要求世界上的窮人繳這麼多所得稅和營業稅並不公平，因為世界上的有錢人連遺產稅或財富稅都不用繳，跨國企業則是輕易就能找到辦法來閃避企業稅，並獲得接連的稅務減免。比較好的會是，有錢人也開始自付費用。畢竟，他們也是從我們日常生活中全都在使用的基礎建設中受惠。為什麼他們不該也開始幫忙為此付費，而不是把財富藏在秘密的銀行帳戶裡？如果他們被要求分配財富，而不是被容許囤積財富，情況會更好。這不會解決所有不平等的問題，但至少是個開始。

除非我們改變對經濟學的思考方式，否則完全的財務和經濟平等永遠無法實現。它純粹是意志的問題。

....

☆ 請留意這篇文章的結構。第一段是介紹問題。第二段交代了這個問題的歷史，描述造成此問題的事件。第三段是延續這番對問題成因的解釋，但層次比較理論。第四段說明不試著去解決問題的後果，最後一段則建議了一個理論上的辦法（改變價值觀）和一個實務上的辦法（課稅）來解決它。

☆ 請留意主題句 (topic sentence) 總是段落中最概括的句子，以及段落中的其他部分是如何以特定的例子或理由來申論主題句的論點。

字詞搭配 Word Partnerships

我們現在要來學習「不平等」這個主題的 15 個關鍵字，以及可搭配這些關鍵字使用的 word partnerships「字詞搭配表」。首先，請看關鍵字語庫。

Task 3

請仔細研讀這些主題字彙和下方的說明。

關鍵語庫 ❶　◎ Track 4.1

名詞	動詞	形容詞	字義
distribution Ⓒ	distribute	distributed	分配
economics Ⓤ	-	-	經濟學
economy Ⓒ	-	economic	經濟
(in)equality Ⓤ	-	equal	(不) 平等
government Ⓒ	govern	governmental	政府、政體
investment ⓊⒸ	invest (in s/th)	-	投資、投入
issue Ⓒ	-	-	議題、問題
legislation Ⓤ	legislate	legislated	立法、法律
market Ⓒ	-	-	市場
poverty Ⓤ	-	-	貧窮、貧困
society Ⓒ	-	social	社會
tax Ⓒ	tax	taxed	稅、稅務
taxation Ⓤ	-	-	課稅、稅款
wealth Ⓒ	-	wealthy	財富
welfare Ⓤ	-	-	福利、福利事業

☆ 需留意哪些名詞是可數，哪些是不可數。而一個名詞是可數或不可數，有時候須視主題而定。

☆ 留意單字的其他詞性形式，如動詞和形容詞。

☆ 請注意 economics 向來都必須有 s，但動詞則要用單數形。例如 Economics is the study of economies. 正確；Economics are the study of economies. 則是錯的。

☆ 請留意 equality「平等」要如何變成否定（不平等）。

☆ investment 用於較廣的層面時，例如政府對經濟體加以投資，必須使用單數、不可數的形式。意即 The government needs to stimulate investment. 是正確的，而 The government needs to stimulate investments. 則是錯的。但若是從個人理財的角度用 investment 來談論個人的私人投資時，那它就是可數，可以用複數形，例如 I have many investments in that industry.。

☆ issue 這個字對於 problem/solution「問題／解決方案」類型文章，以及 argument/opinion「論證／意見」類型文章來說，都是很重要的關鍵字。遇到這個字時，一定要特別留意其用法。

☆ society 可以是複數，但應該要以單數來使用，除非是在比較不同種類的社會。

☆ tax 這個字當然也可以當動詞，用於主動語態或被動語態。tax 當名詞時，可以連同 on 來使用，以指明是對什麼課稅，例如 There should be a tax on wealth.。但是當動詞來用時，則不使用 on，亦即 They should tax wealth. 正確，They should tax on wealth. 則是錯的。

☆ tax 和 taxation 的差別在於，tax 是一種特定的稅，而且這個名詞是可數的；taxation 指的則是一個國家用來為社會項目籌集資金的整個稅收體制，這個名詞不可數。

　　接下來，我們將以 5 個關鍵字為一組，深入地學習與這些字最頻繁搭配的字詞組合及正確用法。

Task 4

請研讀這個字詞搭配表、例句和底下的說明。

搭配在前的動詞	搭配的形容詞	關鍵字
have ensure achieve	equal equitable fair unfair unequal inequitable widespread	**distribution (of s/th)**

PART
1

字詞搭配使用範例 　🎧 **Track 4.2**（收錄本單元 Task 4~Task 20 字詞搭配使用範例）

• The **equal distribution of** wealth must be our objective.
  財富分配之平等必須是我們的目標。

• We must **ensure a widespread distribution of** emergency services.
  我們必須確保緊急服務是廣為分布的。

☆ 這裡的動詞和形容詞都是將意思相似的字詞歸類成一組。不過請記得，同義詞
　 向來都是 topic and collocation specific「特定主題和搭配」。

Task 5
請研讀這個字詞搭配表和例句。

搭配在前的動詞	搭配的形容詞	關鍵字
study do practice work in think about	applied theoretical classical free-market	**economics**

- Those who **study** and **practice economics** in depth know that the subject is flawed.

  那些對經濟學深入研究與實行的人都知道，這個題目有瑕疵。

- **Free-market economics** has brought us to this mess.

  自由市場經濟學把我們帶到了這個困境中。

Task 6

請研讀這個字詞搭配表、例句和底下的說明。

搭配在前面的動詞	搭配的形容詞		關鍵字
restructure reorganise rebuild build control manage regulate run	booming dynamic healthy sound strong ailing depressed sluggish weak advanced developed	free-market planned agricultural industrial service-based domestic local international global	**economy**

字詞搭配使用範例

- We need to **restructure** the **global economy** to make it fair for everyone.

  我們需要重組全球經濟，使它對每個人都公平。

- The way governments are **running** their **local economies** is not fair.

  政府經營地方經濟的方式並不公平。

- We need to **reorganise the economy** from an **agricultural economy** to a more **industrial** and **service-based economy**.
  我們需要把經濟從農業經濟重組成比較以工業和服務為基礎的經濟。

....

☆ 請留意不同類型經濟的說法。

Task 7

請研讀這個字詞搭配表、例句和底下的說明。

搭配在前面的動詞	搭配的形容詞		關鍵字
have achieve establish	complete full	economic financial	
	greater	legal	
demand fight for strive for		political	**(in)equality**
		racial	
promote		sexual	
		gender	
ensure guarantee		social	

字詞搭配使用範例

- There are no societies which **have complete equality** for all classes.
  沒有社會是所有階級都具備完全的平等。

- They are **fighting for greater political equality**.
  他們正為了更大的政治平等而奮鬥。

- **Racial inequality** is a big problem in our society.
  種族不平等是我們社會的大問題。

....

☆ 注意平等的不同類型說法，並留意這個名詞要怎麼構成否定。

請研讀這個字詞搭配表、例句和底下的說明。

搭配在前面的動詞	搭配的形容詞		關鍵字
elect	elected	left-wing	
form	national	right-wing	
install	central	socialist	
disband		communist	
	local		**government**
	provincial	coalition	
bring down	regional	minority	
destabilize			
overthrow		caretaker	
topple		interim	

字詞搭配使用範例

- They **formed** a **minority government**. 他們組成了少數政府。
- The **elected socialist government was overthrown** by the army.
  當選的社會主義政府遭到了軍隊推翻。
- The protests are aimed at **bringing down** the **caretaker government** and
  electing a new one. 抗議人士旨在推倒看守政府並選出新政府。
- A **coalition government was installed** after an inconclusive election.
  聯合政府是在選舉沒有定論後所組成。

☆ 請留意各動詞能以被動來使用。

　　現在，我們來看看各位是否能用一些字詞搭配來擴大對字彙的運用。

Task 9

請從 Task 4 到 Task 8 中選出正確形式的字詞，完成以下段落填空。

If (1) _____ governments are not able to (2) _____ their (3) _____ economies so as to (4) _____ (5) _____ distribution (6) _____ wealth, and make their societies fairer for everyone, then it might be better to (7) _____ central governments and install smaller, (8) _____ ones which are closer to the needs of local people. In fact (9) _____ economics has been a failure in (10) _____ (11) _____ equality for everyone.

範例答案

1. central/national/elected
2. reorganise/restructure/control/manage
3. domestic/local
4. have/achieve/establish/ensure
5. equal/equitable/fair
6. of

7. disband
8. local/provincial/regional
9. classical/free-market
10. ensuring/guaranteeing/ establishing/achieving
11. complete/full/greater

- -

☆ 請留意各組同義字詞，空格中選填同一組內不同的字也是可以的。

☆ 須確認所選用的單字都是正確的形式。請檢查單數或複數，以及動詞的正確形式。例如在空格 (10) 中的動詞必須是 Ving 的形式，因為它是接在介系詞 in 之後。

現在來學習另外 5 個單字。

Task 10

請研讀這個字詞搭配表和例句。

搭配在前面的動詞	搭配的形容詞		關鍵字
make attract encourage promote stimulate increase cut	extra further considerable enormous huge large-scale major massive significant low inadequate	domestic local inward foreign international overseas long-term short-term	**investment (in s/th)**

字詞搭配使用範例

- We need to **make further inward investment** to stimulate the economy.
  我們需要進一步擴大對內投資以刺激經濟。

- The government have **cut long-term investment in** infrastructure.
  政府削減了對基礎建設的長期投資。

- If we can **encourage further local investment**, our economy will grow.
  假如能鼓勵進一步的地方投資,我們的經濟就會成長。

Task 11

請研讀這個字詞搭配表和例句。

搭配在前面的動詞	搭配的形容詞		關鍵字
be raise debate discuss decide settle address tackle deal with focus on	big burning central crucial important key major wider basic fundamental minor side complex thorny controversial	economic environmental political social technical	**issue (of s/th)**

字詞搭配使用範例

- They **raised the issue of** the unequal distribution of wealth, but the
  government said it was just a **side issue** and not worth **tackling**.
  他們點出了財富分配不平等的問題，但政府說它只是次要議題，不值得著墨。

- There **are** so many other **basic political issues** we need to **tackle** before we
  address the issue of free milk for children.
  在解決孩童免費牛奶的問題前，還有許多其他的基本政治議題需要我們去處理。

- Climate change **is a crucial environmental issue** we need to address right now.
  氣候變遷是很要緊的環境議題，我們需要現在就加以因應。

- It's a **controversial issue**. 這是個有爭議的議題。

UNIT 4 不平等 187

請研讀這個字詞搭配表、例句和底下的說明。

搭配在前的動詞	搭配的形容詞		關鍵字
draw up	draft	anti-abortion	
propose		anti-discrimination	
	fresh	employment	
approve	further	environmental	
	new	financial	
enact		gun-control	
pass	effective	health	
introduce	tough	housing	
need	complex	social	**legislation (against s/th)**
require	controversial		
call for	unworkable		
propose			
block			
delay			
amend			
repeal			

字詞搭配使用範例

- They **are drawing up legislation against** gun controls. This will make it possible to buy guns in the supermarket.
  他們在擬訂立法來反制槍枝控管。這將使在超市就可能買得到槍。

- We **need tougher financial legislation** to prevent damage to the economy.
  我們需要更嚴格的金融立法來預防經濟受損。

- If they **pass** this **housing legislation**, free housing will be available to everyone.
  假如他們通過這項住房立法，免費住房就會人人可及。

☆ 注意立法的不同類型說法。

Task 13

請研讀這個字詞搭配表、例句和底下的說明。

搭配在前面的動詞	搭配的形容詞		關鍵字
be	shrinking	competitive	
	declining	domestic	
enter		export	
break into	growing	financial	
		foreign	
withdraw from	important	housing	**market**
	large	international	**(for s/th)**
create	major	labor	
establish		local	
	small		
expand	insignificant	overseas	
develop		stock	
	open		
regulate	over-regulated	tough	

搭配在前面的動詞	搭配的形容詞		關鍵字
be	shrinking	competitive	
	declining	domestic	
enter		export	
break into	growing	financial	
		foreign	
withdraw from	important	housing	**market (for s/th)**
	large	international	
create	major	labor	
establish		local	
	small	overseas	
expand	insignificant	stock	
develop	open	tough	
regulate	over-regulated		

字詞搭配使用範例

- It's a very **competitive labor market**. 這是一個競爭激烈的勞動市場。
- We need to **regulate** the **housing market** so that poor people can afford decent housing. 我們需要監管住房市場，好讓窮人負擔得起像樣的住房。
- They are trying to **develop overseas markets** instead of focussing on problems at home. 他們正試著努力開發海外市場，而不是聚焦於國內的問題。
- They are often told there **is** no **market for** their skills.
  他們經常被告知他們的技能沒有市場。

☆ 注意不同類型市場的說法。

Task 14

請研讀這個字詞搭配表和例句。

搭配在前面的動詞	搭配的形容詞		關鍵字
live in	abject	widespread	
	absolute	urban	
alleviate	extreme		
combat			
reduce	grinding	rural	**poverty**
	severe		
eliminate			
eradicate			

字詞搭配使用範例

- There is a great deal of **widespread rural poverty**, which we must try to **alleviate**. 農村普遍存在著廣泛的貧困問題，我們必須設法去緩解這種現象。

- The task of governments now all over the world should be to **eradicate grinding poverty**. 現在世界各國政府的任務應該是去根除赤貧。

就像前面所做過的，我們再來練習這第二組 5 個單字的字詞搭配應用。

Task 15

請從 Task 10 到 Task 14 中選出正確形式的字詞，完成以下段落填空。

The (1) _____ issue facing our society is the (2) _____ (3) _____ poverty people are (4) _____, especially in all Third World cities where the poor have inadequate housing, hygiene and working conditions. Unless we can (5) _____ this issue, the problem of the poor will never go away. We need to (6) _____ (7) _____ legislation (8) _____ landlords charging high rents, and we need to (9) _____ (10) _____ investment (11) _____ these cities from outside. This will help to (12) _____ (13) _____ and (14) _____ markets (15) _____ the poor, who will thus have new jobs and homes.

1. big/burning/central/crucial/important/key/major/wider/basic/fundamental
2. widespread /abject/absolute/extreme/grinding /severe
3. urban
4. living in
5. address/tackle/deal with
6. enact/pass/introduce
7. new /fresh/further/effective/tough
8. against
9. attract/encourage/promote/stimulate
10. foreign/international/inward
11. in
12. establish/create
13. labor
14. housing
15. for

☆ 請留意各組同義字詞，空格中選填同一組內不同的字也是可以的。

☆ 須確認所選用的單字都是正確的形式。請檢查單數或複數，以及動詞的正確形式。例如在空格 (4) 中便需要用 Ving，因為動詞時態是現在進行式。

現在我們來學習最後一組的 5 個單字。

Task 16

請研讀這個字詞搭配表、例句和底下的說明。

搭配在前面的動詞	搭配的形容詞		關鍵字
have be in live in fit into be a part of be a member of build create establish shape influence	contemporary modern traditional consumer free open fair multiracial multicultural	agricultural capitalist classless democratic industrial matriarchal patriarchal socialist Western	**society**

字詞搭配使用範例

- **Establishing** a **classless society** is the dream of most politicians.
  打造一個無階級的社會是大部分政治人物的夢想。
- If you **are a member of** a **free** and **open**, **multicultural society**, you are pretty lucky. 假如你是自由與開放、多元文化社會的一員，你算是頗為幸運。
- The ideas which have **shaped Western society** are individualism and the free market. 形塑西方社會的思想是個人主義和自由市場。

☆ 請留意 Western 必須用大寫字母。
☆ 注意不同類型社會的說法。

Task 17

請研讀這個字詞搭配表、例句和底下的說明。

搭配在前的動詞	搭配的形容詞		關鍵字	搭配在後的名詞
introduce impose levy put ~ on s/th collect pay increase put up raise cut lower reduce evade avoid	high direct indirect basic redistributive windfall low	capital gains company corporation income inheritance land property purchase sales savings wealth	**tax (on sth)**	payer break rate authorities law measures policy reform

- The government are going to **introduce** a **capital gains tax**, which will hurt the rich. 政府要導入的資本利得稅會傷到有錢人。
- If they **put up basic tax**, this will impact the poor very badly.
  假如他們祭出基本稅，這會對窮人衝擊得非常厲害。
- **Tax law** is very complicated. 稅法非常複雜。
- Instead of **paying savings tax**, the rich are given **tax breaks** so that they can keep their wealth.
  有錢人不用繳存款稅，而是會獲得稅務減免，所以他們能保有財富。

☆ 留意 tax 所能形成的複合名詞。

☆ 注意不同類型「稅」的說法。

Task 18

請研讀這個字詞搭配表和例句。

搭配在前面的動詞	搭配的形容詞	關鍵字
increase put up raise cut reduce lower avoid be exempt from	excessive heavy high low direct indirect company corporate personal redistributive	**taxation**

- **Excessive taxation** puts a heavy burden on the population.
  過度課稅會對民眾造成嚴重的負擔。

- No one should **be exempt from direct taxation**.
  沒有人該免除直接課稅。

- The rich always manage to **avoid personal taxation**.
  富人總是會設法閃避個人課稅。

Task 19

請研讀這個字詞搭配表和例句。

搭配在前面的動詞	搭配的形容詞		關鍵字
have possess accumulate acquire inherit create lose	considerable enormous great vast untold growing increasing shrinking	economic financial material national personal private	**wealth**

字詞搭配使用範例

- A few people **have untold wealth**, and this is not fair.
  少數人擁有數不清的財富,這並不公平。

- The rich have usually **inherited** their **wealth** to begin with.
  有錢人通常是靠繼承財富來起頭。

- The **national wealth is shrinking** rather than **growing** as most of the **wealth** ends up in private hands.
  國民財富是在縮水,而不是成長,因為大部分的財富最終都落入私人手裡。

Task 20

請研讀這個字詞搭配表和例句。

搭配在前面的動詞	搭配的形容詞	關鍵字
live on receive provide pay fund raise reduce be dependent on	state public social basic animal	**welfare (for s/o)**

字詞搭配使用範例

- In a well-ordered society the state **provides basic welfare for** the very poor.
  在秩序井然的社會裡，國家會為非常窮的人提供基本福利。
- The government has cut **social welfare** again. 政府又刪減了社會福利。
- Many people **are dependent on public welfare for** their very survival.
  很多人是依靠公共福利才能生存下去。

接下來，我們來練習這最後一組 5 個單字的字詞搭配應用。

Task 21

請從 Task 16 到 Task 20 中選出正確形式的字詞，完成以下段落填空。

We can only (1) _____ a (2) _____ society if everyone in that society
(3) _____ tax. Tax (4) _____ for the rich are not acceptable. Those
who have (5) _____ (6) _____ wealth should be taxed. Taxation should
not be (7) _____, especially for the poor and middle classes, but it should
be (8) _____, that is, it should distribute wealth fairly among all members
of society, so that no one has to (9) _____ (10) _____ welfare.

1. have/live in
2. fair
3. pays
4. breaks
5. accumulated/acquired/inherited

6. untold/considerable/enormous/great/vast
7. heavy/excessive/high
8. redistributive
9. live on/receive
10. state/public/social/basic

☆ 再提醒一次，請務必留意各組的同義字詞。空格中選填同一組內不同的字也是可以的。

☆ 請確認所選用的單字都是正確的形式。檢查單數或複數，以及動詞的正確形式，確保所套用的單字是正確的形式。

☆ 請留意到在空格 (3) 中，主詞是 everyone，所以動詞需要加上 s。而在空格 (4) 必須使用複數，因為意思是概括的稅務減免。另外，在空格 (5) 中需要使用動詞的過去分詞，因為動詞時態是現在完成式。

　　最後，我們要進行這個部分的最後一個練習，這對於各位記憶 15 個關鍵單字和它們的字詞搭配將有非常大的幫助。記住，多閱讀有助於擴充字彙量，而在文章上下文脈絡中查看大量例子則能幫助你記憶新的用語。

Task 22

請從 Task 1 和 Task 2 的閱讀文章中找出關鍵語庫 ❶ 所列的 15 個關鍵字，並留意這些字在文章中是如何使用的。

常用語塊 Chunks

前面學過了字詞搭配的用法，我們現在要來學一些可用在寫作或談論不平等問題的語塊。

Task 23

研讀這些語塊和底下的說明。

關鍵語庫 ❷

Chunk
❏ be/put s/o at a disadvantage　使 s/o 處在劣勢中
❏ be better (for s/o) to V　（s/o）V 比較好
❏ be better if v.p.　比較好的是，假如 v.p.
❏ be (un)fair that v.p.　（不）公平的是 v.p.
❏ be (un)fair to V　V（不）公平
❏ give s/o s/th　給 s/o s/th
❏ give s/th to s/o　把 s/th 給 s/o
❏ provide (s/o with) s/th　（為 s/o）提供 s/th
❏ the elderly　年長者
❏ the young　年輕人

☆ 別忘了在使用這些語塊時需要改變動詞的時態。

☆ 留意這些語塊是否全都必須用 n.p.、v.p.、Ving 或 V。

☆ 留意哪些語塊要接受詞、哪些不用。還要注意受詞的類型，尤其是需要使用人員受詞 (s/o) 或事物受詞 (s/th) 時。

☆ 當你想要描述一種狀態時，可以用 be at a disadvantage，例如 The poor are always at a disadvantage.。若是想要描述一群人對另一群人所做的不利行動

時，可以用 put s/o at a disadvantage，例如 The rich always put the poor at a disadvantage.。

☆ be better 可以有兩種用法。若想要在它之後接 v.p.，就必須使用 if：It would be better if wealth was equally distributed.。若是要描述行動，就使用 to V：It would be better to distribute wealth equally.。而若是在提出改善的建議，尤其是在寫 argument/opinion 的論說文時，主詞向來必須使用 it is 或 it would be，例如 It would be better if governments took action against this.。

☆ be unfair 有兩個語塊。若想要在這個語塊之後接 v.p.，就必須使用 that：It's unfair that some people are paid millions.。而若想要在語塊之後接動詞，就必須使用 to：It's unfair to expect people to accept less.。注意，主詞向來都是 it is。

☆ give 有兩個語塊。若是要強調給予的人，就把人員受詞 (s/o) 擺在前面：They give their workers a decent wage。而若想要強調所給之物，就把那 (s/th) 擺在前面並使用 to：They give a decent wage to their workers.。此外，give 也能以被動來使用：They were given a pay increase.，They 在此是指拿到所給之物的人。

☆ 各位或許記得在 Unit 2 裡，我們比較過 provide 和 supply 的意思，現在我們要聚焦於 provide 和 give。請留意到 provide 只有一種用法，而 give 卻有兩種。provide 強調所給之物，例如 They provide benefits.。若想要納入關於受提供者的資訊，就把那 (s/o) 直接擺在動詞後面，然後使用 with：They provide their workers with benefits.。注意，寫成 They provide benefits to their workers. 是錯誤的，在此情況下應該要使用 give：They give benefits to their workers.。這個錯誤在台灣很常見，一定要特別留心。

☆ 在描述年長者的群體或年輕人的群體時，前面應該要加定冠詞 the，然後是形容詞，而且必須使用複數形動詞。例如 The elderly are always suffering. 是正確的，而 The elderly is always suffering. 則是錯誤的。

☆ 也可以使用 the old 來代替 the elderly，但不要用 the elders 或 elders，這是錯的。另外，也可以使用 young people 來代替 the young，但不可用 youths，這也是錯的。各位也可以用相同的方式來描述其他的群體，諸如：the poor、the underprivileged、the disadvantaged、the rich、the well off、the privileged，還有其他社會群體：the disabled、the sick、the homeless，

此外也可以用這種方式來寫社會上的不同階級：the middle class、the upper class、the lower class。

☆ 請務必記得，在學習和使用語塊時須特別注意小詞、字尾和語塊的結尾這些細節，確保使用上完全準確。

下一個 Task 將聚焦於大家在使用這些語塊時經常會犯的錯誤。

Task 24

請改正這些句子中使用語塊的常見錯誤。

① It is unfair expect more.

_____

② It is unfair to the rich pay less tax.

_____

③ It would be better for them stop working altogether.

_____

④ The elders are always poor in this society.

_____

⑤ The government would be better if they stopped this unfair practice.

_____

⑥ The old do not understand the youths.

_____

⑦ The poor are always in a disadvantage.

_____

⑧ The poor is unfair that they pay more tax.

_____

⑨ They give benefits their workers.

_____

⑩ They give their workers a good wage, so they were happy to work there.

_____

⑪ They provide a free staff canteen to their workers.

_____

⑫ They would be better to find another job.

_____

⑬ This kind of law always put the poor at a disadvantage.

_____

✅ 答案・中譯・說明　🎧 Track 4.3

① It is unfair **to** expect more. 期望更多是不公平的。

② It is unfair **that** the rich pay less tax. 不公平的是，有錢人繳的稅較少。

③ It would be better for them **to** stop working altogether.
他們最好完全停止工作。

④ The **elderly** are always poor in this society.
在這個社會上，老年人向來都很貧窮。

⑤ **It would** be better if **the government** stopped this unfair practice.
如果政府停止這種不公平的做法，那就更好了。

⑥ **The old/the elderly** do not understand **the young**.
老年人不了解年輕人。

⑦ The poor are always **at** a disadvantage. 窮人向來都處於劣勢中。

⑧ **It is** unfair that **the poor** pay more tax. 不公平的是，窮人繳的稅較多。

⑨ They give benefits **to** their workers. 他們會給職工福利。

⑩ They **gave** their workers a good wage, so they were happy to work there.
他們給職工的工資不錯，所以他們樂於在那裡工作。

⑪ They provide **their workers with** a free staff canteen.
他們為職工提供免費的員工食堂。

⑫ **It would** be better **for them** to find another job.
他們去找別的工作會比較好。

⑬ This kind of law always **puts** the poor at a disadvantage.
這種法律向來都使窮人處於劣勢中。

....

☆ 我已經把錯誤的部分標示出來，各位可以清楚看出哪裡用錯了。

☆ 請將 Task 24 的句子與關鍵語庫 ❷ 的語塊做比較，以確保能清楚看出句中哪
裡用錯了。

☆ 注意，在第 10 句和第 13 句中，錯誤出現在動詞的時態和形式。別忘了聚焦
在動詞上！

☆ 請將正確句子中的完整語塊畫上底線（參照第 1 句的示範），這能幫助你完整
而正確地記住語塊。

　　下一個練習對於記憶語塊將有非常大的幫助。記住，多閱讀有助於擴
充字彙量，而在文章上下文脈絡中查看大量語塊則能幫助你記憶新的用語。

Task 25
請從 Task 1 和 Task 2 的閱讀文章中找出關鍵語庫 ❷ 列出的所有語塊，並
留意這些語塊在文章中是如何使用的。

Task 26
現在請嘗試用前面學過的語塊來寫出你自己的句子。

關鍵字語塊	造句
be/put s/o at a disadvantage	

be better (for s/o) to V (s/o)	
be better if v.p.	
be (un)fair that v.p.	
be (un)fair to V	
give s/o s/th	
give s/th to s/o	
provide (s/o with) s/th	
the elderly	
the young	

☆ 我顯然無法在此改正你的句子,但你可以透過確認語塊所有的小細節,自行改正。再次提醒在寫作中運用語塊時,須特別注意小詞、字尾和語塊的結尾,無論所需要的是 n.p.、v.p.、Ving 還是 V,並且確保你所使用的語塊是完整的。

5 個可作動詞或名詞的單字
5 words which can be verbs or nouns

　　語塊通常會視關鍵字是名詞或動詞而有所不同，現在我們要來看 5 個動詞和名詞同形的單字，並學習使用正確的語塊。

Task 27

看以下幾個名詞和動詞同形的單字。

關鍵語庫 ❸

關鍵字	名詞字義	動詞字義
value	重要性；價值；益處	重視；評價
need	需要；需求	需要；有……必要
change	變化；變更；變遷	更改；交換；變化
question	要討論（或考慮）的問題；懷疑；疑問	對……表示疑問；詢問
start	開始；起點	開始；出發；啟動

Task 28

閱讀句子並判斷關鍵字是動詞或名詞，填入 V 或 N。

① _____ As a society we do not **value** the contribution of those at the bottom.
② _____ If we don't **start** to understand their problems, they will continue to suffer.
③ _____ It's not a perfect solution, but it's a **start**.
④ _____ Some people are beginning to **question** this.
⑤ _____ There is a need for radical social **change**.

⑥ ____ There is no **value** to this work.

⑦ ____ The government is implementing **changes** to the laws.

⑧ ____ The **question** of workers' rights has still not been settled.

⑨ ____ They **started** a petition.

⑩ ____ They **started** paying their workers a better wage.

⑪ ____ We need to **change** our attitude.

⑫ ____ We need to change the **values** of society.

⑬ ____ Workers are not **valued** enough.

✅ 答案・中譯・說明

① V 我們的社會並不重視底層那些人的貢獻。

② V 假如我們不開始去了解他們的問題，他們將會繼續受苦。

③ N 這不是個完美的解決方案，但是個開始。

④ V 有些人開始在質疑這一點。

⑤ N 有需要進行徹底的社會變革。

⑥ N 這項工作沒有價值。

⑦ N 政府正在推行法令變革。

⑧ N 職工權益的問題還是沒有得到解決。

⑨ V 他們發起了一項請願。

⑩ V 他們開始支付更高的工資給職工。

⑪ V 我們需要改變我們的態度。

⑫ N 我們需要改變社會的價值觀。

⑬ V 職工沒有受到足夠的重視。

現在我們來看看在下一個練習中，這些動詞和名詞的不同語塊。

Task 29

請看以下所彙整的語塊及用法說明。

關鍵字語塊	關鍵字詞性	例句＆翻譯
value	*nc*	Their contribution has no value. 他們的貢獻沒有價值。
value s/th	*vt*	Society does not value their contribution. It is not valued. 社會不重視他們的貢獻。它不受重視。
need for	*nc*	There is a real need for change. 改變有實質的需要。
need to V	*vi*	We need to understand their demands. 我們需要去了解他們的需求。
need n.p./Ving	*vt*	They need more recognition. It needs solving urgently. 他們需要更多的認可。這個問題迫切需要解決。
change to s/th	*nc*	They want to make changes to the law. 他們想要對法令進行修改。
change s/th	*vt*	They want to change the law. 他們想要改變法令。
question of	*nu*	It's a question of justice and fairness. 它是正義和公平的問題。
question about s/th	*nc*	I have a couple of questions about this issue. 我對這個議題有幾點疑問。
question s/th	*vt*	Many people are questioning the government's policies. 很多人在質疑政府的政策。
start	*nc*	It's not perfect, but it's a start. 它並不完美，但是個開始。
start to V	*vi*	They are starting to protest in some cities. 他們開始在一些城市抗議。
start n.p./Ving	*vt*	They started listening to their critics./He started his talk. 他們開始去傾聽批評者。／他展開了談話。

start	*vi*	The revolution has started! 革命開始了！

....

☆ 須留意哪些名詞是可數，哪些是不可數。

☆ 別忘了以正確的時態來使用動詞。

☆ value 當名詞時，要連同 have 來使用。在 Unit 9 當中將會學到更多這個名詞的用法。value 在當動詞時，也能以被動來使用。

☆ need 當名詞時，要連同 be、have 或 create 來使用，例如 They created a need for more doctors.。而 need 當動詞時，若想要描述行動，別忘了使用 to V：They need to listen to us.。

☆ change 當名詞時，要連同 make 或 have 來使用：They had a change of plan.。

☆ question 當名詞時，若欲表達「某事需要加以考慮」的想法時，須連同 be 動詞和 of 來使用。例如 It's a question of how much we think their work is worth.，意即這是我們需要加以考慮的事。在表達這種意思時，question 應該使用單數形。而 question 若是連同 about 和動詞 ask 或 have 來使用時，則意指「問題」，在這種含意下的 question 為可數：We were taught not to ask questions.。

☆ 若要在 start 之後接即將展開的一個活動時，須使用 to V 或 Ving：They are going to start protesting.。而若要在它之後接事件時，則應使用 n.p.：They are going to start the protest.。另外，start 也可以不接受詞：It's started!。請注意看例句。

☆ 請仔細學習這些語塊，並把重點放在諸如介系詞和冠詞這些細節。

　　好的，現在讓我們來嘗試正確使用這些語塊。

Task 30

請選用正確形式的單字或語塊，完成下列各句。

① **questions/question**

Don't ask too many ＿＿＿＿＿＿ about the origin of their wealth.

② **change/changes to**

If we don't make ＿＿＿＿＿＿＿ the system, it will collapse.

③ **ask/question**

If you ＿＿＿＿＿＿＿ the figures, the government will lie to you.

④ **a question of/questions of**

It's not just about justice, it's also ＿＿＿＿＿＿＿ honesty.

PART

1

⑤ **start/has started**

The demonstration ＿＿＿＿＿＿＿.

⑥ **values/value**

The rich don't ＿＿＿＿＿＿＿ criticism of their wealth.

⑦ **change to/changes**

The start of the 20th century saw big social ＿＿＿＿＿＿＿.

⑧ **value/values**

Their ＿＿＿＿＿＿＿ is not recognised.

⑨ **value/valued**

Their work is not ＿＿＿＿＿＿＿ at all.

⑩ **need for/need to**

There is no ＿＿＿＿＿＿＿ such a concentration of wealth.

⑪ **changes/change**

They don't want to ＿＿＿＿＿＿＿ their ways.

⑫ **need for/need to**

They ＿＿＿＿＿＿＿ recognise that this situation is unfair.

⑬ **start to/started**

They ＿＿＿＿＿＿ several radical discussion groups which were quickly banned.

⑭ **started to/start**

They ＿＿＿＿＿＿ amass great wealth before the government changed some of the laws.

⑮ **need for/need**

We ＿＿＿＿＿＿ more openness to new ideas.

✅ 答案・中譯・說明　　🔘 Track 4.5

① Don't ask too many <u>questions about</u> the origin of their wealth.
不要問太多關於他們財富來源的問題。

② If we don't make changes to the system, it will collapse.
如果我們不對系統進行更改，它將會崩潰。

③ If you question the figures, the government will lie to you.
假如你質疑這些數字，政府就會對你說謊。

④ It's not just about justice, it's also a question of honesty.
這不僅僅是關乎正義，也是誠實的問題。

⑤ The demonstration has started. 示威已經開始了。

⑥ The rich don't value criticism of their wealth.
有錢人不會重視自身財富所受到的批評。

⑦ The start of the 20th century saw big social changes.
二十世紀初出現了重大的社會變革。

⑧ Their value is not recognised. 他們的價值不受認可。

⑨ Their work is not valued at all. 他們的工作毫不受重視。

⑩ There is no need for such a concentration of wealth. 沒有必要這樣的財富集中。

⑪ They don't want to change their ways. 他們並不想改變自己的方式。

⑫ They need to recognise that this situation is unfair.
他們必須要認知到這樣的情況並不公平。

⑬ They started several radical discussion groups which were quickly banned.
他們開設了好幾個激進的討論群組，但很快就遭到了禁止。

⑭ They started to amass great wealth before the government changed some of the laws. 他們開始聚集很大的財富是在政府改變一些法令前。

⑮ We need more openness to new ideas. 我們需要對新觀念更加開放。

☆ 請確認動詞的時態都正確無誤。

☆ 請拿正確的句子來與關鍵語庫 ❹ 的語塊做比較，確保名詞或動詞語塊都用得正確。

☆ 請將正確句子中的完整語塊畫上底線（參照第 1 句的示範）。這將有助於各位把語塊完整而正確地記起來。

　　接下來，我們要再重複一次前面做過的練習。請詳讀本單元開頭的閱讀文章，並從中把這 5 個動詞和名詞同形的關鍵字語塊全部找到。再次提醒，盡可能地多閱讀有助於擴充字彙量，而在文章上下文脈絡中查看大量語塊則能幫助你記憶新的用語。

Task 31

請從 Task 1 和 Task 2 的閱讀文章中找出關鍵語庫 ❹ 列出的所有語塊，並留意這些語塊在文章中是當動詞還是名詞使用？

Task 32

請練習用關鍵語庫 ❹ 的語塊來造句。

關鍵字語塊	造句
value	
value s/th	

need for	
need to V	
need n.p./Ving	
change to s/th	
change s/th	
question of	
question about s/th	
question s/th	
start	
start to V	
start n.p./Ving	
start	

☆ 我顯然無法在此來改正你的句子，但你可以透過確認語塊所有的小細節，自行改正。再次提醒在寫作中運用語塊時，須特別注意小詞、字尾和語塊的結尾，無論所需要的是 n.p.、v.p.、Ving 還是 V，並且確保你所使用的語塊是完整的。

5 個談論或寫作不平等相關主題常用的片語動詞 5 phrasal verbs for talking or writing about inequality

我們現在要來看一些在寫作或談論不平等相關主題時，常用到的片語動詞。

Task 33

研讀語庫中的片語動詞、例句和其下的說明。

關鍵語庫 ⑤　🎧 Track 4.6

片語動詞	例句
cut back on s/th 縮減政府的資助與服務	• They've cut back on essential services to the poor. 他們削減了對窮人的基本服務。
come up with s/th 對某事有新的構想	• They've come up with a new policy to help the disadvantaged. 他們提出了新政策來幫助弱勢。
draw s/th up 在案子的規劃階段	• They are drawing up a plan for a new scheme. 他們正在為一個新案子擬訂計畫。 • They are drawing a plan up for a new scheme. 他們正在擬訂一個新案子的計畫。 • They are drawing it up. 他們正在規劃。
bring s/th about 造成某事發生	• The cuts have brought about great hardship for many. 刪減為許多人帶來了極大的困難。 • The cuts have brought it about. 這是刪減造成的。 • It was brought about by bad government policies. 這是由糟糕的政府政策所造成的。

trickle down 財富從有錢人往 下流到窮人身上	• The idea is that wealth will trickle down and make all of society better off. 觀念在於，財富會涓滴而下，並使社會全體變得更好過。 • Trickle-down economics has been shown to be a myth. 涓滴式經濟學已被證明是個神話。

☆ 在學習和使用片語動詞時，你必須非常留意動詞有沒有受詞 (s/th)，以及這個受詞是擺在哪個位置。請仔細確認上方語庫中的片語動詞及其受詞的位置。

☆ 在使用 cut back on 和 come up with 時，名詞和代名詞這兩種受詞類型都必須擺在第二個介系詞後面。請看例句。

☆ 在使用 bring about 時，名詞受詞向來必須擺在介系詞後面，例如 The new policy brought about great improvements. 正確，而 The new policy brought great improvements about. 則是錯的。另外，代名詞受詞則必須擺在動詞和介系詞之間，例如 The new policy brought it about. 正確，而 The new policy brought about it. 則是錯的。這個片語動詞也可以用於被動語態。

☆ 在使用 draw s/th up 時，名詞受詞置於介系詞的前後都行，但代名詞受詞必須置於動詞和介系詞之間。請看例句。

☆ trickle-down 也能當成複合形容詞，記得要使用連字號。請看例句。

☆ 請記得片語動詞是動詞，所以還必須考慮動詞要用什麼時態。

　　下一個練習將有助於各位聚焦於受詞的正確擺放位置這些細節上。

Task 34

下列各句中的第一個字是正確的，請按照順序將其後的字詞重組成正確的句子。

EX. **Do brought it know what you about?**

Do you know what brought it about?

① The suffering brought among concentration of the wealth has about great poor

② The services has government all cut on non-essential back

_____

③ They are up of for a plans new kind drawing society

_____

④ Wealth trickle the to poor, should but it down doesn't

_____

PART

1

⑤ We to come ideas with some need up new

_____

⑥ The was about brought by situation bad their policies

_____

✅ 答案・中譯・說明　🔊 Track 4.7

① The concentration of wealth <u>has brought about</u> great suffering among the poor.
財富的集中給窮人帶來了巨大的苦難。

② The government has cut back on all non-essential services.
政府已經削減了所有非必要的服務。

③ They are drawing up plans for a new kind of society.
他們正在擬定一種建立新型社會的計畫。

They are drawing plans up for a new kind of society.
他們正在為建立新型社會擬定計畫。

④ Wealth should trickle down to the poor, but it doesn't.
財富應該要涓滴到窮人身上，但事實並非如此。

⑤ We need to come up with some new ideas. 我們需要提出一些新點子。

⑥ The situation was brought about by their bad policies.
這個局面是由他們糟糕的政策所造成。

☆ 須特別留意受詞的位置。第 3 句可以有兩種不同的解答，就看受詞是擺在哪個位置。

☆ 留意到第 6 句是用被動語態。

☆ 將正確的句子與關鍵語庫 ❺ 中的片語動詞做比較，確認你的用法都正確。

☆ 請將正確句子中的片語動詞畫上底線。這會有助於各位把語塊完整而正確地背下來。（參照第 1 句的示範）

　　來看看這些片語動詞是如何運用在文章脈絡中。

Task 35

請從 Task 1 和 Task 2 的閱讀文章中找出關鍵語庫 ❺ 列出的所有片語動詞，並留意它們在文章中是如何使用的。

Task 36

請練習用關鍵語庫 ❺ 的片語動詞來造句。

片語動詞	造句練習
cut back on s/th	
come up with s/th	
draw s/th up	
bring s/th about	
trickle down	

☆ 再次提醒在寫作時若運用到這些片語動詞時，要特別留意動詞的時態和受詞的位置。

5 個談論或寫作不平等相關主題常用的慣用語 5 idioms for talking or writing about inequality

　　現在各位要學習的是在寫作或談論「不平等」這個主題時，所能運用的一些慣用語。

Task 37

研讀語庫中的慣用語、例句和其下的說明。

關鍵語庫 ⑥　　◎ Track 4.8

慣用語	例句
be economical with the truth 對於某人在說謊或沒有全盤吐實的客氣說法	• Most politicians are always economical with the truth, but he lies quite openly. 大部分的政治人物向來都對實情避重就輕，但他卻是十分公開地說謊。
toe the line 遵照規則或期望	• Citizens are expected to toe the line. If they don't, they are punished. 民眾被期望要嚴守規定。假如不然，他們就會受罰。
the body politic 包括政府與經濟在內的社會整體	• The body politic is rotten to the core. We need to reform society. 這個國家已經腐敗到極點。我們需要改革社會。
big bucks 一大筆錢	• He started his own company and made big bucks. 他開了自己的公司並發了大財。
earn a living 賺足夠的錢來過得舒服	• Most people can't even make enough money to earn a living. 大部分的人甚至賺不到足夠的錢來謀生。

☆ 使用慣用語時唯一能更動的是動詞時態。

☆ 為了讓慣用語有意義，它必須完全準確才行，這意味著你必須將慣用語的所有細節都使用正確。

☆ 注意，以上任何一個慣用語都不能使用受詞。

下一個練習將有助於各位聚焦於使用這些慣用語時，經常會犯的錯誤。

Task 38

改正這些句子中的常見錯誤。

① He is economic with the truth.

_____

② She made a big buck and got very rich.

_____

③ Students must foot a line while they are in college.

_____

④ Body politics is corrupt.

_____

⑤ They can't even earn the life.

_____

⑥ He is financial with the truth.

_____

① He <u>is economical with</u> the truth. 他對實情避重就輕。

② She made big bucks and got very rich. 她賺了一大筆錢，變得很富有。

③ Students must toe the line while they are in college.
　學生在上大學時必須嚴守規定。

④ The body politic is corrupt. 這個國家政體是腐敗的。

⑤ They can't even earn a living. 他們甚至無法謀生。

⑥ He is economical with the truth. 他對實情避重就輕。

☆ 這些錯誤通常是漏掉了小詞、改變了小詞或單字結尾、慣用語不完整。請務必
　聚焦於細節。

☆ 請勿在一個不該有受詞的地方加上了受詞。

☆ 請將正確句子中的慣用語畫上底線。（參照第 1 句的示範）

　　現在我們要練習的是，在文章上下文中找出慣用語。

Task 39

請從 Task 1 和 Task 2 的閱讀文章中找出關鍵語庫 ❻ 列出的所有慣用語，
並留意它們在文章中是如何使用的。

Task 40

請練習用關鍵語庫 ❻ 的慣用語來造句。

慣用語	造句練習
be economical with the truth	
toe the line	

the body politic	
big bucks	
earn a living	

☆ 再次提醒在寫作時若運用到這些慣用語，要特別留意動詞的時態和完整的慣用語包含哪些細節。

易混淆的字詞 easily confused words

❏ 有些單字只能用在特定的主題上，用在別的主題則不適當，或者只能與某些詞搭配使用，而不能與其他詞搭配使用。

❏ 在試著針對容易搞混的單字去了解差別時，需要考量的不只是意思，還有文法和用法。在做接下來的幾個練習時，請務必記得這些重點。

Task 41

請仔細研讀各組易混淆的字詞、例句和其下的說明。

關鍵語庫 ❼ ◉ Track 4.10

易混淆字詞	例句
price (of s/th) (*nc*) 價格、代價	• The price is too high for me. I can't afford it. 價格對我來說太高了。我負擔不起。 • You did something wrong, you must pay the price. 你做錯了事，必須付出代價。 • We did it, but it came at a price. 我們是做了，但嘗到了代價。
cost of s/th (*nc*) **cost s/th** (*vt*) 成本、花費	• The cost of living is too high. 生活費用太高了。 • The cost of doing business there is too high. 在那裡做生意的成本太高。 • It costs $300. 它要花費三百美元。
worker (*nc*) 工人	• The workers are not happy with the working conditions. 工人們對工作條件不滿意。
staff (*nu*) 職員、員工	• We need to increase our staff. 我們需要增加職員。

2	**labor** (*nu*) 勞工 **labor (at s/th)** (*vi*) 勞動	• Our country lacks skilled labor. 我國缺乏技術勞工。 • He labored at it long and hard. 他為此付出了漫長又艱苦地努力。
3	**wage** (*nc*) 工資 **salary** (*nc*) 薪水	• Their hourly wage is quite low. 他們的鐘點工資相當低。 • She gets a thirteen months salary. 她是領十三個月的薪水。
4	**financial** (*adj.*) 財務的 **economic** (*adj.*) 經濟的	• I'm having financial problems at the moment. 我目前有財務問題。 • The country is having economic problems at the moment. 國家目前有經濟問題。
5	**work** (*nu*) 工作 **job** (*nc*) 職務	• There is not so much work available. 現有的工作沒那麼多。 • Even with two jobs some people cannot earn a decent living. 即使身兼二職，有些人也無法過上體面的生活。

☆ price of s/th 和 cost of s/th 的意思和文法非常類似，但用法略有不同。price 是名詞，但 cost 既可以是名詞也可以是動詞。

☆ 若表達的意思是聚焦在「金錢」時，就要用 price of s/th：The price is $200.。此外，price 也能用在慣用語中，諸如 pay the price、come at a price，以概括表示負面的後果。注意，price 千萬不可以當動詞使用。

☆ 若想要表示比較概括的意思而非只是金錢時，則要用 cost：The cost of doing business、the cost of living。此外，cost 也可以當動詞，指某物的價格：It costs $200.。

☆ worker、staff 和 labor 的意思類似，但文法和用法非常不同。

☆ 當指稱的對象是從事手工或工廠工作的單人時，要用 worker。這個名詞是可數的。若只是想要指稱公司的一群員工時，則要用 staff，這個字不能用來指稱單人。此外，這個名詞必須使用複數形動詞：The staff are not happy. 正確；The staff is not happy. 則是錯的。

☆ 想要指稱由人員構成職工的社會階級時，應該用 labor，這個字不能用來指稱單人。另外，這個字還能用來指稱工作本身，尤其是靠雙手的辛苦工作：The labor involved in farming is very hard.。labor 這個字也可以當動詞，用以描述辛苦工作：He labored for many years.。它還能當複合形容詞來用：labor-saving。

☆ wage 和 salary 的文法和用法相同，但意思非常不同。

☆ wage 指的是按鐘點計算或按週支付的工資，通常用於藍領、兼職或臨時工。salary 則是指不是按鐘點計算而是按月支付的工資，通常是屬於全職雇用的白領職工。

☆ financial 和 economic 的文法和用法相同，但意思不同。只有在想要表達個人或家庭的金錢問題時，才使用 financial。若要表達的是國家或國際的金錢問題時，則必須使用 economic。

☆ work 和 job 的意思類似，但文法和用法卻相當不同。work 是用來描述工作的活動，有這個意思時，這個名詞向來都不可數。而若是要描述職業時，則要用可數的 job。

　　在做下一個練習時，請仔細思考句意、文法和用法來選出正確的單字。

Task 42

請選出正確的單字來填入下列各句。

① **cost/price**

If you take part in riots, you must be prepared to pay the _____.

② **economic/financial**

Most families now have _____ problems because the economy is so bad.

③ **Wages/Salaries**

_____ in the advertising industry are generally quite good.

④ **price/cost**

The _____ of living is unfairly high.

⑤ **financial/economic**

The _____ situation is very bad: GDP is down all over the world.

⑥ **labor/workers**

The _____ involved in ship building is immense.

⑦ **work/jobs**

The only _____ available are low paid and temporary.

⑧ **cost/price**

The _____ is on the back.

⑨ **cost/price**

The riots _____ the city thousands of dollars.

⑩ **staffs/workers**

The _____ are protesting about pay.

⑪ **labor/labored**

They _____ to build a better society, and they succeeded.

⑫ **worker/staff**

We have highly skilled _____ in our company.

⑬ **salary/wages**

We pay our restaurant staff good _____, plus tips.

⑭ **Job/Work**

_____ is scarce at the moment. Unemployment is very high.

① If you take part in riots, you must be prepared to <u>pay the price</u>.
假如要參與動亂，你就必須準備好付出代價。

② Most families now have financial problems because the economy is so bad.
大部分的家庭現在都有財務問題，因為經濟太糟了。

③ Salaries in the advertising industry are generally quite good.
廣告業的薪水一般來說相當不錯。

④ The cost of living is unfairly high.　生活費用高得離譜。

⑤ The economic situation is very bad: GDP is down all over the world.
經濟局勢非常差：全世界的 GDP 都在下滑。

⑥ The labor involved in ship building is immense.
造船所涉及的勞動力龐大。

⑦ The only jobs available are low paid and temporary.
唯一能找到的工作都是低薪和臨時的。

⑧ The price is on the back.　價格在背面。

⑨ The riots cost the city thousands of dollars.
暴亂使該城市損失了數千美元。

⑩ The workers are protesting about pay.　工人們正在抗議工資問題。

⑪ They labored to build a better society, and they succeeded.
他們努力打造一個更好的社會並且成功了。

⑫ We have highly skilled staff in our company.
我們公司擁有高技術的員工。

⑬ We pay our restaurant staff good wages, plus tips.
我們付給餐廳員工不錯的工資，外加小費。

⑭ Work is scarce at the moment. Unemployment is very high.
目前的工作稀缺。失業率非常高。

☆ 第 2 句內容是關於家庭的金錢問題，所以用 financial；而第 5 句則是與全球
經濟局勢相關，所以應用 economic。

☆ 第 1 句選用 price 是因為它意指後果；第 4 句選用 cost 則是因為搭配詞 the
cost of living；第 8 句用 price 是因為它是關於物品的金錢價值；而第 9 句需

要的是動詞，所以應選用 cost。

☆ 第 3 句用 salaries 是因為廣告業屬於白領產業；而第 13 句用 wages 則是因為餐廳通常是按鐘點付錢給員工。

☆ 第 6 句用 labor 是因為它意指辛苦的勞動工作；第 10 句選用 workers 是因為 staff 絕不能是複數；而第 12 句則因為指稱的是一群員工而非一位員工，所以必須用 staff。

☆ 第 7 句中的動詞是複數形，所以選用可數的 job；而第 14 句用 work 則是因為動詞是單數形，若想要用 job 就必須寫成 jobs are scarce，使用複數形來意指概括的工作。

　　最後我們還是要來練習從閱讀文章中找出這些容易搞混的單字。當你在文章中每找到一個單字，都必須停下來思考它是意指什麼、它的文法是什麼，以及它是如何使用的。

Task 43

請從 Task 1 和 Task 2 的閱讀文章中找出關鍵語庫 ❼ 列出的所有易混淆字詞，並留意它們在文章中是如何使用的。

Task 44

請練習用關鍵語庫 ❼ 的易混淆字詞來造句。

易混淆字詞	造句練習
price (of s/th)	
cost of s/th cost s/th	
worker	
staff	

labor labor (at s/th)	
wage	
salary	
financial	
economic	
work	
job	

☆ 在寫作中運用這些易混淆的字詞時，記得把重點放在文法、句意和用法上，而不是只注意單字的意思。

　　在你結束這個單元之前，請將下列清單看過，確定你能將所有要點都勾選起來。如果有一些要點你還搞不清楚，請回頭再次研讀本單元的相關部分。

　　□ 我確實閱讀並理解了關於「不平等」的長篇文章。
　　□ 我完全知道字彙在文章中是如何使用，並更加了解到要怎麼用單字來表達特定的主題。
　　□ 我已經學會 15 個關於「不平等」主題的關鍵字，以及可與其搭配使用的動詞和形容詞。
　　□ 我已經練習使用這些搭配詞來描寫「不平等」。

□ 我已經學到了一些同義詞，也了解在運用時需要注意的一些問題。
□ 我學到了很多關於這個主題可以運用的語塊，包括片語動詞以及名詞或動詞為同形的單字。
□ 我已經練習使用這些語塊。
□ 我學到了 5 個關於這個主題的慣用語，且知道如何運用。
□ 我已經理解在運用慣用語時需要特別注意的一些問題。
□ 關於這個主題，我已經能確實掌握一些易混淆字詞的用法。

Unit 5

性別議題
Gender Issues

在本單元裡，我們將探討的是性別相關議題、這些在不同的社會裡所造成的問題，以及對此我們能做些什麼。

Task 1

閱讀文章並盡可能地理解文章內容。請先不要使用字典。

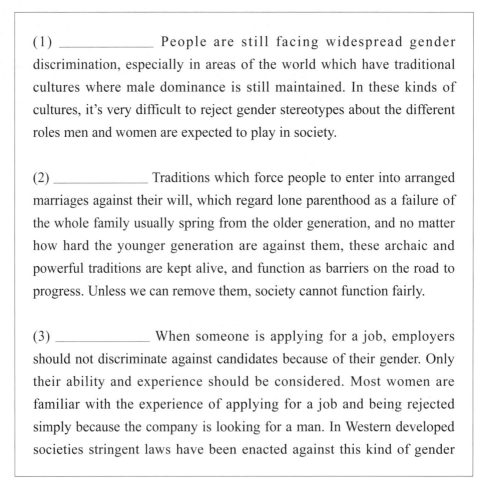

(1) _____ People are still facing widespread gender discrimination, especially in areas of the world which have traditional cultures where male dominance is still maintained. In these kinds of cultures, it's very difficult to reject gender stereotypes about the different roles men and women are expected to play in society.

(2) _____ Traditions which force people to enter into arranged marriages against their will, which regard lone parenthood as a failure of the whole family usually spring from the older generation, and no matter how hard the younger generation are against them, these archaic and powerful traditions are kept alive, and function as barriers on the road to progress. Unless we can remove them, society cannot function fairly.

(3) _____ When someone is applying for a job, employers should not discriminate against candidates because of their gender. Only their ability and experience should be considered. Most women are familiar with the experience of applying for a job and being rejected simply because the company is looking for a man. In Western developed societies stringent laws have been enacted against this kind of gender

discrimination, but nonetheless, there is still a glass ceiling for women in certain industries, which means women can never get to positions of higher management where they are in charge of large groups of people, and large budgets. These functions are usually reserved for men.

(4) _____ Not only are women discriminated against in certain professions, but men are too. For example, midwifery has typically, historically been dominated by women. In the UK, for example, less than 0.4% of midwives are men. Men who have resolved to train for this profession usually run up against the view that it's unsuitable for their gender, and no matter how well qualified they are or how eager they are to do the job, their application is rejected. This form of unconscious sexism is very common, and prevents some professions from becoming popular among the different sexes.

(5) _____ Acceptance of gays, lesbians and transgender people is gradually spreading in society, especially among the young, and their rights are gradually expanding, especially in developed Western societies. However, although more gay, lesbian and trans celebrities are coming out, they still face discrimination in less developed societies. In many Third World countries their situation is deteriorating: they are not allowed to get married, or have or adopt children, and might even face prison sentences. Any attempt to force changes by challenging backwards attitudes in very conservative societies can actually worsen the situation of minorities. Of course, this violates their basic human rights.

(6) _____ The demand for more respect for alternative genders, different orientations and more variety in gender roles needs to be taken seriously. The old stereotype of the man's man has to give way to the new man, and there needs to be greater balance between the sexes in terms of

shared burdens of responsibility for childcare and homemaking. The patriarchy always tries to resist any challenge to the status quo, however, because it is usually men who benefit from that status quo, and they will quickly rule out any changes to their dominant position in society, which they will have no intention of giving up. They usually adopt a hostile attitude towards change, a reaction which is familiar to those who have tried to push-through major moral and political reforms. A complete break with the past is impossible, however, as many of the previous generation cannot accept the new gender roles.

(7) _____ We will have to balance progress with tradition. Any changes will have to be gradual and new laws will need to be phased in, not enacted all at once. The challenge will be for future generations to improve on today's conditions. Everyone has the right to be respected and everyone should have the same life chances, no matter what their gender or their sexual orientation.

Task 2

請從下列句子選出適當的主題句以完成 Task 1 每個段落的填空。

A Another type of discrimination, in addition to gender, is sexual orientation.

B Discrimination can work both ways.

C In addition to the grave financial and economic injustice which many people suffer, the other great issue of our age is gender inequality.

D It is not acceptable in this day and age for people to be accepted or rejected for the opportunity to get a job based on their gender.

E So how can we solve these problems?

F The problem is related to different generations.

G When enough people demand change, it becomes inevitable.

(1) C (2) F (3) D (4) B (5) A (6) E (7) G

譯文

除了許多人遭受的嚴重財務與經濟不公平，當代的另一大議題就是性別不平等。人們仍面臨廣泛的性別歧視，尤其是在世界上仍保持以男性主宰為傳統文化的地方。在這樣的文化中，很難摒棄關於男女被期望在社會上扮演不同角色的性別刻板印象。

這個問題跟不同的世代有關。傳統是強迫人違反意願走入包辦婚姻（奉父母之命成婚），而把單親育兒視為全家的失敗，通常是出自較年長的世代，而且無論較年輕的世代多拚命反對，這些古老又強大的傳統照樣得以保留，並形成進步道路上的障礙。除非我們能消除它們，否則社會將無法公平運行。

在當今時代，根據性別來認可或排除人獲得職務的機會是令人無法接受的。當有人應徵工作時，雇主不該因應聘者的性別而歧視他們。只有能力和經驗才該受到考慮。大部分的女性所熟知的經驗是，應徵工作遭到排除僅僅是因為該公司要找的是男性。在西方已開發社會中，已經制訂了嚴格的法令來預防這類性別歧視，但儘管如此，在某些行業中女性仍存在著玻璃天花板，這意味著她們從來就爭取不到較高層管理的職位來掌管大群的人員和大筆的預算。這些職掌通常是保留給男性。

歧視可以是雙向的。不只是女性在一定的職業中受到歧視，男性也是。例如助產工作一般在歷史上都是由女性所主導。例如在英國，助產士不到 0.4% 是男性。決心為此職業來受訓的男性通常會遭遇到的看法是，這個職業不適合他們的性別，而且無論他們有多符合資格或多有心要任職，應徵就是會遭到排除。這種形式的無意識性別歧視非常普遍，並阻止了某些職業在不同的性別中變得風行。

除了性別，另一類的歧視是性傾向。社會對於男同志、女同志和跨性別的人士的接納度正逐漸擴散，尤其是在年輕人當中，而且他們的權利正逐漸擴大，特別是在已開發的西方社會。不過，雖然更多的男同志、女同志和跨性別的名人出櫃了，但他們在較不開發的社會裡仍面臨歧視。在許多第三世界國家，他們的處境正在惡化：他們不被允許結婚、生育或領養小孩，而且甚至會面臨牢獄之災。在非常保守的社會裡，任何靠挑戰落伍的態度來強迫改變的企圖實際上可能會使弱勢的處境更糟。當然，這侵犯了他們的基本人權。

那我們該如何解決這些問題？對於另類的性別、不同的取向和更多元的性別角色要求更多尊重的需求必須認真地看待。大男人這種舊的刻板印象必須讓位給新好男人，而且在共同負擔育兒和家務責任方面，兩性之間需要有更好的平衡。不過，父權體制向來都試圖抗拒任何對現狀的挑戰，因為從那樣的現狀中得利的通常是男性，而且當自己在社會上無意放棄的主宰地位有了任何改變的可能性，他們馬上就會加以排拒。他們對變革通常是採取敵對的態度，這是那些嘗試去推動重大道德與政治改革的人所熟知的反應。然而，完全

打破過去是不可能的，因為很多過往世代無法接受新的性別角色。

當夠多的人要求改變，它就會變得無可避免。我們必須在進步與傳統之間取得平衡。任何改變都必須是漸進的，而且新法令需要逐步導入，而不是驟然施行。挑戰則在於未來的世代要改善當今的情況。人人都有受到尊重的權利，人人都該有相同的人生機會，無論其性別或性傾向為何。

··

☆ 第一段介紹了問題。第二段描述了這個問題起源於較年長的世代對性別角色的刻板印象。第三和第四段是以男女在雇用平等上的具體問題來看此議題。第五段是從為性別弱勢增進權利的角度來描述性別議題。第六段提出了一些解決方案，並說明為什麼有些解決方案難以實行。最後一段則是以展望未來，更公平的世界來總結。

☆ 請留意主題句 (topic sentence) 總是段落中最概括的句子，以及段落中的其他部分是如何以特定的例子或理由來申論主題句的論點。

字詞搭配 Word Partnerships

　　我們現在將學習「性別議題」這個主題的 15 個關鍵字，以及可搭配這些關鍵字使用的 word partnerships「字詞搭配表」。首先，請看關鍵字語庫。

Task 3

請仔細研讀這些主題字彙和下方的說明。

關鍵語庫 ❶ 　🔊 Track 5.1

名詞	動詞	形容詞	字義
attitude Ⓒ	-	-	態度、意見、看法
culture Ⓒ	-	cultural	文化、文明
discrimination Ⓤ	discriminate against s/th	-	歧視、區別
dominance Ⓤ	dominate s/th	dominant	主宰、優勢
gender Ⓒ	-	-	性別
injustice Ⓒ	-	unjust	不公不義、不公正
law Ⓒ	-	-	法令、法律
marriage Ⓒ	marry s/o	married	婚姻
parenthood Ⓤ	parent s/o	-	生育、父母身份
reform Ⓒ	reform s/th	reformed	改革、改造
rights Ⓒ	-	-	權利
role Ⓒ	-	-	角色、作用
sexism Ⓤ	-	sexist	性別歧視
stereotype Ⓒ	stereotype s/o	stereotypical	刻板印象

tradition Ⓒ	-	traditional	傳統、慣例

☆ 請留意哪些名詞是可數，哪些是不可數。並且要記得，名詞是可數還是不可數，有時候要視主題而定。

☆ 留意單字的其他詞性形式，如動詞和形容詞。

☆ 請注意 discriminate 的動詞形也能用於被動語態。在本單元的後段將會有更清楚的說明。

☆ justice 這個字的名詞形字首為 in-，形容詞形的字首則是 un-。

☆ 注意，parent 除了作名詞用來描述人，也可以當作動詞用來描述活動。例如 My parents (*n.*) did a good job of parenting (*v.*) me.。

☆ 在本單元後段，各位會學到如何使用 right 的單數形，但在概括談論 rights 時，向來都必須以複數形來使用。別忘了 s！

☆ 請留意 stereotype 也能當作動詞使用。

　　接下來，我們將以 5 個關鍵字為一組，深入地學習與這些字最頻繁搭配的字詞組合及正確用法。

Task 4

請研讀這個字詞搭配表、例句和底下的說明。

搭配在前面的動詞	搭配的形容詞		關鍵字
have take adopt change	favourable friendly positive sympathetic responsible right hostile critical negative	prevailing public mental moral sexual conservative backwards inflexible	**attitude (towards s/th)**

- Unfortunately, many people **take** a **hostile mental attitude towards** transgender issues. 不幸的是，很多人對於跨性別議題是採取敵對的態度。

- We need to try to **change** the **prevailing attitude**. 我們需要試著去改變普遍的態度。

- **Conservative attitudes towards** these issues are very difficult to **change**. 對這些議題的保守態度非常難改變。

☆ 動詞和形容詞是以同義詞歸類在一起，不過請記得這裡的同義詞都是「特定主題和搭配」。

Task 5

請研讀這個字詞搭配表、例句和底下的說明。

搭配在前面的動詞	搭配的形容詞		關鍵字
be have create develop foster produce	ancient primitive traditional modern contemporary foreign international mainstream underground vibrant exciting strict repressive	artistic business company corporate dance intellectual legal literary political religious scientific	**culture**

- They **have** a very **primitive culture**. 他們有非常原始的文化。

- They are trying to **create** a **vibrant literary culture**, but the **political culture is** very **strict** and **repressive**.
他們試著要創造出蓬勃的文學文化,但政治文化非常嚴格和壓抑。

....

☆ 請留意不同類型「文化」的說法。

Task 6

請研讀這個字詞搭配表、例句和底下的說明。

搭配在前面的動詞	搭配的形容詞		關鍵字
amount to constitute experience face suffer be opposed to combat end forbid	widespread active blatant direct explicit overt covert indirect positive illegal unlawful institutionalized	age class gender racial religious sexual	**discrimination**

字詞搭配使用範例

- This kind of behavior **amounts to blatant sexual discrimination**, and this is **illegal**. 這種行為相當於公然的性別歧視,這是違法的。

- Many transgender people **have experienced indirect discrimination**.
  許多跨性別人士都經歷過間接的歧視。
- We **are opposed to** all forms of **religious**, **racial**, **age** or **gender discrimination**.
  我們反對一切形式的宗教、種族、年齡或性別歧視。

☆ 請留意「歧視」的不同類型說法。

Task 7

請研讀這個字詞搭配表、例句和底下的說明。

搭配在前面的動詞	搭配的形容詞	關鍵字
have maintain achieve assert assume establish exert	cultural economic male market political	**dominance (over s/th)**

字詞搭配使用範例

- That country still **exerts political dominance over** their former colonies.
  那個國家對於他們以前的殖民地仍發揮著政治上的支配地位。
- In traditional culture, **male dominance is still asserted**.
  在傳統文化中，男性的主導地位仍受到擁護。
- **Economic dominance is maintained** by sanctions against the government.
  經濟優勢是靠著制裁政府來維持。

☆ 留意不同類型的「優勢」。
☆ 注意，各動詞也能以被動語態來使用。

請研讀這個字詞搭配表、例句和底下的說明。

搭配在前的「名詞 + of」	搭配的形容詞	關鍵字	搭配在後的名詞
the issue of	male		issues
the question of	female		relations
the idea of	third		difference
the analysis of	indeterminate		discrimination
the distinction between ~s			bias
		gender	imbalance inequality
搭配在前的動詞			identity role stereotype
see			
recognise			politics
construct			spectrum

字詞搭配使用範例

- **The issue of gender relations** is one of the big problems of our time.
  性別關係的議題是當前最大的問題之一。

- Most people don't **recognize** that they have **gender bias**.
  大部分的人並不承認自己有性別成見。

- Trans people have to **construct** their own **gender identity**.
  跨性別人士必須去建構本身的性別認同。

....

☆ 請注意，gender 這個字能形成很多複合名詞。

現在，我們來看看各位是否能用一些字詞搭配來擴大對字彙的運用。

Task 9

請從 Task 4 到 Task 8 中選出正確形式的字詞，完成以下段落填空。

> (1) _____ gender is very important nowadays. There is still a great imbalance between the genders. If we are not able to (2) _____ people's attitudes (3) _____ gender (4) _____, then we will never be able to (5) _____ a better, more equal culture, one that is not so (6) _____ and which is not so against people who are different. Sexual minorities already (7) _____ widespread discrimination everywhere because straight white males have (8) _____ dominance (9) _____ our culture.

範例答案

1. the issue of/the question of
2. change
3. towards
4. inequality/imbalance
5. have/create/develop/foster/produce

6. repressive/strict
7. face/experience/suffer
8. achieved/asserted/assumed/
   established/exerted
9. over

☆ 請留意各組同義字詞，空格中選填同一組內不同的字也是可以的。

☆ 須確認所選用的單字都是正確的形式。請檢查單數或複數，以及動詞的正確形式。例如在空格 (8) 中的動詞必須使用過去分詞，因為時態是現在完成式。

現在來學習另外 5 個單字。

Task 10

請研讀這個字詞搭配表、例句和底下的說明。

搭配在前面的動詞		搭配的形容詞		關鍵字
be	expose	cruel	economic	
	fight against	grave	financial	
experience	protest against	great	historical	
suffer	speak out against	gross	racial	
		terrible	social	**injustice**
regard s/th as	correct			
	remedy	perceived		
cause				
commit				

字詞搭配使用範例

- They **committed** a **terrible injustice** that was impossible to remedy.
  他們犯下了不可能補救的極度不公義行為。

- Slavery **is a gross historical injustice.** 奴隸制是嚴重的歷史不公。

- Transgender people who are denied their rights **experience** a **great injustice.**
  權利被剝奪的跨性別人士遭到極大的不公平對待。

☆ 請留意各類「不公義」的說法。

Task 11

請研讀這個字詞搭配表、例句和底下的說明。

搭配在前面的動詞		搭配的形容詞		關鍵字
be	obey	harsh	administrative	
become	observe	stringent	case	
		strong	civil	
enforce	adopt		constitutional	**law**
uphold	enact	discriminatory	criminal	**(against**
	pass	unfair	environmental	**s/th)**
break			international	
flout	repeal	new	martial	
violate				

- There **are harsh laws against** gender discrimination.
  有嚴厲的法律來反制性別歧視。

- There **are stringent laws against** this, but they are never **enforced**.
  有嚴格的法律來禁止這種行為，卻從來沒執行過。

- This **discriminatory law was repealed** last year.
  這條歧視性法令去年遭到了廢止。

- A **new law was adopted against** unfair treatment of employees.
  一項禁止對員工不公平對待的新法被採行了。

☆ 留意不同類型的「法律」。

☆ 注意，各動詞也能以被動語態來使用。

Task 12

請研讀這個字詞搭配表、例句和底下的說明。

搭配在前面的動詞	搭配的形容詞		關鍵字
have	good	arranged	
	happy	childless	
propose	successful	mixed	
		modern	
enter into	broken	open	
	disastrous		
make	failed		**marriage**
	unhappy		
annul	loveless		
dissolve			
	first		
save	second		
	previous		

字詞搭配使用範例

- They **entered into a marriage** when they were much too young, and eventually the **marriage was annulled**. 他們太年輕就走入婚姻，最終婚姻告吹了。

- They tried to **save the marriage**, but it was such an **unhappy marriage**, they decided to get divorced.

  他們試著挽救這段婚姻，但這是如此不幸福的婚姻，他們決定離婚。

☆ 留意「婚姻」的不同類型。

☆ 注意，各動詞也能以被動語態來使用。

Task 13

請研讀這個字詞搭配表和例句。

搭配在前面的動詞	搭配的形容詞	關鍵字
choose opt for go for exalt regard ~ as view ~ as	lone single responsible planned	**parenthood**

字詞搭配使用範例

- Most traditional societies **regard parenthood as** absolutely necessary.
  大多數傳統社會都認為生兒育女是絕對必要的。
- Nowadays most couples **opt for planned parenthood**.
  現今大部分的夫妻都是選擇計畫生育。
- **Single parenthood is viewed as** not normal in our society.
  單親家庭在我們的社會中被視為不正常。

Task 14

請研讀這個字詞搭配表、例句和底下的說明。

搭配在前面的動詞	搭配的形容詞		關鍵字
adopt	drastic	constitutional	
bring about	fundamental	democratic	
introduce	great	domestic	
put in place	important	educational	
push through	major	governmental	
implement		institutional	
	comprehensive	legal	**reform**
delay	far-reaching	moral	**(to s/th)**
block	wide-ranging	political	
		prison	
accept	new	social	
welcome	rapid	structural	
		tax	
advocate	much needed		
call for	overdue		
demand			

字詞搭配使用範例

- The new government **put in place far-reaching legal reforms**.
  新政府推行了影響深遠的法律改革。
- The new political party **welcomes constitutional reform**.
  新政黨歡迎憲法改革。
- The **much needed structural reforms to** the system **have now been implemented**. 在制度上深切需要的結構改革現在實行了。

☆ 請留意各動詞也能以被動來使用。

☆ 留意「改革」的不同類型。

　　就像前面所做過的，我們再來練習這第二組 5 個單字的字詞搭配應用。

Task 15

請從 Task 10 到 Task 14 中選出正確形式的字詞，完成以下段落填空。

In some countries there (1) _____ (2) _____ laws (3) _____ sexual minorities. These laws need to be (4) _____ if people are not to (5) _____ a (6) _____ injustice. It needs to be easier to (7) _____ marriage with people of the same gender, for example, and also to (8) _____ a marriage if it fails. The laws against parenthood, for example, also make it difficult for sexual minorities to (9) _____ parenthood. If we can (10) _____ (11) _____ (12) _____ reforms in these areas of the law, then our society will finally join the modern world.

範例答案

1. are
2. harsh/stringent/strong/discriminatory/unfair
3. against
4. repealed
5. experience/suffer
6. cruel/grave/great/gross/terrible
7. enter into
8. annul/dissolve
9. choose/opt for/go for
10. adopt/bring about/introduce/put in place/push through/implement
11. much needed/overdue
12. legal

....

☆ 請留意各組同義字詞，空格中選填同一組內不同的字也是可以的。

☆ 須確認所選用的單字都是正確的形式。請檢查單數或複數，以及動詞的正確形式。例如在空格 (4) 中必須使用過去分詞，因為動詞為被動語態。

現在我們來學習最後一組的 5 個單字。

Task 16

請研讀這個字詞搭配表、例句和底下的說明。

搭配在前面的動詞	搭配的形容詞		關鍵字
have enjoy demand stand up for know give up defend protect violate	basic fundamental inalienable equal legal statutory	animal gay human parental women's	**rights**

字詞搭配使用範例

- If we don't **defend** our **human rights**, they will be taken away from us.
  假如我們不捍衛自己的人權，它將會從我們身上被奪走。

- We need to **stand up for** our **basic human rights**.
  我們需要為自己的基本人權挺身而出。

- In that country they **enjoy inalienable rights** under the law.
  在那個國家，他們依法享有不可剝奪的權利。

☆ 留意「權利」的不同類型。

Task 17

請研讀這個字詞搭配表、例句和底下的說明。

搭配在前面的動詞	搭配的形容詞		關鍵字
have play perform serve accept take s/o's ~ seriously respect s/o's	central critical crucial decisive important key traditional	advisory gender managerial maternal parental political social supervisory	**role**

字詞搭配使用範例

- Women usually **perform the key parental role** here.
  女性在這裡通常是擔負關鍵的父母角色。

- **Traditional gender roles are** no longer **being accepted**.
  傳統的性別角色不再為人所接受。

- Changing attitudes will **play a key role** in changing society.
  改變態度將在社會的變革中發揮關鍵作用。

☆ 動詞語塊 accept、take s/o's ~ seriously 和 respect s/o's 能以被動來使用。

Task 18

請研讀這個字詞搭配表和例句。

搭配在前面的動詞	搭配的形容詞		關鍵字
have fight be	form of blatant obvious unconscious	rampant endemic linguistic	**sexism**

- Some people think using the pronouns 'he' and 'she' **are forms of linguistic sexism**. 有些人認為,使用代名詞 he 和 she 是語言性別歧視的形式。

- We need to **fight** the **blatant sexism** within the industry.
  我們需要對抗業內公然的性別歧視。

- **Sexism is endemic** in our society. 性別歧視在我們的社會中很普遍。

Task 19

請研讀這個字詞搭配表、例句和底下的說明。

搭配在前面的動詞	搭配的形容詞		關鍵字
create produce perpetuate reinforce conform to fit challenge reject	common typical popular traditional negative	cultural gender national racial sexual	**stereotype (about s/th)**

字詞搭配使用範例

- She doesn't really **conform to** the **typical national stereotype**.
  她不太符合典型的國民刻板印象。

- We **reject** all kinds of **racial stereotypes**. 我們拒絕各種的種族刻板印象。

- Many **popular stereotypes about** foreigners are quite **negative**.
  許多對外國人的普遍刻板印象都相當負面。

☆ 注意,這些動詞中有很多可以使用於被動語態。

Task 20

請研讀這個字詞搭配表、例句和底下的說明。

搭配在前面的動詞		搭配的形容詞		關鍵字
be	keep alive	ancient	cherished	
have	maintain	archaic	hallowed	
	uphold	deep-rooted		**tradition**
cherish	hand down	enduring	dominant	**(of s/th)**
continue		long	powerful	
follow	break with	long-held	strong	
	go against			

字詞搭配使用範例

- There **is** a **long-held tradition of** paying dowries to the husband's family.
  附嫁妝給夫家的傳統由來已久。
- They still **cherish** their **ancient traditions**. 他們仍固守古老的傳統。
- It's very difficult to **break with** such a **powerful** and **cherished tradition**.
  要打破這麼強大和珍貴的傳統是非常難的。
- **Traditions of** celebrating marriage **are handed down** from generation to
  generation. 慶祝結婚的傳統是代代相傳的。

☆ 請留意各動詞也能以被動來使用。

接下來，我們來練習這最後一組 5 個單字的字詞搭配應用。

Task 21

請從 Task 16 到 Task 20 中選出正確形式的字詞，完成以下段落填空。

> In a fair society, everyone, regardless of the gender role they have, should
> (1) _____ (2) _____ rights. In the past, all (3) _____
> sexism were quite (4) _____, and (5) _____ rights, for
> example, were not recognised. We have improved a lot since then, and now

women have an equal position in society. We need to accept that everyone, no matter who, has a (6) _____ role to (7) _____ in society. The (8) _____ stereotypes (9) _____ women staying at home and men going out to work, even though the stereotype are very old, need to be (10) _____ and (11) _____ as hopelessly out of date. Only when we can (12) _____ these (13) _____ traditions, will everyone in our society be truly free.

範例答案

1. enjoy/have
2. equal
3. forms of
4. blatant/obvious
5. women's
6. central/critical/crucial/decisive/ important/key
7. play/perform/serve

8. common/typical/traditional
9. about
10. challenged
11. rejected
12. break with/go against
13. ancient/archaic/deep-rooted/ enduring/long/long-held

☆ 再次提醒，請確認選用的單字都是正確的形式。檢查單數或複數，以及動詞的 正確形式。例如在空格 (10) 和 (11) 中必須使用過去分詞，因為動詞為被動式。

　　最後，我們要進行這個部分的最後一個練習，這對於各位記憶 15 個關 鍵單字和它們的字詞搭配將有非常大的幫助。

Task 22

請從 Task 1 和 Task 2 的閱讀文章中找出關鍵語庫 ❶ 所列的 15 個關鍵字， 並留意這些字在文章中是如何使用的。

常用語塊 Chunks

看過了前面字詞搭配的用法，我們現在要來聚焦於這個主題所能運用的語塊。

Task 23

研讀這些語塊和底下的說明。

關鍵語庫 ❷

Chunk
❑ be (un)acceptable (for s/o) to V(s/o)　V 令人（不）可接受
☐ be familiar to s/o　為 s/o 所熟知
☐ be familiar with s/th　熟知 s/th
☐ be in charge of n.p./Ving　掌管 n.p./Ving
☐ be qualified to V　符合資格去 V
☐ be related to n.p./Ving　跟 n.p./Ving 有關
☐ fight/go/be against n.p./Ving　反對 n.p./Ving
☐ have the right to V　有權去 V
☐ intention of Ving　有意 Ving
☐ discriminate against n.p.　歧視 n.p.

☆ 需特別留意哪些語塊要接受詞、哪些不用。還須留意受詞的類型，尤其是需要使用人員受詞 (s/o) 或事物受詞 (s/th) 時。

☆ 留意這些語塊是否全都必須用 n.p.、v.p.、Ving 或 V。且別忘了使用正確的動詞時態。

☆ 在使用 be acceptable to V 時，主詞必須是 it。例如 It is not acceptable to say that. 正確；而 You are unacceptable to say that. 則是錯的。

☆ be familiar 可以有兩種用法，就看你是想要聚焦於所知道的事物，還是知道的人。若要聚焦於「事物」應該用 be familiar to s/o，並以此為主詞：Her story is familiar to most people.，這意味著大部分的人都知道她的故事。若要聚焦於「人」則應該用 be familiar with s/th，並以此為主詞：Most people are familiar with her story.。注意，別忘了要用 be 動詞，而且要改變動詞的時態！

☆ 請留意在英文裡，against 是介系詞而不是動詞，所以它需要連同 be 動詞或 go、fight 來用。這在台灣是很常見的錯誤，必須特別留心！例如 This goes against their rights. 正確，而 This against their rights. 則是錯的；I am against this law. 正確，而 I against this law. 則是錯的。

☆ 注意，使用 have the right to 這個語塊時，right 千萬不可用複數形。

☆ intention 必須連同動詞 have 和 of Ving 來用，不可以用 to V。但是在使用動詞 intend to 時，則要用 to V。例如 I have no intention to break the law. 是錯的；I have no intention of breaking the law. 和 I did not intend to break the law. 則是正確的。

☆ 注意，discriminate against 可以使用主動語態：Employers often discriminate against people based on their gender.。但它也可以用被動語態：People are often discriminated against because of their gender.。

☆ 在學習和使用語塊時須特別注意小詞、字尾和語塊的結尾這些細節，確保使用上完全準確。

　　下一個 Task 將聚焦於大家在使用這些語塊時經常會犯的錯誤。

Task 24

請改正這些句子中使用語塊的常見錯誤。

① All people must have a right to be respected.

_____

② Even if they are qualify for this job, they don't get it.

_____

③ His story familiar to me.

_____

④ I am familiar to this situation.

_____

⑤ It is unacceptable for taking away their rights.

_____

⑥ No one should discriminated against when they apply for a job.

_____

⑦ Most people not against equal rights.

_____

⑧ The situation is familiar with me.

_____

⑨ They have no intention to break the law.

_____

⑩ Who in charge of this?

_____

✔ 答案・中譯・說明　🎧 **Track 5.3**

① All people must <u>have **the** right to</u> be respected. 所有人都須有受尊重的權利。

② Even if they are qualif**ied** for this job, they don't get it.
即使他們有資格勝任這份工作，他們並沒有錄取。

③ His story **is** familiar to me. 他的故事我很熟知。

④ I am familiar **with** this situation. 我對這種處境很熟悉。

⑤ It is unacceptable **to take** away their rights. 剝奪他們的權利是不可接受的。

⑥ No one should **be** discriminated against when they apply for a job.
   在應徵工作時，任何人都不應該受到歧視。

⑦ Most people **are** not against equal rights. 大多數人並不反對平權。

⑧ The situation is familiar **to** me. 這個處境我很熟知。

⑨ They have no intention **of breaking** the law. 他們無意觸法。

⑩ Who **is** in charge of this? 誰負責這個？

☆ 答案中已經把錯誤部分標示出來，各位可以清楚看出哪裡用錯了。

☆ 請將 Task 24 的句子與關鍵語庫 ❷ 的語塊做比較，以確保能清楚看出句中哪裡用錯了。

☆ 第 7 句和第 10 句的錯誤在於 be 動詞。別忘了聚焦在動詞上！

　　下一個練習對於記憶語塊將有非常大的幫助。記住，多閱讀有助於擴充字彙量，而在文章上下文脈絡中查看大量語塊則能幫助你記憶新的用語。

Task 25

請從 Task 1 和 Task 2 的閱讀文章中找出關鍵語庫 ❷ 列出的所有語塊，並留意這些語塊在文章中是如何使用的。

Task 26

現在請嘗試用前面學過的語塊來寫出你自己的句子。

關鍵字語塊	造句
be (un)acceptable (for s/o) to V(s/o)	
be familiar to s/o	
be familiar with s/th	

be in charge of n.p./ Ving	
be qualified to V	
be related to n.p./ Ving	
fight/go/be against n.p./Ving	
have the right to V	
intention of Ving	
discriminate against n.p.	

☆ 我顯然無法在此改正你的句子，但你可以透過確認語塊所有的小細節，自行改正。再次提醒在寫作中運用語塊時，須特別注意小詞、字尾和語塊的結尾，無論所需要的是 n.p.、v.p.、Ving 還是 V，並且確保你所使用的語塊是完整的。

5 個可作動詞或名詞的單字
5 words which can be verbs or nouns

現在我們來看 5 個動詞和名詞同形的單字，並學習使用正確的語塊。

Task 27

請看以下幾個名詞和動詞同形的單字。

關鍵語庫 ❸

關鍵字	名詞字義	動詞字義
balance	平衡；協調；和諧	使平衡；保持平衡
challenge	挑戰；質疑	向……挑戰；對……提出異議
demand	要求；請求；需求	要求；請求；需求
function	功能；職責；作用	運行；起作用
respect	尊敬；尊重；敬意	敬重；尊重；遵守

Task 28

閱讀句子並判斷關鍵字是動詞或名詞，填入 V 或 N。

① _____ People need to **respect** each other.

② _____ Some men experience this as a **challenge** to their power.

③ _____ The **function** of the group is to address gender inequality.

④ _____ The group **functions** as a place where people can share their experiences.

⑤ _____ There is an increasing **demand** for equality.

⑥ _____ There needs to be more of a **balance** between their needs and the requirements of the job.

⑦ _____ They are **challenging** the old ways.

⑧ _____ They are **demanding** more equality.

⑨ _____ Transgender people face immense **challenges**.

⑩ _____ We need to show **respect** for people's stories.

⑪ _____ We need to **balance** their demands with our needs.

✅ 答案・中譯

① V 人需要互相尊重。

② N 有些男人認為這是對他們權力的挑戰。

③ N 這個團體的職能是解決性別不平等問題。

④ V 這個團體的作用如同一個讓人能分享他們經驗的地方。

⑤ N 對於平等的要求與日俱增。

⑥ N 在他們的需求和工作的要求之間需要更多的平衡。

⑦ V 他們在挑戰舊有的方式。

⑧ V 他們要求更加的平等。

⑨ N 跨性別人士面臨著巨大的挑戰。

⑩ N 我們需要對眾人的故事表示尊重。

⑪ V 我們必須去平衡他們的要求和我們的需求。

接著我們來看這些動詞和名詞的不同語塊。

Task 29

請看以下所彙整的語塊及用法說明。

關鍵語庫 ❹ 🎧 Track 5.4

關鍵字語塊	關鍵字詞性	例句 & 翻譯
balance between X (and Y)	nc	We need to find a balance between their needs and ours. 我們必須在他們和我們的需求間找到平衡。

balance X with Y	*vt*	We need to balance human rights with market realities. 我們需要去平衡人權和市場現實。
challenge (to n.p.)	*nc*	It's a clear challenge to the accepted way of doing things. 這是對於公認的做事方式明確的挑戰。
challenge (of n.p.)	*nc*	This is the great challenge of our time. 這是我們當前的重大挑戰。
challenge n.p./ Ving	*vt*	We need to challenge their beliefs. 我們必須去挑戰他們的信仰。
demand (for n.p.)	*nc*	They are facing a demand for equal rights. 他們正面臨對平權的要求。
demand s/th	*vt*	They are demanding equal rights. 他們在要求平等的權利。
function (of s/th)	*nc*	The function of women in society is quite limited. 女性在社會中的作用相當受限。
function	*vi*	Society can't function without the contribution of women. 沒有女性的貢獻，社會就無法運轉。
function as a n.p.	*vi*	The meeting functions as an outlet for people's frustration. 這個聚會的功能是作為讓人們宣洩挫折感的出口。
respect for	*nu*	They have no respect for anyone different from them. 對於任何與他們不同的人，他們都缺乏尊重。
respect n.p./Ving	*vt*	They don't respect them. 他們不尊重他們。

☆ 須留意哪些名詞是可數，哪些是不可數。

☆ 別忘了以正確的時態來使用動詞。

☆ balance 當名詞時，要連同動詞 find、strike 或 have 來使用。注意，雖然 balance 當秤或結餘之意時是可數名詞，但通常是以單數形來使用。另外，balance 當名詞或動詞來用時，語塊中的 X 和 Y 都需要是 n.p. 或 Ving。

☆ 在名詞語塊 challenge to 中，challenge 意指「批評」：a challenge to their power 意即批評他們的權力。而在名詞語塊 challenge of 中，它則是指「困難的事」：the challenge of creating equality 意指創造平等的困難任務。請仔細看例句。

☆ 當 demand 作名詞時，必須與動詞 face、have 或 be 連用。注意，demand 當動詞用時，不可在後面使用 for。

☆ 當 function 作為動詞使用，並想要指明作用是什麼時，就必須用 as a：The media functions as a place where people can tell their stories.。

☆ respect 當名詞時，須連同動詞 have 和 show 來使用。而這個字當動詞時，也能用於被動語態。

☆ 請仔細學習這些語塊，並把重點放在諸如介系詞和冠詞這些細節。

接下來，讓我們來嘗試正確使用這些語塊。

Task 30

請選用正確形式的單字或語塊，完成下列各句。

① **challenge/challenge of**

Changing the law is the great ＿＿＿＿＿＿ our organisation.

② **function of/function**

If we don't have gender equality, society cannot ＿＿＿＿＿＿ smoothly.

③ **between fighting for your rights and/with**

Striking a balance ＿＿＿＿＿＿ not making people feel hostile towards you is always difficult.

④ **function as/function of**

The ＿＿＿＿＿＿ the organisation is to fight for equal rights.

⑤ **functioned of/functioned as**

The meeting _____ an outlet for people's feelings.

⑥ **challenging to /challenging**

They are always _____ tradition.

⑦ **demanding for/demanding**

They are _____ equal pay.

PART
1

⑧ **kindness with firmness/kindness between firmness**

They are trying to balance _____ .

⑨ **respect for/respect**

They don't _____ transgender people.

⑩ **challenge for/challenge to**

Transgender people are a _____ the binary organisation of society.

⑪ **respect/respect for**

We must show _____ everyone.

⑫ **demands/demands for**

We need to listen to their _____ equality.

⑬ **respected/respect for**

Everyone has the right to be _____ .

✔ 答案・中譯・說明 　 🎧 **Track 5.5**

① Changing the law is the great <u>challenge of</u> our organisation.
更改法令是對我們組織的重大挑戰。

② If we don't have gender equality, society cannot function smoothly.
假如沒有性別平等，社會就無法順利運轉。

③ Striking a balance between fighting for your rights and not making people feel hostile towards you is always difficult.
在爭取自己的權利和不讓別人感覺與你敵對之間取得平衡總是很難。

④ The function of the organisation is to fight for equal rights.
該組織的職責是爭取平權。

⑤ The meeting functioned as an outlet for people's feelings.
這個聚會的功能是作為讓人們宣洩情感的出口。

⑥ They are always challenging tradition. 他們總是在挑戰傳統。

⑦ They are demanding equal pay. 他們要求薪酬平等

⑧ They are trying to balance kindness with firmness.
他們正試著要平衡仁慈與堅定。

⑨ They don't respect transgender people. 他們不尊重跨性別人士。

⑩ Transgender people are a challenge to the binary organisation of society.
跨性別人士是對二元（性別）社會組織的挑戰。

⑪ We must show respect for everyone. 我們必須對每個人表示尊重。

⑫ We need to listen to their demands for equality.
我們需要傾聽他們對平等的訴求。

⑬ Everyone has the right to be respected. 每個人都有權受到尊重。

☆ 請拿正確的句子來與關鍵語庫 ❹ 的語塊做比較，確保名詞或動詞語塊都用得正確。並將正確句子中的完整語塊畫上底線（參照第 1 句的示範），這將有助於各位把語塊完整而正確地記起來。

　　接下來，我們要再重複一次前面做過的練習。請詳讀本單元開頭的閱讀文章，並從中把這 5 個動詞和名詞同形的關鍵字語塊全部找到。再次提醒，盡可能地多閱讀有助於擴充字彙量，而在文章上下文脈絡中查看大量語塊則能幫助你記憶新的用語。

請從 Task 1 和 Task 2 的閱讀文章中找出關鍵語庫 ❹ 列出的所有語塊，並留意這些語塊在文章中是當動詞還是名詞使用？

Task 32

請練習用關鍵語庫 ❹ 的語塊來造句。

關鍵字語塊	造句
balance between X (and Y)	
balance X with Y	
challenge (to n.p.)	
challenge (of n.p.)	
challenge n.p./ Ving	
demand (for n.p.)	
demand s/th	
function (of s/th)	
function	
function as a n.p.	

respect for	
respect n.p./Ving	

☆ 我顯然無法在此來改正你的句子，但你可以透過確認語塊所有的小細節，自行改正。再次提醒在寫作中運用語塊時，須特別注意小詞、字尾和語塊的結尾，無論所需要的是 n.p.、v.p.、Ving 還是 V，並且確保你所使用的語塊是完整的。

5 個談論或寫作性別議題常用的片語動詞 5 phrasal verbs for talking or writing about gender issues

我們現在要來看一些在寫作或談論性別議題時，常會用到的片語動詞。

Task 33

研讀語庫中的片語動詞、例句和其下的說明。

關鍵語庫 5 🎧 Track 5.6

片語動詞	例句
rule s/th out 排除……的可能性	• The government has ruled out any further progress. 　政府已經排拒了任何進一步的進展。 • The government has ruled any further progress out. 　政府已經把任何進一步的進展都排拒了。 • The government has ruled it out. 政府把它排拒掉了。 • It has been ruled out. 它遭到了排拒。
phase s/th in 按階段慢慢導入 新的政策或法令	• They are going to phase in the new law. 　他們將逐步實施這項新法。 • They are going to phase the new law in. 　他們要把這項新法逐步實施。 • They are going to phase it in. 他們要把它逐步實施。 • It will be phased in slowly. 它將慢慢地逐步實施。
run up against s/th 遭到對某事物的 反對或抗拒	• The plan ran up against opposition from the public. 　這個計畫遭遇到大眾反對。

spring from s/th 發源於某事物、 起源於	• Her pain sprang from the deep injustice she felt. 她的痛苦來自於她感受到的深刻不公平。
come out (as s/th) 公開表白自己為 男同志、女同志或 跨性別人士	• When Ellen came out there was a big scandal. Ellen 出櫃的時候有個大醜聞。 • When Caitlin Jenner came out as transgender, the world was surprised. 當 Caitlin Jenner 以跨性別者出櫃時，世人都感到很驚訝。

☆ 在學習和使用片語動詞時，你必須非常留意動詞有沒有受詞 (s/th)，以及這個受詞是擺在哪個位置。

☆ rule s/th out 和 phase s/th in 也能在被動語態中使用。這對兩個片語動詞都很常見。

☆ 在使用 run up against s/th 時，主詞是你試著要介紹的新事物，受詞則是它所遭遇到的反對，例如 The proposed law ran up against opposition from lawmakers 即意指立法者反對新法。

☆ 請注意，在使用 run up against s/th 和 spring from s/th 時，不能用受詞把動詞和介系詞隔開來，受詞必須擺在最後。請看例句。

☆ 在使用 come out 時，若是想要指明公告的性質，就該使用 as。請看例句。

☆ 請記得片語動詞是動詞，所以還必須考慮動詞要用什麼時態。

下一個練習將有助於各位聚焦於受詞的正確擺放位置這些細節上。

Task 34

下列各句中的第一個字是正確的，請按照順序將其後的字詞重組成正確的句子。

EX. **Tom as out came gay 2013 in Daley**

Tom Daley came out as gay in 2013.

① We never the rule must of possibility out acceptance

_____

② The years will the new two phased be over next in law

_____

③ They phase the for new in rules will next the event

_____

④ The has against religious run idea groups from opposition up

_____

⑤ Her of from experiences injustice sprang sense her childhood

_____

⑥ Coming is the thing and many hardest gay lesbian out people ever will do

_____

✔ 答案・中譯・說明 **Track 5.7**

① We must never <u>rule out</u> the possibility of acceptance.
我們千萬不可排拒接納的可能性。

We must never <u>rule</u> the possibility of acceptance <u>out</u>.
我們千萬不可把接納的可能性排拒掉。

② The new law will be phased in over the next two years.
新法將會在未來兩年內逐步實施。

③ They will phase in the new rules for the next event.
They will phase the new rules in for the next event.
他們將在下一個賽事逐步使用新規則。

④ The idea has run up against opposition from religious groups.
這個想法遭遇到宗教團體的反對。

⑤ Her sense of injustice sprang from her childhood experiences.
她的不公平感是出自童年的經驗。

⑥ Coming out is the hardest thing many gay and lesbian people will ever do.
出櫃將是許多男女同性戀人士所做過最難的事。

☆ 務必留意受詞的擺放位置。例如 1、3 句可以有兩種不同的解答，就看受詞是擺在哪個位置。

☆ 留意到第 2 句用的是被動式。

☆ 將正確的句子與關鍵語庫 ❺ 中的片語動詞做比較，確認你的用法都正確。並把正確句子中的片語動詞畫上底線，這會幫助你完整而正確地把語塊記起來。

現在來看看這些片語動詞是如何運用在文章脈絡中。

Task 35

請從 Task 1 和 Task 2 的閱讀文章中找出關鍵語庫 ❺ 列出的所有片語動詞，並留意它們在文章中是如何使用的。

Task 36

請練習用關鍵語庫 ❺ 的片語動詞來造句。

片語動詞	造句練習
rule s/th out	
phase s/th in	
run up against s/th	
spring from s/th	
come out (as s/th)	

☆ 再次提醒寫作時若運用到這些片語動詞，需留意動詞的時態和受詞的位置。

5 個談論或寫作性別議題常用的慣用語
5 idioms for talking or writing about gender issues

現在來看看在寫作或談論性別議題時，所能運用的一些慣用語。

Task 37

研讀語庫中的慣用語、例句和其下的說明。

關鍵語庫 6　🔊 Track 5.8

慣用語	例句
a break with the past 打破傳統並開啟新局	• Most activists want a break with the past in gender issues. 大部分的行動人士都想在性別議題上打破過去。
glass ceiling 玻璃天花板（通常專指女性所遭遇的在工作中升級時遇到的一種無形的障礙，使人不能到達較高階層）	• There is a glass ceiling for women in most professions. The top management are always men. 在大多數的職業裡，女性都有玻璃天花板。頂端的管理階層向來都是男性。
the status quo 事物目前在社會上的樣貌、現狀	• The status quo only works for the men. 現狀只對男性管用。
a man's man 不相信各性別間是完全平等的男人，也就是大男人主義	• John is a man's man. He believes a woman's place is in the home, and he lets his wife look after his kids. John 是大男人主義。他相信女性的地盤是在家裡，因此他讓他太太照顧自己的小孩。

| a new man 相信各性別間是完全平等的 男人，也就是新好男人 | • Ted is a new man. He shares the housework with his girlfriend and looks after their kids. Ted 是新好男人。他會和女友分擔家務並照顧小孩。 |

☆ 使用慣用語時唯一能更動的是動詞時態。

☆ 為了讓慣用語有意義，它必須完全準確才行，這意味著你必須將慣用語的所有 細節都使用正確。

☆ 請注意這幾個慣用語都沒有受詞。

下一個練習將有助於各位聚焦於使用這些慣用語時，經常會犯的錯誤。

Task 38

改正這些句子中的常見錯誤。

① I want to break my past.

_____

② He is mans' man.

_____

③ Men must maintain their status in society.

_____

④ The new male believes in equality between the sexes.

_____

⑤ She got as high as she could in her profession, then she reached a glass roof.

_____

① I want <u>a break with the past</u>.

　我想和過去一刀兩斷。

② He is a man's man.

　他是大男人主義。

③ Men must maintain the status quo.

　男人必維護現狀。

④ The new man believes in equality between the sexes.

　新好男人相信兩性平等。

⑤ She got as high as she could in her profession, then she reached a glass ceiling.

　她在職業生涯中取得了最高的成就，然後便觸及了玻璃天花板。

- -

☆ 這些錯誤通常是漏掉了小詞、改變了小詞或單字結尾、慣用語不完整，或者在
　一個不該有受詞的地方加上了受詞。

☆ 請仔細比較錯誤句子和正確解答，務必確實掌握錯在哪以及為什麼是錯的。

☆ 請將正確句子中的慣用語畫上底線。（參照第 1 句的示範）

　　現在我們要練習在文章上下文中找出慣用語。

Task 39

請從 Task 1 和 Task 2 的閱讀文章中找出關鍵語庫 ❻ 列出的所有慣用語，
並留意它們在文章中是如何使用的。

Task 40

請練習用關鍵語庫 ❻ 的慣用語來造句。

慣用語	造句練習
a break with the past	
glass ceiling	

the status quo	
a man's man	
a new man	

☆ 再次提醒在寫作時若運用到這些慣用語，要特別留意動詞的時態和完整的慣用語包含哪些細節。

易混淆的字詞 easily confused words

- 在試著針對容易搞混的單字去了解差別時，需要思考的不僅是意思上的差異，還有文法和用法。
- 要記得，有些單字只能用在特定的主題上，用在別的主題則不適當。
- 容易搞混的單字，其差別常常是在搭配詞的使用上有所不同。

Task 41

請仔細研讀各組易混淆的字詞、例句和其下的說明。

關鍵語庫 ⑦　◎ Track 5.10

易混淆字詞	例句
1	**worsen s/th** (*vt*) 使變得更糟	• This new law might actually worsen the situation. 這條新法實際上可能會使形勢變得更糟。
	deteriorate (*vi*) 惡化	• The situation is deteriorating. 局勢正在惡化。
2	**expand** (*vt*) (*vi*) 擴大	• The boundaries of what's possible are expanding. 關於什麼是有可能的界限正在擴大。
	spread (*vt*) (*vi*) 擴散、傳播	• Her ideas are spreading. More people are accepting them. 她的觀念在傳播。有更多人正在接受它們。
3	**popular** (*adj.*) 受歡迎的	• Although he is a transgender, the star is hugely popular. 儘管是跨性別者，但這位明星極其受歡迎。
	common (*adj.*) 常見的	• Transgenderism is becoming quite common now. 跨性別現在變得相當常見。

4	**chance** (*nc*) 機遇、冒險	• I'm not going to take any chances with my health. 我不想拿我的健康冒任何險。
	opportunity (*nc*) 機會	• Opportunities for higher education are limited in her country. 在她的國家接受高等教育的機會有限。
5	**solve s/th** (*vt*) 解決	• They have solved this problem. 他們已經解決了這個問題。
	resolve to V 決心	• She resolved to live her life the way she wanted to. 她決心照自己想要的方式來過日子。

☆ worsen s/th 和 deteriorate 的意思和用法非常類似，但文法略有不同。別忘了它們都是動詞，所以在使用時必須考慮它們的時態。

☆ worsen s/th 是及物動詞，所以必須使用受詞。它意指 X 使 Y 更糟。

☆ deteriorate 是不及物動詞，所以不可使用受詞。它意指 X 變得更糟了。

☆ expand 和 spread 的文法和用法非常類似，但意思略有不同。別忘了它們都是動詞，所以在使用時必須想到它們的時態。

☆ expand 可以是及物和不及物，根據主題的不同，可以使用或不使用受詞。當你用它來談論性別議題時，通常應該是不連同受詞來用。它意指一件事變得更大，例如 The protest is expanding. 意味著抗議活動的規模越來越大。expand 也能用來描述抽象的概念變得越來越強：The negative reaction is expanding.。

☆ spread 也可以是及物和不及物，同樣根據主題的不同，可以使用或不使用受詞。在用於談論性別議題時，它通常是不連同受詞來用，意指許多事情的數目在增加，例如 The protests are spreading. 意味有更多的抗議在新的地方展開。

☆ popular 和 common 的文法和用法非常類似，但意思截然不同。popular 包括了渴求或想要某事物的概念，但 common 並不包括這個想要或渴求的概念。這兩個單字在台灣常會搞混，所以使用時務必特別留意。

☆ popular 是「風行、受歡迎」的意思，意味著人人都想要，例如 Iphones are very popular. 意味著很多人都想要一支 iphone；Gender reassignment surgery is quite popular. 意味著不少人想要做變性手術。

☆ common 是指「常見」，意味著某事相當正常，例如 Iphones are very

common. 並不意味著很多人都想要，而是意味著它隨處可見；Gender reassignment surgery is quite common. 並不意味著不少人想要去做，而是意味著這種手術相當普遍。

☆ chance 和 opportunity 的文法和用法非常類似，但意思相當不同。

☆ 若想強調運氣、命運或風險時，要用 chance。它也能用在下列的慣用語中：take chances with s/th 意指拿某事冒險，或 life chances 意指你的命運或運氣。

☆ 而若是把「機會」翻譯成英文，則應該要用 opportunity。例如 Women have fewer opportunities than men. 正確；Women have fewer chances than men. 則是錯的。

☆ 各位或許記得在 Unit 2 學過 solution 和 resolution 的差別，它們其實是動詞 solve 和 resolve 的名詞，而動詞 solve 和 resolve 的差別與名詞 solution 和 resolution 的差別十分雷同。但別忘了它們都是動詞，所以在使用時必須考慮時態。

☆ 若是要聚焦於解決一個問題時，應該用 solve。我們在句子或段落中通常會發現 solve 和 problem 彼此相當密切。

☆ 當要表達自己提出的堅毅決定、誓言或承諾時，則應該用 resolve。這無關乎解決問題，不要用 resolve 來描述解決問題，亦即 We can resolve this problem. 的說法是錯的。

　　在做下一個練習時，請仔細思考句意、文法和用法來選出正確的單字。

Task 42
請選出正確的單字來填入下列各句。

① **expanding/spreading**

Acceptance of transgenderism is ＿＿＿＿＿＿＿＿. More places accept it now.

② **worsened/deteriorated**

His mental health ＿＿＿＿＿＿＿ after the operation.

③ **opportunity/chance**

I'm going to take a _____ and have the surgery. I know it's risky.

④ **Chances/Opportunities**

_____ for this kind of work are limited to men only, I'm afraid.

⑤ **resolved to/solved**

She _____ change her gender when he was a little boy.

⑥ **common/popular**

That song was very _____ years ago.

⑦ **worsened/deteriorated**

The new law forbidding transgender people from working in schools only _____ the situation.

⑧ **spreading/expanding**

The type of jobs women can do now is _____.

⑨ **resolve/solve**

They have never been able to _____ this problem.

⑩ **popular/common**

This is a very _____ problem.

✓ 答案・中譯・說明　🎧 **Track 5.11**

① Acceptance of transgenderism is <u>spreading</u>. 對跨性別者的接納正在擴散。

② His mental health deteriorated after the operation.
他的心理健康在手術後惡化了。

③ I'm going to take a chance and have the surgery. I know it's risky.
我要冒險去動手術。我知道它有風險。

④ Opportunities for this kind of work are limited to men only, I'm afraid.
這類工作的機會恐怕是僅限於男性。

⑤ She resolved to change her gender when he was a little boy.
當她還是小男生時，就決心要變性。

⑥ That song was very popular years ago. 那首歌在幾年前非常流行。

⑦ The new law forbidding transgender people from working in schools only worsened the situation. 新法禁止跨性別人士在學校工作，只會使情況變得更糟。

⑧ The type of jobs women can do now is expanding.
現在女性能從事的職業類型正在擴大。

⑨ They have never been able to solve this problem. 他們從未能解決這個問題。

⑩ This is a very common problem. 這是一個很常見的問題。

....

☆ 第 1 句用 spreading 是因為意思表達接納度「擴散」到新的地方；而第 8 句用 expanding 則是因為主詞為 type，而且 type 是單數。

☆ 第 2 句選用 deteriorated 是因為句子裡沒有受詞；而第 7 句用 worsened 則是因為有受詞：the situation。

☆ 第 3 句由於提到了關於風險、幸運或運氣的概念，所以要用 chance；而第 4 句的意思顯然是指機會，所以應使用 opportunities。

☆ 第 5 句需要 resolved 是由於句意與某人所提出的強烈決定有關；第 9 句用 solve 則是因為句子裡包括了單字 problem，而且顯然是關於「問題」，resolved 在此並不適切。

☆ 第 6 句表達的概念與渴求或想要聽歌有關，因此必須用 popular；而第 10 句則與渴求或想要的概念無關，所以應該用 common。

☆ 請將正確答案畫上底線。（參照第 1 句的示範）

　　最後我們還是要來練習從閱讀文章中找出這些容易搞混的單字。當你在文章中每找到一個單字，都必須停下來思考它是意指什麼、它的文法是什麼，以及它是如何使用的。

請從 Task 1 和 Task 2 的閱讀文章中找出關鍵語庫 ❼ 列出的所有易混淆字詞，並留意它們在文章中是如何使用的。

Task 44

請練習用關鍵語庫 ❼ 的易混淆字詞來造句。

易混淆字詞	造句練習
worsen s/th	
deteriorate	
expand	
spread	
popular	
common	
chance	
opportunity	
solve s/th	
resolve to V	

☆ 在寫作中運用這些易混淆的字詞時，記得把重點放在文法、句意和用法上，而不是只注意單字的意思。

在你結束這個單元之前，請將下列清單看過，確定你能將所有要點都勾選起來。如果有一些要點你還搞不清楚，請回頭再次研讀本單元的相關部分。

☐ 我確實閱讀並理解了關於「性別議題」的長篇文章。

☐ 我完全知道字彙在文章中是如何使用，並更加了解到要怎麼用單字來表達特定的主題。

☐ 我已經學會 15 個關於「性別議題」主題的關鍵字，以及可與其搭配使用的動詞和形容詞。

☐ 我已經練習使用這些搭配詞來描寫「性別議題」。

☐ 我已經學到了一些同義詞，也了解在運用時需要注意的一些問題。

☐ 我學到了很多關於這個主題可以運用的語塊，包括片語動詞以及名詞或動詞為同形的單字。

☐ 我已經練習使用這些語塊。

☐ 我學到了 5 個關於這個主題的慣用語，且知道如何運用。

☐ 我已經理解在運用慣用語時需要特別注意的一些問題。

☐ 關於這個主題，我已經能確實掌握一些易混淆字詞的用法。

PART 2

哲學相關議題
Philosophical Issues

Unit 6

安樂死與醫療倫理
Euthanasia and Medical Ethics

閱讀文章 Reading

在 Part 2 中，我們將要閱讀幾篇「論證／意見」(argument/opinion) 類型的文章。本單元所要探討的主題是安樂死與醫療倫理。

Task 1

閱讀文章並盡可能地理解文章內容。請先不要使用字典。

---

(1) _____ Opponents of the practice are up in arms about it. As life expectancy increases due to medical advancements, the problem of euthanasia is becoming increasingly urgent and controversial. Many elderly people are choosing to end their lives as their quality of life deteriorates, and they can no longer manage to do the things they used to be able to do independently. For many people, extreme old age with all the suffering and inconvenience it entails is something to be regarded with horror, especially if they can no longer take care of themselves. However, the issue deserves serious and detailed consideration, because for many doctors and patients, it's a question of medical ethics. There are two sides to the argument, and neither is simple.

(2) _____ The first is that the elderly or the infirm will be pressured by their families into ending their lives earlier. Those concerned will make the decision behind the patient's back to end their life, motivated by such considerations as trying to reduce the financial pressure of prolonged medical care. Naturally, families of those patients who are suffering from a debilitating, chronic illness, and which they are not expected to get over, worry about whether they will have the

---

resources, both emotionally and financially, to care for the sick person for years and years with little support from the government or insurance companies. In this case, the argument goes, they are simply trying to get rid of an expensive and inconvenient burden, and do not really care about the person who is suffering. They say that euthanasia should be proscribed because it is a form of murder, and that no one has the right to decide when to end the life of another person, no matter what their motivation.

(3) _____ The doctor's role is to make diagnoses, cure diseases and save lives at all costs. The practice of medicine is a noble one, and getting doctors involved in killing people is a disgrace to the profession. Opponents also bring up religious arguments, saying that only God has the right to decide when a person will pass away. They also say there is always the possibility that the patient will live long enough to make a full and complete recovery as medical science advances and finds new cures, treatments, and therapies for people who are very ill.

(4) _____ In addition to curing diseases and saving lives, the doctor's role is to alleviate needless or unbearable suffering. If a patient is in a critical condition, they have undergone extensive surgery, and despite having gone under the knife many times, the operations have not been successful; if the drugs the doctor has prescribed have not worked; if the patient is enduring unbearable chronic pain and is unlikely to pull through or recover, and receives a negative prognosis, then it is an act of cruelty to uselessly try to prolong that person's life, especially when that person has requested the doctor's help in ending it because they do not want to burden others with their illness. In that case it is the role of the doctor to fulfil the patients request, and offer constructive, professional advice about the best way to terminate a patient's life. Here the role of the doctor

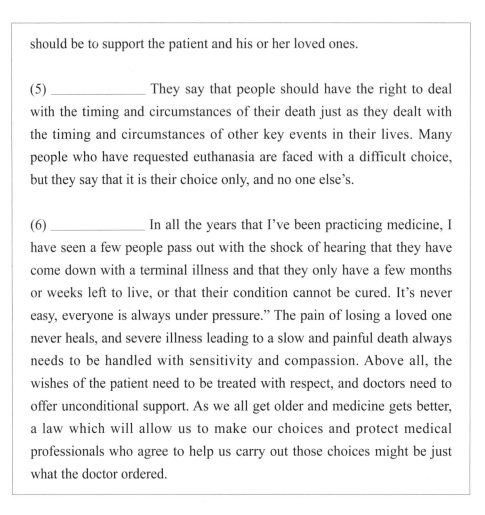

should be to support the patient and his or her loved ones.

(5) _____ They say that people should have the right to deal with the timing and circumstances of their death just as they dealt with the timing and circumstances of other key events in their lives. Many people who have requested euthanasia are faced with a difficult choice, but they say that it is their choice only, and no one else's.

(6) _____ In all the years that I've been practicing medicine, I have seen a few people pass out with the shock of hearing that they have come down with a terminal illness and that they only have a few months or weeks left to live, or that their condition cannot be cured. It's never easy, everyone is always under pressure." The pain of losing a loved one never heals, and severe illness leading to a slow and painful death always needs to be handled with sensitivity and compassion. Above all, the wishes of the patient need to be treated with respect, and doctors need to offer unconditional support. As we all get older and medicine gets better, a law which will allow us to make our choices and protect medical professionals who agree to help us carry out those choices might be just what the doctor ordered.

Task 2

請從下列句子選出適當的主題句以完成 Task 1 每個段落的填空。

A Another argument is that it is unethical for doctors to be involved in decisions about death.

B Dr Maslow, who runs a practice dedicated to helping patients end their lives, says: "It is a bitter pill to swallow to be told that ones life is coming to an end.

C Opponents of euthanasia, who are often fierce and outspoken, say that it is a sick idea and they have a number of more or less convincing arguments.

D Proponents of euthanasia argue that, on the contrary, it is absolutely necessary for doctors to play a role here.

E Tomorrow, the state of Massachusetts will vote on allowing euthanasia.

F Another argument put forward by proponents is that no one else has the right to make crucial decisions for other people, especially in a matter as important as life or death.

◆ 答案‧中譯‧說明

(1) E (2) C (3) A (4) D (5) F (6) B

譯文

　　明天麻州將針對允許安樂死進行投票。反對這種作法的人對此表示強烈反對。隨著預期壽命拜醫療進步所賜而增加，安樂死的問題變得日益迫切和具有爭議。很多老年人選擇結束生命是因為生活品質變壞，他們再也無法勉力做到以往能獨立做到的事。對很多人來說，極高齡以及伴隨其而來的所有痛苦和不便是令人感到恐懼的事，尤其是當他們再也無法照料自己的時候。然而，此課題值得嚴肅與詳細來考慮，因為對很多醫生和病患來說，它是醫療倫理的問題。這個爭論有兩面，而且都不簡單。

　　安樂死的反對者往往激烈且直言不諱的說安樂死是病態的想法，而且他們有一些或多或少令人信服的論點。首先是老年人或體弱多病的人會受到家人壓力而提早結束自己的生命。在為了想要減輕長期醫療照護所帶來的財務壓力這類考量激發下，相關人等會在病患背後決定結束他們的生命。那些苦於使人衰弱的慢性疾病患者，而且預計不會好起來時，他們的家人自然會擔心在沒什麼政府或保險公司的支持下，自己會不會有資源來經年關照生病的人，在情緒與財務上都是。在這種情況下，該論點主張說他們只會試圖擺脫昂貴又不便的負擔，而不會真正去關心正在受苦的人。他們說安樂死應該要被禁止，因為它是一種謀殺的形式，而且沒人有權決定要在什麼時候結束另一個人的生命，無論他們的動機是什麼。

　　另一個論點是，醫生涉入有關死亡的決定是不道德的。醫生的職責是診斷、治療疾病，以及不惜一切的代價來挽救生命。行醫是高尚的，讓醫生參與殺人是這個行業的恥辱。反對者還提出了宗教上的論點，說只有上帝有權決定人會在什麼時候離世。他們還說，隨著醫療科學進步而為非常重病的人找到新的治癒之道、治療和療法，向來都有的可能性是，病患活得夠久就可能整個完全復原。

　　安樂死的支持者則認為恰恰相反的是，醫生在此扮演角色是絕對有必要。除了治病和救命，醫生的作用是減輕不必要或難以忍受的痛苦。假如病患的情況危急，大舉做過了手

術,而且儘管接受多次動刀,手術仍不成功;假如醫生所開的藥不見效;假如病患正承受著難以忍受的慢性疼痛,不太可能熬過去或復原,而且得知預後為負面,那麼徒勞地去嘗試延長此人的生命就是殘忍的行徑,尤其是當此人因為不想讓自己的病症拖累他人而請求醫生幫忙把它結束時。在此情況下,醫生的職責就是要滿足病患的要求,並就終結患者生命的最佳方式提供建設性、專業的建議。醫生在此的角色應該是支持病患和他所愛的人。

支持者所提出的另一個論點是,任何人都無權替其他人做出關鍵決定,尤其是在重要到攸關生死的事情上。他們說,人應該有權自理死亡的時機和情境,一如自理人生中其他關鍵大事的時機和情境。許多要求安樂死的人都面臨著困難的選擇,但他們說這選擇只屬於他們自己,而無關乎別人。

經營業務來專門幫助病患結束生命的馬斯洛醫生說:「被告知生命即將結束,這是一顆難以下嚥的苦藥。在我行醫的這些年來,我看過一些人在聽到自己得到絕症而只剩下幾個月或幾週可活,或者是病情無法治癒時嚇得昏倒了。這從來都不容易,每個人向來都會碰到壓力。」失去所愛之人的痛苦從來都不會癒合,而導致緩慢與痛苦死亡的重症向來都需要以敏感度和愛心來處理。尤有甚者的是,病患的心願需要以尊重來對待,醫生則需要給予無條件的支持。隨著我們都變得更老而醫學變得更好,一項容許我們自己做選擇並保護同意幫助我們實現這些選擇的醫療專業人士的法律,或許正是醫生所建議的。

··

☆ 第一段是以一則非常具體的資訊來開頭,接著便針對安樂死的議題來概括說明其背景。這則非常具體的資訊在一般文章介紹的開頭被稱為 hook「鉤」,因為它會立即勾起你對下文的興趣:你就像是魚上鉤了。注意,在鉤語後面,第一段的其餘資訊是如何屬於概括資訊。

☆ 第二和第三段詳細介紹了反對安樂死的觀點和例子。

☆ 第四和第五段提出相反的觀點,並呈現支持安樂死的論點,有細節和例子。

☆ 最後一段提出馬斯洛醫生贊成安樂死的觀點。我們從文章的組織中可以推論出,這也是作者的觀點。

☆ 請注意,主題句向來是段落中最一般性的句子,而段落中的其他部分又是如何以具體的例子或理由來發展主題句的論點。

字詞搭配 Word Partnerships

　　我們現在要來學習「安樂死與醫療倫理」這個主題的 15 個關鍵字，以及可搭配這些關鍵字使用的 word partnerships「字詞搭配表」。首先，請看關鍵字語庫。

Task 3

請仔細研讀這些主題字彙和下方的說明。

關鍵語庫 ①　 Track 6.1

名詞	動詞	形容詞	字義
advice Ⓤ	advise	-	建言、忠告
choice Ⓒ	choose	chosen	選擇
condition Ⓒ	-	-	情況、環境
consideration Ⓒ	consider s/th	considered	考慮、動機
death Ⓒ	die	dead	死亡
decision Ⓒ	decide	decisive, decided	決定
ethics Ⓒ	-	(un)ethical	倫理、道德標準
illness Ⓒ	-	ill	病症
opponent/proponent Ⓒ	oppose s/th	opposed	反對者／支持者
pain ⓊⒸ	-	painful	痛苦、疼痛
profession Ⓒ	-	professional	職業、專業
recovery Ⓤ	recover	recovered	復原、痊癒
suffering Ⓤ	suffer	-	苦痛、折磨

support U	support	supported	支持、幫助
surgery U	-	-	手術、外科

☆ 需留意哪些名詞是可數，哪些是不可數。

☆ 要記得，名詞是可數或不可數，有時候須視主題而定。

☆ 注意單字的其他詞性形式，包含動詞和形容詞。

☆ 須留意 advice 是不可數名詞，必須連同單數動詞使用。Good advice is important. 正確；Good advices are important. 則是錯的。

☆ choice 是可數名詞，所以可以用 choices。留意其動詞是 choose，不要把動詞跟名詞搞混。

☆ consideration 是可數名詞，所以可以連同複數形動詞來用：There are many considerations.。

☆ 須留意 death 的不同形式。die 是規則動詞：die died died。這些單字非常容易搞混，務必留意！

☆ 留意到 ethics 向來都必須有 s，並可使用複數形動詞，例如 Ethics are important.、Ethics is important. 都正確。

☆ 請特別留意可連同 illness 來使用的不同動詞。當你要描述生病的狀態時，可用 have 和 suffer from；要描述從別人那裡感染傳染病時，可用 get 和 catch；而若要描述「生……病」時，則可用 develop 和 come down with。

☆ opponent 是反對某事，proponent 則是支持某事。在本單元的稍後，各位會看到這兩個單字的字詞組合一模一樣，不過請留意，opponent 有動詞形和形容詞形，而 proponent 則沒有。

☆ 注意，pain 可以是可數也可以是不可數。當用於這個主題和其他的醫療相關主題時，它向來應該連同單數形動詞以單數來使用：The pain is terrible. 正確；The pains are terrible. 則是錯的。

☆ 請注意，professional 既可用作名詞也可以用作形容詞，它還有動詞形式，但意思截然不同，在此不用擔心。

☆ support 可當作動詞與名詞使用，各位在之後會學到更多用法。

☆ surgery 這個字有兩個意思。首先，它可以當作 operation「開刀」的同義詞，這是各位在此會學到的意思。此外，它也可以指醫生的工作時間，類似於

practice 的意思，各位會在本單元後段的關鍵語庫 ❹ 中學到相關用法。例如 I have morning surgery but I'm free in the afternoon. 這句話意指醫生是在早上執業看診。

接下來，我們將以 5 個關鍵字為一組，深入地學習與這些字最頻繁搭配的字詞組合及正確用法。

Task 4

請研讀這個字詞搭配表、例句和底下的說明。

搭配在前的動詞		搭配的形容詞		關鍵字
give (s/o) offer (s/o)	heed listen to	constructive useful valuable helpful	clear general detailed	financial legal medical
pass on provide (s/o with)	act on follow			
	ignore	good excellent	conflicting	**advice**
get obtain receive	reject	practical sensible	expert professional specialist	
take accept		bad wrong		

字詞搭配使用範例　　🎧 **Track 6.2**（收錄本單元 Task 4~Task 20 字詞搭配使用範例）

- The danger of getting a second opinion is that the patient might **get conflicting advice** from the two doctors.
  徵詢第二意見的危險在於，病患或許會從兩位醫生那裡得到相互衝突的建議。

- In order to recover quickly, patients should **follow the medical advice**.
  為了迅速康復，病患應該要遵照醫囑。

- She **gave** the patient **good advice**, but he didn't **act on** it.
  她給了病患好的建言，但他並沒有照做。

• The doctor's **excellent professional advice was ignored**.
醫生極好的專業建言遭到了忽略。

··

☆ 注意，若把建言當成句子的主詞，動詞便能以被動來使用。

Task 5

請研讀這個字詞搭配表和例句。

搭配在前面的動詞	搭配的形容詞		關鍵字
be faced with face	good right	bad wrong	
make	careful informed wise moral	stark difficult hard natural	**choice**

字詞搭配使用範例

• Patients who have received a negative prognosis **are often faced with stark choices**. 得知預後為負面的患者，經常面臨嚴峻的選擇。

• Patients must listen to their doctor, do their own research, and **make an informed choice** about their treatment.
患者必須聽醫生的意見、自行研究，並就他們的治療做出明智的選擇。

• Doctors **face difficult moral choices** all the time.
醫生時時面臨著艱難的道德選擇。

··

☆ 注意，face 和 be faced with 的意思並沒有什麼差別。

Task 6

請研讀這個字詞搭配表、例句和底下的說明。

搭配在前的動詞	搭配的形容詞		關鍵字	搭配在後的動詞
be in a ~	stable critical serious	mental physical	**condition**	improve get better deteriorate get worse

字詞搭配使用範例

- He is very ill, but he **is** currently **in a stable condition**, which is good news.
  他病得很重，但好消息是，目前情況穩定。

- Her **condition** is **not getting better**, and is in fact expected to **deteriorate** even more. 她的情況並沒有好轉，事實上是預計會更加惡化。

☆ 留意到 condition 可以當成動詞的主詞來用。

PART

2

Task 7

請研讀這個字詞搭配表、例句和底下的說明。

搭配在前的動詞	搭配的形容詞		關鍵字
give s/th take s/th into deserve require need receive	careful detailed full serious	adequate due proper special urgent	**consideration**

- Doctors need to **take** the wishes of the family **into consideration**.
  醫生需要把家人的心願納入考慮。

- The problem **requires proper consideration**. 這個問題需要適當的考慮。

- I don't think her request **has received adequate consideration**.
  我認為她的要求沒有得到充分的考慮。

- Many factors need to **be taken into consideration**.
  很多因素都需要納入考慮。

☆ 留意到 give 和 take s/th into 能以被動來使用。

Task 8

請研讀這個字詞搭配表和例句。

搭配在前面的動詞	搭配的形容詞		關鍵字
bring cause lead to mean result in face meet be near approach fear	early premature untimely sudden unexpected instant quick slow	painless painful certain terrible	**death**

字詞搭配使用範例

- As the patient **approaches death**, their breathing becomes more difficult.
  隨著患者瀕臨死亡，他們的呼吸會變得更加困難。

- Some patients who **are facing** an **early death** request euthanasia.
有些面臨早逝的病患會要求安樂死。
- A cancer diagnosis often but not always **leads to an untimely death**.
診斷為癌症經常但並非總是會導致過早死亡。
- Legal euthanasia allows terminally ill patients to **face certain**, **painful death**
bravely. 合法的安樂死容許末期病症的病患勇敢地去面對必然、痛苦的死亡。

現在，我們來看看各位是否能用一些字詞搭配來擴大對字彙的運用。

Task 9

請從 Task 4 到 Task 8 中選出正確形式的字詞，完成以下段落填空。

There are many factors which need to (1) _____ (2) _____ consideration when a person (3) _____ (4) _____ death from a terminal illness. While the patient (5) _____ (6) _____ condition, before their condition (7) _____, he or she needs to (8) _____ the (9) _____ choice of whether to receive euthanasia or not. The patient needs to (10) _____ the doctor's (11) _____ advice and (12) _____ it.

範例答案

1. be taken into/be given
2. serious/careful/detailed/full
3. is facing/is near/is approaching
4. early/untimely/premature/certain
5. is in a
6. stable

7. gets worse
8. make
9. hard/difficult/stark
10. listen to/heed
11. expert/professional
12. act on/follow

☆ 務必確認所選用的單字都是正確的形式。檢查單數或複數，以及動詞的正確形式。例如空格 (3) 中的動詞 face 或 approach 必須使用現在進行式，因為意思

是近在眼前的事。

現在來學習另外 5 個單字。

Task 10

請研讀這個字詞搭配表、例句和底下的說明。

搭配在前的動詞	搭配的形容詞		關鍵字
arrive at come to make reach	big crucial important difficult hard tough final irreversible informed	good rational right sensible wise bad poor unwise wrong	**decision (about s/th) (to V)**

字詞搭配使用範例

- Together with their doctors, patients can **arrive at an informed decision about** their treatment.
  病患能和他們的醫生一起就自己的治療法來做出明智的決定。

- Patients often have to **make the tough decision to** stop treatment.
  患者常常不得不做出停止治療的艱難決定。

- Sometimes it's difficult to **come to a rational decision about** how to proceed.
  對於該怎麼進行下去，有時候很難做出理性的決定。

☆ 當你想要使用 n.p. 時，就必須用 about。
☆ 若是要使用動詞時，則必須用 to。請看例句。

Task 11

請研讀這個字詞搭配表、例句和底下的說明。

搭配在前面的片語	搭配的形容詞		關鍵字
a question of a matter of a code of be bound by	personal	business medical professional legal nursing	**ethics**

字詞搭配使用範例

- Doctors **are bound by a code of professional ethics**.
  醫生是受到職業道德的規範所約束。

- Her **personal ethics** wouldn't allow her to make this decision.
  她的個人道德標準不容許她做出這個決定。

- Euthanasia is **a question of ethics**. 安樂死是一個倫理問題。

·····

☆ 須注意 ethics 的前面需要用片語，而不是動詞。

☆ 留意到倫理的不同類型。

Task 12

請研讀這個字詞搭配表、例句和底下的說明。

搭配在前面的動詞	搭配的形容詞		關鍵字
have suffer from get catch develop come down with	incurable fatal terminal lingering chronic long-term prolonged	mental psychiatric physical respiratory childhood	**illness**

be diagnosed with	debilitating	acute	
	life-threatening	short	
treat	major		
	serious	infectious	**illness**
recover from	severe		
fight off			
	minor		
die of			

- People who **suffer from mental illness** often don't look ill.
  苦於精神疾病的人通常看起來不像有病。

- She **caught a chronic respiratory illness**. 她得了慢性的呼吸道病症。

- They **treated** his **illness** with the latest drugs but he eventually **died of** his
  illness. 他們以最新的藥物來治療他的病，但他終歸是死於這個疾病。

- She **was diagnosed with** a **debilitating** and **incurable illness** and was given 5
  months to live.
  她被診斷出患有一種會使人衰弱的不治之症，只能活 5 個月。

☆ 請留意不同類型疾病的說法。

Task 13

請研讀這個字詞搭配表、例句和底下的說明。

動詞	搭配的形容詞		關鍵字	搭配在後的動詞
be	chief	outspoken		hold that v.p.
	leading	vocal		hold the view that v.p.
	main	vociferous	**opponent /**	maintain that v.p.
			proponent	say that v.p.
	bitter	political	**(of s/th)**	argue that v.p.
	fierce			claim n.p.
	strong			claim that v.p.
	vigorous			

- She **is** an **outspoken opponent of** the law to ban euthanasia.
  在以法律來禁止安樂死上，她是直言的反對者。

- **Proponents of** euthanasia **hold that** it's kinder for the patients and their families.
  安樂死的支持者認為這對病患和家屬比較仁慈。

- **Opponents of** euthanasia **are** often **bitter** and **vociferous**.
  安樂死的反方常是激烈而喧嚷。

....

☆ 注意，當 opponent 或 proponent 是主詞時，動詞的後面就必須用 v.p.。

Task 14

請研讀這個字詞搭配表、例句和底下的說明。

搭配在前的動詞		搭配的形容詞		關鍵字
suffer	alleviate	great	sharp	
bear	control	intense	stabbing	
endure	stop	severe	throbbing	
be in	do something	terrible		
be racked with	for the ~	unbearable	dull	
experience	make the ~ go			
feel	away	acute	abdominal	
go through		agonizing	back	**pain**
have	dull	excruciating	chest	
	ease	extreme	leg	
			muscle	
		constant	shoulder	
		chronic	stomach	
		persistent		

- Often patients **endure terrible persistent pain**, and nothing can **make it go away**. 病患常忍受可怕的持久疼痛，而且沒什麼能把它消除。

- Doctors are often not able to **alleviate** some types of **excruciating pain**.
  醫生往往減輕不了某些類型的劇痛。

- He **is experiencing constant abdominal pain** which doctors cannot **control**.
  他正經歷醫生也無法抑制的持續腹痛。

....

☆ 請注意與身體部位相關的不同類型疼痛該怎麼表達。

☆ 留意到 dull 可以用為形容詞或動詞。

就像前面所做過的，我們再來練習這第二組 5 個單字的字詞搭配應用。

Task 15

請從 Task 10 到 Task 14 中選出正確形式的字詞，完成以下段落填空。

Proponents (1) _____ euthanasia (2) _____ patients have the
right to (3) _____ the decision (4) _____ end their life,
especially if they are (5) _____ a (6) _____ and (7) _____
illness, one which leaves them helpless, and which they are likely to die
from anyway. Opponents, who seem to have little sympathy for the suffering
of others and who (8) _____ often (9) _____ and (10)
_____, (11) _____ , even if the patient (12) _____ (13)
_____ and (14) _____ pain, and doctors can do nothing to (15)
_____ it, only God can take away life.

範例答案

1. of

2. hold that/hold the view that/maintain that/say that/argue that

3. arrive at/come to/make/reach

4. to

5. suffering from/diagnosed with

6. debilitating/life-threatening/major/serious/severe

7. debilitating/life-threatening/major/serious/severe

8. are

9. bitter/fierce/strong/vigorous

10. outspoken/vocal/vociferous

11. hold that/hold the view that/maintain that/say that/argue that

12. is suffering/is bearing/is enduring/is in/is racked with/is experiencing/is feeling/is going through

13. great/intense/severe/terrible/unbearable

14. constant/chronic/persistent

15. alleviate

☆ 請確保所套用的單字是正確的形式,例如在空格 (12) 中,你必須使用現在進行式,因為這裡的意思指疼痛是持續的,沒有終點或結果。

現在我們來學習最後一組的 5 個單字。

Task 16

請研讀這個字詞搭配表、例句和底下的說明。

搭配在前面的動詞	搭配的形容詞		關鍵字
practise	chosen	medical nursing healthcare	
enter go into join		legal	**profession**
搭配在前面的片語		teaching	
be a disgrace to the ~ be at the top of s/o's ~ be by ~		accountancy auditing	

- She was originally a nurse **by profession**, but she studied hard and **entered** the **legal profession**. 她原本是專業護理師，但她努力用功而跨入了法律專業。
- Doctors who assist patients in dying are often regarded as **a disgrace to their profession**. 協助病患死亡的醫生常被視為他們業界的恥辱。

☆ 請注意各種不同專業領域的說法，及有哪些片語可以連同 profession 來使用。

Task 17

請研讀這個字詞搭配表、例句和底下的說明。

搭配在前的動詞	搭配的形容詞		關鍵字
make achieve be in aid speed up delay hamper hinder	amazing astonishing dramatic excellent miraculous good satisfactory significant complete full long-term	limited modest slow steady national economic industrial physical political	**recovery**

- The patient **made** an **astonishing physical recovery**.
  病患的身體有了驚人的恢復。
- The new drug will **aid recovery**. 這種新藥將有助於復原。
- Not following the doctor's advice will **hamper long-term recovery**.
  不聽從醫生的建言會妨礙長期復原。

☆ 請注意，根據不同主題可使用不同的「恢復」說法。

☆ 留意到片語 be in recovery 可用來描述因藥物或酒精成癮而受到治療的人。

Task 18

請研讀這個字詞搭配表和例句。

搭配在前面的動詞		搭配的形容詞		關鍵字
cause (s/o)	alleviate ease reduce	great intense terrible	widespread human	
inflict increase	relieve	unbearable	mental physical	**suffering**
	endure experience	needless unnecessary		

字詞搭配使用範例

- Sometimes prolonging life at the cost of quality of life is to **cause needless suffering**. 有時候以犧牲生活品質為代價來延長生命會造成不必要的苦痛。
- Doctors are supposed to **alleviate human suffering**.
  醫生理當減緩人類的苦痛。
- Many of those who request euthanasia are **enduring unbearable suffering**.
  那些要求安樂死的人很多都在忍受難以忍受的苦痛。

Task 19

請研讀這個字詞搭配表和例句。

搭配在前面的動詞	搭配的形容詞		關鍵字
enjoy have	great complete	tremendous	**support** **(for s/th)** **(of s/o)**
offer provide	full total	adequate sufficient direct	

derive draw on receive	active considerable unflagging unconditional	indirect long-term	**support (for s/th) (of s/o)**

字詞搭配使用範例

- Many terminally ill patients **derive great support** from the knowledge that they can terminate their lives when they want to.
  許多絕症病患得到很大的支持是來自於知道想要時就能結束自己的生命。
- Healthcare workers **provide full long-term support for** those suffering from illnesses of all types. 醫護人員為患有各類病症的人提供了全面的長期支持。
- Patients **enjoy the support of** their doctors. 病患享有醫生的支持。

Task 20

請研讀這個字詞搭配表和例句。

搭配在前面的動詞	搭配的形容詞		關鍵字
have undergo perform need require	major radical extensive invasive minor successful unsuccessful urgent emergency	experimental cosmetic plastic general heart abdominal brain open-heart	**surgery**

字詞搭配使用範例

- This patient will **require urgent surgery**. 這位病患需要緊急手術。

- The patient has **undergone** very **invasive surgery** many times, but the **surgery** has not been **successful**.

  該病患已經接受多次非常侵入式的手術，但手術並不成功。

  接下來，我們來練習這最後一組 5 個單字的字詞搭配應用。

Task 21

請從 Task 16 到 Task 20 中選出正確形式的字詞，完成以下段落填空。

> The (1) _____ profession see their job as (2) _____ (3)
> _____ suffering - for everyone, not just the rich- (4) _____ (5)
> _____ support (6) _____ those who are ill, aiding those who
> have (7) _____ surgery in (8) _____ a (9) _____
> recovery – for the rest of their lives. Those who (10) _____ this
> profession do not see their job as ending life.

範例答案

1. medical/nursing/healthcare
2. alleviating/easing/reducing/relieving
3. human
4. offering/providing
5. adequate/sufficient/direct
6. for
7. undergone/had
8. making/achieving
9. complete/full/long-term
10. practise/enter/go into/join

☆ 同樣的，還是要留意各組的同義字詞，並確認所選用的單字及動詞都是正確的
形式，例如在空格 (2)、(4) 和 (8) 中，你必須使用 Ving，因為動詞是接在介系
詞後面。而空格 (7) 則必須用過去分詞，因為時態為現在完成式。

記住，多閱讀有助於擴充字彙量，而在文章上下文脈絡中查看大量例子則能幫助你記憶新的用語。下一個練習對於各位記憶 15 個關鍵單字和它們的字詞搭配將有非常大的幫助。

Task 22

請從 Task 1 和 Task 2 的閱讀文章中找出關鍵語庫 ❶ 所列的 15 個關鍵字，並留意這些字在文章中是如何使用的。

常用語塊 Chunks

　　前面學過了字詞搭配的用法，我們現在要來學一些可用在寫作或談論安樂死和醫療倫理這類主題的 chunks「語塊」。

Task 23

研讀這些語塊和底下的說明。

關鍵語庫 ❷

Chunk
❏ be (un)ethical (for s/o) (to V)　(s/o)(V)（不）符合道德倫理
❏ care about n.p./Ving　關心 n.p./Ving
❏ care for s/o　關照 s/o
❏ take care of n.p./Ving　照料 n.p./Ving
❏ deal with n.p./Ving　處理 n.p./Ving
❏ get rid of n.p./Ving　送走 n.p./Ving
❏ quality of life　生活品質
❏ manage to V　勉力 V
❏ suffer from n.p./Ving　苦於 n.p./Ving
❏ treat s/th with s/th　以 s/th 來對待 s/th

☆ 必須確認哪些語塊要接受詞、哪些不用，並注意不同類型的受詞：(s/o) 或 (s/th)。

☆ 請留意這些語塊是否全都必須用 n.p.、v.p.、Ving 或 V。並且別忘了使用這些語塊時動詞的時態要正確。

☆ 在使用 be ethical (for s/o) (to V) 時，不需要指明應該要符合道德倫理的人。而在用 to V 來指明符合道德倫理的活動時，必須用 it 來當主詞：It is not ethical (for doctors) to do this. 正確；Doctors are not ethical to do this. 則是錯的。注意，在表示否定時，可以用字首 un-，或是可以用 not 把動詞變為否定：It is not ethical.、It's unethical. 都正確。

☆ 請特別留意 care 這個字的用法。這個字會搞混是因為它可以是名詞或動詞。care for s/o 意指某人對你很重要；care about s/th 則意指 to be concerned about s/th（各位或許還記得在 Unit 1 中學過）；I don't care about that. 的意思就是 That is not my concern.。此外，take care of s/o 意指在人患病時加以照顧：The nurse took really good care of me.。注意，許多人會說 I care you，但這是錯誤的說法，請留心不要犯這樣的錯。

☆ 注意，在使用 get rid of 時，不可以漏掉 of。

☆ 在提到生活品質時，應該說 quality of life，而不是 life quality 或 standard of life。這個語塊必須連同動詞 have 使用。

☆ manage to 意指成功地完成困難之事。

☆ treat 有兩個意思。首先可以用它來描述和其他人的相處方式：She always treated her employees well.；或者也可以用於醫療上的意義：She treated the illness with drugs.。在使用 treat 時，第一個受詞可以是疾病的名稱或病情，或者是受到治療的人。第二個受詞可以是醫療的名稱或療法的類型：The doctor treated the cancer with chemo.、He treated her with chemo.。這個語塊也能以被動來使用：People should be treated with respect.。

☆ 請務必記得，在學習和使用語塊時須特別注意小詞、字尾和語塊的結尾這些細節，確保使用上完全準確。

　　下一個 Task 將聚焦於大家在使用這些語塊時經常會犯的錯誤。

Task 24

請改正這些句子中使用語塊的常見錯誤。

① Do you really care me? Can I believe you?

② Doctors must always ethical.

_____

③ He was on the point of death, but doctors manage to save him.

_____

④ I don't care this, it's none of my business.

_____

⑤ It unethical for nurses to disobey doctors.

_____

⑥ It's important that terminal patients have a good quality life.

_____

⑦ It's not ethic to tell the patient's family.

_____

⑧ Many patients cannot deal pain.

_____

⑨ She is suffering a variety of serious conditions.

_____

⑩ The doctor got rid the visitors so the patient could rest.

_____

⑪ The medical staff took care her during her illness.

_____

⑫ They usually treat morphine with pain.

---

① Do you really <u>care **for**</u> me? Can I believe you?
　你真的關心我嗎？我能相信你嗎？

② Doctors must always **be** ethical. 醫生必須始終合乎道德規範。

③ He was on the point of death, but doctors manag**ed** to save him.
　他在死亡的邊緣，但醫生設法挽救了他。

④ I don't care **about** this, it's none of my business.
　我並不在乎這個，這不關我的事。

⑤ It'**s** unethical for nurses to disobey doctors. 護理師違背醫生是不符合倫理的。

⑥ It's important that terminal patients have a good quality **of** life.
　末期病患有良好的生活品質很重要。

⑦ It's not ethic**al** to tell the patient's family. 告訴病人的家屬是不符合倫理的。

⑧ Many patients cannot deal **with** pain. 很多病患無法忍受疼痛。

⑨ She is suffering **from** a variety of serious conditions. 她正苦於各種嚴重的情況。

⑩ The doctor got rid **of** the visitors so the patient could rest.
　醫生送走了訪客，好讓病患能休息。

⑪ The medical staff took care **of** her during her illness.
　醫療人員在她患病的期間照料她。

⑫ They usually treat **pain** with **morphine**. 他們通常是以嗎啡來治療疼痛。

☆ 我已經把錯誤的部分標示出來，各位可以清楚看出哪裡用錯了。

☆ 請將 Task 24 的句子與關鍵語庫 ❷ 的語塊做比較，以確保能清楚看出句中哪
　裡用錯了。

☆ 請留意到第 3 句的錯誤在於動詞時態。而在第 2、5 句裡，記得要用 be 動詞。
　別忘了聚焦在動詞上！

☆ 請將正確句子中的完整語塊畫上底線（參照第 1 句的示範），這能幫助你完整
　而正確地記住語塊。

下一個練習對於記憶語塊將有非常大的幫助。記住，多閱讀有助於擴充字彙量，而在文章上下文脈絡中查看大量語塊則能幫助你記憶新的用語。

Task 25

請從 Task 1 和 Task 2 的閱讀文章中找出關鍵語庫 ❷ 列出的所有語塊，並留意這些語塊在文章中是如何使用的。

Task 26

現在請嘗試用前面學過的語塊來寫出你自己的句子。

關鍵字語塊	造句
be (un)ethical (for s/o) (to V)	
care about n.p./Ving	
care for s/o	
take care of n.p./Ving	
deal with n.p./Ving	
get rid of n.p./Ving	
quality of life	
manage to V	
suffer from n.p./Ving	

treat s/th with s/th	

....

☆ 我顯然無法在此改正你的句子，但你可以透過確認語塊所有的小細節，自行改正。再次提醒在寫作中運用語塊時，須特別注意小詞、字尾和語塊的結尾，無論所需要的是 n.p.、v.p.、Ving 還是 V，並且確保你所使用的語塊是完整的。

5 個可作動詞或名詞的單字
5 words which can be verbs or nouns

語塊通常會視關鍵字是名詞或動詞而有所不同，現在我們要來看 5 個動詞和名詞同形的單字，並學習使用正確的語塊。

Task 27

請看以下幾個名詞和動詞同形的單字。

關鍵語庫 ❸

關鍵字	名詞字義	動詞字義
burden	重擔；沉重的責任	加負擔於；煩擾；使負荷
cure	治療；療法；療程	治癒；消除（弊病等）；受治療
practice	（醫生、律師等）工作；實施；習慣、常規	開業從事；實行；練習
pressure	壓力；壓迫	迫使；對……施加壓力
request	要求、請求；請求的事；需求	要求、請求；請求給予

Task 28

閱讀句子並判斷關鍵字是動詞或名詞，填入 V 或 N。

① _____ Doctors have to **practice** medicine for many years before they can get a senior position.

② _____ It can be a great financial **burden** on the family.

③ _____ Having a sick family member often places great **pressure** on the whole family.

④ _____ The patient made a **request** for euthanasia.

⑤ _____ You need to apply **pressure** to the wound, like this.

⑥ _____ They **cured** her illness with the new drugs.

⑦ _____ Often patients don't want to **burden** their family with their suffering.

⑧ _____ She developed a good **practice** after a few years.

⑨ _____ The **cure** is often worse than the illness.

⑩ _____ Doctors must not **pressure** vulnerable patients into accepting termination of treatment.

⑪ _____ The patient can **request** more painkiller if they need it.

⑫ _____ He decided to take up the **practice** of medicine.

✅ 答案・中譯・說明

① <u>V</u> 醫生必須執業行醫多年才能得到高級的職位。

② <u>N</u> 它可能會是這個家庭很大的經濟負擔。

③ <u>N</u> 有家庭成員生病常會對全家人造成很大的壓力。

④ <u>N</u> 病患提出了安樂死的請求。

⑤ <u>N</u> 你需要對傷口加壓，就像這樣。

⑥ <u>V</u> 他們是以新藥來治癒她的病症。

⑦ <u>V</u> 通常病患都不想因為自己的苦痛而造成家人的負擔。

⑧ <u>N</u> 她在幾年後養成了一個良好的習慣。

⑨ <u>N</u> 治療之路往往比疾病本身更糟糕。

⑩ <u>V</u> 醫生不可施壓弱勢的病患接受終止治療。

⑪ <u>V</u> 假如需要的話，病患可以要求更多的止痛藥。

⑫ <u>N</u> 他決定開始從事醫療的工作。

☆ 能夠掌握這些字在動詞語塊和名詞語塊上的差別是非常重要的。接下來的練習將幫助各位更加熟悉相關用法。

Task 29

請看以下所彙整的語塊及用法說明。

關鍵字語塊	關鍵字詞性	例句 & 翻譯
burden (of s/th) (on s/o)	*nc*	Her illness placed a great burden of increased financial strain on the family. 她的病對家庭造成很大的負擔在於增加了財務壓力。
burden s/o (with s/th)	*vt*	Patients don't want to burden family with their troubles. 患者不想讓家人負擔他們的煩惱。
cure (for n.p.)	*nc*	They are still looking for a cure for cancer. 他們還在尋找癌症的治癒方法。
cure s/th	*vt*	They cured his disease. They cured him. 他們治癒了他的病症。他們治癒了他。
practice	*nc*	She has a busy practice, with six nurses and many patients. 她的診所業務很忙，有六位護理師及很多病患。
practice (of s/th)	*nu*	The practice of medicine has always been a noble one. 醫療業向來都是崇高之業。
practice	*vt*	He practiced medicine for twenty years. 他執業行醫了二十年。
pressure (of s/th) (on s/o)	*nu*	The pressure of his illness on his family was extreme. 他的病對家庭造成的壓力極大。 The illness put a lot of pressure on his family. 病症對他的家人產生了很大的壓力。
be under pressure	*nu*	The whole family was under quite a lot of pressure. 全家人都承受了相當大的壓力。
pressure s/o (into n.p./ Ving)	*vt*	They pressured him into asking for euthanasia. He was pressured into it. 他們迫使他請求安樂死。他是被迫做這件事的。

PART 2

| request for | *nc* | She put in a request to see the doctor.
她提出了看醫生的要求。 |
| request s/th | *vt* | She requested some time alone.
她要求獨處一段時間。 |

☆ 須留意哪些名詞是可數，哪些是不可數。且別忘了以正確的時態來使用動詞。

☆ burden 當名詞來用時，若想要指明承擔這個負擔的是誰，就需要用 on；若想要指明這個負擔是什麼，就用 of。另外，在描述行動時，它要連同動詞 place 或 put 來使用，若是描述狀態則要用 be 動詞。而 burden 當動詞來用時，必須使用人員受詞，若是要指明負擔的類型，必須使用 with。請仔細看例句。

☆ cure 當名詞使用時，如果想要具體說明被治癒的病症，就需要用 for。而 當 cure 作動詞用時，必須記得加上受詞，這個受詞可以是一種病症或一個人。

☆ practice 這個字當可數名詞時，在醫療英文中有非常特定的意思。它意指由一名醫生或一群醫生所經營的業務，包含了其他任何人員，諸如護理師和病患。請看第一個例句。這個名詞也能用為比較概括的意義 profession。假如想要指明執業的類型，就需要用 of。另外，practice 可當作動詞來描述醫生或其他醫療專業人士的專業活動。在英式英文中，該動詞是以 s 來拼成：practise。

☆ pressure 當名詞有兩個意思。首先可以用動詞 apply ... to 來描述實際的物理壓力：Please apply pressure to this spot.；或者在比喻的意義上用來指壓迫：They are all under a lot of pressure. 意即他們全都受到壓迫。pressure 當名詞來用時，可以連同動詞 put 或 place 來使用，若想要指明承受壓力的是什麼，就應該使用 on，而 under pressure 可連同 be 動詞來使用，用以描述被動。請仔細看 pressure 當名詞來用的例句。另外，pressure 當動詞時，必須有人員受詞，若想要指明壓力是什麼，就需要使用 into。注意，pressure 當動詞時，也能以被動來使用：She was pressured into it by her doctor.。請看例句。

☆ request 當名詞，並想要指明受要求的是什麼時，就需要搭配動詞 put in 或 make 來使用。注意，request 當動詞來用時，請記得必須給它受詞，而且不可以用 for：She requested for some time alone. 是錯的，She requested some time alone. 才正確。

☆ 請仔細學習這些語塊，並聚焦於諸如介系詞這些細節。

好的，現在讓我們來嘗試正確使用這些語塊。

Task 30

請選用正確形式的單字或語塊，完成下列各句。

① **cure/cure for**

As yet, there is no _____ the illness.

② **burden on people/burden people with**

Depressed people often feel they don't want to _____ their problems.

③ **practice/practiced**

He _____ acupuncture for ten years.

④ **pressure into/pressured into**

Many people felt that she had been _____ the decision by her doctor.

⑤ **practise/practice of**

Only special people are attracted to the _____ medicine.

⑥ **pressure on/pressure to**

Please apply _____ the vein.

⑦ **burden on/burden**

Severe illness can put a severe _____ a family's finances.

⑧ **request/request for**

She made a _____ more painkiller.

⑨ **requested for/requested**

The doctor has _____ all family members to be present.

⑩ **pressure/pressure on**

The flu puts great _____ the body's immune system.

⑪ **practice/practices**

There are three medical _____ in our town.

⑫ **cure/cured**

They _____ him the first time he went to the hospital.

⑬ **pressure on/under pressure**

Your immune system is _____.

✅ 答案・中譯・說明   🎧 Track 6.5

① As yet, there is no <u>cure for</u> the illness. 這種病症迄今尚無治癒之道。

② Depressed people often feel they don't want to burden people with their problems.
抑鬱的人往往覺得不希望因為自己的問題而去煩擾別人。

③ He practiced acupuncture for ten years. 他練習針灸十年了。

④ Many people felt that she had been pressured into the decision by her doctor.
很多人覺得，她是迫於醫生的壓力才做出這個決定的。

⑤ Only special people are attracted to the practice of medicine.
只有特殊的人會被行醫工作所吸引。

⑥ Please apply pressure to the vein. 請對靜脈加壓。

⑦ Severe illness can put a severe burden on a family's finances.
重症可能會對家庭的財務造成嚴重負擔。

⑧ She made a request for more painkiller. 她要求要更多止痛藥。

⑨ The doctor has requested all family members to be present.
醫生要求所有的家屬都到場。

⑩ The flu puts great pressure on the body's immune system.
流感對身體的免疫系統造成很大的壓力。

⑪ There are three medical practices in our town. 我們鎮上有三家醫療院所。

⑫ They cured him the first time he went to the hospital.
他第一次去醫院時,他們就把他治癒了。

⑬ Your immune system is under pressure. 你的免疫系統承受了壓力。

. . . .

☆ 記得確認所使用的動詞時態都正確。

☆ 請拿正確的句子來與關鍵語庫 ❹ 的語塊做比較,確保名詞或動詞語塊都用得
正確。

☆ 請將正確句子中的完整語塊畫上底線(參照第 1 句的示範)。這將有助於各位
把語塊完整而正確地記起來。

請詳讀本單元開頭的閱讀文章,並從中把這 5 個動詞和名詞同形的關
鍵字語塊全部找到。再次提醒,盡可能地多閱讀有助於擴充字彙量,而在
文章上下文脈絡中查看大量語塊則能幫助你記憶新的用語。

Task 31

請從 Task 1 和 Task 2 的閱讀文章中找出關鍵語庫 ❹ 列出的所有語塊,並
留意這些語塊在文章中是當動詞還是名詞使用?

Task 32

請練習用關鍵語庫 ❹ 的語塊來造句。

關鍵字語塊	造句
burden (of s/th) (on s/o)	
burden s/o (with s/th)	

cure (for n.p.)	
cure s/th	
practice	
practice (of s/th)	
practice	
pressure (of s/th) (on s/o)	
be under pressure	
pressure s/o (into n.p./ Ving)	
request for	
request s/th	

☆ 我顯然無法在此來改正你的句子，但你可以透過確認語塊所有的小細節，自行改正。再次提醒在寫作中運用語塊時，須特別注意小詞、字尾和語塊的結尾，無論所需要的是 n.p.、v.p.、Ving 還是 V，並且確保你所使用的語塊是完整的。

5 個談論或寫作安樂死與醫療倫理時常用的片語動詞 5 phrasal verbs for talking or writing about euthanasia and medical ethics

我們現在要來看一些在寫作或談論安樂死與醫療倫理時，常會用到的片語動詞。

Task 33

研讀語庫中的片語動詞、例句和其下的說明。

關鍵語庫 **5** (◎) Track 6.6

片語動詞	例句
pass out 失去意識、昏厥	• The patient has passed out. 病患昏倒了。
pass away 過世	• Unfortunately, he passed away during the operation. 他在手術中不幸過世了。
come down with s/th 染上……病 （開始苦於傳染病的症狀）	• I think I'm coming down with the flu. I don't feel well at all. Are you coming down with it too? 我想我染上了流感。我感覺一點都不好。你是不是也得到了？
pull through 從嚴重的病症或受傷中復原	• I don't think she's going to pull through. She will probably die in a few hours. 我不認為她會挺得過去。她八成過幾個小時就會死去。
get over s/th 從嚴重的病症或精神危機中復原	• When her husband died, she never got over it. 當丈夫去世後，她就一直未能釋懷。 • She never got over the death of her husband. 她從來都沒有從丈夫死亡的傷痛中恢復過來。

☆ 一定要非常留心動詞有沒有受詞 (s/th)，以及這個受詞是擺在哪個位置。請仔細確認上方語庫中的片語動詞及其受詞的位置。

☆ 在使用 come down with s/th 和 get over s/th 時，兩類的受詞——名詞和代名詞都必須接在介系詞之後。請仔細看例句。

☆ 語庫中其他的片語動詞都沒有受詞。

☆ 請記得片語動詞是動詞，所以你也必須想到所用動詞的時態。

下一個練習將有助於各位聚焦於受詞的正確擺放位置這些細節上。

Task 34

下列各句中的第一個字是正確的，請按照順序將其後的字詞重組成正確的句子。

EX. **She so passed blood she lost out much that**

She lost so much blood that she passed out.

① Do will think through you she pull ?

_____

② He to cancer away due passed

_____

③ I don't get leaving I will my ever think over boyfriend me

_____

④ Many coming with the colleagues of are down my flu

_____

⑤ The out made several him pass pain times

_____

① Do you think she will <u>pull through</u>? 你認為她會熬過去嗎？

② He passed away due to cancer. 他因癌症而過世。

③ I don't think I will ever get over my boyfriend leaving me.
　我想我永遠都無法忘懷我男朋友離我而去的事。

④ Many of my colleagues are coming down with the flu.
　我的很多同事都得到流感。

⑤ The pain made him pass out several times. 疼痛使他昏倒了好幾次。

··

☆ 將正確的句子與關鍵語庫 ❺ 中的片語動詞做比較，確認你的用法都正確。

☆ 請將正確句子中的片語動詞畫上底線，這將幫助你完整而正確地把語塊記起
　來。（參照第 1 句的示範）

　　現在來看看這些片語動詞是如何運用在文章脈絡中。

Task 35

請從 Task 1 和 Task 2 的閱讀文章中找出關鍵語庫 ❺ 列出的所有片語動詞，
並留意它們在文章中是如何使用的。

Task 36

請練習用關鍵語庫 ❺ 的片語動詞來造句。

片語動詞	造句練習
pass out	
pass away	
come down with s/th	

pull through	
get over s/th	

....

☆ 再次提醒，在寫作時若運用到這些片語動詞，要特別留意動詞的時態和受詞的位置。

5 個談論或寫作安樂死與醫療倫理時常用的慣用語 5 idioms for talking or writing about euthanasia and medical ethics

現在來看看在寫作或談論這個主題時，所能運用的一些慣用語。

Task 37

研讀語庫中的慣用語、例句和其下的說明。

關鍵語庫 ❻　 Track 6.8

慣用語	例句
bitter pill to swallow 不得不忍受的苦事； 難以接受的事	• She has terminal cancer. This news is a very bitter pill to swallow. 她得了末期癌症。這個消息真是令人難以接受。
just what the doctor ordered 正合需要；問題的完美解方（不一定是在醫療上）	• I was so tired I took a day off work and stayed in bed. I felt much better the next day. It was just what the doctor ordered. 我累到請了一天假沒上班並躺在床上。隔天我就覺得好多了。這正是我所需要的。
go/be under the knife 接受手術、開刀	• He passed away while he was under the knife. It was a difficult operation and his chances were small. 他在接受手術時過世了。這是一個困難的手術，他的機會很小。
behind s/o's back 在某人不知情下做某事	• They will always gossip about you behind your back. Be careful what you say to them! 他們總會在你的背後說閒話。對他們說話要小心！
be up in arms about s/th 憤怒抗議某事；強烈反對	• They are up in arms about the new rules for doctors. 他們強烈反對對醫生的新規定。

☆ 使用慣用語時唯一能更動的是動詞時態，或者在此處的某些案例中則是代名詞。

☆ 為了讓慣用語有意義，它必須完全準確才行，這意味著你必須將慣用語的所有細節都使用正確。

☆ 請注意這幾個慣用語都沒有受詞，不要連同受詞來使用。

下一個練習將有助於各位聚焦於使用這些慣用語時，經常會犯的錯誤。

Task 38

改正這些句子中的常見錯誤。

① A nice cup of tea is just what I ordered from the doctor.

_____

② They lifted up their arms in anger about it.

_____

③ I'm going under a knife tomorrow. I'm nervous.

_____

④ The news was a bitter medicine to swallow.

_____

⑤ They often laugh about him behind a back.

_____

⑥ The doctor gave him a bitter pill to swallow.

_____

✔ 答案・中譯・說明　◎ Track 6.9

① A nice cup of tea is just what the doctor ordered. 一杯好茶正合我意。

② They were up in arms about it. 他們對這件事強烈反對。

③ I'm going under the knife tomorrow. I'm nervous.
   我明天就要動手術了。我很緊張。

④ The news was a bitter pill to swallow. 這個消息令人難以接受。

⑤ They often laugh about him behind his back. 他們常在他背後嘲笑他。

⑥ ~~The doctor gave him a bitter pill to swallow.~~ ~~醫生給了他難吞的苦藥。~~

....

☆ 不要在一個不該有受詞的地方加上了受詞。

☆ 在第 5 句中，代名詞必須配合主題。此處的主題是 him，所以需要用 his。

☆ 請注意，第 6 句完全是錯誤的。因為慣用語是在隱喻，而這一句不是以隱喻的
   意義來使用，它在此是照字面的意思，意指醫生給了他一些難吞的藥。這不是
   慣用語的正確用法。

☆ 請仔細比較錯誤句子和正確解答，務必確實掌握錯在哪以及為什麼是錯的。

　　現在我們要練習的是，在文章上下文中找出慣用語。

Task 39

請從 Task 1 和 Task 2 的閱讀文章中找出關鍵語庫 ❻ 列出的所有慣用語，
並留意它們在文章中是如何使用的。

Task 40

請練習用關鍵語庫 ❻ 的慣用語來造句。

慣用語	造句練習
bitter pill to swallow	
just what the doctor ordered	
go/be under the knife	

behind s/o's back	
be up in arms about s/th	

☆ 再次提醒在寫作時若運用到這些慣用語，要特別留意動詞的時態和完整的慣用語包含哪些細節。

❏ 在試著針對容易搞混的單字去了解差別時,需要思考的不僅是意思上的差異,還有文法和用法。

❏ 別忘了,有些單字只能用在特定的主題上,用在別的主題則不適當。

❏ 另外要記得,容易搞混的單字,其差別常常是在搭配詞的使用上有所不同。

在做接下來幾個練習時,務必記得這些重點。

Task 41

請仔細研讀各組易混淆的字詞、例句和其下的說明。

關鍵語庫 ❼ 🔊 **Track 6.10**

易混淆字詞	例句
1	**be ill** (*adj.*) 生病	• She is actually quite seriously ill and might die. 她實際上病得相當重,可能會死。
	be sick (*adj.*) 生病的;對……厭煩的	• I am sick of this nonsense. 我受夠了這些廢話。 • The economy is sick. 經濟病了(不景氣)。 • Your ideas are quite sick. 你的觀念蠻病態的。 • The little boy was sick in the car. 小男孩暈車了。
2	**diagnosis** (*nc*) 診斷	• The second doctor gave the same diagnosis as the first one. 第二位醫生所給的診斷跟第一位一樣。
	prognosis (*nc*) 【醫】預後	• The prognosis is not positive. The patient will probably die quite soon. 預後並不正面。病患大概很快就會死了。

3	**treatment** (*nc*) 治療	• The treatment is working well. 治療效果很好。
	therapy (*nc*) 療法	• Her therapy included medication, counselling, and physiotherapy. 她的療法包括藥物、諮商和物理療法。
4	**prescribe** (*vt*) 開藥	• He prescribed some drugs for her illness. 他為她的病症開了一些藥。
	proscribe (*vt*) 禁絕	• This drug is proscribed in this country. 這種藥在這個國家是被禁止的。
5	**heal** (*vt*)(*vi*) 癒合、治癒	• My broken heart will never heal. 我破碎的心永遠不會癒合了。 • I can heal the wound, but not the scar. 我能治好這個傷口，但疤痕不行。
	recover (from s/th) (*vi*) 從某事中復原、 恢復	• He recovered from the illness very quickly. 他從病症中復原得非常快。 • Although she was very sick, she recovered well. 雖然她病得非常重，但復原良好。

☆ be ill 和 be sick 的意思和文法非常類似，但用法略有不同。在 Task 12 中我們學過 illness 當名詞要怎麼使用。若想要具體描述某人深受病症所苦時，則要使用 be ill。

☆ be sick 可以當成 be ill 的同義詞來使用，但 be sick 還能表達 be ill 所不能表達的情況，例如當你想要描述比較概括的糟糕狀態，而且與健康或身體無關時：the economy is sick、the idea is quite sick、his sense of humour is a bit sick。此外，若要描述你受夠了、厭倦了、對某事膩了，或者想要描述嘔吐時，也能使用 be sick of s/th：Are you going to be sick? 意即「你要吐了嗎？」。

☆ diagnosis 和 prognosis 的文法和用法相同，但意思略有不同。它們都是可數名詞，複數形為 -ses：diagnoses、prognoses，但我們幾乎從不使用這些字的複數形式。

☆ diagnosis 要連同動詞 make 或 give 來使用，描述找出病症是什麼和由什麼所

造成的過程。diagnosis 通常是短期的,並聚焦於治療。

☆ 若想要描述病症對治療會不會有反應的長期結果時,則要使用 prognosis。

☆ treatment 和 therapy 確實是非常接近的同義詞,尤其是用於醫療的主題時,但 therapy 的意思和用法比 treatment 稍微廣泛一些。

☆ 當你想要特定聚焦於用來治病的醫療時,應使用 treatment。此外,treatment 也能用於主題不是醫療時,意指「行事之道」:She gave him the silent treatment. 意指「她對他視若無睹」。

☆ 而若想要描述以比較一般的方法來使人好轉時,則應使用 therapy。therapy 也能用於比較整體的醫療取向,諸如 art therapy、music therapy、speech therapy 等等。這些療法並不能使用 treatment。

☆ prescribe 和 proscribe 的文法相當類似,但意思和用法非常不同。首先要注意,這兩個字都是動詞,所以必須確認所用的時態是否正確。prescribe 是用來描述醫生決定要用什麼藥來治病的過程,這個字的名詞是 prescription。而 proscribe 則是用來描述事物遭到禁止,這個動詞通常應該要以被動來使用。

☆ heal 和 recover 的文法和意思相似,但用法略有不同。它們都是意指在某些健康問題後有所好轉,但各自的健康問題則略有不同。使用 heal 時,它的主詞應為病症或傷口:The wound healed very quickly. 正確;The patient healed very quickly. 則是錯的。但使用 recover 時,主詞則必須用人:The patient recovered very quickly. 正確;The wound recovered very quickly. 則是錯的。注意,這兩個字都是動詞,所以必須對所用的時態非常留心。

☆ 當你要具體描述一個傷口,或是身上破碎或受損的東西時,要使用 heal。這個動詞加受詞或不加受詞都可以,而且在描述精神上的痛苦時,也能使用這個動詞。請看例句。

☆ 若要描述病情好轉的一般過程時,則要使用 recover。這個動詞不能用來描述傷口或破碎的東西,如果要指明病症,就必須使用 from 且加上一個受詞。請看例句。

在做下一個練習時,請仔細思考句意、文法和用法來選出正確的單字。

Task 42

請選出正確的字詞來填入下列各句。

① **treatment/therapy**

He got VIP _____ after winning the Oscar for best actor.

② **be very ill/was very ill**

He _____ for a while and then recovered.

③ **recovered/healed**

Her broken heart never _____.

④ **prognosis/diagnosis**

Her _____ is quite good, she will be on her feet in a few months.

⑤ **sick/ill**

I'm getting quite _____ of being ill.

⑥ **sick/illness**

She is still quite _____, so we are going to keep her in the hospital for one more night.

⑦ **recovered/recovered from**

She _____ her illness in record time.

⑧ **was sick/was ill**

She _____ all over her coat. The smell was disgusting.

⑨ **diagnosis/prognosis**

The _____ was wrong, so the treatment was also wrong.

⑩ **proscribed/prescribed**

The doctor _____ some very strong painkillers.

⑪ **therapy/treatment**

The first doctor prescribed music _____, but that didn't work at all.

⑫ **prescribed/proscribed**

The medicine the doctor wants to use is actually _____ here, so we will need to find another type of drug.

PART
2

⑬ **therapy/treatment**

The _____ was very expensive because of the drugs the doctor prescribed.

⑭ **recover/heal**

The wound will _____ very quickly if you use this ointment.

✔ 答案・中譯・說明   ◉ **Track 6.11**

① He got VIP treatment after winning the Oscar for best actor.
在拿下奧斯卡最佳演員後，他獲得了貴賓級的待遇。

② He was very ill for a while and then recovered.
他有一陣子病得很重，後來復原了。

③ Her broken heart never healed. 她破碎的心從未癒合。

④ Her prognosis is quite good, she will be on her feet in a few months.
她的預後相當好，過幾個月就會康復了。

⑤ I'm getting quite sick of being ill. 我對生病變得相當厭煩。

⑥ She is still quite sick, so we are going to keep her in the hospital for one more night.
她還是病得相當重，所以我們打算讓她在醫院多住一晚。

⑦ She recovered from her illness in record time.
她在破紀錄的時間內從病症中復原。

⑧ She was sick all over her coat. The smell was disgusting.

她吐到整個外套都是。味道令人作嘔。

⑨ The diagnosis was wrong, so the treatment was also wrong.

診斷錯了，所以治療也錯了。

⑩ The doctor prescribed some very strong painkillers.

醫生開了一些非常強的止痛藥。

⑪ The first doctor prescribed music therapy, but that didn't work at all.

第一位醫生開立了音樂療法，但那一點都不見效。

⑫ The medicine the doctor wants to use is actually proscribed here, so we will need to find another type of drug.

醫生想用的藥在這裡實際上是被禁用的，所以我們需要找另一類的藥物。

⑬ The treatment was very expensive because of the drugs the doctor prescribed.

治療費用非常貴是因為這個醫生所開的藥。

⑭ The wound will heal very quickly if you use this ointment.

如果你使用這款藥膏，傷口會癒合得非常快。

....

☆ 第 1 句選填 treatment 是因為話題跟醫療並不相干。第 11 句用 therapy 是因為字詞組合 music therapy。而第 13 句的話題是關於醫生所開的藥物，所以應使用 treatment。

☆ 第 2 句需要用過去式是因為 recovered 也是過去式。請務必留意正確的動詞時態！第 5 句使用 sick 是因為語塊 be sick of。第 6 句的空格中需要的是形容詞而非名詞，因此要用 sick。而第 8 句的意思顯然是關於嘔吐，所以必須用 was sick。

☆ 第 3 句需要 healed 是因為意思與某樣破碎的東西有關，即使它只是一個隱喻。第 7 句需要用 recovered from 是因為句子裡有受詞：her illness。而第 14 句用 heal 則是因為主題是一個傷口。

☆ 第 4 句是關於疾病的長期病程，所以必須用 prognosis。而第 9 句的內容是關於治療用藥的適切性，所以應該用 diagnosis。

☆ 第 10 句選填 prescribed 是因為句子是關於醫生所推薦的藥物。而第 12 句用 proscribed 則是因為意思是該種藥物受到禁止。

最後我們還是要來練習從閱讀文章中找出這些容易搞混的單字。當你在文章中每找到一個單字，都必須停下來思考它是意指什麼、它的文法是什麼，以及它是如何使用的。

Task 43

請從 Task 1 和 Task 2 的閱讀文章中找出關鍵語庫 ❼ 列出的所有易混淆字詞，並留意它們在文章中是如何使用的。

Task 44

請練習用關鍵語庫 ❼ 的易混淆字詞來造句。

易混淆字詞	造句練習
be ill	
be sick	
diagnosis	
prognosis	
treatment	
therapy	
prescribe	
proscribe	

heal	
recover (from s/th)	

在你結束這個單元之前，請將下列清單看過，確定你能將所有要點都勾選起來。如果有一些要點你還搞不清楚，請回頭再次研讀本單元的相關部分。

☐ 我確實閱讀並理解了關於「安樂死與醫療倫理」的長篇文章。
☐ 我完全知道字彙在文章中是如何使用，並更加了解到要怎麼用單字來表達特定的主題。
☐ 我已經學會 15 個關於「安樂死與醫療倫理」主題的關鍵字，以及可與其搭配使用的動詞和形容詞。
☐ 我已經練習使用這些搭配詞來描寫「安樂死與醫療倫理」。
☐ 我已經學到了一些同義詞，也了解在運用時需要注意的一些問題。
☐ 我學到了很多關於這個主題可以運用的語塊，包括片語動詞以及名詞或動詞為同形的單字。
☐ 我已經練習使用這些語塊。
☐ 我學到了 5 個關於這個主題的慣用語，且知道如何運用。
☐ 我已經理解在運用慣用語時需要特別注意的一些問題。
☐ 關於這個主題，我已經能確實掌握一些易混淆字詞的用法。

Unit 7

基改食品與科學
GM Food and Science

閱讀文章 Reading

　　本單元所要探討的是「基因改造食品與科學」的相關議題。在這裡要閱讀的同樣也是「論證／意見」(argument/opinion) 類型的文章。

Task 1

閱讀文章並盡可能地理解文章內容。請先不要使用字典。

(1) _____ The population forecast for 2070 is expected to be around 9.4 billion, which is a huge number of people. All these people are going to need three square meals a day, which is huge amount of food to provide. Scientists have long been looking into ways to increase food production, and as it happens, GM (genetic modification) turns out to be the solution. However, people are worried about the safety of GM food, both in the long-term effects on the environment, and in the short term, on people's health; and the issue is not without controversy.

(2) _____ GM food is the branch of science called genetics. In this science, scientists take a gene from one living organism and put it into another living organism to create a new, modified organism. For example, most of the corn grown in the world today has been modified so that it can grow without the use of chemicals needed to kill insects, or that is more resistant to extreme weather conditions such as drought or heavy rainfall. According to Dr Wendy Cook, a scientist at a government-run lab that does research into food production, people's fears about GM food need to be put into perspective. "We have been altering plants for thousands of years by selective breeding," she says. "For example, rice

was originally a wild grain that humans learned to domesticate and make it easier to use by a long process of trial and error. What GM does is to speed up that process, so that instead of it taking thousands of years, it now only takes a few. It's an enormous scientific and social advance. Most people in the world live on rice, and when the crop fails, there is famine. GM can shorten the growth season of crops, so that they are ready to harvest earlier and more often. In my view, GM food is actually the best thing since sliced bread," she jokes, "because without it we would not be able to feed the global population as it currently stands, not to mention 50 years into the future."

(3) _____ We can carry out certain slight modifications to food which will benefit both the consumer and those companies who produce food. Nowadays with fewer people eating out because of the pandemic, people are buying more food and preparing it at home. However, this food soon goes off if it is not consumed quickly. One of the purposes of GM food is to lengthen this shelf life, so that the commercial food products people buy can last longer. GM can also be used to enhance the foods we eat so that they can be a source of proper nutrition. For example, we can make them contain more or fewer calories according to the needs of the consumer, and in this way we can make sure they have a healthy diet.

(4) _____ Many people are worried that it may be damaging to the health. Because it has not been around that long, we have not had the opportunity or the time to really study and assess the possible dangers of GM food, and we do not know what the long-term effects will be. Will it damage our physical or even environmental health? Some researchers claim that the sharp rise in the number of people who are allergic to more

kinds of food may be directly attributed to GM. Tom Watts is an organic farmer who is strongly opposed to any kind of GM food. "Compared with three generations ago, there is more GM food now. Most junk food that people consume nowadays, for example, is very unhealthy because it is made from GM ingredients. We just don't know if it is good for people's health, or if it will be bad for them in the long term. I wouldn't eat that kind of food for all the tea in China. I worry about the long-term impact on people's health. There have been no studies done into the potential, irreparable harm GM food could be causing. For example, there have been no tests into the possibility that we may pass on some of the genetic changes to future generations. We definitely need to research this more." Opponents like Tom recognise the pressing need for more food for future generations, but they worry that our focus on GM is like putting all our eggs in one basket. Organic agriculture may also be a way forward, they think. "Why are we risking our future on a method that might not be safe? We need to test other methods to see if they can also help to relieve the problem of global hunger, not just rely on GM."

(5) _____ "Organic farming is a different kettle of fish", she says. "It simply won't work on the scale we need if population growth continues at the current rate. It's not correct to say that GM has not been tested. Those who do hard, experimental science know that it works by rigorous and frequent testing. The scientific evidence points to the fact that GM food as we are using it today is safe and beneficial for humanity." As the debate stands at the moment, it's hard to say who is right. But listening to both sides of the argument certainly gives one plenty of food for thought.

Task 2

請從下列句子選出適當的主題句以完成 Task 1 每個段落的填空。

A Another benefit of GM food is undoubtedly commercial.

B For scientists like Dr Cook, these concerns are not appropriate.

C It turns out, however, that most people's fears are unfounded, or based on a lack of information about exactly what GM food is, and an exaggerated idea of the risks involved.

D One of the main objections to GM food is that scientists often cannot guarantee its safety standards.

E One of the most worrying predictions of the future 50 years is the amount of food needed for a growing population.

答案・中譯・說明

(1) E (2) C (3) A (4) D (5) B

譯文

　　對於未來 50 年，最令人擔憂的預測之一就是人口增長所需要的糧食量。2070 年的人口預測預計是 94 億左右，人口數龐大。所有這些人都將需要一日三頓的飽餐，待提供的糧食數量龐大。科學家長期以來一直在探尋增加糧食產量的方法，而基改（基因改造）恰好就是解決方案。不過，人們擔心基改食品的安全性，無論是對環境的長期效應，還是短期內對人們健康的影響；而且此議題並非沒有爭議。

　　然而，事實證明，大多數人的擔心是沒有根據的，或是基於對基改食品究竟是什麼缺乏確切的資訊，以及對所涉及風險的誇大想法。基改食品是所謂遺傳學的科學分支。在這門科學中，科學家是從一個活的有機體中取出基因，把它放進另一個活的有機體，以創造出新的、改造過的有機體。例如現今世界上所種植的玉米大部分都經過改良，使它們在不使用殺蟲劑的情況下就能生長，或是比較抵抗得了極端的氣候條件，諸如乾旱或大量降雨。在政府轄下對糧食生產做研究的實驗室裡，科學家 Wendy Cook 博士表示，人們對基改食品的恐懼需要持平看待。「幾千年來，我們靠著選擇性育種改變植物。」她說。「例如稻米原本是野生穀物，人們學著去栽種，並靠著嘗試錯誤的漫長過程，使它比較容易運用。基改所做的就是加速這個過程，使它不用花上成千上萬年，現在只要花上幾年。它是重大的科學與社會進步。世界上大部分的人都是靠稻米為生，當作物歉收時，就會發生饑

荒。基改能縮短作物的生長季，使它可以更早和更頻繁收成。以我的看法，基改食品實際上是有史以來最棒的東西。」她開玩笑說。「因為沒有它的話，我們在目前的情況下就會無法餵飽全球的人口，更遑論未來的 50 年。」

　　基改食品的另一個好處無疑是在商業上。我們可以對食物進行某些細微的改良，這將使消費者和那些生產糧食的公司都受惠。如今外食的人因為疫情而變少，人們開始購買更多的食物在家料理。不過，假如沒有快速消耗掉，這些食物很快就會變質。基改食品的目標之一就在於延長這樣的保質期，使民眾所買的商業食品保質期更長。基改還能用來提升我們所吃的食物，使它能當成適當營養的來源。例如我們可以根據消費者的需求，使它含有較多或較少的卡路里，而如此一來，我們就能確保他們有健康的飲食。

　　反對基改食品的主要理由之一是，科學家經常無法保證其安全標準。很多人擔心它可能會損害健康。由於它問世沒那麼久，我們沒有機會或時間來好好探究和評估基改食品的可能危險，而且我們不曉得它長期影響會是怎樣。它會損害我們的身體或者甚至是環境健康嗎？有些研究人員宣稱，對更多種食物過敏的人數激增或許可直接歸因於基改。Tom Watts 是有機農民，對任何一種基改食品都強烈反對。「比起三代以前，現在有更多的基改食品。例如現今人們所消費的垃圾食物大部分都非常不健康，因為它是由基改的食材所製成。我們不曉得它對人們的健康是不是有益，或者長期來說，它對他們會不會有害？不管再好，我都不會吃那種食物。我擔心這對眾人健康的長期影響。目前沒有針對基改食品可能造成的潛在的、無法彌補的危害所進行的研究。例如對於我們或許會把一些基因變化遺傳給未來的世代，這個可能性並沒有受過檢驗。我們必定需要多加研究這點。」像 Tom 這樣的反對者也意識到未來各代子孫對於更多食物的迫切需求，但他們擔心，聚焦於基改就像是把所有的雞蛋放在一個籃子裡。他們認為，有機農業也可能是一個前進的方向。「我們為什麼要以不見得安全的方法來拿未來冒險？我們需要測試其他的方法，看看它們是否也能幫忙紓解全球飢餓的問題，而不是光靠基改。」

　　對於像 Cook 博士這樣的科學家來說，這些疑慮並不適當。「有機農業是不同的一碼事。」她說。「假如人口繼續以目前的速率增長下去，它壓根應付不了我們所需要的規模。說基改沒有受過檢驗並不正確。那些努力從事實驗科學的人都知道，它是靠嚴格與頻繁的檢驗來運作。科學證據所指出的事實在於，我們現今所採用的基改食品對人類是安全和有益的。」就眼前的爭論來看，很難說誰是對的。但是，傾聽爭論雙方的意見肯定會帶給人不少的省思。

☆ 第一段是以概括的資訊來介紹主題，概述基改食品的重要性和爭議性。

☆ 第二和第三段用細節和例子介紹了支持基改食品的主張。

☆ 第四段是在提出相反的觀點，並呈現反對基改食品的主張，同樣有細節和例子。

☆ 最後一段是在總結，再次強調了基改食品的好處，但最終是開放看待此事。

字詞搭配 Word Partnerships

我們現在要來學習「基改食品與科學」這個主題的 15 個關鍵字，以及可搭配這些關鍵字使用的 word partnerships「字詞搭配表」。首先，請看關鍵字語庫。

Task 3

請仔細研讀這些主題字彙和下方的說明。

關鍵語庫 ❶　　⊚ **Track 7.1**

名詞	動詞	形容詞	字義
advance Ⓒ	advance	advanced	進步、前進、發展
calorie Ⓒ	-	-	卡路里
danger Ⓒ	-	dangerous	危險、威脅
diet Ⓒ	diet	-	飲食、食物
food Ⓤ	-	-	食物、食品
evidence Ⓤ	-	-	證據
growth Ⓤ	grow	grown	成長、增長
harm Ⓤ	harm	harmed	危害、損傷
health Ⓤ	-	healthy	健康（狀況）
modification Ⓒ	modify	modified	改造、修改
nutrition Ⓤ	-	nutritional	營養（物）
organism Ⓒ	-	-	有機體、生物
product Ⓒ	produce	produced	產品、產量
safety Ⓤ	save	safe	安全

| science C | - | scientific | （自然）科學 |

☆ 需留意哪些名詞是可數，哪些是不可數。而名詞是可數或不可數，有時候須視主題而定。

☆ 注意單字的其他詞性形式，包含動詞和形容詞。

☆ diet 當名詞和動詞用都行：I have a healthy diet. 是當名詞；I'm dieting. 則是當動詞，意指控制體重。

☆ 注意，food 是不可數名詞：This food is delicious. 正確；These foods are delicious. 則是錯的。

☆ evidence 這個字也是不可數名詞，必須連同單數形動詞來使用：The evidence is clear. 正確；The evidence are clear. 則是錯的。

☆ 須留意 harm 既可以當名詞，也可以當動詞使用。

☆ 請留意 health (n.) 和 healthy (adj.) 的差別。此字的這兩個形式很容易搞混，使用時要特別小心！

☆ modification 經常以複數形來使用。

☆ 請留意 safety 的不同形式。這些字非常容易搞混，務必留意！

　　接下來，我們將以 5 個關鍵字為一組，深入地學習與這些字最頻繁搭配的字詞組合及正確用法。

Task 4

請研讀這個字詞搭配表、例句和底下的說明。

搭配在前面的動詞	搭配的形容詞			關鍵字
be make	big considerable dramatic enormous great tremendous	important significant major notable rapid steady	economic educational medical political scientific social technical technological	**advance (in s/th)**

- Scientists **have made rapid technological advances**.
  科學家造就了快速的科技進步。

- There **have been enormous** and **significant advances in** the field of genetics.
  遺傳學的領域有重大而顯著的進步。

☆ 留意「進步」的不同類型。

Task 5

請研讀這個字詞搭配表、例句和底下的說明。

搭配在前面的動詞		搭配的形容詞	關鍵字
contain have	burn ~ off	more	
	count	few	**calorie**
consume	watch	fewer	
eat			

字詞搭配使用範例

- Soft drinks **contain more calories** than any other type of food.
  汽水所含的卡路里比其他任何類型的食物還多。

- If you **consume** a lot of **calories**, you need to **burn them off** to avoid putting
  on weight.　假如你消費了大量的卡路里，就必須把它燃燒掉，以免體重增加。

- I can't eat sweet food. I'm **counting** my **calories**.
  我不能吃甜食。我在計算我的卡路里。

Task 6

請研讀這個字詞搭配表、例句和底下的說明。

搭配在前面的動詞		搭配的形容詞		關鍵字
be exposed to face be in poses~to sth involve be aware of assess foresee	identify realize recognize spot lessen minimize reduce avoid ignore	big considerable enormous extreme grave great serious real terrible	immediate imminent impending constant possible	**danger (of s/th)**

字詞搭配使用範例

- We need to **be aware of** the **possible grave dangers of** GM food.
  我們必須意識到基改食品可能存在的嚴重危險。

- GM **poses a great danger to** the environment that we cannot yet foresee.
  基改對環境造成了我們還無法預見的極大危險。

☆ 使用 pose 時，介系詞必須用 to，而不是 of。

☆ 注意，be in danger of 是語塊，不可以用 be in the danger of。

Task 7

請研讀這個字詞搭配表、例句和底下的說明。

搭配在前面的動詞		搭配的形容詞		關鍵字
eat have live on survive on	feed s/o on be on	balanced good healthy sensible bad poor unhealthy	staple vegan vegetarian	**diet (of s/th)**

- In Asia and Africa, most people **live on** a **staple diet of** rice.
  在亞洲和非洲，大部分的人都是以稻米為主食。

- **I'm on** a **diet** because I'm trying to lose weight.
  我在節食，因為我正試著減重。

- It's not possible to **survive on** an **unhealthy diet of** American junk food.
  要靠美式垃圾食物這種不健康的飲食活下去並不可能。

☆ be on a diet 意指「嘗試減重」。

Task 8

請研讀這個字詞搭配表、例句和底下的說明。

搭配在前的動詞	搭配的形容詞			關鍵字
eat have consume enjoy like be short of go short of cook make prepare	delicious tasty adequate enough sufficient staple plain simple fine gourmet	cheap bad poor unhealthy healthy nourishing nutritious wholesome	canned cold cooked fast fresh frozen GM hot junk leftover organic processed raw rotten	**food**

字詞搭配使用範例

- The rice harvest failed this year, so hundreds of people **are short of food**.
  今年稻米收成不好，所以好幾百人糧食短缺。

- Most people in the world don't **consume enough food**.

  世界上大部分的人都沒有充足的糧食可消耗。
- Most of the **food** people **eat** in the developed world is quite **unhealthy**.

  在已開發世界，人們所吃的食物泰半都相當不健康。

....

☆ be short of 是指「沒有足夠的」。

Task 9

請從 Task 4 到 Task 8 中選出正確形式的字詞，完成以下段落填空。

Thanks to the fact that scientists (1) _____ (2) _____ advances (3) _____ food science, most of the food we (4) _____ nowadays is much more (5) _____ than it was 50 years ago. It is more abundant, and it (6) _____ (7) _____ calories, which makes it easier for people to (8) _____ a (9) _____ diet, and which means fewer people (10) _____ the danger (11) _____ becoming obese.

範例答案

1. have made
2. great/big/considerable/dramatic/
   enormous/tremendous
4. eat/have/consume
3. in
5. healthy/nourishing/nutritious/
   wholesome

6. has/contains
7. fewer
8. eat/have
9. balanced/good/healthy/sensible
10. face/are exposed to
11. of

....

☆ 請留意各組同義字詞，空格中選填同一組內不同的字也是可以的。

☆ 須確認所選用的單字都是正確的形式。請檢查單數或複數，以及動詞的正確形式。例如在空格 (1) 中，動詞 make 必須使用現在完成式，因為這句的意思是在說明一個結果；在空格 (6) 中，別忘了動詞必須加上 s；而在空格 (10) 中不能用 be in，因為空格後所接的字是 the。

Task 10

請研讀這個字詞搭配表、例句和底下的說明。

搭配在前面的動詞	搭配的形容詞		關鍵字	搭配在後面的動詞
be have look for collect come up with find gather offer provide show	considerable substantial clear compelling conclusive convincing good hard solid strong flimsy inadequate insufficient scant available current	anecdotal empirical experimental factual false medical scientific statistical	**evidence (for n.p.) (that v.p.)**	confirm demonstrate establish point to show suggest support

字詞搭配使用範例

- The **evidence shows that** GM food is totally safe.
  證據顯示，基改食品是完全安全的。

- We **have considerable scientific evidence that** there is no harm to the environment. 我們有相當多的科學證據可以證明對環境並沒有危害。

- Scientists **have provided compelling statistical** and **experimental evidence for** their hypothesis.
  科學家們為他們的假設提供了有說服力的統計和實驗證據。

☆ 留意到 evidence 也能作為主詞使用。
☆ 學會「證據」的不同類型。

Task 11

請研讀這個字詞搭配表、例句和底下的說明。

搭配在前面的動詞	搭配的形容詞		關鍵字	搭配在後面的名詞
be continue see achieve maintain sustain encourage promote stimulate control	considerable dramatic enormous strong tremendous fast rapid slow modest steady	long-term short-term economic industrial population	**growth (in s/th)**	season rate area industry

字詞搭配使用範例

- We need to **maintain modest growth**. 我們需要維持適度的成長。
- There **is strong growth in** this field. 這個領域有強勁的成長。
- If we cannot **control economic growth**, we will be in trouble in a few generations. 假如我們無法控制經濟成長,再過幾代後就會陷入困境。
- We **have seen tremendous growth in** the field of genetics. It's **a growth industry**. 我們在遺傳學的領域看到了巨大的成長。這是個成長的產業。

......

☆ 請留意這個名詞能構成的複合名詞。
☆ 學會說明不同類型的「成長」。

Task 12

請研讀這個字詞搭配表、例句和底下的說明。

搭配在前面的動詞	搭配的形容詞		關鍵字
cause do inflict mean come to suffer keep s/o from prevent protect s/o from	considerable great serious untold irreparable lasting permanent potential	economic emotional environmental mental physical psychological	**harm**

PART

2

字詞搭配使用範例

- GM could **cause untold harm** to future generations.
  基改可能會對後代造成無數的危害。

- The companies who control agriculture **mean no harm**, but they do actually
  inflict considerable harm on the environment.
  掌控農業的公司無意為害，但實際上他們確實對環境造成相當大的傷害。

··

☆ 學會說明「危害」的不同類型。

☆ 在使用 mean 時，通常必須以否定來使用：they mean no harm 意指「它們的
意圖不是要造成危害」。

Task 13

請研讀這個字詞搭配表、例句和底下的說明。

搭配在前面的動詞		搭配的形容詞		關鍵字
be in	recover	excellent	environmental	
have	regain	full	general	
enjoy		good	mental	
	damage	perfect	physical	
maintain	harm		public	**health**
look after	ruin	bad		
	undermine	declining		
improve		delicate		
		ill		
		poor		

字詞搭配使用範例

- The food we eat can irreparably **ruin our health**, so that often it is impossible to **recover our health** many years later. 我們所吃的食物可能會無可挽回地摧殘我們的健康，因此往往在多年後要恢復健康是不可能的。

- She **is in declining health** now, but when she was young, she **enjoyed excellent health**. 她現在的健康狀況每況愈下，可是在她年輕的時候，身體極為健康。

☆ 請留意不同類型的「健康」。

Task 14

請研讀這個字詞搭配表、例句和底下的說明。

搭配在前面的動詞		搭配的形容詞		關鍵字
involve	carry out	considerable	further	
need	introduce	extensive		
require	make	major	important	**modification**
			necessary	**(to s/th)**
cause	receive	minor	significant	
	undergo	slight		
			certain	

- The original design **is undergoing major modifications.**
  原本的設計正在進行大幅度的修改。

- Scientists **introduce slight modifications** to the genetic structure.
  科學家將微幅的改造導入基因結構。

- It **will involve some modifications to** our initial concept.
  這會牽涉到把我們起初的概念加以部分改造。

....

☆ 注意，certain modifications 意指「未經指明的改造」。certain 在此並非意指「一定」。

Task 15

請從 Task 10 到 Task 14 中選出正確形式的字詞，完成以下段落填空。

All the (1) _____ and (2) _____ evidence – meaning personal experience and tests conducted in laboratories - (3) _____ the fact that (4) _____ these (5) _____ modifications (6) _____ the genetic structure of organisms – no matter how small these modifications are - could (7) _____ (8) _____ harm to our (9) _____ and (10) _____ health – both to us and to our environment - that cannot be reversed. The (11) _____ growth (12) _____ these industries and methods needs to (13) _____, therefore.

範例答案

1. anecdotal/scientific/empirical/
   experimental/statistical
2. anecdotal/scientific/empirical/
   experimental/statistical
3. points to/shows/suggests/
   confirms/demonstrates

6. to
7. cause/do/inflict
8. irreparable/lasting/permanent
9. physical
10. environmental
11. fast/rapid

| 4. carrying out/introducing/making | 12. in |
| 5. minor/slight | 13. be controlled |

☆ 在空格 (3) 中，一定要記得加上 s，因為時態是現在簡單式，而且主詞是第三人稱。

☆ 在空格 (4) 中必須使用 Ving，因為這些字是動詞 could 的主詞：introducing modifications could ...。

Task 16

請研讀這個字詞搭配表和例句。

搭配在前的片語	搭配的形容詞		關鍵字
a/the source of ~	adequate	inadequate	
	good	poor	
搭配在前面的動詞	proper		**nutrition**
suffer from			
enjoy			
get			

字詞搭配使用範例

- Rice is **the** main **source of nutrition** for many people in the world.
  稻米是世界上許多人主要的營養來源。

- Many people in the developing world **suffer from inadequate nutrition**, while those in the developed world **enjoy good nutrition**.
  開發中國家的許多人正苦於營養不足，而已開發國家的人則享有良好的營養。

Task 17

請研讀這個字詞搭配表、例句和底下的說明。

搭配在前面的動詞	搭配的形容詞		關鍵字
be have modify	developing growing living simple complex higher modified	aquatic biological human marine	**organism**

PART

2

字詞搭配使用範例

- The sea is full of **marine organisms** that are so small they cannot be seen with the naked eye. 海裡到處都是小到用肉眼看不見的海洋生物。
- There are **simple organisms** and **complex organisms**.
  有簡單的有機體和複雜的有機體。
- Homo Sapiens is usually counted as a **higher organism**.
  智人通常被認為是較高等的有機體。

☆ 請留意「有機體（生物）」的不同類型。

Task 18

請研讀這個字詞搭配表、例句和底下的說明。

搭配在前面的動詞	搭配的形容詞		關鍵字
be buy sell market promote	innovative new quality	agricultural beauty cereal commercial consumer diary food	**product**

| develop

launch | everyday
natural
manufactured | household
industrial
meat
pharmaceutical
software
waste | **product** |
|---|---|---|---|

字詞搭配使用範例

- They **produce natural food products**. 他們是生產天然食品。
- They **launched this innovative household product** a few years ago.
  他們在幾年前推出了這款創新的家用產品。
- This **is** the most popular breakfast **cereal product** on the market.
  這是市面上最受歡迎的早餐穀片產品。

☆ 留意不同類型「產品」的說法。

Task 19

請研讀這個字詞搭配表、例句和底下的說明。

搭配在前的動詞	搭配的形容詞		關鍵字	搭配在後的名詞	
ensure
guarantee

improve

enforce | extra
greater

perfect | air
child
fire
food
home
industrial
nuclear
occupational
passenger
personal
public
road
traffic | **safety** | controls
improvements
limits
measures
precautions
procedures

guidelines
laws | standards

violation
hazard
risk

inspection |

- We need to ensure that **food safety standards** are **enforced**.
  我們需要確保食物安全標準受到落實。
- **Safety precautions** are taken in the factory to make sure that **food safety laws** are followed. 工廠內採取了安全預防措施來確保食品安全法規受到遵循。

☆ 留意「安全」的不同類型。

☆ safety 可以構成很多複合名詞，請留意哪些複合名詞有 s，哪些沒有。

Task 20

請研讀這個字詞搭配表、例句和底下的說明。

搭配在前面的動詞	搭配的形容詞		關鍵字
do work in study go against	hard basic applied experimental	agricultural environmental food marine biological medical behavioural political social computer information	**science**

- Those who **do hard science** know that it is important to keep an open mind about the result.
  那些做硬科學研究的人都知道，對結果保持開放的心態很重要。
- **Experimental science** has given us most of our technological advances.
  實驗科學為我們帶來了大部分的科技進步。
- **Hard science** allows no room for error. 硬科學不容許有失誤的空間。

- Your beliefs **go against basic science**. 你的信仰與基礎科學相悖。
- The **social sciences** include psychology and linguistics.
  社會科學包括了心理學和語言學。

....

☆ 留意「科學」的不同類型。

☆ 在這裡，hard science 並非意指困難的科學。它是指純科學。

接下來，我們來練習這最後一組 5 個單字的字詞搭配應用。

Task 21

請從 Task 16 到 Task 20 中選出正確形式的字詞，完成以下段落填空。

Those who (1) _____ (2) _____ science know that they have to (3) _____ strict safety (4) _____ to make sure the (5) _____ products they (6) _____ are totally safe for the consumer to eat. GM scientists can (7) _____ a (8) _____ organism to create new food, but they have to make sure that everyone who eats it (9) _____ (10) _____ nutrition from their food.

範例答案

1. do/work in/study
2. food
3. enforce/ensure/guarantee
4. guidelines/laws/standards
5. food

6. develop/market/promote/sell
7. modify
8. living
9. is getting
10. adequate/good/proper

....

☆ 同樣的，還是要留意各組的同義字詞。

☆ 請確認所選用的單字都是正確的形式。檢查單數或複數，以及動詞的正確形式。

記住，多閱讀有助於擴充字彙量，而在文章上下文脈絡中查看大量例子則能幫助你記憶新的用語。下一個練習對於各位記憶 15 個關鍵單字和它們的字詞搭配將有非常大的幫助。

Task 22

請從 Task 1 和 Task 2 的閱讀文章中找出關鍵語庫 ❶ 所列的 15 個關鍵字，並留意這些字在文章中是如何使用的。

常用語塊 Chunks

前面學過了字詞搭配的用法，我們現在要來學一些可用在寫作或談論基改食品和科學這類主題的 chunks「語塊」。

Task 23

研讀這些語塊和底下的說明。

關鍵語庫 ❷

Chunk
❏ be allergic to n.p./Ving　對 n.p./Ving 過敏
❏ be good (for s/o) (to V) (that v.p.)　　(to V)(that v.p.) 對 s/o 有益
❏ be bad (for s/o) (to V) (that v.p.)　　(to V)(that v.p.) 對 s/o 有害
❏ be damaging to n.p./Ving　損害 n.p./Ving
❏ be made of n.p./Ving　由 n.p./Ving 製成
❏ compared with n.p./Ving　比起 n.p./Ving
❏ pass s/th on to s/o　把 s/th 傳給 s/o
❏ worry about n.p./Ving/that v.p.　擔心 n.p./Ving/that v.p.
❏ be worried about n.p./Ving/that v.p.　擔心 n.p./Ving/that v.p.
❏ be resistant to n.p./Ving　抵抗得了 n.p./Ving

☆ 須留意這些語塊是否全都必須用 n.p.、Ving 或 V。

☆ 注意哪些語塊要接受詞、哪些不用。還要留意受詞的類型，尤其是需要使用人物受詞 (s/o) 或事物受詞 (s/th) 時。

☆ 別忘了在使用這些語塊時需要改變動詞的時態。

☆ 在使用 be good 和 be bad 時，可以在 for 之後接一個名詞受詞，也可以在 to

之後接動詞，或是在 that 之後接動詞片語，或是把它們全部加在一起：It's good for people to know that their food is safe.。

☆ 動詞 damage 和語塊 be damaging to n.p. 之間有細微的差別。當你想把重點放在「行動」時，要使用動詞：GM foods damage the soil.；而若想要描述「狀態」時，則要使用語塊：GM crops are damaging to the soil.。

☆ 在使用 be made of 時，後面必須接一種物質：It is made of wheat.；若是物質加起來不只兩種，就必須使用 be made from：It is made from wheat and soya.；而假如想要描述做出東西的人，則需要使用 be made by：It's made by scientists in a laboratory.。注意，It is made by wheat. 是很常見的錯誤。請務必要非常小心這些語塊的正確用法。

☆ 請留意到必須用 compared with，而不是 compared to。例如 Compared with organic food, GM food is cheaper. 正確；而 Compared to organic food, GM food is cheaper. 則是錯的。

PART

2

☆ 在使用 pass s/th on to s/o 時，必須以事物為第一個受詞，人物為第二個受詞。而第一個事物受詞也能擺在 on 和 to 之間，例如 They might pass their DNA on to other animals. 和 They might pass on their DNA to other animals.，兩者都正確。

☆ 請特別留意 worry 的用法。你可以把它當作動詞使用，後接 about n.p.：People worry about the safety.，或是後接 that v.p.：People worry that it is not safe.。此外，worry 的過去分詞 worried 還可以當形容詞用，同樣後接 about n.p. 或 that v.p.：People are worried about the safety.、People are worried that it might not be safe.。以上兩種用法都正確，而且意思上的差異非常少，但第二種用法比較常見，也比較自然。

☆ 請留意哪些語塊要用 be 動詞，而且別把它給忘了！

　　下一個 Task 將聚焦於大家在使用這些語塊時經常會犯的錯誤。

請改正這些句子中使用語塊的常見錯誤。

① Compare with eggs from free-range chickens, these factory-produced eggs taste terrible.

_____

② GM rice is good that eating.

_____

③ It was found that the new food damaging to people's health.

_____

④ It's good for people are concerned about it.

_____

⑤ Many people allergic to GM foods.

_____

⑥ Compared to real meat, it tastes just as good.

_____

⑦ Most of their products are made by mushrooms.

_____

⑧ People are worry about this issue.

_____

⑨ People have been found to be allergy with wheat.

_____

⑩ People worry food safety.

_____

⑪ Some GM crops damaging the environment.

_____

⑫ The burger is made from meat.

_____

⑬ The meat was made from scientists in a laboratory.

_____

⑭ These crops are resistant certain kinds of insects.

_____

⑮ They might pass their genes to other species.

_____

⑯ They might pass to other scientists their secrets.

_____

⑰ This kind of rice resistant to cold weather.

_____

⑱ Too much meat is bad to your health.

_____

⑲ When they heard the news, people are worried about it.

_____

① <u>Compar**ed** with</u> eggs from free-range chickens, these factory-produced eggs taste terrible. 與自由放養雞的蛋相比，這些工廠生產的蛋味道遭透了。

② GM rice is good **to eat**. 基改稻米吃起來很不錯。

③ It was found that the new food **was** damaging to people's health.
據發現，這種新食品會損害人們的健康。

④ It's good **that** people are concerned about it. 民眾關切它是件好事。

⑤ Many people **are** allergic to GM foods. 很多人對基改食品過敏。

⑥ Compared **with** real meat, it tastes just as good.
與真正的肉相比，它一樣好吃。

⑦ Most of their products are made **of** mushrooms.
他們的大部分產品是由菇類所製成。

⑧ People are worr**ied** about this issue. 人們很擔心這個議題。

⑨ People have been found to be allerg**ic to** wheat. 據發現人會對小麥過敏。

⑩ People worry **about** food safety. 民眾擔心食品安全。

⑪ Some GM crops **are** damaging **to** the environment.
有些基改作物對環境是有害的。

⑫ The burger is made **of** meat. 這個漢堡是用肉做的。

⑬ The meat was made **by** scientists in a laboratory.
該肉品是由科學家在實驗室裡所製成。

⑭ These crops are resistant **to** certain kinds of insects.
這些作物抵抗得了某幾種蟲。

⑮ They might pass their genes **on** to other species.

They might pass **on** their genes to other species.
它們或許會把基因傳給其他的物種。

⑯ They might pass **on their secrets** to other scientists.

They might pass **their secrets on** to other scientists.
他們或許會把機密告訴其他的科學家。

⑰ This kind of rice **is** resistant to cold weather. 這種米抵抗得了寒冷的氣候。

⑱ Too much meat is bad **for** your health. 太多肉對你的健康有害。

⑲ When they heard the news, people **were** worried about it. 人們聽到消息時都很擔心。

☆ 將 Task 24 的句子與關鍵語庫 ❷ 的語塊做比較，以確保能清楚看出句中哪裡用錯了。

☆ 第 19 句的錯誤在於動詞時態。而在第 5、11 和 17 句中，必須使用 be 動詞。別忘了聚焦在動詞上！

☆ 請將正確句子中的完整語塊畫上底線（參照第 1 句的示範），這能幫助你完整而正確地記住語塊。

Task 25

請從 Task 1 和 Task 2 的閱讀文章中找出關鍵語庫 ❷ 列出的所有語塊，並留意這些語塊在文章中是如何使用的。

Task 26

現在請嘗試用前面學過的語塊來寫出你自己的句子。

關鍵字語塊	造句
be allergic to n.p./Ving	
be good (for s/o) (to V) (that v.p.)	
be bad (for s/o) (to V) (that v.p.)	
be damaging to n.p./Ving	
be made of n.p./Ving	
compared with n.p./Ving	
pass s/th on to s/o	

worry about n.p./ Ving/that v.p.	
be worried about n.p./ Ving/that v.p.	
be resistant to n.p./ Ving	

☆ 我顯然無法在此改正你的句子，但你可以透過確認語塊所有的小細節，自行改正。再次提醒在寫作中運用語塊時，須特別注意小詞、字尾和語塊的結尾，無論所需要的是 n.p.、v.p.、Ving 還是 V，並且確保你所使用的語塊是完整的。

5 個可作動詞或名詞的單字
5 words which can be verbs or nouns

　　語塊通常會視關鍵字是名詞或動詞而有所不同，現在我們要來看 5 個動詞和名詞同形的單字，並學習使用正確的語塊。

Task 27

看以下幾個名詞和動詞同形的單字。

關鍵語庫 ❸

關鍵字	名詞字義	動詞字義
study	學習；研究；調查；課題	學習；研究；細看；努力
test	測試；檢驗；考驗	試驗；檢驗；分析；受試驗
research	（學術）研究；調查，探究	作學術研究；調查，探究
use	使用（權）；效用；益處；用途	使用；利用
risk	危險，風險；危險率	使遭受危險；冒……的風險

Task 28

閱讀句子並判斷關鍵字是動詞或名詞，填入 V 或 N。

① ＿＿＿ If we continue to **use** animals as food, the environment will suffer.

② ＿＿＿ Scientists **are researching** ways to improve crop yield.

③ ＿＿＿ The products have all been rigorously **tested**.

④ ＿＿＿ The **research** shows that there are no harmful effects.

⑤ ＿＿＿ The **risks** are well known and accepted.

⑥ ＿＿＿ The **study** of nutrition is very important.

⑦ ＿＿＿ The **tests** were inconclusive.

⑧ ＿＿＿ The **use** of antibiotics for animal farming is very dangerous.

⑨ ＿＿＿ The food has been through a variety of **tests** before it is put onto the market.

⑩ ＿＿＿ We need to **study** the effects on humans.

⑪ ＿＿＿ We **risk** a famine if we don't try to create new species of rice.

✔ 答案・中譯・說明

① V 假如我們繼續用動物來當作食物，環境就會遭殃。

② V 科學家們正在研究改善作物產量的方式。

③ V 這些產品全都被嚴格地檢驗過了。

④ N 研究顯示，這並沒有危害性的影響。

⑤ N 風險眾所皆知且為人所接受。

⑥ N 對營養學的探究非常重要。

⑦ N 檢驗結果沒有定論。

⑧ N 在動物養殖業中使用抗生素非常危險。

⑨ N 這種食品在上市前已經經過了各種檢驗。

⑩ V 我們需要研究這對人類的效果。

⑪ V 如果不嘗試創造水稻的新物種，我們要冒著遭受飢荒的風險。

Task 29

請看以下所彙整的語塊及用法說明。

關鍵語庫 ④ 🎧 **Track 7.4**

關鍵字語塊	關鍵字詞性	例句＆翻譯
study (of s/th)	nc	Further studies have shown the results are quite safe. 進一步的研究顯示，結果是相當安全的。
study s/th	vt	We need to study the impacts on the environment more. 我們需要多去研究對環境的衝擊。

test (of s/th)	*nc*	It's a test of our ingenuity. 這是對我們創意力的考驗。
test s/th	*vt*	They tested the food very carefully before they sold it. 在販售食物前，他們檢驗得非常仔細。
test (s/th) for s/th	*vi*	They tested it for allergies, but they found nothing. 他們測試了它的過敏性，但什麼都沒發現。
research (into s/th)	*nu*	They are constantly conducting research into this. 他們不斷對此做研究。
research s/th	*vt*	They are researching the possibility. 他們正在探究可能性。
use (of s/th) (for s/th)	*nc*	The use of pesticides for killing insects is very harmful. 使用殺蟲劑來殺蟲是非常有害的。
use s/th to V	*vt*	They are using chemicals to spray the land. 他們正在使用化學藥劑噴灑土地。
use s/th for n.p.	*vt*	They are using pesticides for pest control. 他們是用殺蟲劑來控制害蟲。
risk (of s/th) (to s/th)	*nc*	The risks of failure to us all are very great. 對我們大家來說，失敗的風險都非常大。
risk s/th	*vt*	They risked everything. 他們是拿一切來冒險。

☆ 須留意哪些名詞是可數，哪些是不可數。

☆ 別忘了以正確的時態來使用動詞。

☆ 在說到名詞 study 時，可以使用動詞 conduct、carry out 和 do。當 study 作為名詞使用時，若想要指明研究的主題就必須用 of，但若 study 是動詞則不需要。請仔細看關鍵語庫 ❹ 及 Task 28 裡的例句。

☆ test 當名詞使用時，若是想指明檢驗的對象就需要用 of。當動詞使用時，test s/th 和 test s/th for s/th 之間有小小的差別。假如想要表達的觀念是「做檢驗時不知道會找到什麼」，那就用 test s/th。而若想要表達的觀念是「你正在尋找某樣東西，但不知道會不會在那裡找到」，那就用 test s/th for s/th。注意，

test 當動詞時，能以被動來使用。請仔細看關鍵語庫 ❹ 及 Task 28 裡的例句。

☆ 請注意，research 當名詞時是不可數的。如果想要指明研究的主題，需要用 into，而可以和名詞 research 連用的動詞為 conduct、carry out 和 do。不過，當 research 是動詞時就不可以用 into：They are researching the possibility. 正確；They are researching into the possibility. 則是錯的。

☆ 當 use 作為名詞使用時，如果想要指明「所用的物質」，就用 of；若是想要指明「結果」，就用 to。請看例句。不過須特別留意，use 當動詞時，可以使用 to V 或 for n.p，但不能使用 for Ving：They are using pesticides for controlling insects. 是錯的；They are using pesticides for insect control. 才正確。此外，請注意這個動詞也能用於被動語態。

☆ risk 作為名詞使用時，若想要指明「風險是什麼」，需要用 of；若想要指明「結果」，則需要用 to。請看例句。注意，risk 當動詞時，不可使用 of：They risked of failure. 是錯的。

☆ 請仔細學習這些語塊，並把重點放在諸如介系詞和冠詞這些細節。

　　好的，現在讓我們來嘗試正確使用這些語塊。

Task 30

請選用正確形式的單字或語塊，完成下列各句。

① **are used/ used**

Chemicals _____ too frequently in modern farming.

② **use of antibiotics for/use for antibiotics of**

Further _____ farming is very dangerous.

③ **a test of/test**

It's _____ man's ability to shape his environment.

④ **test of/test**

Scientists _____ the new food very thoroughly.

⑤ **tested/test**

The products are all _____ carefully.

⑥ **research/researches**

The _____ will probably show that nothing is wrong with the food.

⑦ **risk to/risk of**

There is no _____ having an allergic reaction.

⑧ **research/research into**

They are doing _____ the plant's DNA.

⑨ **researching/researching into**

They are _____ the species.

⑩ **testing it for/testing**

They are _____ any possible allergic reactions.

⑪ **to better results/for better results**

They are using natural methods _____.

⑫ **risk/risk of**

They dare not _____ it.

⑬ **risks of/risks to**

They don't care about the _____ our health.

⑭ **do further study of/study of**

We need to _____ the food to find out if it's safe.

⑮ **study/study of**

We need to further _____ the safety of the food.

⑯ **to test/for testing**

We use the most rigorous methods _____ the results.

① Chemicals <u>are used</u> too frequently in modern farming.
化學藥劑太頻繁地被使用於現代農業中。

② Further use of antibiotics for farming is very dangerous.
在養殖時進一步使用抗生素是非常危險的。

③ It's a test of man's ability to shape his environment.
這是對人類形塑環境能力的考驗。

④ Scientists test the new food very thoroughly.
科學家們對新食物檢驗得非常徹底。

⑤ The products are all tested carefully. 產品全都經過精心測試。

⑥ The research will probably show that nothing is wrong with the food.
這項調查很可能會表明食物沒有任何問題。

⑦ There is no risk of having an allergic reaction.
並不具有產生過敏反應的風險。

⑧ They are doing research into the plant's DNA.
他們在針對植物的 DNA 進行研究。

⑨ They are researching the species. 他們正在研究這個物種。

⑩ They are testing it for any possible allergic reactions.
他們正針對任何可能的過敏反應在檢驗它。

⑪ They are using natural methods for better results.
他們使用天然的方法是為了更好的結果。

⑫ They dare not risk it. 他們不敢拿它來冒險。

⑬ They don't care about the risks to our health.
他們不在乎對於我們健康的風險。

⑭ We need to do further study of the food to find out if it's safe.
我們需要對食品做進一步的研究，以查明它是否安全。

⑮ We need to further study the safety of the food.
我們需要進一步探究食品的安全性。

⑯ We use the most rigorous methods to test the results.
我們是用最嚴格的方法來檢驗結果。

....

☆ 記得確認所使用的動詞時態都正確。

☆ 請拿正確的句子來與關鍵語庫 ❹ 的語塊做比較，確保名詞或動詞語塊都用得正確。

☆ 請將正確句子中的完整語塊畫上底線（參照第 1 句的示範）。這將有助於各位把語塊完整而正確地記起來。

　　請詳讀本單元開頭的閱讀文章，並從中把這 5 個動詞和名詞同形的關鍵字語塊全部找到。再次提醒，盡可能地多閱讀有助於擴充字彙量，而在文章上下文脈絡中查看大量語塊則能幫助你記憶新的用語。

Task 31

請從 Task 1 和 Task 2 的閱讀文章中找出關鍵語庫 ❹ 列出的所有語塊，並留意這些語塊在文章中是當動詞還是名詞使用？

Task 32

請練習用關鍵語庫 ❹ 的語塊來造句。

關鍵字語塊	造句
study (of s/th)	
study s/th	
test (of s/th)	
test s/th	

test (s/th) for s/th	
research (into s/th)	
research s/th	
use (of s/th) (for s/th)	
use s/th to V	
use s/th for n.p.	
risk (of s/th) (to s/th)	
risk s/th	

5 個談論或寫作基改食品與科學時常用的片語動詞 5 phrasal verbs for talking or writing about GM food and science

我們現在要來看一些在寫作或談論基改食品與科學時，常會用到的片語動詞。

Task 33

研讀語庫中的片語動詞、例句和其下的說明。

關鍵語庫 ❺　💿 Track 7.6

片語動詞	例句
go off 變得腐爛、變質	• Food goes off very quickly unless it is treated with chemicals. 食物變質得非常快，除非經過化學藥劑處理。
eat out 到餐館吃飯， 即外食	• Most people now eat out. 大部分的人現在都外食。
turn out that **v.p. /to V** 導致某事、結果 是……	• It turns out that the new meat substitute is healthier than meat. 事實證明，新的肉類替代品比肉要來得健康。 • It turned out to be a failure. 結果證明是失敗的。
live on s/th 把某物當成主要的 食物或餐飲、 靠……生活	• Most people don't have enough food to live on. 大部分的人並沒有足夠的食物來賴以為生。 • They live on rice and water. 他們是靠稻米和水為生。

look into s/th 調查某事的原因或 要怎麼做某事	• We are looking into it. 我們正在調查它。
	• We are looking into why so many people are allergic to it. 我們正在研究為什麼這麼多人對它過敏。
	• They are looking into ways to make it safer. 他們在尋找使它更安全的方式。

☆ 請記得，你必須非常留意動詞有沒有受詞 (s/th)，及這個受詞是擺在哪個位置。

☆ 留意到 go off 和 eat out 沒有受詞。

☆ 注意，turn out 沒有受詞，但如果想要說明發生了什麼事，可以用 that v.p. 或 to V。而在使用這個片語動詞時，必須用 it 來當主詞，例如 A good thing turned out. 是錯的，It turned out to be a good thing. 才正確。請仔細看例句。

☆ 使用 live on s/th 時，必須把兩類的受詞（名詞和代名詞）都放在介系詞後面。請看例句。

☆ 同樣的，在使用 look into s/th 時，名詞和代名詞這兩類受詞也必須接在介系詞後面。此外，這個片語動詞後面也能接 wh- v.p.，而不是受詞。請看例句。

☆ 請記得片語動詞是動詞，所以還必須考慮動詞要用什麼時態。

Task 34

下列各句中的第一個字是正確的，請按照順序將其後的字詞重組成正確的句子。

EX. **Most quickly off very food it not is goes if refrigerated**

Most food goes off very quickly if it is not refrigerated.

① During pandemic, eating people stopped the out

_____

② It out a positive good to turned force for be

_____

③ It no that turned there the was change to sample out

_____

④ They time fish most on of live the

_____

⑤ Scientists have fish into are the where looking gone

_____

⑥ They into urgently look to it need

_____

✅ 答案・中譯・說明　　🔊 **Track 7.7**

① During the pandemic, people stopped <u>eating out</u>.
在疫情期間，民眾都停止外食。

② It turned out to be a positive force for good.
結果證明，這是一種積極正向的力量。

③ It turned out that there was no change to the sample.
結果證明，樣本沒有變化。

④ They live on fish most of the time. 他們很多時候都是以魚為主食。

⑤ Scientists are looking into where the fish have gone.
科學家們正在調查這些魚去哪兒了。

⑥ They need to look into it urgently. 他們需要緊急調查此事。

....

☆ 將正確的句子與關鍵語庫 ❺ 中的片語動詞做比較，確認你的用法都正確。

☆ 請將正確句子中的片語動詞畫上底線。（參照第 1 句的示範）這將幫助你完整
而正確地把語塊記起來。

Task 35

請從 Task 1 和 Task 2 的閱讀文章中找出關鍵語庫 ❺ 列出的所有片語動詞，
並留意它們在文章中是如何使用的。

Task 36

請練習用關鍵語庫 ❺ 的片語動詞來造句。

片語動詞	造句練習
go off	
eat out	
turn out that v.p. /to V	
live on s/th	
look into s/th	

☆ 再次提醒在寫作時若運用到這些片語動詞時，要特別留意動詞的時態和受詞的位置。

5 個談論或寫作基改食品與科學時常用的慣用語 5 idioms for talking or writing about GM food and science

現在來看看在寫作或談論這個主題時,所能運用的一些慣用語。

Task 37

研讀語庫中的慣用語、例句和其下的說明。

關鍵語庫 6 ◎ **Track 7.8**

慣用語	例句
I wouldn't do it for all the tea in China. 即使把世上的錢全部給我,我都不會去做。	• I wouldn't eat GM food for all the tea in China. It's too risky. 不管再好,我都不會吃基改食品。它風險太大了。
(don't) put all your eggs in one basket 不拿一切來賭一把冒險,分散風險	• We shouldn't just focus on GM food to solve the problem of global hunger. We shouldn't put all our eggs in one basket. 我們不該只聚焦於用基改食品來解決全球飢餓的問題。我們不該把所有的雞蛋放在一個籃子裡。
best thing since sliced bread 有史以來最棒的事,形容某些東西非常出色	• Many people believe GM food is the best thing since sliced bread. 很多人相信基改食品是有史以來最棒的東西。
different kettle of fish 與所討論的主題截然不同的事	• We are not talking about the taste of GM food, but its convenience. That's a totally different kettle of fish. 我們在談論的不是基改食品的味道,而是其便利性。那完全是另一回事。

| **food for thought**
引人深思的事 | • His lecture has certainly given me lots of food for thought. 他的演說確實是帶給了我諸多的省思。 |

. . . .

☆ 第二個是諺語，所以必須用完整的慣用語作為固定片語，什麼都不要改，唯一能改變的是代名詞：put all my eggs in one basket。

☆ 為了讓慣用語有意義，它必須完全準確才行，這意味著你必須將慣用語的所有細節都使用正確。

☆ 注意，以上這些慣用語都不能使用受詞。

　　下一個練習將有助於各位聚焦於使用這些慣用語時，經常會犯的錯誤。

Task 38

改正這些句子中的常見錯誤。

① Can we talk about a different kettle of fish?

_____

② Do you want to put all your eggs in my basket?

_____

③ I would do it for all the tea in China.

_____

④ I wouldn't do it for all the tea in India.

_____

⑤ I wouldn't do it with all the tea in China.

_____

⑥ It's not a good idea to put all the eggs in one basket.

_____

⑦ This new scientific development is the best thing since bread was sliced.

_____

⑧ You've given me lots of food for my thoughts.

_____

✔ 答案・中譯・說明　　◎ **Track 7.9**

① ~~Can we talk about a different kettle of fish?~~

② ~~Do you want to put all your eggs in my basket.~~

③ ~~I would do it for all the tea in China.~~

④ I wouldn't do it for all the tea in China. 無論如何我都不會這麼做。

⑤ I wouldn't do it for all the tea in China. 無論如何我都不會這麼做。

⑥ It's not a good idea to put all your eggs in one basket.
　　把所有的雞蛋放在一個籃子裡不是好主意。

⑦ This new scientific development is the best thing since sliced bread.
　　這項新的科學發展是有史以來最棒的東西。

⑧ You've given me lots of food for thought. 你帶給了我諸多的省思。

....

☆ different kettle of fish 不能以第 1 句中這種方式來介紹新主題。這個慣用語只
　　能用來指出某人所說的與談話無關。

☆ 不能以第 2 句這種方式來使用 put all your eggs in one basket，這個慣用語向
　　來都必須為否定，因為它是一種警示。而且，請注意必須使用 one basket，
　　而不是 my basket。另外，在第 6 句中必須使用代名詞以搭配句子的主題。此
　　處是在警告某人，或是加以勸告，所以必須使用 your。

☆ 留意第 7 句和第 8 句的細節。

　　現在我們要練習的是，在文章上下文中找出慣用語。

Task 39

請從 Task 1 和 Task 2 的閱讀文章中找出關鍵語庫 ❻ 列出的所有慣用語，
並留意它們在文章中是如何使用的。

Task 40

請練習用關鍵語庫 ❻ 的慣用語來造句。

慣用語	造句練習
I wouldn't do it for all the tea in China.	
(don't) put all your eggs in one basket	
best thing since sliced bread	
different kettle of fish	
food for thought	

易混淆的字詞 easily confused words

- 在這部分，我們要來學習一些易混淆的單字，其中三組是聚焦於意思的差別，另外兩組單字則是聚焦於文法的差別。
- 要記得，有些單字只能用在特定的主題上，用在別的主題則不適當。
- 另外須注意，容易搞混的單字，其差別常常是在搭配詞的使用上有所不同。在做這部分的接下來幾道習題時，要記得這些重點。

Task 41

請仔細研讀各組易混淆的字詞、例句和其下的說明。

關鍵語庫 ⑦　 🔊 **Track 7.10**

	易混淆字詞	例句
1	**prediction** (*nc*) 預判；預測	• His prediction was wrong. 他的預測錯了。 • Her predictions are usually correct! 她的預判通常是正確的！
	forecast (*nc*) 預測；預報	• The weather forecast is good: it will be sunny! 氣象預報是好的：它會是晴天！ • The financial forecast for the next quarter is not good. 下一季的財務預測並不好。
2	**view** (*nc*) 看法	• What's your view? 你的看法是什麼？ • Would you like to share your views on this? 你要分享對這點的看法嗎？
	perspective (*nc*) 看待；觀點	• We need to put this into perspective. 我們得換個角度看待這件事。

3	**correct** (*adj.*) 正確的	• That is not correct. It's wrong. 這並不正確。它是錯的。
	appropriate (*adj.*) 適當的；恰當的	• This is not appropriate. Maybe we can talk about it another time? 這並不恰當。也許我們可以改天再談？
4	**amount** (*nc*) 數量；總數	• There is a huge amount of work to be done. 有大量的工作待辦。 • Large amounts of water are used in the process. 在這個過程中要使用大量的水。
	number (*nc*) 數字；數目；號碼	• There is a huge number of jobs to be done. 有大量的工作待做。 • A large number of people are required to complete the process. 需要大量的人員來完成這個過程。
5	**most** (*adv.*) 大部分的	• Most people would agree. 大部分的人都會認同。 • Most things are just like that. 大部分的東西都是像那樣。
	most of the (*adv.*) 大多數的	• Most of the people (we asked) said they agreed. （我們所問到）大多數的人都說認同。 • Most of the things (in the box) are like that. （箱子裡）大多數的東西都是像那樣。

☆ forecast 和 prediction 有相同的文法和非常類似的意思，但用法相當不同。prediction 是指比較一般的預測，而且我們知道是誰在做預測。 forecast 則是特定關於天氣或經濟事務方面的預測，而且我們不知道是誰在做預測。

☆ 將 forecast 連同 weather、financial、economic 等等來當成複合名詞使用，在這種情況下，就無法表達預測的來源。若想要表達預測從何而來時，則應使用 prediction，但 prediction 不能連同 weather、financial、economic 等等來當成複合名詞使用。

☆ view 和 perspective 有相同的文法和非常類似的意思，但用法相當不同。view 可當成 opinion 的同義詞來用：What's your view?、My view is that ... 等等。

☆ 而 perspective 也指意見，但它加上了相對重要的觀念或想法。因此在表達時若想要納入相對重要的觀念想法時，就應使用 perspective，例如 His perspective is not right. 這句話意味著他視為重要的事其實並非真的重要。另外，put s/th into perspective 意指對什麼重要和什麼不重要取得正確的看法。注意，From my perspective 也能用來當成 In my view 的同義詞，但是須留意介系詞。

☆ correct 和 appropriate 的文法相同，但意思和用法非常不同。它們的差別在於所採用的標準。總之，它們並非同義詞。

☆ 當所採用的標準是在情境之外時，就用 correct，例如談到真實性、準確度、事實等。

☆ 而當所採用的標準是來自說話者之間的處境時，就用 appropriate，例如 That is not an appropriate remark.，這句話意味著可能是時間不適合、地點不適合這種言論、該說法跟主題不搭軋，甚或是言論中包含了不適合的用語，但言論的事實準確性並未受到質疑。注意，當你想要表達否定的意思時，也可以用 inappropriate（不適當的）。

☆ amount 和 number 的意思類似，但文法和用法截然不同。它們的意思都是在描述事物的數量，而區別在於被量化的事物類型。當被量化的事物是不可數名詞時，要用 amount；而被量化的事物是可數名詞時，則使用 number。

☆ most 和 most of the 在台灣經常被誤用，所以必須非常留心。

☆ 在描述一般事物時用 most，這意味著你之前在內文或談話中並沒有提過它：Most people would agree. 意指「普遍的人」都會同意。

☆ 若想要描述特定的事物時就用 most of the，這意味著你之前在內文或談話中已經提到過它：Most of the people (we asked) said they agreed. 意指「（我們問過的）大多數人」都說同意。we asked 就是特定：先前已經提過了。

☆ 請注意，most of X 是很常見的錯誤用法，例如 Most of people agree 的說法是錯誤的，你是指一般人還是特定的人？文法錯了就意味著它沒有意義。記得，概括和特定的區別在英文裡是非常重要的。

在做下一個練習時，請仔細思考句意、文法和用法來選出正確的單字。

Task 42

請選出正確的單字來填入下列各句。

① **amount/number**

A huge _____ of radium is needed for the project.

② **view/perspective**

From my _____, GM food is of great benefit to us all.

③ **prediction/forecast**

His _____ that the experiment would succeed was correct.

④ **perspective/view**

In my _____, the science behind the experiment is correct.

⑤ **correct/appropriate**

It is not _____ to say that the earth is flat. It's nonsense.

⑥ **Most of the/Most of**

_____ problems come from mistakes with the experiments.

⑦ **Most/Most of**

_____ people think GM food is safe, but that's because they don't know the risks. .

⑧ **forecast/predictions**

So far, her _____ have all come true.

⑨ **prediction/forecast**

The economic _____ for the next few years is quite negative.

⑩ **forecast/prediction**

The _____ said it would rain this afternoon.

⑪ **amount/number**

We have a large _____ of scientists working on the project.

⑫ **view/perspective**

We need to put his remarks into _____. He may not be correct about everything.

⑬ **appropriate/correct**

What you said was _____. Everyone thought you were being rude.

答案・中譯・說明　　🔊 **Track 7.11**

① A huge amount of radium is needed for the project. 這項工程需要大量的鐳。

② From my perspective, GM food is of great benefit to us all.
在我看來，基改食品對我們所有人都有很大的好處。

③ His prediction that the experiment would succeed was correct.
他對實驗會成功的預判正確。

④ In my view, the science behind the experiment is correct.
以我的看法，這個實驗背後的科學原理是正確的。

⑤ It is not correct to say that the earth is flat. It's nonsense.
說地球是平的是不對的。它是無稽之談。

⑥ Most of the problems come from mistakes with the experiments.
大多數的問題來自於實驗時的錯誤。

⑦ Most people think GM food is safe, but that's because they don't know the risks.
大部分的人認為基改食品是安全的，但那是因為他們不知道風險。

⑧ So far, her predictions have all come true. 到目前為止，她的預言全都成真了。

⑨ The economic forecast for the next few years is quite negative.
接下來幾年的經濟預測相當負面。

⑩ The forecast said it would rain this afternoon. 預報說今天下午會下雨。

⑪ We have a large number of scientists working on the project.
我們有為數眾多的科學家在投入這項計畫。

⑫ We need to put his remarks into perspective. He may not be correct about everything. 我們需要正確地看待他的言論。他可能不是每件事都對。

⑬ What you said was inappropriate. Everyone thought you were being rude.
你說的話是不適當的。每個人都認為你很粗魯。

....

☆ 第 1 句選擇 amount 是因為 radium 不可數；而第 11 句選擇 number 則是因為 scientists 是可數的。

☆ 第 2 句需要 perspective 是因為固定片語 From my perspective；第 4 句需要 view 是因為固定片語 In my view；而第 12 句需要 perspective 是因為意思有表達出相對重要性。

☆ 在第 3 和第 8 句中必須用 prediction 是因為句子的主詞是人；而第 9 和第 10 句則因為是特定關於天氣或經濟事務方面的預測，所以要用 forecast。

☆ 第 5 句需要 correct 是因為這個陳述在事實上是不準確的；而第 13 句中，雖然我們不知道說話者所說的話在事實上是否準確，但說話者在錯誤的時間說話了，所以要用 inappropriate。

☆ 在第 6 句中提到問題是從實驗中得知，意味著這些問題是在之前就提過，也就是「特定的」，所以應該用 most of the。而第 7 句則是需要 most，再次提醒，Most of X 的用法是錯的。

　　最後我們還是要來練習從閱讀文章中找出這些容易搞混的單字。當你在文章中每找到一個單字，都必須停下來思考它是意指什麼、它的文法是什麼，以及它是如何使用的。

Task 43

請從 Task 1 和 Task 2 的閱讀文章中找出關鍵語庫 ❼ 列出的所有易混淆字詞，並留意它們在文章中是如何使用的。

Task 44

請練習用關鍵語庫 ❼ 的易混淆字詞來造句。

易混淆字詞	造句練習
prediction	
forecast	
view	
perspective	
correct	
appropriate	
amount	
number	
most	
most of the	

在你結束這個單元之前，請將下列清單看過，確定你能將所有要點都勾選起來。如果有一些要點你還搞不清楚，請回頭再次研讀本單元的相關部分。

☐ 我確實閱讀並理解了關於「基改食品與科學」的長篇文章。

☐ 我已經學會 15 個關於「基改食品與科學」主題的關鍵字，以及可與其搭配使用的動詞和形容詞。

☐ 我已經練習使用這些搭配詞來描寫「基改食品與科學」。

☐ 我已經學到了一些同義詞，也了解在運用時需要注意的一些問題。

☐ 我學到了很多關於這個主題可以運用的語塊，包括片語動詞以及名詞或動詞為同形的單字。

☐ 我已經練習使用這些語塊。

☐ 我學到了 5 個關於這個主題的慣用語，且知道如何運用。

☐ 關於這個主題，我已經能確實掌握一些易混淆字詞的用法。

Unit 8

民主與政府
Democracy and Government

閱讀文章 Reading

本單元所要探討的主題是「民主與政府」。在這裡要閱讀的同樣也是「論證／意見」(argument/opinion) 類型的文章。

Task 1

閱讀文章並盡可能地理解文章內容。請先不要使用字典。

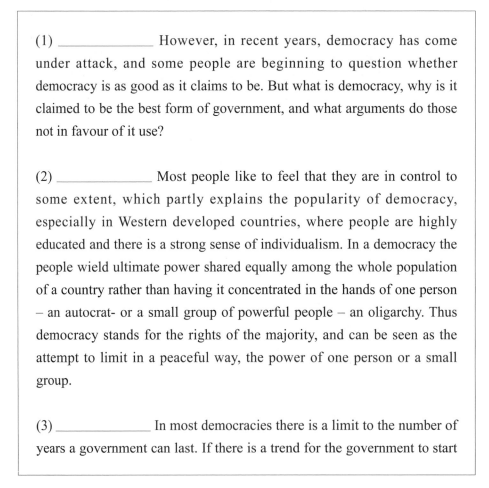

(1) _____ However, in recent years, democracy has come under attack, and some people are beginning to question whether democracy is as good as it claims to be. But what is democracy, why is it claimed to be the best form of government, and what arguments do those not in favour of it use?

(2) _____ Most people like to feel that they are in control to some extent, which partly explains the popularity of democracy, especially in Western developed countries, where people are highly educated and there is a strong sense of individualism. In a democracy the people wield ultimate power shared equally among the whole population of a country rather than having it concentrated in the hands of one person – an autocrat- or a small group of powerful people – an oligarchy. Thus democracy stands for the rights of the majority, and can be seen as the attempt to limit in a peaceful way, the power of one person or a small group.

(3) _____ In most democracies there is a limit to the number of years a government can last. If there is a trend for the government to start

adopting unpopular policies, or a leader starts to show autocratic tendencies and starts implementing unpopular measures, and thus both leader and government start to lose popular support, they can be voted out and an alternative can be voted in. On the other hand, if the government is popular, they can woo eligible voters to continue to support them and they can be voted in again.

(4) _____ In countries which have autocracy, it's difficult to do away with a leader who is unwilling to go. This means that protests become more common as people stand up for their rights. If enough people protest, this can lead to calls for anti-government revolution, which means that the transfer of power can become violent, the economy can suffer and ordinary people can lose their livelihoods and even their lives.

(5) _____ First, is the idea that career politicians in a democracy have no real desire to enact real necessary reforms because being elected again when the country holds the next general election is their only concern. Most politicians are caught between the devil and the deep blue sea. On the one hand they need to show they are effective, and on the other hand they need to get re-elected. One group of people might be happy with their performance – those who have benefitted from their policies, while another group may not – those who have not benefitted, or who have actually been harmed by their policies. Opponents of democracy argue that it's impossible to implement real necessary structural change to society while those in charge of implementing it are always changing their game plan, or simply do nothing and stand by for the next election.

(6) _____ The invention of the internet and the prevalence of

false information is a real danger and weakness of democracy. It is difficult to measure, for example, whether something is true or not, when it is all over the internet and millions of people believe it to be true. Politicians and journalists have their work cut out to make sure people have access to the real truth. The sheer number of lies on social media is related to the rise of extremist parties who put up unsuitable candidates, who, once they have achieved power though democratic means, try to subvert democracy and hold on to power indefinitely. Political history, both recent and not so recent, is rich in examples of these. We need to find ways to reduce the number of lies on the internet. If we can do this, the number of extremist political candidates might decrease.

(7) _____ Professor John Hopkins, a political researcher from Another Nameless University, says we can't really prohibit extremist groups from participating. "If we ban extremist political parties, we go against the function of democracy, the whole point of which is that everyone participates. In a modern democracy, everyone should be interested in politics, whether mainstream politics, or niche issues such as gender identity or getting involved in environmental politics. Moderates often feel inhibited by the number of extremists who want to be elected. Against their better judgement, they would rather not vote at all than vote for a candidate who is not moderate. This is a problem. We can't say to a certain group of people who have extreme views, you have to stand on the side and simply watch while all the moderates exercise their right to power. This would weaken the absolute authority of democracy. For democracy to really work, it has to represent everybody, or it represents nobody."

However, even if you want to play devil's advocate and say that democracy is finished, it is still a measure of the attractiveness of democracy as a system, that in spite of its many drawbacks, most developing countries are fighting to establish genuine multi-party democracies.

Task 2

請從下列句子選出適當的主題句以完成 Task 1 每個段落的填空。

A Another negative aspect of democracy, related to this cause, is the rise of extremism.

B Another reason for the success of democracy is that in general a government must change every few years.

C But what about the arguments against democracy?

D Democracy can also be seen as a peaceful way to carry out a transfer of power.

E Democracy is supposed to be the most perfect system of government mankind has yet devised.

F The reasons why democracy is well established in most of the Western world is that no one likes to feel that they are controlled.

G The second argument against democracy is that in this age of post-truth, it easily leads to election fraud, or elections which are not fair and open.

✔ 答案・中譯・說明

(1) E　(2) F　(3) B　(4) D　(5) C　(6) G　(7) A

譯文

　　民主政治理應是人類迄今設計出來的最完美的政府制度。不過近年來，民主卻受到了攻擊，有些人開始質疑民主是否有像它所宣稱的那麼好。但民主是什麼？為什麼被宣稱是最佳的政府形式？以及那些不贊同它的人用了哪些論點？

　　在大多數的西方國家，民主制度能得到確立的原因就在於，沒有人喜歡感覺到自己被控制了。大多數的人都喜歡感覺到自己在某種程度上是可以掌控的，這也部分解釋了民主

之所以得人心，尤其是在西方的已開發國家，人民受過高度教育，並有強烈的個人主義意識。在民主政治中，人民擁有最終極的權力，且這權力是由國家的全體人民平等共享，而不是集中於一人（獨裁者）或是一小群有權力者（寡頭政治）的手上。因此，民主象徵著多數人的權利，並可看作是試圖以和平的方式來限制一人或一小群人的權力。

民主能成功的另一個原因是，一般來說，政府必須每隔幾年就輪替一次。在大多數的民主國家都有限制政府所能執政的年數。假如政府有開始採取不得人心的政策的趨勢，或者一個領導人開始顯現出專制的傾向並開始實行不得人心的措施，因而領導人和政府都開始失去民眾的支持，則他們可以被投票淘汰，而替代者可以被投票當選。另一方面，假如政府得人心，他們能爭取到合格選民繼續支持他們，並能再次當選。

民主也能視為以和平的方式來完成權力移轉。在獨裁統治的國家，要廢除一個不願意下台的領導人很難。這意味著隨著人民捍衛自己的權利，抗議活動就會變得越來越常見。假如抗議的人夠多，可能會引起反政府革命的呼聲，這意味著權力轉移可能會變得暴力，經濟可能會遭殃，一般民眾則可能會失去生計，甚至是性命。

但是那些反對民主的論點呢？首先，有一種觀點是，民主國家的職業政客並沒有想要去實施真正必要改革的渴望，因為在該國舉行下屆大選時能否再次當選是他們唯一關切的問題。大部分的政治人物都是左右為難。一方面，他們需要證明自己稱職，另一方面，他們則需要獲得連任。一群人可能對他們的表現感到滿意——那些受惠於其政策的人，而另一群人則不見得滿意——那些沒有受惠或實際上是受到其政策所害的人。反對民主的人士認為，對社會真正必要的結構變革不可能實行，當主導實行的人總是在改變其行動策略，或者乾脆什麼都不做，以留待下一次的選舉。

反對民主的第二點主張是，在這個後真相的時代，它很容易造成選舉舞弊，或是不公平、不公開的選舉。網際網路的發明和不實資訊盛行是民主真正的危險與弱點。例如，當某件事在網際網路上到處傳播，數以百萬計的人都相信它為真時，就難以去衡量它是否為真。政治人物和新聞記者要確保民眾獲取真正的真相會傷透腦筋。社群媒體上的大量謊言與極端主義政黨的興起有關，他們推出了不合適的候選人，一旦透過民主手段取得政權，就會試著去顛覆民主，並無限期地把持權力。無論是近期或沒那麼近期的政治史上都有很多這樣的例子。我們需要設法去降低網際網路上的謊言數。假如我們能做到這點，極端主義政治候選人的數量或許就會減少。

民主與這個成因有關的另一個負向層面是極端主義的興起。另一所不具名大學的政治研究員 John Hopkins 教授說，我們無法真正禁止極端團體參與。「如果我們禁止極端主義政黨，我們將違背民主的功能，民主的關鍵要點就是每個人都參與。在現代民主中，人人都該對政治感興趣，無論是主流政治還是諸如性別、身分認同或參與環境政治等小眾議題。溫和派覺得受到想要當選的極端派人數所阻卻。在明知不可為之下，他們寧可壓根不去投票，也不願投給不是溫和派的候選人。這是個問題。我們不能對某群抱持極端看法的人說，你們必須靠邊站在一旁，僅僅是觀看，而由所有的溫和派來行使他們的權力。這

會削弱絕對民主的絕對權威。民主要想真正發揮作用，就必須代表每一個人，否則一個人都代表不了。」

不過，即使你想要唱反調說民主完了，它仍然是衡量民主制度吸引力的標準。儘管它的缺陷很多，大部分的開發中國家還是奮力要建立真正的多黨式民主。

....

☆ 第一段是在介紹主題和論點。它概括的論述是，儘管民主政治通常被視為最佳的政府形式，但還是有反對它的主張。

☆ 第二段討論了支持民主政治的一個主要論點，即民主賦予每個人權力，讓每個人都覺得自己能掌控並參與其中。

☆ 第三段提出支持民主政治的另一項論點，即權力受到任期限制。

☆ 第四段提出另一個支持民主政治的相關主張，指出民主國家中的權力轉移通常很和平，不像那些沒有民主的國家。

☆ 第五段提出了反對民主政治的否定論點。首先是，政治人物缺乏真正的實權，因為他們總是必須考慮能否獲得連任。這意味著他們做不了任何真正有意義或激進的事。

☆ 第六段所提出的另一項否定論點是關於媒體上的不實資訊對民主的衝擊。

☆ 第七段是在說明錯誤的資訊是如何導致極端主義，而這會讓很多溫和派不願去參與民主。專家說，這是民主的問題。

☆ 結論是，儘管有否定的主張，世界上大多數的國家仍然認為民主政治是最佳的政府形式。

我們現在要來學習「民主與政府」這個主題的 15 個關鍵字，以及可搭配這些關鍵字使用的「字詞搭配表」。首先，請看關鍵字語庫。

Task 3

請仔細研讀這些主題字彙和下方的說明。

關鍵語庫 ① 🎧 Track 8.1

名詞	動詞	形容詞	字義
authority Ｕ	-	-	權威、權力、當權者
candidate Ｃ	-	-	候選人、應試者
democracy Ｃ	-	democratic	民主、民主國家
election Ｃ	elect	elected	選舉、當選
government Ｃ	govern	governed	政府、政體
history Ｕ	-	historical	歷史、沿革
majority Ｕ	-	-	多數、多數黨（派）
party Ｃ	-	-	政黨、黨派
policy Ｃ	-	political	政策、方針
politician Ｃ	-	-	政治人物、政客
politics Ｕ	-	political	政治
power Ｃ	-	powerful	權力、政權
revolution Ｃ	revolt	-	革命、大變革
system Ｃ	-	systematic	制度、體制、體系
voter Ｃ	vote	-	選民、有投票權者

☆ 需留意哪些名詞是可數，哪些是不可數。

☆ 要記得，名詞是可數或不可數，有時候須視主題而定。

☆ 注意單字的其他詞性形式，包含動詞和形容詞。

☆ authority 意指權力時為不可數。它有時候有別的意思而可以是可數的，但在這個主題上，它必須作不可數名詞來使用。

☆ 注意，使用 government 時，如果有用形容詞的話，通常必須在形容詞前面加 the，若不使用形容詞的話，則直接在名詞前面加 the。而所用的動詞和任何代名詞則是單數或複數形皆可：The government are doing their best.、The government is doing its best. 都正確。

☆ majority 在此專指當選代表組成政府或發動投票的必要最低人數。majority 也能用來意指 the most，在這種情況下則必須使用 the majority of X 和複數形動詞，例如 The majority of the people are in favour. 意指「大部分的人都支持」。

☆ party 在此專指政黨。這個字有其他許多的意思和用法，但在此的主題是政治。

☆ 留意到 politics 向來都有 s，但這個字其實是不可數的，所以必須記得使用單數形動詞：Politics is a nasty business. 正確；Politic is a nasty business. 和 Politics are a nasty business. 都是錯的。

接下來，我們將以 5 個關鍵字為一組，深入地學習與這些字最頻繁搭配的字詞組合及正確用法。

Task 4

請研讀這個字詞搭配表、例句和底下的說明。

搭配在前的動詞		搭配的形容詞		關鍵字
have	give up	absolute	governmental	**authority (over s/th) (to V)**
	relinquish	complete	judicial	
assert		full	legal	
establish	abuse		parental	
exercise			presidential	
assume				
take on				

use show demonstrate	challenge defy deny rebel against reject undermine			**authority (over s/th) (to V)**

字詞搭配使用範例　🎧 **Track 8.2**（收錄本單元 Task 4~Task 20 字詞搭配使用範例）

• Autocrats **exercise absolute authority over** their people.
　獨裁者們對其人民是行使絕對權威。

• The government said the protests **challenged** its **authority**.
　政府表示，抗議活動挑戰了其權威。

• The protestors **deny the authority of** the government **to** ban protests.
　抗議人士否認政府禁止抗議活動的權力。

• The leader doesn't want to **give up** his **authority**.　領導人不想放棄他的權威。

☆ 請留意「權威」的不同類型。

Task 5

請研讀這個字詞搭配表、例句和底下的說明。

搭配在前面的動詞		搭配的形容詞		關鍵字
be have put o/self forward as stand as field nominate put up be nominated as	run as back support vote for choose select reject	potential prospective likely possible good ideal suitable unsuitable successful	congressional ministerial parliamentary presidential	**candidate (for s/th)**

- She **put herself forward as** a **candidate for** the party, but no one **voted for** her.
  她自薦為該黨的候選人，但沒人投票給她。

- He **was nominated as** a **possible congressional candidate**.
  他獲提名為可能的國會候選人。

- Our party is **fielding** a lot of **good candidates** in this election.
  本黨在這次選舉中派出了許多優秀的候選人。

☆ 留意不同類型的「候選人」。

Task 6

請研讀這個字詞搭配表、例句和底下的說明。

搭配在前面的動詞		搭配的形容詞		關鍵字
be　　　　fight for have　　　establish believe in　restore support		genuine true full political	constitutional multi-party parliamentary Western	**democracy**
搭配在前面的片語				
the road to ~ the spread of ~				

字詞搭配使用範例

- In this country we **have genuine democracy**.　在本國，我們有真正的民主。

- In many countries in the developing world they are **fighting for true democracy**.
  在開發中世界的很多國家，他們正為了真正的民主而奮戰。

- After many years as an autocracy, the country began to **restore political democracy**. But **the road to democracy** is very slow.
  歷經多年的獨裁政治，該國開始恢復政治民主。但通往民主之路非常緩慢。

☆ 留意「民主」的不同類型。

Task 7

請研讀這個字詞搭配表和例句。

搭配在前面的動詞		搭配的形容詞		關鍵字
be	stand for	fair	federal	
		free	general	
have	lose		local	
hold		democratic	local government	
	win		mayoral	
call		multi-party	municipal	**election**
	rig		national	
contest		rigged	presidential	
fight				
		fresh		
		new		
		early		

字詞搭配使用範例

- She is **standing for election**. She is an excellent candidate.
  她正參加選舉。她是優秀的候選人。

- They **are holding local government elections** this month.
  他們這個月在舉行地方政府選舉。

- Many observers are claiming the **general election was rigged**, and that it was not **free** or **fair**. We therefore need a **fresh election**.
  很多觀察人士宣稱大選受到人為操縱，它不是自由或公平的。因此，我們需要重新選舉。

Task 8

請研讀這個字詞搭配表、例句和底下的說明。

搭配在前面的動詞	搭配的形容詞		關鍵字
be　　　　swear in have 　　　　bring down elect　　destabilize 　　　　overthrow form　　topple install	left-wing right-wing coalition minority caretaker interim transitional military puppet	federal central local national provincial Communist Socialist	**government**
搭配在前面的片語			
a change of ~ the ~ of the day a member of ~ the best form of ~ the best system of ~			

PART
2

字詞搭配使用範例

- The country used to **have a military government**, but they recently **elected** an **interim government**. They are slowly moving towards full democracy.
  這個國家以往是有一個軍事政府，但他們最近推選出了一個臨時政府。他們正慢慢邁向完全的民主。

- The extremists are trying to **bring down the government**.
  極端派正試圖推翻政府。

- This crisis will **destabilize the coalition government**.
  這場危機將動搖聯合政府。

☆ 留意「政府」的不同類型。

現在，我們來看看各位是否能用一些字詞搭配來擴大對字彙的運用。

Task 9

請從 Task 4 到 Task 8 中選出正確形式的字詞，完成以下段落填空。

The country is going to (1) _____ a (2) _____ government this week, after the previous leader (3) _____ his (4) _____ authority and the people turned against him. This is the first time in many generations that the country (5) _____ (6) _____, (7) _____ elections, and although it will not be full democracy, three main parties have been formed and hope to win seats in the legislature. Many ordinary people (8) _____ (9) _____ candidates and the public has been enthusiastic about the process. The international community is strongly supporting the country on (10) _____ (11) _____ democracy.

範例答案

1. elect
2. transitional/caretaker/interim
3. abused
4. absolute/complete/full
5. will hold /will have
6. free/fair/democratic/multi-party

7. free/fair/democratic/multi-party
8. are putting themselves forward as/are standing as
9. possible/likely
10. the road to
11. genuine/true/full

☆ 請留意各組同義字詞，空格中選填同一組內不同的字也是可以的。

☆ 須確認所選用的單字都是正確的形式。請檢查單數或複數，以及動詞的正確形式。例如在空格 (3) 中的動詞 abuse 必須使用過去簡單式，因為領導人再也不在位了；在空格 (5) 中需要用 will V，因為選舉是在未來發生；而在空格 (8) 中則需要用現在進行式，因為它是還沒有結果的活動。

現在來學習另外 5 個單字。

Task 10

請研讀這個字詞搭配表、例句和底下的說明。

搭配在前面的動詞	搭配的形容詞		關鍵字
have　　　　trace go down in　distort make　　　rewrite pass into	contemporary long short early recent official recorded	ancient art cultural economic family human literary local medieval modern political world	**history (of s/th)**
搭配在前面的片語			
change the course of ~ period of ~ the rest is ~ a sense of ~			

字詞搭配使用範例

- This country **has** a **long history of** democracy.
  這個國家有悠久的民主歷史。

- His government will **go down in history** as one of the worst ever.
  他的政府將作為歷來最糟糕的政府之一而名留史冊。

- Now they are trying to **distort** and **rewrite official history** by saying the election never happened.
  現在他們正試圖扭曲和改寫官方歷史，說選舉從未發生過。

- This **period of art history** is fascinating.
  藝術史的這段時期引人入勝。

☆ 留意「歷史」的不同類型。

Task 11

請研讀這個字詞搭配表、例句和底下的說明。

搭配在前面的動詞		搭配的形容詞		關鍵字
have command	maintain retain	huge large massive overwhelming substantial	bare narrow slight slim tiny	
achieve gain get secure win	lose overturn indicate show	absolute outright overall clear simple	two-thirds increased working parliamentary government	**majority**
defend	believe in support	comfortable decisive	necessary requisite	
搭配在前面的片語				
the rights of the ~				

字詞搭配使用範例

- After the election the government **commands a massive majority**, so they can now do whatever they like.
  選舉結束後，政府獲得了絕大多數選票，所以他們現在可以做任何想做的事情。
- The government **majority was overturned** in the last election, so now they have to listen to the other parties.
  政府多數在上次的選舉中被推翻，所以現在他們必須傾聽其他政黨的意見。
- They **have gained a two-thirds working majority**, which is enough to form a government. 他們獲得了三分之二的有效多數，這足以組成一個政府。

....

☆ 若是以 majority 為句子的主詞，achieve、gain、secure、lose 和 overturn 就能以被動來使用。請看例句。

☆ 注意，你可以用幾分之幾來描述 majority：two-thirds、three-quarters 等等。

Task 12

請研讀這個字詞搭配表、例句和底下的說明。

搭配在前面的動詞		搭配的形容詞		關鍵字
establish form found set up dissolve wind up ban join	have links with expel s/o from resign from vote for elect put in power return to power become the leader of lead become a member of belong to	political centre left-wing right-wing majority minority extremist moderate opposition parliamentary governing ruling	Communist fascist populist progressive radical reactionary revolutionary democratic socialist	**party**

字詞搭配使用範例

- They **set up the party** in 1971 and since then many people have **joined** it and **become members of** it.

  他們是在 1971 年成立了該黨，此後很多人便加入成為其中一員。

- After the scandal, he **resigned from the party**. They also **expelled** many others **from** the party.

  在醜聞之後，他便退出了該黨。他們還把其他很多人從政黨中開除。

- The **party was put in power** by the people of this country.

  該黨是靠這個國家的人民來取得權力的。

- He **became the leader of** the **democratic socialist party** at a very young age.

  他在非常年輕的時候就當上了民主社會黨的領導人。

☆ 留意「政黨」的不同類型。

☆ expel s/o from、vote for、elect 和 put in power 能以被動來使用。

請研讀這個字詞搭配表、例句和底下的說明。

搭配在前的動詞	搭配的形容詞			關鍵字
be have operate implement adopt carry out follow establish develop formulate frame shape introduce	clear coherent deliberate strict controversial official public popular unpopular government	party domestic national regional international	agricultural conservation economic educational energy environmental financial foreign housing industrial immigration military pandemic social transport	**policy (of s/th)**

字詞搭配使用範例

- The government started to **implement** a **controversial immigration policy**.
  政府開始實行有爭議的移民政策。

- It's the role of government to **formulate** and **adopt domestic economic policy**.
  制定和採取國內的經濟政策是政府的角色。

- The government's **pandemic policy** is not totally **coherent**. No one
  understands it. 政府的防疫政策並非完全一致的。沒有人理解它。

- The **official policy of** deporting non-white people is quite unpopular.
  驅逐非白人的官方政策相當不得人心。

☆ 留意「政策」的不同類型。

Task 14

請研讀這個字詞搭配表、例句和底下的說明。

搭配在前面的動詞	搭配的形容詞			關鍵字
elect bribe	leading prominent senior experienced veteran	influential astute clever shrewd corrupt	career professional local left-wing right-wing	**politician**

字詞搭配使用範例

- They **elected** a **shrewd career politician** to represent their interests.
  他們推選了一位精明的職業政治人物來代表他們的利益。

- The **prominent**, but **corrupt politician was bribed**.
  那位知名但腐敗的政治人物被賄賂了。

☆ 注意，如果要以 politician 為主詞，該動詞就能以被動來使用。

Task 15

請從 Task 10 到 Task 14 中選出正確形式的字詞，完成以下段落填空。

Although the party (1) _____ a (2) _____ majority, they became hugely unpopular after their (3) _____ politician was found to be (4) _____. He was taking money and then ordering his party to carry out (5) _____ (6) _____ policies which were deeply (7) _____ as well, especially amongst environmental activists. Although he (8) _____ his party, the corruption was so deep that his party (9) _____ and all the other members had to resign. The scandal will (10) _____ the (11) _____ history (12) _____ politics in this country as one of the worst this century.

1. had/commanded	7. unpopular
2. huge/large/massive/overwhelming/substantial	8. was expelled from
3. senior/leading/prominent	9. was dissolved
4. corrupt	10. go down in
5. controversial	11. official
6. environmental/energy	12. of

☆ 注意，在空格 (1) 中，你必須使用過去簡單式，因為整段是在講歷史事件。而在空格 (8) 和 (9) 中，動詞則需要使用被動式。

現在我們來學習最後一組的 5 個單字。

Task 16

請研讀這個字詞搭配表、例句和底下的說明。

搭配在前的動詞	搭配的形容詞		關鍵字
enter go into	county local	mainstream gender	democratic electoral multiparty
abandon retire from	domestic internal national	sexual identity	party office
be interested in be involved in be active in be engaged in participate in	global international world	environmental	**politics**
dominate	contemporary modern		
reshape	practical		

- She **reshaped contemporary international politics** by her emphasis on the environment. 她以強調環境來重塑了當代的國際政治。

- Young people **are getting more involved in sexual** and **gender politics**. 年輕人更加地涉及到兩性與性別政治。

- I hate my job, there is too much **office politics**. 我討厭我的工作，有太多的辦公室政治角力。

- He took up music when he **retired from mainstream politics**. 他開始從事音樂是在他從主流政治中退下時。

☆ 請注意，politics 向來都必須有 s，而且動詞必須是單數形。

☆ 留意「政治」的不同類型。

Task 17

請研讀這個字詞搭配表、例句和底下的說明。

搭配在前面的動詞			搭配的形容詞		關鍵字
have hold wield	restore s/o to return s/o to share	fall from lose give up	absolute ultimate considerable	economic legal political popular	
come to rise to	exercise use confer	renounce relinquish	enormous limited		
assume seize take	give s/o~ grant s/o~ to	delegate devolve	arbitrary		**power**
搭配在前面的片語					
abuse of ~ balance of ~ bid for ~ the exercise of ~ a position of ~ the ~ behind the throne be power-hungry					

- Lady Macbeth was **power-hungry** and became **the power behind the throne**.
  馬克白夫人是渴求權力的,並且成為幕後的掌權者。

- **Exercising absolute power** can have a corrupting influence on someone.
  行使絕對權力可能會對某人產生腐敗性的影響。

- In the UK the Queen **has limited power**, while parliament **holds ultimate power**. 在英國,女王的權力有限,而議會則握有最高的權力。

- In a multi-party democracy, when one party **assumes power**, the other party has to **relinquish** it.
  在多黨式民主中,當一個政黨掌權時,另一黨必須放棄該政權。

☆ 留意「權力」的不同類型。

Task 18

請研讀這個字詞搭配表、例句和底下的說明。

搭配在前面的動詞	搭配的形容詞		關鍵字
have　　foment 　　　　stage carry out conduct　crush 　　　　put down fight 　　　　call for	successful bloody violent bloodless peaceful popular political communist anti-communist anti-democratic anti-government proletarian world	agrarian agricultural computer cultural economic environmental industrial political scientific sexual social technological	**revolution**
搭配在前面的片語			
the outbreak of the ~ ~ from above ~ from below The threat of ~			

- Activists want to **carry out an environmental revolution**.
  行動人士想要進行環境革命。

- The army were called in to **crush the anti-communist revolution**.
  軍隊受命來鎮壓反共革命。

- The people are **calling for a political revolution**.
  人民正呼喚一場政治革命。

- **The outbreak of the revolution** stopped all further economic progress in that country. 革命的爆發阻止了該國所有進一步的經濟進展。

☆ 須留意，不只是政治，其他方面也能有「革命」。

Task 19

請研讀這個字詞搭配表、例句和底下的說明。

搭配在前面的動詞		搭配的形容詞		關鍵字
have	organize	current	comprehensive	banking
	simplify	existing	effective	court
build			efficient	economic
create	destabilize	modern		educational
design	undermine	new	viable	examination
develop	weaken		workable	government
devise		old		healthcare
set up	abandon	old-		justice
adopt	scrap	fashioned	inefficient	legal
apply	do away	outdated	ineffective	national
implement	with	traditional	wasteful	insurance
introduce				political
	replace	standard	imperfect	prison
manage	restore			school
operate		perfect	flexible	tax
run				**system (of s/th)**

use strengthen modernize improve	criticize rebel against defend support blame	complex complicated elaborate simple	rigid stable	taxation university voting welfare	**system (of s/th)**

字詞搭配使用範例

- Don't **blame** the **system** for your own failures.
  不要把你自身的失敗歸咎於體制。

- Revolutionaries usually want to **do away with** the **outdated system**.
  革命人士通常是想要廢除過時的制度。

- They want to **replace the old system** and **set up a new**, **more modern**, **comprehensive system**.
  他們想要取代掉舊制度，並建立一個新的、更現代化、更周全的制度。

- We **have** a **perfect system of** collecting votes in this country. Let's not criticize it. 我們在這個國家有完善的收集選票系統。咱們就別批評它了。

....

☆ 留意到「制度」可以有很多不同的類型。

Task 20

請研讀這個字詞搭配表和例句。

搭配在前面的動詞	搭配的形容詞			關鍵字
woo persuade convince urge warn influence	eligible registered unregistered proxy overseas	floating uncommitted undecided	wavering first time new potential ordinary	**voter**

- They are trying to **persuade floating voters** to vote for them, but these voters say they are still **undecided**.

  他們正試著說服浮動選民投票給他們，但這些選民說，他們仍然沒有做出決定。

- Many **overseas voters** have not been able to register their vote. As **unregistered voters**, they will not be able to vote.

  很多海外選民還無法登記投票。身為未登記選民，他們將無法投票。

- Their campaign was aimed at **influencing** and **wooing first time voters**.

  他們的競選活動所瞄準的是去影響和爭取首投族選民。

Task 21

請從 Task 16 到 Task 20 中選出正確形式的字詞，完成以下段落填空。

> Those who are (1) _____ politics know that the most important part of the system is the voter. Most democracies have (2) _____ a (3) _____ system to ensure that governments (4) _____ (5) _____ power for a short time only. The key to the system is the voters. There are a number of different types of voters: those who are (6) _____ – they haven't yet decided who they will vote for, those who live (7) _____, and (8) _____ voters, who can ask someone else to vote for them. Parties spend a lot of efforts trying to (9) _____ voters to vote for them. Without these voters, the only way to transfer power would be by (10) _____ a (11) _____ revolution. However, as revolutions are rarely not violent, they are also only rarely (12) _____.

範例答案

1. interested in/involved in/active in/engaged in
2. built/created/designed/developed/devised/set up/adopted/applied/
   implemented/introduced
3. comprehensive/effective/efficient

4. have/hold/wield

5. limited

6. floating/uncommitted/undecided/wavering

7. overseas

8. proxy

9. woo/persuade/convince/urge

10. carrying out/conducting

11. violent/bloody

12. successful

☆ 須留意在空格 (1) 中，動詞要用過去分詞，因為它是被動式；在空格 (2) 中也需要用過去分詞，因為動詞是現在完成式；而在空格 (10) 中，因為 by 的關係，則是需要用 Ving。

　　記住，多閱讀有助於擴充字彙量，而在文章上下文脈絡中查看大量例子則能幫助你記憶新的用語。下一個練習對於各位記憶 15 個關鍵單字和它們的字詞搭配將有非常大的幫助。

Task 22

請從 Task 1 和 Task 2 的閱讀文章中找出關鍵語庫 ❶ 所列的 15 個關鍵字，並留意這些字在文章中是如何使用的。

常用語塊 Chunks

前面學過了字詞搭配的用法，我們現在要來學一些可用在寫作或談論這個主題的 chunks「語塊」。

Task 23

研讀這些語塊和底下的說明。

關鍵語庫 ❷

Chunk
❏ be well-established　深受確立
❏ be supposed to V　理當、應該要 V
❏ be (im)possible to V　（不）可能 V
❏ be (un)willing to V　（不）願意 V
❏ lead to n.p.　帶來、導致 n.p.
❏ mean that v.p.　意味著 v.p.
❏ reason for n.p.　n.p. 的原因
❏ reason why v.p.　為什麼 v.p. 的原因
❏ relate to n.p.　與 n.p. 有關
❏ In general, v.p.　一般來說，v.p.

☆ 須留意哪些語塊要接受詞、哪些不用。還要留意到受詞的類型，尤其是需要使用人物受詞 (s/o) 或事物受詞 (s/th) 時。

☆ 須留意這些語塊是否全都必須用 n.p.、Ving 或 V。

☆ 別忘了在使用這些語塊時需要改變動詞的時態。

☆ 注意哪些語塊必須連同 be 動詞來用，並確保這個動詞使用的時態正確，與主詞一致。

☆ be supposed to 意指某事應該要做卻沒有做。

☆ 注意否定形 im- 和 un-。

☆ lead to 和 mean that 的意思或多或少相同。用在想要表達結果時，結果是接續在動詞後。X means that Y / X leads to Y。Y 是結果。注意，lead to 後面接 n.p.，而 mean that 後面則接 v.p.。

☆ 留意到 reason 有兩個語塊，一是連同 for n.p.，一是連同 wh- v.p.。而這裡的 wh- 向來都是 why：There are many reasons why people do not vote.。

☆ In general 之後都是接句子。把它擺在句子的開頭，以表明你是在概括意指某事物。別忘了逗號 (,)。

下一個 Task 將聚焦於大家在使用這些語塊時經常會犯的錯誤。

Task 24

請改正這些句子中使用語塊的常見錯誤。

① The link between democracy and civil rights is well-establish.

_____

② We need to well establish democracy in our country.

_____

③ In a democracy everyone is suppose to vote.

_____

④ Politicians supposed to be honest and truthful.

_____

⑤ It's impossible having democracy in an autocratic system.

_____

⑥ Most politicians unwilling to standing down when their term of office ends.

_____

⑦ Democracy lead to freedom for all.

_____

⑧ Democracy usually mean that everyone over a certain age has the right to vote.

_____

⑨ The reason because some people cannot vote is that they are too young.

_____

⑩ Another reason about the situation is that many people didn't vote.

_____

⑪ The reason for people didn't vote is that they didn't believe in the candidates.

_____

⑫ Many people say they do not relate the candidates.

_____

⑬ In general most Western countries are democracies.

_____

☑ 答案・中譯・說明 ◉ **Track 8.3**

① The link between democracy and civil rights <u>is well-establish**ed**</u>.
民主和公民權利之間的聯繫深受確立。

② ~~We need to well establish democracy in our country.~~

③ In a democracy everyone is suppos**ed** to vote.
在民主政治中，每個人都應該要投票。

④ Politicians **are** supposed to be honest and truthful. 政治人物理當要誠實與實在的。

⑤ It's impossible **to have** democracy in an autocratic system.
在專制制度中不可能有民主。

⑥ Most politicians **are** unwilling to **stand** down when their term of office ends.
大部分的政治人物在他們的任期結束後都不願意下台。

⑦ Democracy lead**s** to freedom for all. 民主引領所有人通往自由。

⑧ Democracy usually mean**s** that everyone over a certain age has the right to vote.
民主通常意味著，每個人超過一定的年齡就有選舉權。

⑨ The reason **why** some people cannot vote is that they are too young.
有些人之所以不能投票的原因是他們太年輕了。

⑩ Another reason **for** the situation is that many people didn't vote.
造成這個情況的另一個原因是，很多人沒去投票。

⑪ The reason **why** people didn't vote is that they didn't believe in the candidates.
人們之所以不投票的原因是，他們不信任候選人。

⑫ Many people say they do not relate **to** the candidates.
很多人說，他們與候選人不相關。

⑬ In general**,** most Western countries are democracies.
一般來說，大部分的西方國家都是民主國家。

. . . .

☆ 注意，第 2 句整句都是錯的，因為 well establish 不能以這種方式來用。請仔細看關鍵語庫 ❷ 的語塊，並確保把它用得正確。

☆ 在第 7 句和第 8 句中，必須確保動詞與主詞一致。主詞是 Democracy，所以動詞必須加上 s。而在第 13 句中，記得要用逗號。

☆ 請將正確句子中的完整語塊畫上底線，這能幫助你完整而正確地記住語塊。

　　下一個練習對於記憶語塊將有非常大的幫助。記住，多閱讀有助於擴充字彙量，而在文章上下文脈絡中查看大量語塊則能幫助你記憶新的用語。

Task 25

請從 Task 1 和 Task 2 的閱讀文章中找出關鍵語庫 ❷ 列出的所有語塊，並留意這些語塊在文章中是如何使用的。

Task 26

現在請嘗試用前面學過的語塊來寫出你自己的句子。

關鍵字語塊	造句
be well-established	
be supposed to V	
be (im)possible to V	
be (un)willing to V	
lead to n.p.	
mean that v.p.	
reason for n.p.	
reason why v.p.	
relate to n.p.	
In general, v.p.	

☆ 我顯然無法在此改正你的句子，但你可以透過確認語塊所有的小細節，自行改正。再次提醒在寫作中運用語塊時，須特別注意小詞、字尾和語塊的結尾，無論所需要的是 n.p.、v.p.、Ving 還是 V，並且確保你所使用的語塊是完整的。

5 個可作動詞或名詞的單字
5 words which can be verbs or nouns

語塊通常會視關鍵字是名詞或動詞而有所不同，現在我們要來看 5 個動詞和名詞同形的單字，並學習使用正確的語塊。

Task 27

請看以下幾個名詞和動詞同形的單字。

關鍵語庫 3

關鍵字	名詞字義	動詞字義
control	支配；控制；調節；抑制	控制；支配；管理；克制
limit	界限；限度；範圍	限制；限定
measure	措施；手段；（判斷等的）基準	測量；計量；打量；估量
protest	抗議，異議，反對	抗議，聲明；對……提出異議
support	支撐（物）；支持（度）	支撐；支持；資助

Task 28

閱讀句子並判斷關鍵字是動詞或名詞，填入 V 或 N。

① ＿＿＿ The government has no **control** over the press.

② ＿＿＿ In order to **control** people's ideas, the press is not free.

③ ＿＿＿ In non-democratic countries the media is under the **control** of the government.

④ ＿＿＿ In non-democratic countries the media is **controlled by** the government.

⑤ ＿＿＿ The vote is **limited** to one vote per person.

⑥ ＿＿＿ There are usually term **limits** on political office in a democracy.

⑦ _____ The government **limits** the spread of information.

⑧ _____ Free access to the media is a **measure** of political maturity.

⑨ _____ We can clearly **measure** the effects of this policy on the country.

⑩ _____ **Protests** erupted around the country after the announcement.

⑪ _____ We are **protesting** about low wages and conditions.

⑫ _____ **Support** for the president is at an all-time low.

⑬ _____ If we do not **support** the protestors, they will lose their battle.

✓ 答案・中譯

① N 政府無從掌控新聞界。

② V 為了要控制人民的思想，新聞界並不自由。

③ N 在非民主國家，媒體是受到政府掌控。

④ V 在非民主國家，媒體是受到政府掌控。

⑤ V 這個投票是每人限投一票。

⑥ N 在民主國家中，政治職務通常有任期限制。

⑦ V 政府限制了資訊的傳播。

⑧ N 自由使用媒體是政治成熟度的衡量基準。

⑨ V 我們能明確地衡量這項政策對國家帶來的效應。

⑩ N 在聲明宣布後，全國各地便爆發了抗議活動。

⑪ V 我們正在抗議低工資和工作條件。

⑫ N 對總統的支持度創了歷史新低。

⑬ V 假如我們不支持抗議人士，他們就會輸掉這場戰役。

Task 29

請看以下所彙整的語塊及用法說明。

關鍵字語塊	關鍵字詞性	例句＆翻譯
control (of s/th)	nc	They exercised their control of the news by shutting it down. 他們透過關閉新聞來執行他們對新聞的控管。
control s/th	vt	They want to control the result of the election. 他們想要掌控選舉的結果。
limit (on s/th)	nc	We will not put a limit on the number of people who can attend. 我們不會在可參加的人數上設限。
limit s/th (to s/th)	vt	They limited the number of candidates to two. 他們把候選人的數目限制在兩人。
measure (of s/th)	nu	It's a measure of the country's political maturity. 這是該國政治成熟度的一個衡量基準。
measure	nc	They have put in place measures to control the crowd. 他們已經採取了控制群眾的措施。
measure s/th	vt	It will be difficult to measure the impact. 很難去衡量其產生的衝擊。
protest (about s/th)	nc	The protests are about the war. 抗議活動是針對戰爭而來。
protest (about s/th)	vi	The citizens dare not protest. They want to protest about wages. 公民不敢抗議。他們想要抗議工資問題。
support (for s/th)	nu	We are giving you our support. 我們會給予你支持。
support s/th	vt	Everyone is supporting you. 每個人都在支持你。

☆ 留意哪些名詞是可數，哪些是不可數；使用動詞時務必確認時態正確性。

☆ control 當名詞時，可與 have、exercise、lose、be under the control of 或 be in control 這些動詞一起連用。而 control 當動詞來用時，必須要有受詞，另外還要留意到，control 能以被動來使用。

☆ limit 當名詞時，要連同動詞 put 或 be 動詞來用，且必須使用介系詞 on。而 limit 當動詞用時，可以在介系詞後面用第二個受詞，且這個動詞也能以被動來使用。

☆ measure 當名詞時有兩個不同的意思，這取決於你所使用的語塊。當你要表達評估和理解某事的方式時，要用 a measure of，在這個用法中的 measure 是不可數的。此外，measure 也能連同動詞 put in place 或 implement 來使用，以表示掌控或限制，而這個用法中的 measure 則是可數的。注意，measure 當動詞時是指以量化來評估某事，而且必須使用受詞。

☆ protest 當名詞來用時，可以用介系詞 about 來指明抗議是針對什麼而來。而 protest 當動詞來用時，若想加上受詞，必須先用 about。

☆ support 當名詞使用時是不可數的。若是想要指明支持的標的或對象，就必須使用 for。而想要把 support 當動詞來用時，則必須給它受詞。

☆ 請仔細學習這些語塊，並把重點放在諸如介系詞和冠詞這些細節。

Task 30

請選用正確形式的單字或語塊，完成下列各句。

① **controlled/was controlled**

By controlling the media, the government _____ the country.

② **measure/measure of**

It's a _____ the president's popularity that he was elected three times.

③ **supports/support**

No one _____ the president.

④ **protests/protests about**

The _____ are getting violent.

⑤ **protests/protest about**

The country is so well governed that there is nothing left to _____.

⑥ **measure/measure of**

The effect of his speech was difficult to _____.

⑦ **control/control of**

The government lost _____ the country after the protests.

⑧ **is limited to/limit on**

The number of people who can attend the protest _____ 200,000.

⑨ **limit on/limited to**

There is a _____ the number of times a candidate can stand for election.

⑩ **measures/measure of**

They put in place _____ to control voting so that everyone had the chance to vote.

⑪ **supports/support**

We need your _____ to win this election.

✔ 答案・中譯・說明　🔊 **Track 8.5**

① By controlling the media, the government <u>controlled</u> the country.
靠著掌控媒體，政府便掌控了國家。

② It's a measure of the president's popularity that he was elected three times.
判斷這位總統深得人心的指標就在於，他當選了三次。

③ No one supports the president. 沒有人支持總統。

④ The protests are getting violent. 抗議活動變得暴力了。

⑤ The country is so well governed that there is nothing left to protest about.
這個國家治理得如此好,沒有什麼可抗議的了。

⑥ The effect of his speech was difficult to measure.
他的演說效應難以衡量。

⑦ The government lost control of the country after the protests.
政府在抗議過後便失去了對國家的掌控。

⑧ The number of people who can attend the protest is limited to 200,000.
能參加抗議的人數被限制在二十萬人以內。

⑨ There is a limit on the number of times a candidate can stand for election.
候選人能參加競選的次數是有限制的。

⑩ They put in place measures to control voting so that everyone had the chance to vote.
他們採取了控制投票的措施,使每個人都有機會投票。

⑪ We need your support to win this election.
我們需要你的支持來贏得這場選舉。

⋯⋯⋯⋯⋯⋯⋯⋯⋯⋯⋯⋯⋯⋯⋯⋯⋯⋯⋯⋯⋯⋯⋯⋯⋯⋯⋯⋯⋯

☆ 記得確認所使用的動詞時態都正確。

☆ 請拿正確的句子來與關鍵語庫 ❹ 的語塊做比較,確保名詞或動詞語塊都用得正確。

☆ 請將正確句子中的完整語塊畫上底線(參照第 1 句的示範)。這將有助於各位把語塊完整而正確地記起來。

　　再次提醒,盡可能地多閱讀有助於擴充字彙量,而在文章上下文脈絡中查看大量語塊則能幫助你記憶新的用語。

Task 31

請從 Task 1 和 Task 2 的閱讀文章中找出關鍵語庫 ❹ 列出的所有語塊,並留意這些語塊在文章中是當動詞還是名詞使用?

Task 32

請練習用關鍵語庫 ❹ 的語塊來造句。

關鍵字語塊	造句
control (of s/th)	
control s/th	
limit (on s/th)	
limit s/th (to s/th)	
measure (of s/th)	
measure	
measure s/th	
protest (about s/th)	
support s/th	
support (for s/th)	

☆ 我顯然無法在此來改正你的句子，但你可以透過確認語塊所有的小細節，自行改正。再次提醒在寫作中運用語塊時，須特別注意小詞、字尾和語塊的結尾，無論所需要的是 n.p.、v.p.、Ving 還是 V，並且確保你所使用的語塊是完整的。

5 個談論或寫作民主與政府時常用的片語動詞 5 phrasal verbs for talking or writing about democracy and government

我們現在要來看一些在寫作或談論民主與政府相關主題時，常會用到的片語動詞。

Task 33

研讀語庫中的片語動詞、例句和其下的說明。

關鍵語庫 ⑤　⊙ **Track 8.6**

片語動詞	例句
stand by (for s/th) 等待、期望某事自發	• The crowd are standing by for the new president to appear. 群眾正留待新總統現身。
stand for s/th 代表、支持、容忍	• The candidate stands for stability at home and expansion abroad. 該候選人主張國內穩定和海外擴張。 • The public will not stand for it. It will be very unpopular. 大眾不會容忍的。它會非常不得人心。
carry out s/th 實行、完成	• As soon as it was elected, the new government began to carry out reforms. 新政府一當選就開始實行改革。
stand up for s/th 以發言或行動來支持	• The party is standing up for the rights of LGBT+ people. 該黨為跨性別人士的權利挺身而出。
do away with s/th 廢止、廢除	• The party wants to do away with injustice and poverty. 該黨想要去除不義與貧窮。

☆ 記得，你必須非常留意動詞有沒有受詞 (s/th)，以及這個受詞是擺在哪個位置。請仔細確認上方語庫中的片語動詞及其受詞的位置。

☆ 須留意 stand by 沒有受詞，假如想要指明受詞，就必須加上 for。這個片語動詞也能當名詞來用：be on standby。

☆ stand for 有兩個不同的意思，就看動詞是肯定還是否定。當它是肯定時，意指 represent「代表」；當它是否定時，則意指 will not tolerate「不容忍」。請看例句。

☆ 留意到 stand up for s/th 和 do away with s/th 有兩個介系詞。

☆ 請記得片語動詞是動詞，所以還必須考慮動詞要用什麼時態。

　　下一個練習將有助於各位聚焦於受詞的正確擺放位置這些細節上。

Task 34

下列各句中的第一個字是正確的，請按照順序將其後的字詞重組成正確的句子。

EX. **We with do will corruption away**

　　We will do away with corruption.

① There big the by standing crowd the was airport a waiting at president for

_____

② The will for not public stand level corruption of this

_____

③ The honesty stands party and integrity for

_____

④ The first reforms out carried 100 new in their government year

_____

⑤ Everyone stand rights up should for workers'

_____

⑥ We away this to want with do law

_____

✅ 答案・中譯・說明　🎧 **Track 8.7**

① There was a big crowd <u>standing by</u> at the airport waiting for the president.
有廣大的群眾留待機場等著總統。

② The public will not stand for this level of corruption.
大眾不會容忍這種程度的腐敗。

③ The party stands for honesty and integrity./The party stands for integrity and honesty. 該黨主張誠實與誠信。

④ The new government carried out 100 reforms in their first year.
新政府在頭一年就完成了一百項改革。

⑤ Everyone should stand up for workers' rights.
每個人都該為勞工的權利挺身而出。

⑥ We want to do away with this law.
我們想要廢除這條法律。

PART 2

☆ 將正確的句子與關鍵語庫 ❺ 的片語動詞做比較，確認你的用法都正確。

☆ 請將正確句子中的片語動詞畫上底線，這將幫助你完整而正確地把語塊記起來。（參照第 1 句的示範）

Task 35

請從 Task 1 和 Task 2 的閱讀文章中找出關鍵語庫 ❺ 列出的所有片語動詞，並留意它們在文章中是如何使用的。

請練習用關鍵語庫 ❺ 的片語動詞來造句。

片語動詞	造句練習
stand by (for s/th)	
stand for s/th	
carry out s/th	
stand up for s/th	
do away with s/th	

5 個談論或寫作民主與政府時常用的慣用語 5 idioms for talking or writing about democracy and government

Task 37

研讀語庫中的慣用語、例句和其下的說明。

關鍵語庫 ⑥ 🎧 **Track 8.8**

慣用語	例句
game plan 行動策略；（比賽前）的戰略計畫	• They don't even have a game plan for their first year. 他們甚至沒有第一年的行動策略。
have s/o's work cut out 面對難事	• The country is in such a mess that the new government will have their work cut out to solve everything. 國家陷入一片混亂，新政府將不得不面對重重的困難以解決一切問題。
be between the devil and the deep blue sea 陷入兩難	• It's not an easy choice. We are between the devil and the deep blue sea. 這不是個容易的選擇。我們左右為難。
play devil's advocate 為了激化辯論而提出困難的問題	• She's a good party member, but she likes to create discussion by playing devil's advocate. 她是個好黨員，但她喜歡唱反調來引發討論。
against s/o's better judgement 即使認為它是錯的仍做某事	• She stood for election, against her better judgement. Of course, she lost. 她在明知不可為之下參加競選。當然，她選輸了。

☆ be between the devil and the deep blue sea 和 be between a rock and a hard place 的意思相同，就是在兩個選項同樣糟糕下陷入兩難，或是面對困難時的選擇。

☆ 在 have s/o's work cut out 中，唯一能改變的是所有格形容詞 have her work cut out，當然，還有動詞時態。

☆ 為了讓慣用語有意義，它必須完全準確才行，這意味著你必須將慣用語的所有細節都使用正確。

☆ 請注意這幾個慣用語都沒有受詞，不要連同受詞來使用。

Task 38

改正這些句子中的常見錯誤。

① They were elected without a plan for the game.

_____

② The country is in a mess. The new government will have its work cut for them.

_____

③ We are between a devil and a sea.

_____

④ Even though I didn't agree with his policies, against someone's better judgement I voted for him.

_____

⑤ I don't want to play advocate for the devil, but I think this strategy could be wrong.

_____

✅ 答案・中譯・說明　⊚ Track 8.9

① They were elected without a game plan. 他們是在沒有戰略計畫下當選的。

② The country is in a mess. The new government will have its work cut out.
國家亂成一團。新政府將會傷透腦筋。

③ We are between the devil and the deep blue sea. 我們正陷入兩難。

④ Even though I didn't agree with his policies, against my better judgement I voted for him. 即使不認同他的政策，但我還是在明知不可為之下投票給他。

⑤ I don't want to play devil's advocate, but I think this strategy could be wrong.
我不想要唱反調，但我認為這項策略可能是錯的。

··

☆ 請仔細比較錯誤句子和正確解答，務必確實掌握錯在哪以及為什麼是錯的。

　　現在我們要練習在文章上下文中找出慣用語。

Task 39

請從 Task 1 和 Task 2 的閱讀文章中找出關鍵語庫 ❻ 列出的所有慣用語，並留意它們在文章中是如何使用的。

Task 40

請練習用關鍵語庫 ❻ 的慣用語來造句。

慣用語	造句練習
game plan	
have s/o's work cut out	
be between the devil and the deep blue sea	
play devil's advocate	
against s/o's better judgement	

··

☆ 再次提醒在寫作時若運用到這些慣用語，要特別留意動詞的時態和完整的慣用語包含哪些細節。

易混淆的字詞 easily confused words

- ❏ 要記得，有些單字只能用在特定的主題上，用在別的主題則不適當。
- ❏ 另外，容易搞混的單字，其差別常常是在搭配詞的使用上有所不同。
  在做接下來幾個練習時，務必記得這些重點。

Task 41

請仔細研讀各組易混淆的字詞、例句和其下的說明。

關鍵語庫 7　🔊 Track 8.10

	易混淆字詞	例句
1	**trend** (*nc*) 趨勢	• The market trend is going up right now. 市場趨勢目前正在上升。 • The trend for democracy is increasing around the world. 全世界的民主趨勢正在增長。 • The iphone is the latest trend among young people. iphone 是年輕人的最新潮流。
	tendency (*nc*) 傾向	• He has a tendency to get angry. 他有生氣的傾向。 • He tends to get angry quite easily. 他往往相當容易就發怒。
2	**reduce** (*vt*) 降低	• We need to reduce the number of people who don't vote. 我們必須降低不投票的人數。
	decrease (*vi*) 減少	• The number of people who do not vote is decreasing. 不投票的人數在減少。
3	**aspect** (*nc*) 層面	• The problem has many different aspects. 該問題有許多不同的層面。
	side (*nc*) 邊、側	• The sun always shines on the other side of the street. 太陽總是照在街道的另一邊。

4	**prohibit** (*vt*) 禁止	• The law prohibits people from voting twice. 法律禁止民眾投兩次票。
	inhibit (*vt*) 阻卻	• The cold weather inhibited many voters from going out to vote. 寒冷的天氣阻卻了許多選民外出去投票。
5	**function** (*nc*) 功能	• The function of democracy is to allow all citizens to participate in choosing their government. 民主的功能是容許所有的公民參與來選擇政府。
	cause (*nc*) 成因	• The cause of the surprising win of the party is still unknown. 該黨出人意料地獲勝的原因仍然未知。

☆ trend 和 tendency 在華文中的意思非常類似，但在英文中雖然文法相同，但是意思和用法卻相當不同。

☆ 想要描述經濟、政治、政府、服裝時尚、音樂和藝術等等較廣大世界的概括走向時，可以用 trend。這個字具有一般、概括的意思。

☆ 若是要聚焦於一人的個人行為時，可以用 tendency。例如 He has the tendency to V 意指 he often V。實際上，這個字在英文中的使用頻率非常低，我們根本不會使用這個名詞，而是會用動詞形式的 tend to。例如 He often gets angry. 就跟 He tends to get angry easily. 相同。請看上面的例句。

☆ reduce 和 decrease 的意思相同，但文法和用法不同。

☆ 意指行動是為了把某事變小而做時，可以用 reduce。

☆ 意指某事變小並且是自行發生時，可以用 decrease。注意，decrease 不能連同受詞來用，例如 We need to decrease the number of people who do not vote. 是錯的。

☆ aspect 和 side 的文法相同，但意思和用法是不同的。總之，不能把它們當成同義字。

☆ 使用 aspect 時要非常留心。這個字不但意思與華文中的「方面」稍有不同，使用方式也並不相同。當你要聚焦於看一件事情的不同方式時，可以用 aspect。注意，這裡所指的事情並非實物，而是一個情況或事件，它是在比喻從不同的角度來看一個情況或事件，彷彿它就是物件，並討論該情況或事件的不同部分。「方面」在華文中用得比 aspect 在英文中要頻繁許多。一般來說，

當華文的句子中有「方面」這個詞時，在英文的句子中並不需要翻譯出來。

☆ 如果要描述的是一個實體物質的位置或一部分時，就用 side。有時候人們會
把它當成 hand 的同義詞來用。但是請注意，On the one hand, on the other
hand. 正確；On the one side, on the other side. 向來都是錯的。

☆ prohibit 和 inhibit 有相同的文法和非常類似的意思，但用法略有不同。這兩個
字都是動詞，但經常以 ___ed 形式的形容詞連同 be 動詞來使用：It is
prohibited by law.、She is rather inhibited.。

☆ 若要表達某事為法律所禁止時，就用 prohibit。但若某事是基於某個原因而遭
到阻絕或阻止，但不是因為法律時，則用 inhibit。請看上面的例句。

☆ function 和 cause 的文法相同，但意思和用法截然不同。我們在此是聚焦於這
些單字當名詞來用，但它們也可以是動詞。

☆ 當想要表達某事是如何運作以及為什麼是以這種方式運作時，就用 function 這
個名詞。所強調的是「如何」，而不是「為什麼」。

☆ 而若想要表達某事為什麼會這樣運作或某事發生的原因時，則可以用 cause
這個名詞。

在做下一個練習時，請仔細思考句意、文法和用法來選出正確的單字。

Task 42

請選出正確的單字來填入下列各句。

① **trends/tendencies**

Politicians have to keep an eye on common and popular _____
to make sure they understand the people they represent.

② **inhibited/prohibited**

She is very shy, so she feels _____ when she has to talk to large
groups of people.

③ **cause/function**

The _____ of the disaster is still unknown, but we are looking into all aspects of it.

④ **decreased/reduced**

The government _____ the number of places where people can vote, so this effected the result.

⑤ **inhibit/prohibit**

The law doesn't _____ this.

⑥ **prohibits/inhibits**

The law _____ anyone running for president more than two times.

⑦ **sides/aspect**

They set up a committee to look at all the _____ of the disaster.

⑧ **trend/tendency**

This politician has the _____ to ignore what people tell him.

⑨ **reduced/decreased**

This year, the number of people who didn't vote _____.

⑩ **cause/function**

We are pleased to say that the _____ of democracy is very smooth in our country.

⑪ **sides/aspects**

We will address all _____ of the situation in our report.

⑫ **aspects/sides**

You can see the building from two different _____ if you stand here.

① Politicians have to keep an eye on common and popular trends to make sure they understand the people they represent.

政治人物必須關注普遍和民心的趨勢，以確保自己了解所代表的民眾。

② She is very shy, so she feels inhibited when she has to talk to large groups of people.

她非常害羞，所以當她必須和一大群人交談時便會感到卻步。

③ The cause of the disaster is still unknown, but we are looking into all aspects of it.

災害的成因還不明，但我們正在對此做各方面的調查。

④ The government reduced the number of places where people can vote, so this effected the result.

政府減少了民眾可以去投票的地點數，所以這影響了結果。

⑤ The law doesn't prohibit this. 法律不禁止這個。

⑥ The law prohibits anyone running for president more than two times.

法律禁止任何人競選總統超過兩次。

⑦ They set up a committee to look at all the aspects of the disaster.

他們成立了委員會來檢視這次災害的所有層面。

⑧ This politician has the tendency to ignore what people tell him.

這位政治人物有忽視別人告訴他的話的傾向。

⑨ This year, the number of people who didn't vote decreased.

今年，未投票的人數減少了。

⑩ We are pleased to say that the function of democracy is very smooth in our country.

我們很高興地說，民主的功能在我國是非常順暢的。

⑪ We will address all aspects of the situation in our report.

我們會在報告中論及這個局勢的所有層面。

⑫ You can see the building from two different sides if you stand here.

假如站在這裡，你就能從兩個不同的側面看到這棟建築。

☆ 第 1 句選填 trend 是因為主題為「民眾和當前趨勢」等概括的事；第 8 句則是在講一人的行為，而不是概括的走向，所以要用 tendency。

☆ 第 2、5、6 句中都包含了因為某種原因而受到「阻絕、禁止」的意涵。在第 2 句中，受阻的原因與個人的害羞有關，所以應選用 inhibited；而第 5、6 句則

都與法律有關，所以必須用 prohibit。

☆ 第 3 句需要 cause 是由於陳述聚焦於災害為什麼會發生的「原因」；第 10 句則因為陳述聚焦於民主在此例中運作得如何，順暢不順暢，而不是民主的原因，所以必須用 function。

☆ 第 4 句使用 reduced 是因為某人正在執行這個行動，屬於 transitive「及物動詞」的意思：某人對別的事採取行動；第 9 句則沒有人在對某事採取行動，行動純粹是自行發生，所以這是 intransitive「不及物的」，應使用 decreased。

☆ 第 7 句選用 aspects 是因為災害不是實物，而是一個情況或事件，第 11 句需要 aspects 也是基於相同的原因；第 12 句是在談論實物（建築物），所以必須選用 sides。

最後我們還是要來練習從閱讀文章中找出這些容易搞混的單字。當你在文章中每找到一個單字，都必須停下來思考它是意指什麼、它的文法是什麼，以及它是如何使用的。

Task 43
請從 Task 1 和 Task 2 的閱讀文章中找出關鍵語庫 ❼ 列出的所有易混淆字詞，並留意它們在文章中是如何使用的。

Task 44
請練習用關鍵語庫 ❼ 的易混淆字詞來造句。

易混淆字詞	造句練習
trend	
tendency	
reduce	

decrease	
aspect	
side	
prohibit	
inhibit	
function	
cause	

☆ 在寫作中運用這些易混淆的字詞時，記得把重點放在文法、句意和用法上，而不是只注意單字的意思。

　　在你結束這個單元之前，請將下列清單看過，確定你能將所有要點都勾選起來。如果有一些要點你還搞不清楚，請回頭再次研讀本單元的相關部分。

☐ 我確實閱讀並理解了關於「民主與政府」的長篇文章。
☐ 我完全知道字彙在文章中是如何使用，並更加了解到要怎麼用單字來表達特定的主題。
☐ 我已經學會 15 個關於「民主與政府」主題的關鍵字，以及可與其搭配使用的動詞和形容詞。

□ 我已經練習使用這些搭配詞來描寫「民主與政府」。

□ 我已經學到了一些同義詞，也了解在運用時需要注意的一些問題。

□ 我學到了很多關於這個主題可以運用的語塊，包括片語動詞以及名詞或動詞為同形的單字。

□ 我已經練習使用這些語塊。

□ 我學到了 5 個關於這個主題的慣用語，且知道如何運用。

□ 我已經理解在運用慣用語時需要特別注意的一些問題。

□ 關於這個主題，我已經能確實掌握一些易混淆字詞的用法。

Unit 9

個人主義
Individualism

本單元所要探討的是「個人主義」的哲學思想，以及與此思想不同的另一種觀點。在這裡要閱讀的同樣也是「論證／意見」(argument/opinion) 類型的文章。

Task 1

閱讀文章並盡可能地理解文章內容。請先不要使用字典。

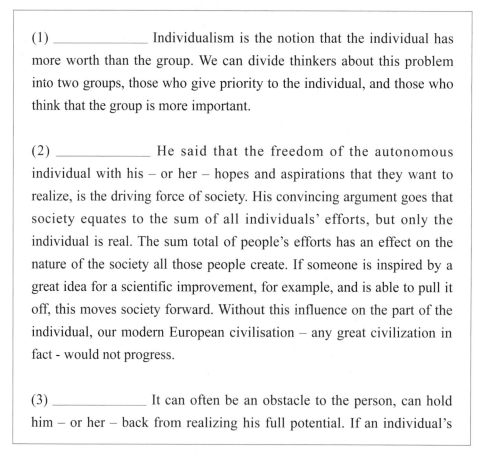

(1) _____ Individualism is the notion that the individual has more worth than the group. We can divide thinkers about this problem into two groups, those who give priority to the individual, and those who think that the group is more important.

(2) _____ He said that the freedom of the autonomous individual with his – or her – hopes and aspirations that they want to realize, is the driving force of society. His convincing argument goes that society equates to the sum of all individuals' efforts, but only the individual is real. The sum total of people's efforts has an effect on the nature of the society all those people create. If someone is inspired by a great idea for a scientific improvement, for example, and is able to pull it off, this moves society forward. Without this influence on the part of the individual, our modern European civilisation – any great civilization in fact - would not progress.

(3) _____ It can often be an obstacle to the person, can hold him – or her – back from realizing his full potential. If an individual's

plan falls through, or if his longstanding, cherished ambition is thwarted, he can blame society for it, rather than taking personal responsibility for his own failings. Society, then, exists for the benefit of the individual.

(4) _____ Some high fliers might be tempted to take advantage of group, pull rank, and work the system to their advantage without an offer of help to their fellow human beings. Kant's idea is based on the fundamental mistake that people are inherently good in their intentions.

(5) _____ He put forward the opposite theory, that the group is more important than the individual. Bentham pointed out that the individual cannot obtain complete personal fulfilment without the backing of society. The individual has to be educated, fed, and looked after when they are sick, and all these things happen when society is united. Without them, the individual, no matter how great, no matter how high he rises, cannot hope to be successful. The great individual has to build on what society can offer.

(6) _____ He said that the happiness of the greatest number is the same as the greatest happiness. It's not only the movers and shakers who deserve to be happy, but the average Joe has the right to happiness too. Bentham believed that the individual should sacrifice his personal happiness in exchange for the greater happiness of belonging to a coherent social group. In other words, happiness is found in being useful to the group, which is why Bentham called his theory Utilitarianism, which means 'being useful'. For most people, it's a fair exchange: I offer my help to the group and hope for support when I need it in turn.

(7) _____ How many of us are content to let someone else have the last cookie? How many of us can be content with a situation in

which our needs are placed secondary to the - often quite different - needs of the group? How many of us want to avoid massive disappointment? We are all selfish and all want to stay ahead of the competition in the great game of life. Leading a quiet and full life sometimes means putting yourself first and others last.

(8) _____ The fact of the matter is that in practice, situations arise which call on us to make decisions taking into account innumerable factors. In some situations, individualism and self-interest might influence our decision, in others, the hope that the group will benefit will prevail over self-interest. These two theories, Individualism and Utilitarianism, have spread throughout the world, and now most of our politics, society and economics are based on their interaction.

Task 2

請從下列句子選出適當的主題句以完成 Task 1 每個段落的填空。

A Bentham further expanded his idea to include the notion of happiness.

B In the first group, we have the great German 19th century philosopher Kant.

C In the second group we have the equally great English 18th century philosopher Bentham.

D Of course, these two theories exist on a theoretical spectrum which is entirely abstract.

E Society can also affect a person in a negative way.

F The downside to that way of thinking is that it gives rise to pure selfishness.

G The controversial aspect of Bentham's ideas is that for many people, exchanging the personal happiness that you might find on your own for the greater happiness of the group is a sacrifice that they are not prepared to make.

H The theory of individualism is at the heart of Western philosophy.

(1) H　(2) B　(3) E　(4) F　(5) C　(6) A　(7) G　(8) D

[譯文]

　　個人主義理論是西方哲學的核心。個人主義的思維是，認為個人比群體更要有價值。我們可以把有關這個問題的思想家分為兩類，一類是優先考慮個人，另一類認為群體更為重要。

　　在第一類中，我們有十九世紀偉大的德國哲學家康德。他說，自主個人的自由以及他們想要實現之希望與抱負，是社會的驅動力。他令人信服的論點是，社會等同於所有個人努力的總和，但只有個人是真實的。眾人努力的總和會對所有這些人所創造出的社會本質產生影響。例如，假如某人在科學進步上受到很棒的觀念啟發並有能力完成它，這就會把社會往前推進。少了這股對個人部分的影響力，現代的歐洲文明、事實上是任何偉大的文明就不會進步。

　　社會也能以負面的方式來影響一個人。它往往會成為人們的阻礙，壓抑他或她去充分發揮他的潛能。假如一個人的計畫落空，或者他長期懷抱的雄心壯志受挫了，他可能會以此來責怪社會，而不是為本身的缺失負起個人責任。所以說，社會是為了個人的利益而存在著。

　　這種思考方式的缺點是，它會引發純然的自私。有些野心勃勃的人或許會受到誘惑去占群體的便宜、濫用職權，以及把制度操弄到對自己有利，而不對同胞人類提供幫助。康德的思想是奠基於一個根本的錯誤，即人天生就是意圖善良。

　　在第二類中，我們有同樣偉大的英國十八世紀哲學家邊沁。他提出了相反的理論，認為群體比個人更重要。邊沁指出，沒有社會的支持，個人不可能取得完全的個人成就。個人必須受教育、被撫養，以及生病時被照料，而這些事全都是發生在社會團結一致的時候。少了它們，個人無論多優秀，無論升到多高的位置，都無法指望成功。偉大的個人必須建立在社會所能提供的基礎上。

　　邊沁把他的觀念進一步擴展到納入幸福的思維。他說，最多數人的幸福就與最大的幸福相同。不僅是那些有權有勢的人值得幸福，一般人也有幸福的權利。邊沁相信，個人應該犧牲自己的個人幸福，以換取屬於一個和諧社會群體的更大幸福。換句話說，幸福在於對群體有用，這就是為什麼邊沁把他的理論稱為功利主義，意思是「有用」。對大部分的人來說，它是公平的交換：我對群體提供我的幫助，並希望在我需要的時候能得到支援。

　　邊沁的觀念中有爭議的方面在於，對很多人來說，用自己可能會找到的個人的幸福來換取群體的更大幸福是他們並未準備要付出的犧牲。我們有多少人會甘於讓別人來吃最後一塊餅乾？我們有多少人能甘於這樣一種情況：為了常常是相當不同的群體需求而使自己的需求居於次要地位？我們有多少人會想要避免巨大的失望？我們全都是自私的，都想要

在人生這場偉大的比賽中居於領先地位。過一種安靜和圓滿的生活有時候意味著要把自己放在第一位，把他人放在最後。

當然，這兩種理論是存在於全然抽象的理論光譜上。事實則是在實踐中，出現的一些情況使得我們在做決定時需要考慮無數的因素。在某些情況下，個人主義和利己主義或許會影響到我們的決定，而在其他情況，寄望群體受益的希望則會勝過個人利益。個人主義和功利主義這兩種理論已經傳播到了全世界，現在我們的政治、社會與經濟大部分都是奠基於它們的相互作用之上。

....

☆ 第一段介紹了主題和概括資訊，概述了兩種主要的哲學論點。

☆ 第二和第三段介紹了康德關於個人是文明驅動力的論點。

☆ 第四段描述了康德論點的缺點。

☆ 第五和第六段描述了相反的主張：邊沁的功利主義。

☆ 第七段描述了邊沁論點的缺點。

☆ 最後一段總結，強調在哲學中看似清楚又容易的事，在現實生活中則比較混亂而沒那麼簡單。

☆ 在閱讀時，務必試著跟隨雙方的論點，看出文章是如何組織的。

字詞搭配 Word Partnerships

我們現在要來學習「個人主義」這個主題的 15 個關鍵字，以及可搭配這些關鍵字使用的「字詞搭配表」。首先，請看關鍵字語庫。

Task 3

請仔細研讀這些主題字彙和下方的說明。

關鍵語庫 ❶　⊙ **Track 9.1**

名詞	動詞	形容詞	字義
ambition Ⓒ	-	ambitious	野心、雄心、抱負
argument Ⓒ	argue	-	主張、論據、論點
aspect Ⓒ	-	-	層面、方面、觀點
aspiration Ⓒ	aspire to s/th	-	抱負、志向、渴望達到的目的
civilization Ⓒ	civilize	civilized	文明、文明國家
disappointment Ⓒ	disappoint	disappointed	失望、令人掃興的事
fulfilment Ⓤ	fulfil	(un)fulfilled	實踐、實現、完成
group Ⓒ	group	-	群、組、類、群體
happiness Ⓤ	-	happy	幸福、快樂、幸運
individual Ⓒ	-	-	個人、個體
life Ⓒ	live	alive	人生、生活
potential Ⓤ	-	-	潛能、潛力、可能性
responsibility Ⓤ	-	responsible for	責任
selfishness Ⓤ	-	selfish	自私、自我中心

| spectrum C | - | - | 光譜 |

....

☆ 需留意哪些名詞是可數，哪些是不可數。

☆ 要記得，名詞是可數或不可數，有時候須視主題而定。

☆ 注意單字的其他詞性形式，包含動詞和形容詞。

☆ 注意，ambition、argument、aspect 和 aspiration 都是可數的，且通常必須使用複數形，尤其是 aspirations。例如 Everyone has aspirations 正確，而 Everyone has an aspiration 不算錯，但極不自然。

☆ 須留意 argument 有兩個意思：「吵架」和「論點」。在此的意思是「論點」。

☆ disappointed 也能當成被動式的動詞來用：People are often very disappointed by their lives.。注意，disappointed 以被動式來用時，就跟連同 be 動詞來用的形容詞形式相同。

☆ 留意 fulfilment、fulfil 和 fulfilled 的拼法。留心這些雙 l。

☆ 注意，group 也能當作動詞來用，意指把東西分組或歸類。

☆ spectrum 的複數形是 spectra，但請盡量避免使用複數。雖然這個字可數，但它通常是以單數來使用。

　　接下來，我們將以 5 個關鍵字爲一組，深入地學習與這些字最頻繁搭配的字詞組合及正確用法。

Task 4

請研讀這個字詞搭配表、例句和底下的說明。

搭配在前面的動詞		搭配的形容詞		關鍵字
lack	achieve	driving	modest	**ambition** **(to V)**
have	realise	great		
		naked	secret	
cherish	limit	burning		
harbour	restrain	high	youthful	
nurture	frustrate			

abandon　　thwart give up	main overriding ultimate personal lifelong longstanding life's	frustrated thwarted unfulfilled	**ambition (to V)**

字詞搭配使用範例　🎧 **Track 9.2**（收錄本單元 Task 4~Task 20 字詞搭配使用範例）

- His **great ambition** was to be an astronaut, but his **ambition was never realised**.
  他的偉大志向是當太空人，但他的抱負從未實現。

- She **cherished** the **youthful**, **burning ambition to** become a doctor and save
  the world.　她抱持著青春、炙熱的雄心壯志要成為一名醫生並拯救世人。

- His **high ambition was frustrated** by his lack of social support.
  他的遠大抱負因他缺乏社會支援而受挫。

☆ 請注意動詞 achieve、realise、limit、thwart 和 restrain 能以被動來使用。

Task 5

請研讀這個字詞搭配表、例句和底下的說明。

搭配在前面 的動詞	搭配的形容詞		關鍵字	搭配在後的動詞
advance deploy offer present put forward develop accept agree with	basic general main good major powerful sound	reasoned spurious tenuous weak balanced logical rational	**argument (for n.p.) (against n.p.) (that v.p.)**	go that v.p. run that v.p. be based on s/th

illustrate support underline consider hear listen to dismiss reject	strong valid compelling conclusive convincing persuasive plausible controversial	**argument (for n.p.) (against n.p.) (that v.p.)**	

字詞搭配使用範例

- He **put forward** both the **arguments for** and the **arguments against** the proposal. Both **arguments** were ultimately pretty **weak**, and they **were rejected**.
  他提出了贊成該提案和反對該提案的論點。這兩個論點最終都相當薄弱，被否決了。

- She **offered** a **compelling argument**, and everyone **supported** it.
  她提出了一個令人信服的論點，每個人都支持它。

- The **argument goes that** everyone has the right to be respected.
  該主張認為，每個人都有受尊重的權利。

- He **deployed** the **argument that** individualism drives society.
  他標舉著個人主義驅動社會的主張。

☆ 注意，要在 argument 之後接名詞時，必須依觀點來使用 for 或 against；而若想要接 v.p. 時，則必須使用 that。

Task 6

請研讀這個字詞搭配表、例句和底下的說明。

搭配在前面的動詞	搭配的形容詞		關鍵字
have be consider	central crucial essential fundamental important	encouraging exciting fascinating interesting	**aspect (of s/th)**

cover deal with discuss examine explore focus on look at study demonstrate illustrate	key main major principle basic broad general curious puzzling	alarming controversial disturbing negative	**aspect (of s/th)**

字詞搭配使用範例

- The most **disturbing aspect of** the argument is that it's so compelling, even though it's wrong.
  這個論點最令人困擾的方面是，它如此有說服力，儘管它是錯的。
- I want to **deal with** this **fundamental aspect** now.
  我現在想要來討論這個基本層面。
- The most **interesting aspect of** the question is what to do about the group.
  這個問題最有意思的方面是該怎麼處理這個小組。

☆ 注意，aspect 只能用來描述考慮抽象思維的不同方式。它所能描述的單字只有像是 argument、question、problem、idea 等等。

Task 7

請研讀這個字詞搭配表、例句和底下的說明。

搭配在前的動詞		搭配的形容詞		關鍵字
have	achieve fulfil meet realize satisfy	high lofty failed	career personal national social political	**aspiration (towards s/th)**

- He **has high career aspirations** that he wants to **fulfil** in the first twenty years of his life. 他有遠大的生涯抱負想要在他人生的頭二十年就實現。

- Most countries in the world **have** their own **national aspirations towards** self-governance. 世界上大多數的國家都有朝向自己民族自治的渴望。

- Most people aim to **realize** their **personal aspirations**, and most people hope that society can help them **achieve their aspirations**. 大多數人的目標是實現他們的個人抱負，而且大部分的人都希望社會能幫助自己達成抱負。

☆ 注意「抱負」的不同類型。

☆ 留意這些例句都是如何以複數來使用 aspirations。

Task 8

請研讀這個字詞搭配表、例句和底下的說明。

搭配在前的動詞	搭配的形容詞		關鍵字
bring ~ to create destroy save	ancient early modern advanced great primitive	Greek Roman Egyptian European Western Eastern industrial human	**civilization**

字詞搭配使用範例

- The Romans **brought civilisation** to the four corners of the world.
羅馬人把文明帶到了世界的各個角落。

- Individualism could **destroy Western civilization** if everyone does only what they want. 如果每個人都只做自己想做的事，個人主義可能會推毀西方文明。

....

☆ 注意不同類型的「文明」。

☆ 注意哪幾種 civilization 必須使用大寫字母，哪幾種則不行。

　　現在，我們來看看各位是否能用一些字詞搭配來擴大對字彙的運用。

Task 9

請從 Task 4 到 Task 8 中選出正確形式的字詞，完成以下段落填空。

Kant (1) ＿＿＿＿＿ the (2) ＿＿＿＿＿ argument (3) ＿＿＿＿＿ it is the (4) ＿＿＿＿＿ ambition to succeed which makes people (5) ＿＿＿＿＿ (6) ＿＿＿＿＿ civilisations, with special technology and high cultural achievements. Their (7) ＿＿＿＿＿ aspirations (8) ＿＿＿＿＿ self-fulfilment and independence are the driving forces behind society. It's this aspect of his argument which most people (9) ＿＿＿＿＿ his most (10) ＿＿＿＿＿.

範例答案

1. advanced/deployed/offered/presented/put forward
2. compelling/conclusive/convincing/persuasive/plausible
3. that
4. driving/great/naked/burning/high/main/overriding/ultimate/personal
5. create
6. advanced/modern/great
7. high/lofty
8. towards
9. consider
10. encouraging/exciting/fascinating/interesting/controversial

....

☆ 請留意各組同義字詞，空格中選填同一組內不同的字也是可以的。

☆ 須確認所選用的單字都是正確的形式。請檢查單數或複數，以及動詞的正確形式。例如空格 (1) 中的動詞必須使用過去簡單式，因為康德已經不在世上了。

Task 10

請研讀這個字詞搭配表和例句。

搭配在前的動詞	搭配的形容詞		關鍵字
have be come as avoid	big huge massive great bitter crushing grave serious terrible	slight inevitable personal	**disappointment**

字詞搭配使用範例

- His failure to achieve his ambition **came as** a **grave disappointment** to him.
  未能完成他的雄心壯志對他來說是極大的失望。

- Life **is a crushing disappointment** for many people.
  對很多人來說，人生是徹底失望的。

Task 11

請研讀這個字詞搭配表和例句。

搭配在前面的動詞		搭配的形容詞		關鍵字
have	provide s/o with	great	intellectual personal	**fulfilment**
derive gain find obtain		complete perfect partial	physical sexual	

- Complete isolation from society cannot **provide** everyone **with personal fulfilment**. 與社會完全隔絕就無法為人們提供個人的成就。

- Every individual deserves to **derive** at least **partial fulfilment** from their lives. 每個個人都應該從他們的人生中獲得至少部分的實現。

Task 12

請研讀這個字詞搭配表、例句和底下的說明。

搭配在前面的動詞	搭配的形容詞		關鍵字
form found set up start divide s/th into s/th manage run be a member of ~ become a member of ~ join belong to leave	big large wide small coherent tight select overlapping different	age blood cultural discussion ethnic family minority peer pop pressure racial rock self-help social study theatre	**group (of s/th)**

- Society **is** often **formed** of quite **different** but **coherent** and **overlapping groups**. 社會通常是由一些相當不同但又相互關連的群體所組成。

- Most people **become a member of** a **group of** like-minded people, and thus never change their minds about important issues. 大部分的人會成為志同道合的群體中的一員，因此他們在重要的議題上從不改變自己的想法。

- Most people **belong to** a coherent **social** and **ethnic** group.
  大部分的人都會歸屬於一個相互凝聚的社會和種族群體。

....

☆ 留意到「群體」的不同類型。

☆ 注意，動詞 be/come a member of ~、join、belong to、leave 不能使用被動
　　語態，但其他的動詞都可以。

Task 13

請研讀這個字詞搭配表和例句。

搭配在前面的動詞	搭配的形容詞		關鍵字
achieve find be filled with feel glow with weep with bring s/o buy s/o wish s/o	deep great perfect pure true lasting future	domestic earthly family human marital personal	**happiness**

字詞搭配使用範例

- When she achieved her dream, she **was weeping with perfect happiness**.
  當她實現自己的夢想時，喜極而泣。

- Most people **find personal happiness** when they are part of a group, but some
  individuals only **achieve true happiness** when they are on their own.
  大部分的人在身為群體的一分子時會找到個人的幸福，但有些個人則是只有當他們獨自
  一人時才能獲得真正的幸福。

Task 14

請研讀這個字詞搭配表、例句和底下的說明。

搭配在前面的片語	搭配的形容詞		關鍵字
concern for the ~ the freedom of the ~ a group of ~s the needs of the ~ respect for the ~ vary from ~ to ~ each ~	outstanding talented key powerful creative	average ordinary private autonomous independent isolated like-minded	**individual**
搭配在前面的動詞			
treat s/o as			

PART

2

字詞搭配使用範例

- **Concern for the ordinary individual** is the driving force of humanitarian efforts. 關切平凡的個人是人道努力的驅動力。
- We must **treat** everyone **as an autonomous individual**.
  我們必須把每個人都當成自主的個體來對待。
- Society is nothing more than **a group of individuals**.
  社會不過就是一群的個體。

☆ 使用 a group of 時，名詞 individual 必須加上 s。

Task 15

請從 Task 10 到 Task 14 中選出正確形式的字詞，完成以下段落填空。

Bentham was a proponent of the argument that (1) _____ the (2) _____ individual is less important than social stability. He saw society as consisting of (3) _____ groups to which people (4) _____, so sometimes people (5) _____ of more than one social group, and they (6) _____ (7) _____ fulfilment as members. The happiness that one person can (8) _____ on their own is not as (9) _____ as the happiness which that person can (10) _____ as a member of a happy group. The problem with Bentham's idea is that he never found a reliable way of measuring happiness. For most people, putting the needs of the group first makes it hard for individuals to (11) _____ (12) _____ disappointment when the needs of the group do not match their own personal needs.

範例答案

1. the freedom of
2. private/autonomous/independent
3. coherent/tight/select/overlapping/different
4. belong
5. are members
6. derive/gain/find/obtain
7. personal/complete/perfect
8. achieve/find
9. deep/great/perfect/pure/true/lasting
10. achieve/find
11. avoid
12. bitter/crushing/grave/serious/terrible/personal

☆ 務必確認所選用的單字都是正確的形式。例如,在空格 (5) 中必須使用 members,因為主詞是 people。

請研讀這個字詞搭配表和例句。

搭配在前的動詞	搭配的形容詞		關鍵字
have lead live enjoy change dominate take over build start make	good happy lonely miserable sad unhappy hard easy active busy hectic exciting	full peaceful quiet normal ordinary healthy sheltered double new	**life**

PART
2

字詞搭配使用範例

- In order to **lead** a **good** and **happy life**, there must be a balance between individualism and the group.
  為了過美好而幸福的生活，個人主義和群體之間必須有所平衡。

- If you let selfish desires **take over your life**, you will not be happy.
  假如讓自私的慾望接管你的人生，你就不會幸福。

- Most people just want to **live** a **quiet** and **peaceful life**.
  大部分的人只想要過安靜平和的生活。

- The spy was found to **have lead** a **double life**.
  那名間諜被發現過著雙重生活。

請研讀這個字詞搭配表、例句和底下的說明。

搭配在前面的動詞		搭配的形容詞	關鍵字
have	develop	considerable	
show	exploit	enormous	
	unlock	great	**potential**
be aware of		limitless	**(for s/th)**
see	fulfil	full	**(to V)**
	reach		
	realize	unfulfilled	
	recognize	untapped	

字詞搭配使用範例

• Society can either help an individual to **reach her full potential**, or it can prevent her from **unlocking** it.
社會既能幫助個人充分發揮潛能，也能阻止個人解鎖潛能。

• Most people do not see the **limitless potential** in themselves, and need help from others to **recognize** it.
大部分的人沒有看到自己身上無限的潛能，需要由別人幫忙來認識到這一 潛能。

• The young man **showed great potential for** business.
這個年輕人在生意上展現出巨大的潛能。

• Many people **have** the **potential to do** this, but only a few **realize** it.
很多人都有潛能做到這樣，但只有少數人意識到這一點。

☆ 留意到你需要用 for n.p. 或 to V，但千萬不能用 for Ving。

Task 18

請研讀這個字詞搭配表、例句和底下的說明。

搭配在前面的動詞		搭配的形容詞		關鍵字
have	abdicate	full	financial	
	evade	total	legal	
take	shift	great	ministerial	
accept			moral	
assume	admit	heavy	parental	
bear	claim	weighty	social	
shoulder				
take on	deny	direct		**responsibility**
	disclaim	overall		**(for s/th)**
share		primary		
lay		ultimate		
place ~ on		special		
delegate ~ to		collective		
devolve ~ to		joint		
hand over ~ to		shared		
		individual		
		personal		

字詞搭配使用範例

- We all have to **bear** the **responsibility for** our own decisions.
  我們都必須為自己的決定承擔責任。

- Some people want to **abdicate** all **responsibility for** their lives and just
  become a sheep in a flock.
  有些人想要放棄對自己人生的一切責任，而只是成為羊群中的一隻羊。

- They **denied responsibility for** any wrongdoing.
  他們否認對任何不當行為負有責任。

- We are going to **devolve responsibility for** this project **to** you. We hope you
  will **take** overall **responsibility for** it.
  我們將把這個專案的責任移交給你。希望你會為它負起全責。

☆ 留意到「責任」的不同類型。

Task 19

請研讀這個字詞搭配表和例句。

搭配在前面的片語	搭配的形容詞	關鍵字
an act of ~ greed and ~ be full of ~	pure utter ruthless narrow egoistic downright	**selfishness**
搭配在前面的動詞		
have be promote give rise to		

字詞搭配使用範例

- Our modern way of life often **gives rise to pure selfishness**.
  我們現代的生活方式常常會導致純粹的自私。

- Capitalism **promotes downright selfishness**. 資本主義促使了徹頭徹尾的自私。

- Without some idea of the needs of the group, society will **be full of narrow selfishness**. 如果沒有對群體的需求有一些想法，社會將會充滿狹隘的自私。

Task 20

請研讀這個字詞搭配表、例句和底下的說明。

搭配在前面的片語	搭配的形容詞		關鍵字
across the ~ at one end of the ~ at the other end of the ~ at opposite ends of the ~	full complete entire whole broad wide	narrow political social theoretical	**spectrum (of s/th)**
搭配在前面的動詞			
cover be exist on			

- We **exist on opposite ends of** the **political spectrum**. He's on the right and I'm on the left. 我們處於政治光譜的兩個極端。他在右，我在左。

- **At one end of the spectrum** we have those who believe in individualism, and **at the other end of the spectrum** we have those who believe in the group. We **are at opposite ends of the spectrum**.

  在光譜的一端，我們有那些相信個人主義的人，而在光譜的另一端，我們則有那些相信群體的人。我們是在光譜的兩個極端。

- An open society should **cover** the **complete political spectrum**.

  一個開放的社會應該要涵蓋完整的政治光譜。

....

☆ 留意到「光譜」的不同類型。

☆ spectrum 的複數是 spectra，但盡量避免使用複數。

Task 21

請從 Task 16 到 Task 20 中選出正確形式的字詞，完成以下段落填空。

Everyone (1) _____ (2) _____ potential (3) _____ (4) _____ a (5) _____ and (6) _____ life, with the (7) _____ spectrum (8) _____ both joy and sorrows. Society helps those individuals to not (9) _____ (10) _____ selfishness and to (11) _____ responsibility (12) _____ their actions and how they impact other people. No one can blame others for their faults.

範例答案

1. has/shows

2. considerable/enormous/great/limitless/full

3. to

4. have/lead/live

5. full/peaceful/quiet/good/happy
6. full/peaceful/quiet/good/happy
7. full/complete/entire/whole
8. of
9. give rise to
10. pure/utter/ruthless/narrow/egoistic/downright
11. take/accept/assume/bear/shoulder/take on
12. for

．．．

☆ 須留意在空格 (1) 中，動詞要加上 s，因為主詞是 Everyone，而且 everyone 後面必須用單數動詞。

　　記住，多閱讀有助於擴充字彙量，而在文章上下文脈絡中查看大量例子則能幫助你記憶新的用語。下一個練習對於各位記憶 15 個關鍵單字和它們的字詞搭配將有非常大的幫助。

Task 22

請從 Task 1 和 Task 2 的閱讀文章中找出關鍵語庫 ❶ 所列的 15 個關鍵字，並留意這些字在文章中是如何使用的。

常用語塊 Chunks

前面學過了字詞搭配的用法，我們現在要來學一些可用在寫作或談論這個主題的 chunks「語塊」。

Task 23

研讀這些語塊和底下的說明。

關鍵語庫 ❷

<table>
<tr><th>Chunk</th></tr>
<tr><td>

❏ an obstacle to n.p./Ving　阻礙 n.p./Ving

❏ be inspired by n.p./Ving　受到 n.p./Ving 啟發、鼓舞

❏ take s/th into account　考慮到 s/th

❏ be the same (as s/th)　（跟 s/th）相同

❏ equate to n.p./Ving　等同於 n.p./Ving

❏ give priority to n.p./Ving　把 n.p./Ving 視為優先

❏ be united (in n.p./Ving)　（在 s/th 上）團結一致

❏ be successful (at n.p./Ving)　（在 s/th 上）成功

❏ be content (with n.p./Ving)　甘於、滿足於 n.p./Ving

❏ be content to (V)　滿足於（V）

</td></tr>
</table>

☆ 須留意哪些語塊要接受詞、哪些不用。還要留意到受詞的類型，尤其是需要使用人物受詞 (s/o) 或事物受詞 (s/th) 時。

☆ 須留意這些語塊是否全都必須用 n.p.、Ving 或 V。

☆ 別忘了在使用這些語塊時需要改變動詞的時態。

☆ 注意，在使用 obstacle to 時，必須使用 be 動詞。假如想要用於否定，可以把動詞變為否定或使用 no：There is no obstacle to it.、There isn't an obstacle to it.。兩者都正確。

☆ inspired 可以用於主動式的句子中：It inspires people。但是我們通常會以被動來使用這個字，如同此處。

☆ 使用 take s/th into account 時，可以把名詞受詞擺在動詞和介系詞之間，或者擺在 account 後面：We need to take human nature into account.、We need to take into account human nature. 兩者都正確。但如果受詞是代名詞，它就只能擺在動詞和介系詞之間：We need to take it into account. 正確；We need to take into account it. 則是錯的。

☆ 請注意，使用 be the same as 時，必須使用 the，而且必須使用 as，而不是 with：It is not the same with this. 是錯的；It is not the same as this. 才正確。

☆ equate 是動詞，所以必要時記得要加上 s，並使用正確的時態。注意，不要用 be 動詞。

☆ 使用 united 時，若想要指明受詞，就必須使用 in。

☆ 使用 successful 時，若想要指明受詞，就必須使用 at。若要把這變成否定，就用 unsuccessful。

☆ 使用 content 時，若想要指明一個 n.p. 或 Ving 受詞，就必須使用 with。若想要指明一個行動受詞，則必須使用 to V。

下一個 Task 將聚焦於大家在使用這些語塊時經常會犯的錯誤。

Task 24

請改正這些句子中使用語塊的常見錯誤。

① A successful leader always take into account the weakness of his followers.

_____

② Do we give priority for the individual or for the group?

_____

③ He successful due to his ambition and drive.

_____

④ If we are united for our efforts, we will be stronger.

_____

⑤ Individualism is not the same with selfishness.

_____

⑥ It's difficult to get people to be unite.

_____

⑦ Many people inspired by his example.

_____

⑧ Most people are content with have a peaceful life.

_____

⑨ Most people are successful in finding a balance between self-interest and the needs of the group.

_____

⑩ Philosophy often equate individualism with selfishness.

_____

⑪ Self-interest the same as selfishness.

_____

⑫ She was inspire by their collective effort.

_____

⑬ She was not content to her life.

_____

⑭ Society can sometimes be an obstacle for people's happiness.

_____

⑮ Society doesn't equate with group effort.

_____

⑯ There no obstacles to our ambition and greed.

_____

⑰ We must take human frailty onto account.

_____

✅ 答案・中譯・說明　💿 **Track 9.3**

① A successful leader always take**s** into account the weakness of his followers.
一個成功的領導人向來都會考慮到他追隨者的弱點。

② Do we <u>give priority</u> **to** the individual or to the group?
我們該優先考慮的是個人還是團體？

③ He **is** successful due to his ambition and drive. 他是靠企圖心和衝勁而成功。

④ If we are united **in** our efforts, we will be stronger.
假如我們在努力上團結一致，我們就會更強。

⑤ Individualism is not the same **as** selfishness. 個人主義和自私並不相同。

⑥ It's difficult to get people to be unit**ed**. 要讓人團結一致很難。

⑦ Many people **are** inspired by his example. 很多人受到他的例子所啓發。

⑧ Most people are content with **have** a peaceful life.
大部分的人都對平和的生活感到滿意。

Most people are content **to have** a peaceful life.
大部分的人都甘於過著平和的生活。

⑨ Most people are successful **at** finding a balance between self-interest and the needs of the group.
大部分的人都成功地在自身利益和群體需要之間找到平衡。

⑩ Philosophy often equate**s** individualism with selfishness.
哲學常把個人主義等同於自私。

⑪ Self-interest **is** the same as selfishness. 自利就等同於自私。

⑫ She was inspir**ed** by their collective effort.
她是受到他們的集體努力所鼓舞。

⑬ She was not content **with** her life. 她不滿足於自己的生活。

⑭ Society can sometimes be an obstacle **to** people's happiness.
社會有時候可能成為人們幸福的阻礙。

⑮ Society doesn't equate **to** group effort. 社會並不等同於群體努力。

⑯ There **are** no obstacles to our ambition and greed.
這對我們的野心和貪婪沒有任何阻礙。

⑰ We must take human frailty **into** account. 我們必須考慮到人性的脆弱。

☆ 第 1 句和第 10 句的錯誤在於動詞時態：在使用現在簡單式時，若主詞是第三人稱，別忘了動詞要加上 s！而在第 3、7、11、16 句中，記得要用 be 動詞。別忘了聚焦在動詞上！

☆ 請將正確句子中的完整語塊畫上底線，這能幫助你完整而正確地記住語塊。

　　下一個練習對於記憶語塊將有非常大的幫助。記住，多閱讀有助於擴充字彙量，而在文章上下文脈絡中查看大量語塊則能幫助你記憶新的用語。

Task 25

請從 Task 1 和 Task 2 的閱讀文章中找出關鍵語庫 ❷ 列出的所有語塊，並留意這些語塊在文章中是如何使用的。

Task 26

現在請嘗試用前面學過的語塊來寫出你自己的句子。

關鍵字語塊	造句
an obstacle to n.p. /Ving	

be inspired by n.p. /Ving	
take s/th into account	
be the same (as s/th)	
equate to n.p./Ving	
give priority to n.p. /Ving	
be united (in n.p./Ving)	
be successful (at n.p./Ving)	
be content (with n.p./Ving)	
be content to (V)	

☆ 我顯然無法在此改正你的句子，但你可以透過確認語塊所有的小細節，自行改正。再次提醒在寫作中運用語塊時，須特別注意小詞、字尾和語塊的結尾，無論所需要的是 n.p.、v.p.、Ving 還是 V，並且確保你所使用的語塊是完整的。

5 個可作動詞或名詞的單字
5 words which can be verbs or nouns

語塊通常會視關鍵字是名詞或動詞而有所不同，現在我們要來看 5 個動詞和名詞同形的單字，並學習使用正確的語塊。

Task 27

請看以下幾個名詞和動詞同形的單字。

關鍵語庫 ❸

關鍵字	名詞字義	動詞字義
exchange	交換；交流；交易；匯兌	交換；兌換；調換職務（或位置）
hope	希望；可能性；期待	希望；盼望；期待
influence	影響（力）；作用；勢力	影響；感化；左右
offer	提供；提議；出價；報價	提供；提議；出示；出（價）
sacrifice	祭品；獻祭；犧牲（的行為）	犧牲；獻出

Task 28

閱讀句子並判斷關鍵字是動詞或名詞，填入 V 或 N。

① _____ Everyone **hopes** to achieve their dreams.
② _____ If we **exchange** our personal freedom for the benefit of the group, everybody will be better off.
③ _____ It's not a fair **exchange**.
④ _____ It's too much of a **sacrifice** to expect people to give up their ambitions.
⑤ _____ Some people feel that society has not much to **offer** them.
⑥ _____ Sometimes we have to **sacrifice** our own pleasure for the needs of the group.

⑦ _____ The Greeks had the biggest **influence** on Western philosophy.

⑧ _____ There is no **hope** of ever achieving social harmony.

⑨ _____ Western thinking about individualism **influences** everything in our society.

⑩ _____ What's on **offer** is social harmony in the broadest sense.

✅ 答案・中譯・說明

① V 每個人都希望達成夢想。

② V 如果我們用個人的自由來換取群體的利益，每個人就會更好過。

③ N 這不是公平的交易。

④ N 期望人們放棄他們的野心，這犧牲太大了。

⑤ V 有些人覺得，社會可給予他們的並不多。

⑥ V 有時候我們不得不為了群體的需要而犧牲自身的快樂。

⑦ N 希臘人對西方哲學的影響力最大。

⑧ N 社會和諧是永遠沒有希望實現的。

⑨ V 西方有關個人主義的思想影響了我們社會的一切。

⑩ N 這裡所提供的是最廣義的社會和諧。

Task 29

請看以下所彙整的語塊及用法說明。

關鍵語庫 ④　🎧 Track 9.4

關鍵字語塊	關鍵字詞性	例句 & 翻譯
exchange (of)	*nc*	The open exchange of ideas is very important. 公開的思想交流是非常重要的。
(in) exchange (for)	*nc*	Many give up their freedoms in exchange for stability. 許多人放棄自由以換取穩定。

exchange s/th (for s/th)	*vt*	He exchanged his freedom for financial security. 他用自由換取了財務保障。
hope (of s/th)	*nc*	There's no hope of social stability. 社會穩定是沒有希望的。
hope (for n.p.)	*vi*	Many hope for total fairness in society. 許多人希望社會全然公平。
hope (that v.p.)	*vi*	There's hope that things will get better for the individual. 對個人來說，情況有希望變好。
hope (to V)	*vi*	We can only hope to succeed. 我們只能希望會成功。
influence (of s/th) (on s/th)	*nc*	The influence of society on people's decisions is big. 社會對人們決策方面的影響是很大的。
influence s/th	*vt*	It did not influence my decision at all. 它絲毫沒有影響到我的決定。
offer (of s/th)	*nc*	The offer of support is very welcome. 非常歡迎提供支援。
offer s/th to s/o	*vt*	Group membership offers many advantages to people. 團體會員資格提供了很多優勢給人們。
offer (to V)	*vi*	They offered to help with expenses. 他們提出要在費用上給予幫助。
sacrifice	*nc*	Parents usually make many sacrifices for their children. 父母通常會為他們的子女做出很多犧牲。
sacrifice s/th (to s/o) (for s/th)	*vt*	They sacrificed their freedom to the government. 他們為政府犧牲了自由。

☆ 留意哪些名詞是可數，哪些是不可數；使用動詞時務必確認時態正確性。

☆ 注意，exchange 作為名詞時是可數的，但向來都應以單數來使用：There are

many fair exchanges. 是錯的；It's an unfair exchange. 則正確。另外要留意到，你可以使用名詞片語 in exchange for s/th。而當 exchange 是動詞時，必須使用受詞，若想要指明所交換的兩樣東西，可以使用兩個受詞。請看例句。

☆ hope 當動詞來用時，可以使用 for n.p. 或 hope that v.p.。請務必留心 n.p. 和 v.p.，以及所需使用的不同小詞。你也可以使用 hope to V，在這種情況下，意指 plan to「計畫去……」。

☆ influence 當名詞來用時，可以使用動詞 have 和 be。另外，若想要指明帶來影響的事物時，必須使用介系詞 of 和 on：He talked about the big influence of peer pressure.、Security is a big influence on people.。注意，influence 當動詞來用時，不可以使用任何介系詞：It influenced on me. 是錯的；It influenced me. 才正確。

☆ offer 當名詞使用時，若想要指明被提供的事物，必須使用 of。而當動詞使用時，可以有兩個受詞，但須留意哪個受詞是事物、哪個是人物。此外，如果想要後接一個行動，則必須使用 to V。請仔細看所有的例句。

☆ sacrifice 當名詞時，必須使用動詞 make 或 be 動詞：It's no sacrifice.。而若是把 sacrifice 用作動詞時，則要特別留意所使用的受詞：They sacrificed their freedom to the government. 意思指「他們把自由交給政府」；They sacrificed their freedom for safety. 指的則是「他們交出自由來換取別的東西（安全）」。

☆ 請仔細學習這些語塊，並把重點放在諸如介系詞、所需受詞等這些細節。

Task 30

請選用正確形式的單字或語塊，完成下列各句。

① **in exchange for/exchange it for**

Giving up your personal freedom ＿＿＿＿＿＿ social stability is a good choice for many people.

② **influence of/influence on**

His ideas had a big ＿＿＿＿＿＿ society.

③ **sacrificing/sacrificing for**

Is it worth _____ your youth in the hopes that the future will be better?

④ **hope that/hope for**

Most of us _____ a better life for our children.

⑤ **offer/offers**

Social stability _____ many benefits to individuals.

⑥ **offer to/offer of**

Society can _____ help with things the individual cannot do on their own.

⑦ **exchange for/exchange of**

The _____ personal freedom for group safety seems fair to many people.

⑧ **hope for/hope of**

The _____ a better future motivates many people to undergo present suffering.

⑨ **influence on/influence of**

The _____ his ideas on our world is enormous.

⑩ **sacrifice/sacrifice to**

The _____ is difficult for many.

⑪ **hope that/hope to**

Most people _____ be able to provide for themselves.

⑫ **offer of/offer to**

They made him an _____ a government position he couldn't refuse.

⑬ **influenced/influence on**

This idea _____ future generations.

⑭ **hope for/hope that**

We _____ the group will meet those needs we cannot meet by ourselves.

⑮ **exchange of/exchange**

Western people are unwilling to _____ their freedom for the good of society.

✔ 答案・中譯・說明   🎧 **Track 9.5**

① Giving up your personal freedom <u>in exchange for</u> social stability is a good choice for many people.
放棄個人自由以換取社會穩定對許多人來說是個好選擇。

② His ideas had a big influence on society. 他的觀念對社會有很大的影響力。

③ Is it worth sacrificing your youth in the hopes that the future will be better?
犧牲青春來寄望未來會更好是否值得？

④ Most of us hope for a better life for our children.
我們大多數的人都盼望我們的孩子過上更好的生活。

⑤ Social stability offers many benefits to individuals.
社會穩定帶給個人很多益處。

⑥ Society can offer to help with things the individual cannot do on their own.
社會可以在個人無法自行做到的事情上提供幫助。

⑦ The exchange of personal freedom for group safety seems fair to many people.
以個人自由來換取群體安全對許多人來說似乎是公平的。

⑧ The hope of a better future motivates many people to undergo present suffering.
對更美好未來的期望會促使很多人去忍受眼前的苦難。

⑨ The influence of his ideas on our world is enormous.
他的思想對世界的影響力是巨大的。

⑩ The sacrifice is difficult for many. 這個犧牲對很多人來說是困難的。

⑪ Most people hope to be able to provide for themselves.
大多數的人都希望能夠自給自足。

⑫ They made him an offer of a government position he couldn't refuse.
他們向他提議了一個他無法拒絕的政府職位。

⑬ This idea influenced future generations. 這個觀念影響了未來世代。

⑭ We hope that the group will meet those needs we cannot meet by ourselves.
我們希望該團體會滿足我們無法自行滿足的那些需求。

⑮ Western people are unwilling to exchange their freedom for the good of society.
西方人不願意以他們的自由來換取社會公益。

☆ 記得確認所使用的動詞時態都正確。

☆ 請拿正確的句子來與關鍵語庫 ❹ 的語塊做比較,確保名詞或動詞語塊都用得正確。

☆ 請將正確句子中的完整語塊畫上底線(參照第 1 句的示範)。這將有助於各位把語塊完整而正確地記起來。

再次提醒,盡可能地多閱讀有助於擴充字彙量,而在文章上下文脈絡中查看大量語塊則能幫助你記憶新的用語。

Task 31

請從 Task 1 和 Task 2 的閱讀文章中找出關鍵語庫 ❹ 列出的所有語塊,並留意這些語塊在文章中是當動詞還是名詞使用?

Task 32

請練習用關鍵語庫 ❹ 的語塊來造句。

關鍵字語塊	造句
exchange (of)	
(in) exchange (for)	
exchange s/th (for s/th)	
hope (of s/th)	
hope (for n.p.)	
hope (that v.p.)	
hope (to V)	
influence (of s/th) (on s/th)	
influence s/th	
offer (of s/th)	
offer s/th to s/o	
offer (to V)	
sacrifice	
sacrifice s/th (to s/o) (for s/th)	

☆ 我顯然無法在此來改正你的句子，但你可以透過確認語塊所有的小細節，自行改正。再次提醒在寫作中運用語塊時，須特別注意小詞、字尾和語塊的結尾，無論所需要的是 n.p.、v.p.、Ving 還是 V，並且確保你所使用的語塊是完整的。

5 個談論或寫作個人主義時常用的片語動詞 5 phrasal verbs for talking or writing about individualism

我們現在要來看一些在寫作或談論個人主義相關主題時，常會用到的片語動詞。

Task 33

研讀語庫中的片語動詞、例句和其下的說明。

關鍵語庫 ⑤　🔘 **Track 9.6**

片語動詞	例句
point s/th out 指出	• He pointed the truth out. 他把事實真相指出來。 • He pointed out the truth. 他指出了事實真相 • He pointed it out. 他把它指出來。 • He pointed out that society helps us to do things we cannot do ourselves. 　他指出，社會幫助我們做我們自己做不到的事情。
pull s/th off 成功完成	• He pulled the difficult achievement off. 　他把那項困難的成就完成了。 • He pulled off the difficult achievement. 　他完成了那項困難的成就。 • He pulled it off. 他把它做成了。
build (s/th) on s/th 把某事當成其他事的基礎、建立於	• They built on the failures of the past. 　他們是奠基在過去的失敗上。 • They built the new society on the failures of the past. 　他們在過去失敗的基礎上建立了新社會。 • The new society was built on the failures of the past. 　新社會是奠立在過去失敗的基礎上。

stay ahead (of s/th) 有競爭力、贏得、準備好、保持領先	• Other societies are catching up. We need to stay ahead of other societies. 別的社會正迎頭趕上。我們必須保持領先（其他社會）。 • We need to stay ahead of them. 我們必須保持領先他們。 • We need to stay ahead. 我們必須保持領先。
fall through 失敗、落空	• His attempt to create a better society fell through. 他想創造更美好社會的企圖沒能實現。

☆ 記得，你必須非常留意動詞有沒有受詞 (s/th)，以及這個受詞是擺在哪個位置。請仔細確認上方語庫中的片語動詞及其受詞的位置。

☆ point out 若連同名詞受詞來用，可以擺在動詞和介系詞之間，或是介系詞之後。不過若是使用代名詞受詞，則必須擺在動詞和介系詞之間。注意，這個片語動詞後面也能使用 that v.p.。請看例句。

☆ pull off 若連同名詞受詞來用，可以擺在動詞和介系詞之間，或是介系詞之後。不過若是使用代名詞受詞，則必須擺在動詞和介系詞之間。請看例句。

☆ 使用 build on 時，可以選擇要不要指明新的事物（如例句中的 the new society），on 後接的受詞則是舊事物。這個片語動詞中不要用代名詞，但要用名詞片語來說明新舊事物是什麼。另外，這個片語動詞也能以被動來使用。

☆ 使用 stay ahead (of s/th) 時，若要指明想要贏得的事，名詞和代名詞這兩類受詞都必須擺在介系詞之後。請看例句。

☆ 注意，fall through 沒有受詞。

☆ 請記得片語動詞是動詞，所以還必須考慮動詞要用什麼時態。

下一個練習將有助於各位聚焦於受詞的正確擺放位置這些細節上。

Task 34

下列各句中的第一個字是正確的，請按照順序將其後的字詞重組成正確的句子。

EX. **His through to persuade ideas accept people attempt his fell to**
His attempt to persuade people to accept his ideas fell through.

① Every the is of on built the advance achievements past

_____

② He out there benefit was by pointed great to the be that had joining group

_____

③ He truth out the pointed

_____

④ His a through of society dream fair fell

_____

⑤ In it's of important the to age ahead competition our stay

_____

⑥ They understand out until didn't he pointed it it

_____

⑦ They off pulled plan the

_____

✅ 答案・中譯・說明 🎧 **Track 9.7**

① Every advance <u>is built on</u> the achievements of the past.
每一次的進展都是奠基在過去的成就。

② He pointed out that there was great benefit to be had by joining the group.
他指出，加入這個團體會有很大的益處。

③ He pointed out the truth. 他指出了真相。

He pointed the truth out. 他把真相指出來了。

④ His dream of a fair society fell through. 他所夢想的公平社會落空了。

⑤ In our age it's important to stay ahead of the competition.
在我們這個時代，於競爭中保持領先是很重要的。

⑥ They didn't understand it until he pointed it out.
直到他把它指出來，他們才了解。

⑦ They pulled the plan off. 他們把計畫做成了。

They pulled off the plan. 他們做成了這個計畫。

....

☆ 將正確的句子與關鍵語庫 ❺ 的片語動詞做比較，確認你的用法都正確。

☆ 請將正確句子中的片語動詞畫上底線，這將幫助你完整而正確地把語塊記起
　 來。（參照第 1 句的示範）

Task 35

請從 Task 1 和 Task 2 的閱讀文章中找出關鍵語庫 ❺ 列出的所有片語動詞，
並留意它們在文章中是如何使用的。

Task 36

請練習用關鍵語庫 ❺ 的片語動詞來造句。

片語動詞	造句練習
point s/th out	
pull s/th off	
build (s/th) on s/th	
stay ahead (of s/th)	
fall through	

5 個談論或寫作個人主義時常用的慣用語 5 idioms for talking or writing about individualism

Task 37

研讀語庫中的慣用語、例句和其下的說明。

關鍵語庫 **6**　🔊 **Track 9.8**

慣用語	例句
an/the average Joe 一般人	• The average Joe wants to be happy and fulfilled just as much as a great individual. 一般人和偉大的人都一樣，希望自己能快樂與充實。
be a high flier 成為在事業上有極高抱負的成功職業人士	• Not everyone can be a high flier because there isn't much room at the top. 不是人人都當得了位高權重的人，因為頂層沒那麼多空間。
movers and shakers 有影響力、有權勢的人	• The movers and shakers of the world have decided to keep things as they are. 世上有權有勢的人決定保持現狀。
pull rank 因為社會地位較高而占到某種便宜；濫用職權	• Although he was at the back of the queue, he pulled rank and was given first priority. 雖然他排在隊伍的後段，但他因自己的地位而被給予第一優先權。
work the system 知道要怎麼把規則操作到對自己有利	• He doesn't have much natural ability, but he got where he is because he knows how to work the system. 他沒多少天生的能力，但他能有今天的地位是因為他知道要如何善用體制。

☆ 為了讓慣用語有意義，它必須完全準確才行，這意味著你必須將慣用語的所有

細節都使用正確。

☆ 請注意這幾個慣用語都沒有受詞，不要連同受詞來使用。

Task 38

改正這些句子中的常見錯誤。

① A normal Joe wants to be happy too.

_____

② Although he is flying high, he still helps those in need.

_____

③ He is a mover and a shaker in our society.

_____

④ He knows how the system works.

_____

⑤ He pulled out his rank and got better service.

_____

☑ 答案・中譯・說明　　◉ **Track 9.9**

① The average Joe wants to be happy too. 平凡人也想要幸福。

② Although he is a high flier, he still helps those in need.
　 雖然他是位高權重的人，他還是會幫助有需要的人。

③ He is one of the movers and shakers in our society.
　 他在我們的社會上是一個有權有勢的人。

④ He knows how to work the system. 他知道要怎麼善用體制。

⑤ He pulled rank and got better service. 他利用職權而得到了較好的服務。

☆ 請仔細比較錯誤句子和正確解答，務必確實掌握錯在哪以及為什麼是錯的。

現在我們要練習的是，在文章上下文中找出慣用語。

Task 39

請從 Task 1 和 Task 2 的閱讀文章中找出關鍵語庫 ❻ 列出的所有慣用語，並留意它們在文章中是如何使用的。

Task 40

請練習用關鍵語庫 ❻ 的慣用語來造句。

慣用語	造句練習
an/the average Joe	
be a high flier	
movers and shakers	
pull rank	
work the system	

☆ 再次提醒在寫作時若運用到這些慣用語，要特別留意動詞的時態和完整的慣用語包含哪些細節。

易混淆的字詞 easily confused words

☐ 要記得，有些單字只能用在特定的主題上，用在別的主題則不適當。

☐ 另外，容易搞混的單字，其差別常常是在搭配詞的使用上有所不同。

在做接下來幾個練習時，務必記得這些重點。

Task 41

請仔細研讀各組易混淆的字詞、例句和其下的說明。

關鍵語庫 ⑦ 🎧 **Track 9.10**

易混淆字詞		例句
1	**expand** (*vi*, *vt*) 擴展	• We can expand this idea to include all forms of antisocial behavior. 我們可以把這個觀念擴展到包含所有形式的反社會行為。 • The notion of personhood has expanded to include business entities. 人格的概念已經擴展到包含商業實體。
	spread (*vi*, *vt*) 傳播、散布、延伸	• The media is the best way to spread ideas. 媒體是傳播思想的最佳方式。 • The idea is spreading. 這個想法正在傳播。
2	**rise** (*vi*) 攀升、升起	• The number of people who feel trapped by society's expectations is rising. 覺得被社會期望所束縛的人數正在上升。
	arise (*vi*) 形成、產生、出現	• What has arisen here is something very unexpected. 在此所發生的是非常出乎意料的事。

3	**notion** (*nc*) 觀念、概念	• Most people have the notion that individualism is a good thing. 大部分的人都有的觀念是，個人主義是件好事。
	theory (*nc*) 理論	• There are many theories, but none of them really explain the phenomenon. 理論有很多，但沒有一個能真正解釋此現象。
4	**affect** (*nc*, *vt*) 影響	• His ideas affected social science and philosophy in a number of ways. 他的思想在若干方面影響了社會科學與哲學。
	effect (*nc*, *vt*) 作用、效果	• The effect was instantaneous. 效果立竿見影。 • It won't take effect until next month. 它要到下個月才會生效。 • Changes to the system were effected almost immediately. 對系統的修改幾乎是立即生效。
5	**person** (*nc*) 單人	• One person disagreed. 有一人不認同。
	people (*nc*) 眾人	• Some people are like that. 有些人就像是那樣。

PART
2

☆ expand 和 spread 的文法相同，但意思和用法相當不同。它們都可以用來描述抽象的概念，諸如觀念或思想。並請留意它們有兩種用法，帶受詞 (*vt*) 或不帶受詞 (*vi*)。

☆ 若要描述一個概念是如何變得更大以納入更多的概念時，就用 expand。而若要描述一些概念是如何增加，或者一個觀念影響的範圍如何擴大時，則須用 spread。

☆ rise 和 arise 看起來非常類似，似乎是有關連的，但實際上這兩個字只有文法類似，意思和用法則非常不同。注意，這兩個字都沒有受詞，在 Unit 3 裡，各位學過 rise 意指 increase「增加」，arise 則意指 happen「發生」。

☆ rise 是用來表示增加或以朝上的方向來走。注意，其動詞變化是不規則形：rise、rose、risen。

☆ 若是要描述事情已經發生時，就用 arise：A strange situation has arisen.。注意，這個動詞相當正式，動詞變化也是不規則形：arise、arose、arisen。

☆ notion 和 theory 的文法相同，但意思和用法略有不同。它們指的都是抽象的概念。notion 是 idea 或 concept 的同義詞，theory 則是指可能解釋某種現象的想法。在科學中，理論是透過實驗來檢驗，看看它是否正確地解釋了一些事情。我們也把一些著名的思想稱為 theories，諸如 the Theory of Relativity「相對論」、the Theory of Utilitarianism「功利主義理論」。

☆ 當要描述專門在解釋某事物的概念或想法時，使用 theory。想要指明某事不存在於物理現實中，而只作為一個抽象概念而存在時，也可以使用 theory。我們經常拿理論來對比現實，這種情況便稱為 practice：It might work in theory, but in practice, I don't know if it will work.。

☆ affect 和 effect 這兩個字聽起來幾乎一樣，也都可以作名詞或動詞，但其實意思和用法大不相同。

☆ 若想找另一個可表達 influence 的單字時，可把 affect 當作動詞使用：The idea has affected our society. 意即「我們的社會受到了這個觀念所影響」。另外，affect 當動詞時，也能以被動來使用：She was affected by his ideas.。請注意，affect 當名詞時是一個專門用於心理學領域中的特殊詞彙，因此在寫作時，不要把 affect 當名詞來用。

☆ 如果想要用另一個非常正式的單字來表達 do 或 carry out 時，可以將 effect 作為動詞使用：We should suspend the law until changes to it can be effected.。注意，當你這樣使用 effect 時，必須記得使用被動語態。另外，若是想用另一個字來表示 result，可把 effect 當名詞使用。effect 也能當名詞用於下列片語中：take effect、have an effect on s/th、put s/th into effect，這些全都表示某件事將作為另一件事的結果而發生。

☆ person 和 people 的區別非常容易。people 就是 person 的不規則複數形：一個人用 person，兩人以上用 people。person 的另一個複數形是 persons，但這用得不多，各位也絕不要用。像這樣的不規則形複數有更多，而且全都跟人有關：一個 man，兩個以上 men；一個 woman，兩個以上 women；一個 child，兩個以上 children。

☆ 注意，當想要指明一個特定的人時，就用 person。反之，若腦海中沒有浮現任何特定的人，只是想要描述一般的人時，就用 people。

在做下一個練習時，請仔細思考句意、文法和用法來選出正確的單字。

Task 42

請選出正確的單字來填入下列各句。

① **risen/arisen**

A new type of thinking about freedom has _____.

② **rising/arising**

Discontent among society's outcasts is _____.

③ **theory/notion**

In _____, it should work, but in practice it often doesn't.

④ **affected/effected**

Our society has been _____ by the ideas of the ancient Greeks.

⑤ **People/Person**

_____ are strange, there's no denying it.

⑥ **person/people**

She is the kind of _____ who likes ideas.

⑦ **has spread/has expanded**

The idea of Christmas _____ all over the world.

⑧ **has spread/has expanded**

The idea that everyone is equal under the law _____ to include the idea that everyone is the same.

⑨ **affect/effect**

The new laws will take _____ next week.

⑩ **notion/theory**

The _____ that society is greater than the individual was first put forward by Bentham.

⑪ **theory/notion**

The _____ has been tested again and again and it still doesn't hold true.

⑫ **are expanding/are spreading**

They _____ the rumour that our society is under threat.

⑬ **spread/expand**

They intend to _____ the law to include legal immigrants as well as illegal ones.

⑭ **affect/effect**

We don't know what the _____ will be.

✅ 答案．中譯．說明　🔊 **Track 9.11**

① A new type of thinking about freedom has arisen.
一種關於自由的新型思維產生了。

② Discontent among society's outcasts is rising.
社會棄兒的不滿情緒正在攀升。

③ In theory, it should work, but in practice it often doesn't.
理論上，這應該行得通，但實際上常常不然。

④ Our society has been affected by the ideas of the ancient Greeks.
我們的社會受到古希臘人的思想所影響。

⑤ People are strange, there's no denying it. 無可否認的是，人很奇怪。

⑥ She is the kind of person who likes ideas. 她是喜歡創意的那種人。

⑦ The idea of Christmas has spread all over the world.
耶誕節的概念已經傳遍了世界各地。

⑧ The idea that everyone is equal under the law has expanded to include the idea that everyone is the same.
法律之下、人人平等的觀念已經擴展到納入了人人相同的觀念。

⑨ The new laws will take effect next week. 新法將於下週生效。

⑩ The notion that society is greater than the individual was first put forward by Bentham. 社會大於個人的思維是由邊沁首先提出的。

⑪ The theory has been tested again and again and it still doesn't hold true.
這個理論經過了再三檢驗，還是沒有成立。

⑫ They are spreading the rumour that our society is under threat.
他們正在散布有關我們的社會受到威脅的謠言。

⑬ They intend to expand the law to include legal immigrants as well as illegal ones.
他們意圖把法律擴展到包括合法移民以及非法的。

⑭ We don't know what the effect will be. 我們不知道影響會是什麼。

☆ 第 1 句選用 arisen 是因為表達的意思是 happened；第 2 句選用 rising 是因為表達的意思是 increasing。

☆ 第 3 句需要 theory 是因為片語 in theory v.p..., but in practice v.p....；第 10 句用 notion 是因為意思純粹指一個觀念或想法，若在此使用 idea 也是可以的；第 11 句則是在講檢驗一個觀點或理論，因此需用 theory。

☆ 第 4 句所表達的意思是 influence 而不是 do 或 carry out 的被動正式說法，因此應選擇當動詞用的 affected；第 9 句選用當名詞的 effect 是因為片語 take effect，表示某事將作為另一件事的結果而發生；而第 14 句的意思同樣是指「結果」，因此也應用 effect。注意，affect 千萬不可當名詞用。

☆ 第 5 句不是在講特定的一個人，而是所有的一般人，因此要用 people；而第 6 句用 person 則是因為句子只在講一個人 she。

☆ 在第 7 句中必須用 has spread 是因為句意指的是受耶誕節所影響的地區變大；第 8 句使用 expanded 是因為本句表達的觀念是把意義擴展到納入了新的相關

意義；第 12 句選用 are spreading 是因為這是及物動詞，意指很多事在傳布；而第 13 句中，因為某事物（法律之事）是在規模和範疇上增加，而不是數目，因此應該用 expand。

最後我們還是要來練習從閱讀文章中找出這些容易搞混的單字。當你在文章中每找到一個單字，都必須停下來思考它是意指什麼、它的文法是什麼，以及它是如何使用的。

Task 43

請從 Task 1 和 Task 2 的閱讀文章中找出關鍵語庫 ❼ 列出的所有易混淆字詞，並留意它們在文章中是如何使用的。

Task 44

請練習用關鍵語庫 ❼ 的易混淆字詞來造句。

易混淆字詞	造句練習
expand	
spread	
rise	
arise	
notion	
theory	

affect	
effect	
person	
people	

在你結束這個單元之前，請將下列清單看過，確定你能將所有要點都勾選起來。如果有一些要點你還搞不清楚，請回頭再次研讀本單元的相關部分。

□ 我確實閱讀並理解了關於「個人主義」的長篇文章。

□ 我完全知道字彙在文章中是如何使用，並更加了解到要怎麼用單字來表達特定的主題。

□ 我已經學會 15 個關於「個人主義」主題的關鍵字，以及可與其搭配使用的動詞和形容詞。

□ 我已經練習使用這些搭配詞來描寫「個人主義」。

□ 我已經學到了一些同義詞，也了解在運用時需要注意的一些問題。

□ 我學到了很多關於這個主題可以運用的語塊，包括片語動詞以及名詞或動詞為同形的單字。

□ 我已經練習使用這些語塊。

□ 我學到了 5 個關於這個主題的慣用語，且知道如何運用。

□ 我已經理解在運用慣用語時需要特別注意的一些問題。

□ 關於這個主題，我已經能確實掌握一些易混淆字詞的用法。

Unit 10

道德
Morality

本單元將要探討道德是什麼，以及它在整個西方史中是如何以不同的形式來顯現。在這裡要閱讀的同樣也是「論證／意見」(argument/opinion) 類型的文章。

Task 1

閱讀文章並盡可能地理解文章內容。請先不要使用字典。

---

(1) _____ It's a branch of moral philosophy that determines how we judge whether actions are good or bad, and it establishes a set of moral principles to help us decide what good and bad are. The main issue in morality is whether those principles are absolute — meaning the same standards apply in all times and places- or whether they are relative to different societies — meaning, they don't apply to all times and places. There are arguments for and against both views.

(2) _____ Wherever people have come together to live a communal life, questions of conflict have arisen, and how we resolve those conflicts is the work of morality. Morality can exist in three forms: conventions, rules and laws. Conventions are the common standards of behaviour. We can also call these traditions. For example, if a man makes a mistake which causes you to be hurt, is it fair to blame him? If his intention is not to hurt you, then conventions tell us that we should not lay into him to get revenge but that we should let him off. However, if his intention is to take out his frustration and anger on you, then he should take the blame, and that is where rules and laws come in. 'Without

morality,' says Dr Grouper,' all hell would break lose, with each person pursuing their own selfish interest. Such a devil-may-care attitude would mean that society - any group - would eventually collapse.'

(3) _____ Moreover, different societies in different places have established different moral codes. According to Dr Grouper the history of morality in the West can be roughly divided into three parts, pre-Christian, Christian and post-Christian.

(4) _____ The Greek philosopher Plato gave a list of four virtues: wisdom, courage, self-control and fairness. According to him, morality consists of developing these four qualities. If each person developed these four qualities to the best of their abilities, society would be harmonious. 'This theory was controversial though,' says Dr Grouper, 'because wisdom can take many different forms. If I am very hungry, and as bold as brass, I might decide that it's wise to take some of your food. But you will probably think it's wise to try to stop me from taking your food by hitting back at me. The moral ideal of acting wisely, which I cling to, might be very different in comparison with your moral ideal, to which you are no less committed. In fact, it might be totally opposed to yours. It is constantly necessary to come to some kind of happy compromise between my desires and your desires. Plato's response to this argument was the creation of laws. The laws decide what kind of behaviour is prohibited, and what kind of unacceptable or anti-social behaviour is controlled.

(5) _____ These common values were derived from teachings found in the Bible and were widespread and formed the basis of society during this period. They became ancient traditions which were preserved and handed down through the centuries. The Church claimed that people

had to love each other, to have faith in God, and hope in a better life after death, and they were expected to devote themselves to the Church, which in turn encouraged the healthy development of these three virtues – love, faith and hope. All through their childhood, little children were taught that God loved them and would look after them in the future life after death, as long as they acted in a good way and didn't do things which were mostly forbidden.

(6) _____ The argument against it is that there is no way of judging whether this claim is true or not. For those people who are unprincipled, or who find it almost impossible to measure up to the standards imposed by the Church, the promise of a future better life in heaven is regarded as a lie. The argument against this view of morality is that it doesn't explain why there is so much suffering in the world. The child thinks, if God loves me, and I love him in return, why do I still have to suffer? Perhaps God is as cold as ice and as hard as nails? Perhaps God is even dead, as the famous German philosopher Nietzsche maintained. If God is dead, where does that leave us?

Task 2

請從下列句子選出適當的主題句以完成 Task 1 每個段落的填空。

A 'Believing in some kind of public or private morality is important,' says Dr Wendy Grouper, Professor of Moral Philosophy from the University of Somewhere, 'because in the absence of a god to tell us, we need a guide to help us decide for ourselves what good is and how to do it, and what moral evil is and how to avoid doing it.'

B During the post-Christian period, society is no longer guided by this view of morality.

C In medieval Europe, when Christianity was very strong, the Church emphasised the cardinal virtues of love, faith and hope.

D Morality at the most basic level, consists of deciding what kind of acts are good, and what kind of acts are bad, and how we establish and judge standards of good and bad.

E The ancient Greeks considered goodness to be the performance of what they called virtue.

F Throughout history, in different times and places, the question of what is good conduct and what is immoral conduct has been defined differently.

✓ 答案・中譯・說明

(1) D   (2) A   (3) F   (4) E   (5) C   (6) B

譯文

　　道德在最基本的層次上,包括決定什麼樣的行為是善、什麼樣的行為是惡,以及我們如何確立和判斷善惡的標準。它是道德哲學的一個分支,以決定我們要如何去判斷行為是善還是惡,並確立一套道德原則來幫助我們決定善惡是什麼。道德的主要課題在於,這些原則是否為絕對的(意味著相同的標準隨時隨地都適用),或者它們是否相對於不同的社會而言(意味著它們並非隨時隨地都適用)。兩種看法都有支持或反對的主張。

　　「相信著某種公共或私人的道德是很重要的。」某地大學的道德哲學教授 Wendy Grouper 博士說。「因為少了神來告訴我們,我們就需要一個指引以幫助我們為自己決定善是什麼、要怎麼去做,以及道德之惡是什麼和要怎麼避免去做。」只要是人們聚在一起過著公共生活的地方,衝突的問題就會出現,而我們該如何化解這些衝突便是道德的工作。道德能以三種形式存在:習俗、規則和法律。習俗是行為的共同準則。我們也可以稱之為傳統。例如,若是某人犯了一個錯誤而造成你受到傷害,責怪他是否公平?如果他的意圖不是要傷害你,那習俗就會告訴我們,我們不該為了報復而痛擊他,應該饒恕他。可是,如果他的意圖是要把挫折與憤怒發洩在你身上,那他就該承擔責備,而這就是規則和法律派得上用場的地方。Grouper 博士說:「沒有了道德,每個人都在追求自己的私利,那麼天下就會大亂。這種肆無忌憚的態度意味著,社會、任何群體最終都會崩潰。」

　　綜觀歷史,在不同的時間和地點,關於什麼是善舉和什麼是不道德之舉的問題定義會有所不同。此外,不同地方的不同社會將確立不同的道德規範。Grouper 博士表示,西方的道德史可大致區分為三部分:前基督教、基督教、後基督教。

　　古希臘人認為,善就是他們所謂的美德的表現。希臘哲學家柏拉圖列出了四種美德:智慧、勇敢、節制、正義。他認為,道德就是由發展這四種特質而構成。如果每個人都能

盡其最大能力發展這四種特質，社會就會變得和諧。「只不過這套理論是有爭議的。」Grouper 博士說。「因為智慧可以呈現為很多不同的形式。假如我非常餓並且膽大妄為，我或許就會認定拿走你的一些食物算是明智的。但你八成會認為，透過反擊我來試圖阻止我拿走你的食物是明智的。」我對於明智行事所堅持的道德理想，與你同樣堅定不移的道德理想比起來或許大不相同。事實上，它或許是跟你的全然相反。不斷在我的慾望和你的慾望之間達到某種愉快的妥協是必要的。柏拉圖對這項主張的回應是法律的創造。法律決定了什麼樣的行為是被禁止的、什麼樣的不可接受或對反社會的行為加以控制。

在中世紀的歐洲，基督教非常強大，教會所強調的基本美德是信、望、愛。這些共同的價值觀是從《聖經》中發現的教義中衍生出來的，並廣為傳播而在這段時期構成社會的基礎。它們成為被保存下來並在幾個世紀間傳承的古老傳統。教會宣稱人們必須彼此相愛、信仰上帝、寄望死後的生命會更好，並被期望要把自己奉獻給教會，繼而由它來鼓勵健全發展出這三種美德——信、望、愛。在童年時期，小孩們就被教導說上帝愛他們，並且會在未來的死後生命中照顧他們，只要他們以善的方式行事，而不要做那些多數是被禁止的事。

在後基督教時期，社會不再受這種道德觀所指引。反對它的論點在於，沒有辦法判斷這樣的主張是否正確。對於那些不講原則的人，或是發現幾乎不可能達到教會所施加之標準的人來說，未來在天堂過上更好生活的承諾被視為一個謊言。反對這種道德觀的論點在於，它不能解釋為什麼世界上會有這麼多苦難。孩子會認為，如果上帝愛我，而我也以愛祂作為回報，為什麼我還是得受苦？也許上帝像冰一樣冷，像釘子一樣硬？也許上帝已經死了，正如著名的德國哲學家尼采所堅稱的那樣。如果上帝死了，那我們該何去何從？

☆ 第一段是以道德的一般定義來介紹主題，所陳述的主要論點在於：有些人認為道德是相對的，有些人則認為它是絕對的。

☆ 第二段是告訴我們為什麼道德對於幫助人們一起生活是非常重要的。這段介紹了道德的三種存在形式：習俗、規則和法律。

☆ 第三段介紹了西方道德史的三個主要時期。

☆ 第四段是在檢視對前基督教時期的道德觀，支持和反對的論點主張。

☆ 第五段是在檢視基督教時期的道德觀。

☆ 第六段是在檢視反對後基督教時期道德觀的論點主張。

字詞搭配 Word Partnerships

我們現在要來學習「道德」這個主題的 15 個關鍵字，以及可搭配這些關鍵字使用的「字詞搭配表」。首先，請看關鍵字語庫。

Task 3

請仔細研讀這些主題字彙和下方的說明。

關鍵語庫 ①　 Track 10.1

名詞	動詞	形容詞	字義
behaviour Ⓒ	behave	-	行為、舉止、態度
code Ⓒ	-	-	守則、法規、規則
compromise Ⓒ	compromise	-	妥協、折衷（辦法）
conduct Ⓤ	conduct	-	舉止、行為、品行
development Ⓒ	develop	developed	發展、進化、新情況
evil Ⓒ	-	evil	邪惡
good Ⓤ	-	good	善、好事、慷慨的行為
ideal Ⓒ	-	ideal	理想、完美的典範
morality Ⓤ	-	moral, immoral, amoral	道德、品行、道德觀
philosophy Ⓤ	-	philosophical	哲學、哲理、人生觀
principle Ⓒ	-	(un)principled	原則、原理、主義、信條
standard ⓊⒸ	-	-	標準、規格、規範
tradition Ⓒ	-	traditional	傳統、慣例、常規

| values Ⓒ | - | valued | 價值（觀）、重要性 |
| virtue Ⓒ | - | virtuous | 美德、德行 |

☆ 在心理學的領域中，behaviour 是可數名詞，但除非是在心理學領域，否則它應該當不可數名詞使用。

☆ 留意到 compromise 也可以是一個動詞。

☆ 注意，code 和 conduct 經常一起使用。請仔細研讀這兩個單字的字詞搭配表，了解它們是如何一起使用。

☆ 留意到 evil、good 和 ideal 也可以當作形容詞。

☆ 形容詞 moral 有兩種不同的否定形。意指某事惡劣、邪惡或不善時，使用 immoral；意指道德全然付之闕如時，不管是善或惡的道德，應使用 amoral。請留意這兩種否定詞的拼法。

☆ 注意形容詞 principled 是如何形成否定。若說某人 unprincipled「不講原則」，就是指某人毫無道德可言。

☆ values 向來都有 s。如果沒有加 s 的話，意思就會變成「值錢」。此外須留意，values 的形容詞是 valued，而 valuable 則是 value 的形容詞，意指值錢。不要在意思和用法上把這兩個全然不同的字給搞混。

　　接下來，我們將以 5 個關鍵字為一組，深入地學習與這些字最頻繁搭配的字詞組合及正確用法。

Task 4

請研讀這個字詞搭配表、例句和底下的說明。

搭配在前面的動詞	搭配的形容詞		關鍵字
be on s/o's best ~ control influence alter change modify display exhibit show	normal strange good acceptable anti-social bad unacceptable undesirable deviant problem	animal criminal disruptive human sexual social violent	**behaviour (towards s/th)**

字詞搭配使用範例　　🔊 **Track 10.2**（收錄本單元 Task 4~Task 20 字詞搭配使用範例）

- Children are expected to **be on their best behaviour** at all times.
  孩童被期望要隨時表現出最好的行為舉止。

- Morality exists to help people **control their anti-social behaviour**.
  道德的存在是為幫助人控制自己的反社會行為。

- **Showing good behaviour** is the result of education and training.
  表現出良好的行為是教育和訓練的結果。

- **Behaviour** can **be influenced** by friends, family, intoxicants and other factors.
  行為會受到朋友、家人、麻醉品和其他因素所影響。

....

☆ 留意到「行為」的不同類型。

☆ 動詞 control、influence、alter、change 和 modify 能以被動來使用。

請研讀這個字詞搭配表、例句和底下的說明。

搭配在前面的動詞		搭配的形容詞		關鍵字
have	comply with	strict	civil	
be	follow		criminal	
		ethical	disciplinary	
devise	break	moral	penal	
draw up	infringe		highway	
establish	violate			
formulate				
lay down				**code (of s/th)**
搭配在後面的短語				
~ of behaviour				
~ of conduct				
~ of ethics				
~ of honor				
~ of practice				

字詞搭配使用範例

- Morality on one level is a type of **code of conduct**. Anyone who **infringes this code** is seen as immoral. 道德在某種程度上，是一種行為的準則。任何違反這一準則的人就會被視為不道德。

- Doctors and other professionals have a **strict ethical code** they have to follow. 醫生和其他的專業人士有嚴格的倫理守則必須遵循。

- I have a driving test next week, so I am learning **the highway code**. 我下星期有一個駕駛考試，所以我正在學公路法規。

- A strict **code of ethics** for teachers **has been drawn up**. 一份針對教師的嚴格倫理守則訂立出來了。

☆ 留意「法規」的不同類型，以及動詞能以被動來使用。

請研讀這個字詞搭配表、例句和底下的說明。

搭配在前面的動詞		搭配的形容詞		關鍵字
agree on arrive at come to work out find make reach look for seek	offer suggest accept reject	acceptable fair good happy honourable possible reasonable sensible suitable	ideal muddled uneasy unsatisfactory inevitable necessary	**compromise (between s/th and s/th)**

字詞搭配使用範例

- Both parties must **agree on** a **suitable compromise**, otherwise the deal cannot move forward.
  雙方必須就適當的妥協達成共識，否則交易就無法向前推進。

- People must **work out** a **sensible compromise** when their desires come into conflict with each other.
  當人們的慾望彼此間相互衝突時，他們就必須想出一個明智的妥協方式。

- We **found** a **muddled compromise**. It's not perfect, but it's the best we can do.
  我們找到了一個馬馬虎虎的折衷方案。它並不完美，卻是我們所能做到最好的了。

- Morality exists when we have to **arrive at** a **compromise between** what I want, and what is acceptable to others.
  當我們必須在自己想要什麼和他人可接受什麼之間達成妥協，道德即告存在。

☆ 請留意不同動詞所需搭配使用的介系詞。

Task 7

請研讀這個字詞搭配表、例句和底下的說明。

搭配在前面的動詞	搭配的形容詞		關鍵字
be engage in regulate explain	good bad discreditable disgraceful immoral improper	business human personal police professional sexual	**conduct**
搭配在前面的片語			
a code of ~ rules of ~ standards of ~	unprofessional unseemly aggressive violent criminal illegal unlawful wrongful		

字詞搭配使用範例

- This **is disgraceful conduct**. You will have to resign.
  這是不名譽的行為。你將不得不辭職。

- He was not able to **explain** his **improper conduct**, so he was fired.
  他無法解釋自己的不當行為,所以遭到了開除。

- Morality tries to **regulate conduct**.
  道德試圖規範行為。

- Morality consists of **rules of conduct**.
  道德是由行為準則所構成。

....

☆ 留意不同類型的「行為、舉止」。

Task 8

請研讀這個字詞搭配表、例句和底下的說明。

搭配在前面的動詞		搭配的形容詞		關鍵字
aid	arrest	full	child	
allow	halt		commercial	
assist	prevent	gradual	economic	
encourage		slow	educational	
enhance	discourage		emotional	
facilitate	hinder	rapid	evolutionary	
	inhibit	fast	historical	
favour	restrict		human	
foster	slow	sustainable	industrial	
permit		healthy	intellectual	**development (of s/th)**
promote	finance		personal	
stimulate			physical	
support	monitor		property	
	oversee		psychological	
accelerate			regional	
speed up	trace		rural	
			sexual	
			social	
			software	
			spiritual	
			suburban	
			urban	

字詞搭配使用範例

- The role of teachers is to **promote** the **healthy intellectual** and **personal development of** their pupils. 教師的角色是在促進學生智力和個人發展的健全。
- The role of government is to stimulate **sustainable suburban** and **urban economic development**. 政府的作用是在促進郊區和城市可長可久的經濟發展。
- Without the **development of** new ideas, society would still be stuck in the past. 如果沒有新觀念的發展，社會將仍然停留在過去。

....

☆ 留意到「發展」的不同類型。

現在，我們來看看各位是否能用一些字詞搭配來擴大對字彙的運用。

Task 9

請從 Task 4 到 Task 8 中選出正確形式的字詞，完成以下段落填空。

> Morality consists of a code (1) _____ that has been (2) _____ to make it easier for people to (3) _____ a (4) _____ compromise (5) _____ their own desires (6) _____ socially (7) _____ behaviour. The slow development (8) _____ (9) _____ conduct throughout history has ensured a stable society. If we can all control our (10) _____ behaviour, society will be safer and more pleasant for everyone.

範例答案

1. of behaviour/of conduct/of ethics/of practice
2. devised/drawn up/established/formulated/laid down
3. agree on/arrive at/come to/work out/find/make/reach
4. fair/good/happy/possible/reasonable/sensible/suitable/necessary
5. between
6. and
7. acceptable
8. of
9. a code of/rules of/standards of
10. social

....

☆ 請留意各組同義字詞，空格中選填同一組內不同的字也是可以的。

☆ 須確認所選用的單字都是正確的形式。請檢查單數或複數，以及動詞的正確形式。例如空格 (2) 的動詞必須使用過去分詞，因為它是被動語態。

現在來學習另外 5 個單字。

Task 10

請研讀這個字詞搭配表、例句和底下的說明。

搭配在前面的動詞	搭配的形容詞		關鍵字
be do commit combat fight resist turn away from	great lesser	moral social	**evil**
搭配在前面的片語			
the forces of ~ good and ~ the root of ~			

字詞搭配使用範例

- Those who **do evil** shall have evil **done** to them.
  那些作惡之人會自食惡果。

- **The forces of evil** in society are many, and we need to **combat** them.
  社會上的邪惡勢力很多,我們必須與它們戰鬥。

- Morality teaches us to **turn away from evil**.
  道德教導我們遠離邪惡。

- Sometimes life only gives us the choice of **doing** the **lesser evil**.
  有時候,人生只給我們兩害相權取其輕的選擇。

Task 11

請研讀這個字詞搭配表、例句和底下的說明。

搭配在前面的動詞	搭配的形容詞	關鍵字
do commit	the common no	
搭配在前面的片語		**good**
a force for ~ for s/o's own ~ for the ~ of s/th ~ and evil a power of ~ be up to no ~		

字詞搭配使用範例

- **The common good** is what is best for most people.
  共同利益亦即對大多數人來說是最好的。

- People who only **do good** are rare in this world.
  只做善事的人在這個世界上十分罕見。

- Morality is seen by most people as **a force for good** in the world.
  道德被大多數人視為世間一種向善的力量。

- This cup of hot tea has **done** me **a power of good**!
  這杯熱茶對我很有好處！

- It's **no good** complaining all the time. You have to be better.
  一直抱怨是不好的。你必須變得更好。

- That naughty boy **is up to no good** again.
  那個調皮的男孩又不懷好意了。

☆ 注意許多能連同 good 來使用的片語。

Task 12

請研讀這個字詞搭配表、例句和底下的說明。

搭配在前面的動詞		搭配的形容詞		關鍵字
be	conform to	high	aesthetic	
	live up to	lofty	artistic	
have		noble	ethical	
support	fall short of		moral	
be committed to	abandon	unattainable	political	
be devoted to	betray		democratic	
believe in			liberal	**ideal**
espouse	embody		revolutionary	**(of s/th)**
	reflect		socialist	
cling to				
pursue				
strive for				
achieve				
attain				
be true to				

字詞搭配使用範例

- Many people still **cling to** the **political ideal of** a society which is totally equal.
  很多人仍然堅持一個完全平等的社會的政治理想。

- Our society today **falls short of** the **ideal** by a long way.
  我們現今的社會與理想相去甚遠。

- Many people **are committed to** the **moral ideal of** perfect behaviour.
  很多人固守著完美行為的道德理想。

☆ 留意到「理想」的不同類型。

請研讀這個字詞搭配表、例句和底下的說明。

搭配在前面的動詞	搭配的形容詞		關鍵字
have believe in preserve protect strengthen lack be contrary to go against attack be concerned with	common sense changed objective	conventional traditional personal private public social political sexual Christian	**morality (of s/th)**
搭配在前面的片語			
standard(s) of ~ the role of ~ an attack upon ~ the source of ~ the basis of ~			

字詞搭配使用範例

- The Church tried to **strengthen Christian morality**.
  教會試圖去強化基督教的道德。

- Nowadays we only **believe in common sense morality**.
  如今我們只相信常識道德。

- Many people **believe standards of morality** are lower than before.
  很多人認為道德的標準比以前要低。

- Some people believe that humanity **lacks objective morality**.
  有些人相信，人類缺乏客觀的道德。

- His behaviour **was against traditional morality**. 他的行為違背了傳統道德。

....

☆ 留意「道德」的不同類型。

☆ Christian 的第一字母必須大寫，因為它是一個當形容詞用的「名稱」。

Task 14

請研讀這個字詞搭配表、例句和底下的說明。

搭配在前面的動詞	搭配的形容詞		關鍵字
have determine develop adopt embrace espouse formulate articulate reject	competing differing prevailing basic general underlying	ancient classical contemporary Eastern experimental modern moral natural personal political religious social Western	**philosophy (of s/th)**

字詞搭配使用範例

- The **prevailing philosophy** we **have** in the West is neo-liberalism.
  我們在西方所盛行的哲學是新自由主義。
- Kant **developed** the **moral philosophy of** individualism.
  康德發展出個人主義的道德哲學。
- He **has** no **underlying moral philosophy**, which makes him dangerous.
  他沒有基本的道德理念，這使他很危險。

....

☆ Eastern 和 Western 的第一個字母必須大寫，因為它們是方位的名稱。

☆ 留意「哲學」的不同類型。

請從 Task 10 到 Task 14 中選出正確形式的字詞，完成以下段落填空。

Societies (1) _____ a (2) _____ philosophy when they need to find ways of solving conflicts. If societies (3) _____ (4) _____ and (5) _____ morality, then both personal and public life will be without conflicts. Laws are often a way of (6) _____ morality because when people break the law, they also (7) _____ morality. In a perfect world, there would be no laws or rules, people would behave properly at all times. However, this (8) _____ ideal (9) _____ (10) _____ – we cannot reach it because human beings cannot (11) _____ evil. (12) _____ always go together- sometimes people (13) _____ good, and sometimes they (14) _____ evil. But usually, unfortunately, (15) _____ evil dominate. This is why we need morality.

範例答案

1. develop/adopt/embrace/espouse
2. moral
3. have/believe in
4. private/public
5. public/private
6. preserving/protecting/strengthening
7. are contrary to/go against/attack
8. high/lofty/noble

9. is
10. unattainable
11. combat/fight/resist/turn away from
12. good and evil
13. do/commit
14. do/commit
15. the forces of

....

☆ 注意，在空格 (6) 中必須使用 Ving，因為動詞是接在介系詞 of 之後。介系詞後面全部都需要用 Ving。而在空格 (7) 中記得要用 are，因為主詞是複數：they。

現在我們來學習最後一組的 5 個單字。

Task 16

請研讀這個字詞搭配表、例句和底下的說明。

搭配在前面的動詞	搭配的形容詞		關鍵字
be　　　　　　stick to have establish lay down apply ~ to s/th explain	basic broad general universal central fundamental essential key	democratic ethical legal market moral political scientific theoretical	**principle (that v.p.) (of n.p.)**
搭配在前面的片語			
be against s/o's ~s to V a set of ~s a matter of ~			

字詞搭配使用範例

- **It's against my principles to** eat meat. I'm a vegetarian.
  吃肉有違我的原則。我是個素食主義者。

- As **a matter of principle** I won't do it. I don't want to be involved in illegal activity. 出於原則，我不會去做這件事。我可不想涉及非法活動。

- Morality **establishes the general principle that** as I do to you, so will I be done by. 道德所確立的基本原則是，我對你做的也將使我蒙受。

··

☆ 留意到「原則」的不同類型。

☆ 還要留意到能連同 principle 來使用的片語，以及這些片語有哪些需要以複數來使用：principles。

請研讀這個字詞搭配表、例句和底下的說明。

搭配在前面的動詞		搭配的形容詞		關鍵字
have be of a ~ boast enjoy define judge establish set achieve meet reach	fall short of apply enforce provide improve raise lower maintain sustain	high low poor minimum acceptable adequate decent proper reasonable improved rising clear objective	academic accounting advertising educational environmental ethical health intellectual moral safety technical trading	**standard (of s/th)**

字詞搭配使用範例

- Our country **boasts the finest educational standards** in the world.
  我國擁有世界上最好的教育水準。

- We will not be able to **maintain** our current **high standards** if we don't get a higher budget. 如果我們得不到更高的預算，將會無法維持現有的高標準。

- Morality **provides a standard of** behaviour for everyone to follow.
  道德提供了讓每個人遵循的行為標準。

- Your work **is not of an acceptable standard**.
  你的作業不是一個可接受的水準。

☆ 須留意「標準」的不同類型。

Task 18

請研讀這個字詞搭配表、例句和底下的說明。

搭配在前的動詞	搭配的形容詞			關鍵字
have be cherish continue follow keep alive maintain preserve uphold hand down break (with) go against establish start revive	age-old ancient archaic centuries-old deep-rooted enduring living long-established well-established long unbroken fine great powerful	cherished hallowed dominant powerful strong local national native folk popular oral	academic artistic cultural ideological literary military musical philosophical political religious sporting teaching theatrical	**tradition (of s/th)**

字詞搭配使用範例

- The **fine tradition of** marriage **was established** centuries ago and **is still upheld** today. 婚姻的良好傳統在幾世紀前就已確立，至今仍然堅持著。
- Our society **follows** many **powerful traditions** that are meaningless in modern life. 我們的社會所遵循的許多強大傳統在現代生活中毫無意義。
- Old people usually try to **uphold well-established traditions,** while young people usually try to **go against** them.
  老年人通常會試圖維護深受確立的傳統，而年輕人通常試圖違背它們。

Task 19

請研讀這個字詞搭配表、例句和底下的說明。

搭配在前面的動詞	搭配的形容詞		關鍵字
be have hold cherish encourage foster hold onto preserve maintain	dominant conservative conventional traditional common shared universal	aesthetic Christian cultural democratic Eastern educational ethical family human middle-class moral political social spiritual Western	**values (of s/th)**

字詞搭配使用範例

- Most people **hold** quite **conservative values**.
  大部分的人都是抱持著相當保守的價值觀。
- We want to **hold onto** our **common moral values**.
  我們想要堅守我們共同的道德價值。
- **Western values are** still quite **Christian**. 西方的價值觀仍是頗為基督教。

☆ 須留意「價值（觀）」的不同類型。

☆ 注意，values 向來必須連同 s 來使用。value 不加 s 則完全是別的意思。

Task 20

請研讀這個字詞搭配表、例句和底下的說明。

搭配在前面的動詞	搭配的形容詞		關鍵字
have be espouse emphasise extol preach	cardinal great special chief inherent negative positive old-fashioned traditional	Christian civic domestic ethical moral political public	**virtue** **(of s/th)**

PART

2

字詞搭配使用範例

- Our society **has** at least the **great virtue of** being more or less free.
  我們的社會至少具有一種很棒的美德，即或多或少還算自由。

- The Christian era **extoled** the **cardinal virtues of** love, faith and hope.
  基督教時代頌揚愛、信、望等基本美德。

- If you want to be a member of our society, you need to **espouse the civic virtues** we all follow.
  假如想要成為我們社會的一分子，你就需要奉行我們都遵循的公民美德。

....

☆ 留意到「美德」的不同類型。

Task 21

請從 Task 16 到 Task 20 中選出正確形式的字詞，完成以下段落填空。

In medieval Europe, when Christianity was very strong, the Church (1) _____ the (2) _____ virtues (3) _____ love, faith and hope. These (4) _____ (5) _____ standards that could be used to help people guide their behaviour: everyone had to at least try them. The (6) _____ principle behind these virtues was the idea of loving your neighbour. If we all loved each other, society would be harmonious. Many of the (7) _____ traditions (8) _____ Western culture, kept alive throughout the ages, (9) _____ these ethical values (10) _____ society.

範例答案

1. emphasised/extoled/preached
2. cardinal/great/special/chief
3. of
4. established
5. acceptable/adequate/decent/proper/reasonable
6. central/fundamental/essential/key
7. age-old/ancient/archaic/centuries-old/deep-rooted
8. of
9. cherished/encouraged/fostered
10. of

☆ 在空格 (1)、(4) 和 (9) 中，必須使用過去簡單式，因為摘要所講的中世紀歐洲是已告終的時期。別忘了動詞時態！

記住，多閱讀有助於擴充字彙量，而在文章上下文脈絡中查看大量例子則能幫助你記憶新的用語。下一個練習對於各位記憶 15 個關鍵單字和它們的字詞搭配將有非常大的幫助。

Task 22

請從 Task 1 和 Task 2 的閱讀文章中找出關鍵語庫 ❶ 所列的 15 個關鍵字，並留意這些字在文章中是如何使用的。

常用語塊 Chunks

前面學過了字詞搭配的用法，我們現在要來學一些可用在寫作或談論這個主題的 chunks「語塊」。

Task 23

研讀這些語塊和底下的說明。

關鍵語庫 ❷

Chunk
❏ be controversial　有爭議的
❏ be derived from n.p./Ving　源自 n.p./Ving
❏ be opposed to n.p. Ving　反對 n.p. Ving
❏ be relative (to n.p./Ving)　相對於 (n.p./Ving)
❏ be unprincipled (about s/th)　（對某事）不講原則
❏ be widespread　廣為散布
❏ in comparison with n.p./Ving　與 n.p./Ving 相比
❏ consist of n.p./Ving　構成自 n.p./Ving
❏ devote o/self to s/o/Ving　獻身於做某事；致力於……
❏ explain (s/th) (to s/o)(wh- v.p.)　向 s/o 解釋 s/th

☆ 須留意哪些語塊要接受詞、哪些不用。還要留意到受詞的類型，尤其是需要使用人物受詞 (s/o) 或事物受詞 (s/th) 時。

☆ 須留意這些語塊是否全都必須用 n.p.、Ving 或 V。

☆ 別忘了在使用這些語塊時需要改變動詞的時態。

☆ 這些語塊有很多必須使用 be 動詞。並注意，使用 be controversial 和 be widespread 時，不可使用受詞。

☆ 在 Unit 7 中，各位學過 compared with 要怎麼用。在此所學的則是 in comparison with 要怎麼用。

☆ 注意，在 consist of 中不可使用 be 動詞。consist 就是動詞。

☆ 使用 devote 時，第一個受詞必須是 -self 單字：oneself、herself、myself。第二個受詞則可以是人員受詞或 Ving。

☆ explain 可以接受詞也可以不接受詞。你也可以用 wh- 單字再加上 v.p. 來使用。

下一個 Task 將聚焦於大家在使用這些語塊時經常會犯的錯誤。

Task 24

請改正這些句子中使用語塊的常見錯誤。

① Some standards of behaviour controversial in different parts of the world.

_____

② Moral values often derived from traditions that are so old no one remembers their origin.

_____

③ Most people is opposed to values which cause harm to the environment.

_____

④ Some people think morality is absolute but actually it relative to different times and places.

_____

⑤ Most politicians is unprincipled when it comes to their career.

_____

⑥ Evil is spread wide.

_____

⑦ In comparison to the past, the present is always better.

_____

⑧ Morality is consist of a mix of manners and values.

_____

⑨ Some people devote their time for helping others.

_____

⑩ Can you explain why morality to be relative.

_____

⑪ Please explain me this.

_____

✔ 答案・中譯・說明 🎧 **Track 10.3**

① Some standards of behaviour **are** <u>controversial</u> in different parts of the world.
有些行為標準在世界上的不同地方是有爭議的。

② Moral values **are** often derived from traditions that are so old no one remembers their origin. 道德價值常是源自久到沒有人記得起源的傳統。

③ Most people **are** opposed to values which cause harm to the environment.
大多數的人都反對對環境造成危害的價值觀。

④ Some people think morality is absolute but actually it **is** relative to different times and places.
有些人認為道德是絕對的，但事實上它是相對於不同的時間和地點。

⑤ Most politicians **are** unprincipled when it comes to their career.
大部分的政治人物在職涯中都不講原則。

⑥ Evil is **widespread**. 邪惡是廣為散布的。

⑦ In comparison **with** the past, the present is always better.
與過去相比，現在總是更好。

⑧ Morality **consists** of a mix of manners and values.
品德構成自禮貌與價值觀的混合。

⑨ Some people devote their time **to helping** others.
有些人奉獻自己的時間去幫助他人。

⑩ Can you explain why morality **is** relative?
你能不能解釋道德為什麼是相對的？

⑪ Please explain **this to me**. 請向我解釋一下這點。

....

☆ 請注意，從第 1 句到第 5 句中，錯誤都在於 be 動詞：別忘了加上時態正確的 be 動詞和人員；在第 8 句中則不應該有 be 動詞，別忘了聚焦在動詞上！至於其他句則多是錯在介系詞，請務必將介系詞使用正確。

☆ 請將正確句子中的完整語塊畫上底線，這能幫助你完整而正確地記住語塊。

　　下一個練習對於記憶語塊將有非常大的幫助。記住，多閱讀有助於擴充字彙量，而在文章上下文脈絡中查看大量語塊則能幫助你記憶新的用語。

Task 25

請從 Task 1 和 Task 2 的閱讀文章中找出關鍵語庫 ❷ 列出的所有語塊，並留意這些語塊在文章中是如何使用的。

Task 26

現在請嘗試用前面學過的語塊來寫出你自己的句子。

關鍵字語塊	造句
be controversial	
be derived from n.p./Ving	
be opposed to n.p. Ving	

be relative (to n.p./Ving)	
be unprincipled (about s/th)	
be widespread	
in comparison with n.p./Ving	
consist of n.p./Ving	
devote o/self to s/o/Ving	
explain (s/th) (to s/o) (wh- v.p.)	

☆ 我顯然無法在此改正你的句子,但你可以透過確認語塊所有的小細節,自行改正。再次提醒在寫作中運用語塊時,須特別注意小詞、字尾和語塊的結尾,無論所需要的是 n.p.、v.p.、Ving 還是 V,並且確保你所使用的語塊是完整的。

5 個可作動詞或名詞的單字
5 words which can be verbs or nouns

　　語塊通常會視關鍵字是名詞或動詞而有所不同，現在我們要來看 5 個動詞和名詞同形的單字，並學習使用正確的語塊。

Task 27

請看以下幾個名詞和動詞同形的單字。

關鍵語庫 ❸

關鍵字	名詞字義	動詞字義
act	行為；行動；節目	扮演；舉動像；行動；起作用
blame	責備，指責；責任	指責；把……歸咎（於）；歸因於
claim	（根據權利而提出的）要求；主張，聲稱	聲稱；主張；提出要求；索取
form	外形；類型；形式；表格	形成；構成；塑造；（物體）成形
guide	指導者；指導；指南	為……領路；帶領；引導；指導

Task 28

閱讀句子並判斷關鍵字是動詞或名詞，填入 V 或 N。

① _____ He put forward the **claim** that he was the judge of all moral matters.
② _____ In some places, good morality takes the **form** of being kind and deferring to the elders of the group.
③ _____ It's a good idea to **act** with care wherever you are in the world.
④ _____ Morality **guides** us in our relationships with others and with society.
⑤ _____ Some **acts** are regarded as evil all over the world.
⑥ _____ Some people **claim** to be the origin of all morality.

⑦ ＿＿ The **blame** falls squarely on the shoulders of the evildoer in most societies.

⑧ ＿＿ There is an unstated code of conduct which **forms** the basis of morality.

⑨ ＿＿ Watching the behaviour of others can often serve as a **guide** to the social and moral values of a place.

⑩ ＿＿ You can only **blame** yourself if your behaviour doesn't meet the standards of your society.

✅ 答案・中譯・說明

① N 他提出主張說自己就是所有道德事務的審判者。

② N 在某些地方，良好的道德表現形式為善待和聽從群體中的長輩。

③ V 無論你在世界的哪個角落，小心行事是一個好主意。

④ V 道德在我們與他人以及與社會的關係方面引導著我們。

⑤ N 有些舉動在全世界都被視為邪惡。

⑥ V 有些人聲稱自己是所有道德的起源。

⑦ N 在大部分的社會中，責怪都是直接落在為惡者的肩上。

⑧ V 有一種心照不宣的行為守則，它形成了道德的基礎。

⑨ N 觀察他人的行為通常可充當了解一個地方之社會與道德價值的指南。

⑩ V 如果你的行為不符合所在社會的標準，你只能怪你自己。

Task 29

請看以下所彙整的語塊及用法說明。

關鍵語庫 ④　🎧 Track 10.4

關鍵字語塊	關鍵字詞性	例句＆翻譯
act (of s/th)	*nc*	It was an act of revenge, so it was acceptable. 這是一種報復行為，所以可以接受。

act (as n.p.)	*vi*	Morality sometimes acts as a check on selfish behaviour. 道德有時候能充當對自私行為的約束。
blame (for n.p.)	*nu*	He took the blame for his actions. He didn't put the blame on someone else. 他為自己的行徑承擔責怪。他並沒有把責任歸咎於別人。
blame s/o (for s/th)	*vt*	Don't blame yourself for his mistake. 不要為了他的錯誤而責怪你自己。
claim that v.p.	*nc*	He put forward the claim that he was the ruler. 他提出宣稱說，自己才是管理者。
claim (to V) (that v.p.)	*vi*	Some people claim to be better than others. 有些人宣稱自己比他人強。 They claim that they are better. 他們宣稱說，自己是更好的。
claim s/th as s/th	*vt*	He claimed the idea as his own. 他宣稱這個構想為他所有。
form of s/th	*nc*	Morality is a form of social control. 道德是社會控制的一種形式。
form s/th	*vt*	Morality forms the basis of social behaviour. 道德形成了社會行為的準則。
guide to s/th	*nu*	Let these rules be a guide to your behaviour. 就讓這些規則來成為你行為的指引。
guide s/th/s/o	*vt*	The rules guided my behaviour when I joined the club. 我加入社團時，規則便指引了我的行為。

PART
2

☆ 留意哪些名詞是可數，哪些是不可數；使用動詞時務必確認時態正確性。

☆ act as 的意思是 be like「像是某事」。請看上面的例句，你也可以用不同的方式來表達：Sometimes morality is like a check on selfish behaviour.。

☆ 當 blame 用作名詞時，可以與動詞 take 或 put 連用。而若是用作動詞，請留

意必須先用人員受詞，再用 for 和事物受詞來指明應受責怪的行動。請看例句。

☆ claim 當名詞來用時，可用 that 然後接 v.p.。此外，名詞 claim 還可連同動詞 put forward 或 make 來用：He made the claim that morality is necessary.。 而 claim 當動詞時類似於 announce「宣告」或 make an announcement「加以宣告」。注意，使用 claim s/th as s/th 時，它是意指「擁有某事物」。

☆ 請留意，form 當動詞使用時，不可用 of。

☆ guide 指「人」時，當然是可數，但這裡的 guide 指的是 standard「標準」， 所以是不可數。注意，guide 當名詞來用時，需要使用 to，但若是當動詞使用 則不可以。另外，guide 當動詞時，能以被動用法來使用：She was guided by her belief.。

☆ 請仔細學習這些語塊，把重點放在諸如介系詞和冠詞等細節，以及這些單字的 不同字義。

Task 30

請選用正確形式的單字或語塊，完成下列各句。

① **guide you/guide to**

A good _____ knowing what to do is to watch the behaviour of others'.

② **forms of/forms**

Having good manners _____ one part of social morality.

③ **claims to/claims that**

He _____ he didn't know the law.

④ **claims that/claims to**

He _____ know right from wrong, but his actions show otherwise.

⑤ **guide you/guide**

If you don't know how to behave, watch others and let them _____.

⑥ **blame for/blame me for**

If you want to _____ your mistakes, that is not fair.

⑦ **act of/act as**

In some cultures it's also seen as an _____ wickedness to break the law.

⑧ **claimed the idea as/claim the idea as**

She _____ her own, but we all know it was his first.

⑨ **act as/act of**

Social rules usually _____ a guide to morality.

⑩ **claim that/claim to**

Some people often make the _____ they are better than others.

⑪ **blame for/blame me for**

The _____ this must lie elsewhere. I am not responsible.

⑫ **is a form of/forms of**

The law _____ social control.

✅ 答案・中譯・說明　🎧 **Track 10.5**

① A good <u>guide to</u> knowing what to do is to watch the behaviour of others'.
了解該怎麼做的一個好方法是去觀察他人的行為。

② Having good manners forms one part of social morality.
具有善良風俗是形成社會道德的一部分。

③ He claims that he didn't know the law. 他聲稱自己不懂法律。

④ He claims to know right from wrong, but his actions show otherwise.
他宣稱能明辨是非，但他的行徑卻顯示不然。

⑤ If you don't know how to behave, watch others and let them guide you.
　　如果你不知道要怎麼表現，就觀摩他人並讓他們來引導你。

⑥ If you want to blame me for your mistakes, that is not fair.
　　如果你想要因為你的錯誤而責怪我，那就不公平了。

⑦ In some cultures it's also seen as an act of wickedness to break the law.
　　在某些文化中，違法也被視為一種邪惡的行為。

⑧ She claimed the idea as her own, but we all know it was his first.
　　她宣稱這個構想是為她所有，但我們全都知道起先是他的。

⑨ Social rules usually act as a guide to morality.
　　社會規則通常是充當道德的指南。

⑩ Some people often make the claim that they are better than others.
　　有些人常宣稱說，自己比他人要好。

⑪ The blame for this must lie elsewhere. I am not responsible.
　　這件事的責任歸屬肯定是在別處。並非由我來負責。

⑫ The law is a form of social control. 法律是社會控制的一種形式。

　　再次提醒，盡可能地多閱讀有助於擴充字彙量，而在文章上下文脈絡中查看大量語塊則能幫助你記憶新的用語。

Task 31

請從 Task 1 和 Task 2 的閱讀文章中找出關鍵語庫 ❹ 列出的所有語塊，並留意這些語塊在文章中是當動詞還是名詞使用？

Task 32

請練習用關鍵語庫 ❹ 的語塊來造句。

關鍵字語塊	造句
act (of s/th)	
act (as n.p.)	

blame (for n.p.)	
blame s/o (for s/th)	
claim that v.p.	
claim (to V) (that v.p.)	
claim s/th as s/th	
form of s/th	
form s/th	
guide to s/th	
guide s/th/s/o	

☆ 我顯然無法在此來改正你的句子，但你可以透過確認語塊所有的小細節，自行改正。再次提醒在寫作中運用語塊時，須特別注意小詞、字尾和語塊的結尾，無論所需要的是 n.p.、v.p.、Ving 還是 V，並且確保你所使用的語塊是完整的。

5 個談論或寫作道德相關主題常用的片語動詞 5 phrasal verbs for talking or writing about morality

我們現在看一些在寫作或談論道德相關主題時，常會用到的片語動詞。

Task 33

研讀語庫中的片語動詞、例句和其下的說明。

關鍵語庫 ⑤　◎ **Track 10.6**

片語動詞	例句
hit back (at s/th) 為捍衛自己而對某事加以反擊	• Some people are beginning to hit back at the idea that good social behavior is important. 有些人正開始對「良好的社會行為很重要」這個觀念進行反擊。
lay into s/o 在肢體或言詞上攻擊某人	• He laid into me, but I defended myself successfully. 他痛罵了我一頓，但我成功地為自己辯護。
measure up to s/th 符合……的要求	• Some people never measure up to the standards of society. 有些人從未達到社會的標準。
take s/th out on s/o 向（某人）發洩、拿（某人）出氣	• He took out all his frustration on his children. 他把所有的挫折都發洩在他的孩子身上。
let s/o off (with s/th) 給某人非常輕的懲罰、讓逃走，免受……	• The police let him off with just a warning. 警察只是警告之後就放了他一馬。 • The judge let him off. He was free to go. 法官放過了他。他可以走了。 • Although he did wrong, he was let off. 他雖然做錯了，但還是被放過了。

☆ 記得，你必須非常留意動詞有沒有受詞 (s/th)，以及這個受詞是擺在哪個位置。請仔細確認上方語庫中的片語動詞及其受詞的位置。

☆ 使用 hit back 時，如果想要指明對象，就需要用介系詞 at。

☆ 使用 lay into s/o 時，名詞和代名詞這兩類受詞必須接在介系詞之後。

☆ 使用 measure up to 時，名詞和代名詞這兩類的受詞都必須接在第二個介系詞之後。

☆ 使用 take s/th out on s/o 時，它是指對別人生氣，而不是對讓你生氣的事，因為惹你生氣的事比你要強大。請特別留意兩個不同的介系詞和兩種不同的受詞。

☆ 如果沒有用 with 來指明 let s/o off 的受詞，這就意味著絲毫沒有懲罰。注意，這個片語動詞也能以被動來使用。

下一個練習將有助於各位聚焦於受詞的正確擺放位置這些細節上。

Task 34

下列各句中的第一個字是正確的，請按照順序將其後的字詞重組成正確的句子。

EX. **The him off let he police realised once wrong was they man the**
The police let him off once they realised he was the wrong man.

① Young generation at are back the the of hitting social people rules older

_____

② The him so hit first the the laid bystander bystander criminal into

_____

③ Sometimes measure impossible to imposed the it's to standards by up society

_____

④ Even are you you you take should never if it someone out on angry weaker than

_____

⑤ Although let committed he crime, judge him the the off

---

① Young people are <u>hitting back at</u> the social rules of the older generation.
年輕人正在對老一代的社會規則進行反擊。

② The criminal hit the bystander first, so the bystander laid into him.
罪犯先襲擊了旁觀者，所以旁觀者便對他加以痛擊。

③ Sometimes it's impossible to measure up to the standards imposed by society.
有時候要達到社會所施加的標準是不可能的。

④ Even if you are angry, you should never take it out on someone weaker than you.
即使你很生氣，你也絕不該把憤怒發洩在比你弱小的人身上。

⑤ Although he committed the crime, the judge let him off.
雖然他犯了罪，但法官還是放過了他。

⋯⋯⋯⋯⋯⋯⋯⋯⋯⋯⋯⋯⋯⋯⋯⋯⋯⋯⋯⋯⋯⋯⋯⋯⋯⋯⋯⋯⋯⋯⋯⋯⋯⋯⋯⋯⋯⋯

☆ 將正確的句子與關鍵語庫 ❺ 的片語動詞做比較，確認你的用法都正確。

☆ 請將正確句子中的片語動詞畫上底線，這將幫助你完整而正確地把語塊記起來。（參照第 1 句的示範）

Task 35

請從 Task 1 和 Task 2 的閱讀文章中找出關鍵語庫 ❺ 列出的所有片語動詞，並留意它們在文章中是如何使用的。

Task 36

請練習用關鍵語庫 ❺ 的片語動詞來造句。

片語動詞	造句練習
hit back (at s/th)	

lay into s/o	
measure up to s/th	
take s/th out on s/o	
let s/o off (with s/th)	

5 個談論或寫作道德相關主題常用的慣用語 5 idioms for talking or writing about morality

Task 37

研讀語庫中的慣用語、例句和其下的說明。

關鍵語庫 6 🎧 Track 10.8

慣用語	例句
all hell breaks loose 開始陷入一片混亂	• If we don't have morality to guide us, all hell will break loose in society. 如果我們沒有道德來作為指引，那麼社會將會陷入一片混亂。
devil may care 什麼都不在乎的態度；無所顧忌	• Some people have a devil may care attitude to morality. They think that social norms don't matter. 有些人對道德是抱持著無所顧忌的態度。他們認為社會常規無關緊要。
as cold as ice / as hard as nails 冷酷無情；無感	• The judge accused the criminal of being as cold as ice and as hard as nails, with no remorse towards his victims. 法官指控那個罪犯冷酷無情，對被害人毫無悔意。
as bold as brass 自以為是、不尊重；極其膽大妄為	• The criminal was as bold as brass and told the judge he didn't care about his opinion. 那個罪犯膽大妄為，他告訴法官說他不在乎他的意見。

☆ 為了讓慣用語有意義，它必須完全準確才行，這意味著你必須將慣用語的所有細節都使用正確。

☆ 請注意這幾個慣用語都沒有受詞，不要連同受詞來使用。

☆ 在 all hell breaks loose 中可以改變動詞時態，而這也是唯一能改變的部分。

改正這些句子中的常見錯誤。

① The criminal was hard-hearted and cold as ice.

② Some children are as bold as copper and need to be taught to respect their elders.

③ The murderer was as hard as a nail and showed no mercy to his victims.

④ Some people have the attitude that the devil may care.

⑤ Some people think if we don't respect social morality, the hell will break lose.

✅ 答案・中譯・說明　🎧 **Track 10.9**

① The criminal was hard-hearted and as cold as ice.
那個罪犯是鐵石心腸的，像冰一樣冷酷。

② Some children are as bold as brass and need to be taught to respect their elders.
有些孩子極其膽大妄為，需要加以教導以尊重長輩。

③ The murderer was as hard as nails and showed no mercy to his victims.
這個凶手冷酷無情，對受害人沒有絲毫憐憫。

④ Some people have a devil may care attitude.
有些人是抱持著無所顧忌的態度。

⑤ Some people think if we don't respect social morality, all hell will break loose.
有些人認為假如不尊重社會道德，一切會變得一團糟。

☆ 請仔細比較錯誤句子和正確解答，務必確實掌握錯在哪以及為什麼是錯的。

現在我們要練習的是，在文章上下文中找出慣用語。

Task 39

請從 Task 1 和 Task 2 的閱讀文章中找出關鍵語庫 ❻ 列出的所有慣用語，並留意它們在文章中是如何使用的。

Task 40

請練習用關鍵語庫 ❻ 的慣用語來造句。

慣用語	造句練習
all hell breaks loose	
devil may care	
as cold as ice	
as hard as nails	
as bold as brass	

☆ 再次提醒在寫作時若運用到這些慣用語，要特別留意動詞的時態和完整的慣用語包含哪些細節。

易混淆的字詞 easily confused words

❑ 要記得，有些單字只能用在特定的主題上，用在別的主題則不適當。

❑ 另外，容易搞混的單字，其差別常常是在搭配詞的使用上有所不同。

❑ 在這個部分，各位將會學到兩組的三個單字和三組的兩個單字。

Task 41

請仔細研讀各組易混淆的字詞、例句和其下的說明。

關鍵語庫 ❼　🎧 Track 10.10

	易混淆字詞	例句
1	**child** (*nc*) 孩子	• The one child policy was successful in lowering the birthrate. 一胎化政策成功地降低了生育率。
	children (*nc*) 孩子	• People should teach their children to show respect. 人們應該教他們的孩子表現出尊重。
	childhood (*nc*) 童年	• Childhood is the most important part of life for learning about correct behavior. 童年是人生中在學習正確的行為部分，最重要的一環。
2	**convention** (*nc*) 慣例、常規	• You have to know the conventions of correct social behavior. 你必須知道正確社會行為的慣例。
	rule (*nc*) 規則	• You have to obey the rules if you want to be a member of the club. 如果想要成為社團的成員，你就必須遵守規則。
	law (*nc*) 法律	• You have to follow the law if you want to be a good member of society. 如果想要成為社會良好的一分子，你就必須遵守法律。

3	**consider** (*vt*) 認為	• Most people consider it polite to shake hands. 大部分的人都認為握手是禮貌。 • It is usually considered polite to shake hands. 握手通常被認為是有禮貌的。
	regard (*vt*) 把……看作	• Most people regard themselves as well brought up. 大部分的人都自認為教養良好。 • Most people are regarded as well brought up if they know the social conventions. 假如懂得社會常規，大部分的人就會被視為教養良好。
4	**forbid** (*vt*) 禁絕	• They were forbidden to get married. 他們被禁止結婚。 • Their marriage was forbidden. 他們的婚姻遭禁。
	prohibit (*vt*) 禁止	• Drugs are prohibited in this country. 毒品在這個國家是被禁止的。 • The laws in this country prohibit drug use. 這個國家的法律禁用毒品。
5	**almost** (*adv.*) 幾乎	• It is almost impossible to join the club. 要加入這個社團幾乎是不可能的。
	mostly (*adv.*) 大多數地	• The members are mostly very rich people. 會員大多數是非常有錢的人。

☆ child、children 和 childhood 這三個字在文法、意思和用法上都相當不同。

☆ 若是只提到一個人時要用 child，提到超過一個人時則用 children。children 是 child 的不規則複數，記住，一個 child，兩個 children。

☆ 而若是要提及兩歲到十二歲這段時期時，應使用 childhood。字尾 -hood 意指時期：adulthood「成年」，或是空間區域：neighborhood「鄰里」。

☆ convention、rule 和 law 的文法相同，但意思和用法略有不同。conventions「慣例」是不成文的規則，rules「規則」是成文和不成文都行，而 laws「法律」向來都是成文的規定。

☆ 若要描述在某個處境中正確的行為方式時，應使用 convention，其同義詞是

tradition。

☆ 若要描寫或談論關於一個小型組織的規範（如社團或健身房），就用 rule，這些規則通常是由成員本身來決定。rule 還能用於描述比賽或運動的規則。rule 也能用來描述把社會維繫在一起的不成文法律，規範可被接受或不可接受的行為或說法。注意，rule 要連同動詞 make、follow、obey 或 break 來用。

☆ 在寫作或談論國家的成文法典或商業交易時，使用 law。法律通常是由立法者在立法機構所通過，如果違反了法律，就會有刑責。law 也能用於談論或寫作自然定律，例如 laws of physics「物理定律」、the law of gravity「萬有引力定律」等等。注意，law 可連同動詞 pass、follow、obey 或 break 來用，但不能連同 make 來用。

☆ consider 和 regard 的意思和用法相同，但文法稍點不同。它們都意指以某種方式來思考某事，且都必須有受詞。

☆ consider 連同 to V 以被動來使用時，是在描述對一個情況的思考方式：He was considered to be against the law.；它也能以主動來使用：People considered it to be against the law.。注意，It was considered as against the law. 則是錯的。

☆ 想要描述以某種方式來看待一個情況時，應使用 regard。它要連同 as s/th 來用，如 They regarded him as a gentleman.、He was regarded as a gentleman. 正確，而 He was regarded to be a gentleman. 則是錯的。

☆ forbid 和 prohibit 的文法相同，但意思和用法略有不同。它們都意指某事不被允許，且都能用於被動語態。

☆ 當某事因為慣例或無關乎法律的非正式原因而不被容許時，使用 forbidden，其後必須接 to V。而當某事違反法律時，則使用 prohibited。

☆ almost 和 mostly 看起來似乎非常相似，因為都包含了單字 most，但其實它們在意思和用法上都非常不同。

☆ 當某事差不多是這樣的時候用 almost：It is almost lunchtime. 正確，It is mostly lunchtime. 則是錯的。

☆ 當某事是大部分的時候都會做時用 mostly：He is mostly quite polite. 正確，表示大部分的時候他都有禮貌。而 He is almost polite. 則是錯的。

在做下一個練習時，請仔細思考句意、文法和用法來選出正確的單字。

Task 42

請選出正確的單字來填入下列各句。

① **mostly/almost**

I _____ forgot to tell you.

② **laws/rules**

In most countries if you break the _____, you go to jail.

③ **laws/conventions**

In most countries if you break the social _____, you will not go to jail.

④ **mostly/almost**

It's _____ impossible to change social conventions.

⑤ **consider/regard**

Many people _____ it important to follow the rules.

⑥ **child/childhood**

My _____ was a happy one.

⑦ **forbidden/prohibited**

Parking in the managers' carpark is _____ by the management.

⑧ **almost/mostly**

People _____ follow the law.

⑨ **childs/children**

She had three _____.

⑩ **forbidden/prohibited**

Smoking in public areas is _____.

⑪ **rules/conventions**

Social _____ can be just as strict as laws.

⑫ **almost/mostly**

The club rules _____ don't allow this kind of behaviour.

⑬ **rule/law**

The _____ of gravity is one of the laws of physics.

⑭ **laws/rules**

The _____ of tennis are hard to follow.

⑮ **regarded/considered**

The social conventions are often _____ as just as important as the laws.

⑯ **rule/law**

They passed a _____ to stop this from happening.

⑰ **rules/laws**

We are going to make some new _____ for the club.

⑱ **child/children**

When I was a _____, I lived in the UK.

◇ 答案・中譯・說明   ◎ **Track 10.11**

① I almost forgot to tell you. 我差點忘了要告訴你。

② In most countries if you break the laws, you'll go to jail.
在大部分的國家如果違法了，你就會入獄。

③ In most countries if you break the social conventions, you will not go to jail.
在大部分的國家，如果違反了社會習俗，你並不會入獄。

④ It's almost impossible to change social conventions.
要改變社會習俗幾乎是不可能的。

⑤ Many people consider it important to follow the rules.
很多人認為遵守規則很重要。

⑥ My childhood was a happy one. 我的童年是快樂的。

⑦ Parking in the managers' carpark is forbidden by the management.
在經理人的停車場上停車受到管理階層所禁絕。

⑧ People mostly follow the law. 民眾大多會遵循法律。

⑨ She had three children. 她有三個孩子。

⑩ Smoking in public areas is prohibited. 公共場所禁止吸菸。

⑪ Social conventions can be just as strict as laws.
社會習俗可以像法律一樣嚴格。

⑫ The club rules mostly don't allow this kind of behaviour.
社團的規定大多不容許這種行為。

⑬ The law of gravity is one of the laws of physics.
萬有引力定律是物理學的定律之一。

⑭ The rules of tennis are hard to follow. 網球規則很難遵守。

⑮ The social conventions are often regarded as just as important as the laws.
社會習俗常被視為跟法律一樣重要。

⑯ They passed a law to stop this from happening.
他們通過了一項法律來阻止這種情況發生。

⑰ We are going to make some new rules for the club.
我們將為社團制訂一些新規則。

⑱ When I was a child, I lived in the UK. 我小時候是住在英國。

....

☆ 第 1、4 句選填 almost 是因為意思是「近乎」。第 8、12 句選用 mostly 則是
因為意指大部分的人或各種行為的大部分。

☆ 在第 2 句中提到了 jail「牢獄」，因此應該使用 laws；第 3、11 句需要

conventions 是因為 social conventions 乃非常常見的字詞組合；第 13 句需要 law 是因為短語 the law of gravity「萬有引力定律」；第 14 句講的是網球比賽，所以要用 rules；第 16 句用 law 是因為 pass；第 17 句需要 rule 則是因為動詞是 make 而非 pass，注意，law 不能連同 make 來用。

☆ 第 5 句選用 consider 是因為此句子的後半段有 to follow；而第 15 句選用 regarded 則是因為句子的後半段有 as s/th。

☆ 第 6 句中，說話者是在指稱他是孩子時的人生，因此要用 childhood；第 9 句提到有三個孩子，所以要用複數的 children；而第 18 句使用 child 則是因為 a。

☆ 第 7 句選用 forbidden 是因為，它實際上並非公法，而是這座停車場的私人規則；第 10 句用 prohibited 則是因為在公共場所吸菸實際上是有法律來阻絕。

　　最後我們還是要來練習從閱讀文章中找出這些容易搞混的單字。當你在文章中每找到一個單字，都必須停下來思考它是意指什麼、它的文法是什麼，以及它是如何使用的。

Task 43

請從 Task 1 和 Task 2 的閱讀文章中找出關鍵語庫 ❼ 列出的所有易混淆字詞，並留意它們在文章中是如何使用的。

Task 44

請練習用關鍵語庫 ❼ 的易混淆字詞來造句。

易混淆字詞	造句練習
child	
children	

childhood	
convention	
rule	
law	
consider	
regard	
forbid	
prohibit	
almost	
mostly	

在你結束這個單元之前，請將下列清單看過，確定你能將所有要點都勾選起來。如果有一些要點你還搞不清楚，請回頭再次研讀本單元的相關部分。

□ 我確實閱讀並理解了關於「道德」的長篇文章。

□ 我完全知道字彙在文章中是如何使用，並更加了解到要怎麼用單字來表達特定的主題。

□ 我已經學會 15 個關於「道德」主題的關鍵字，以及可與其搭配使用的動詞和形容詞。

□ 我已經練習使用這些搭配詞來描寫「道德」。

□ 我已經學到了一些同義詞，也了解在運用時需要注意的一些問題。

□ 我學到了很多關於這個主題可以運用的語塊，包括片語動詞以及名詞或動詞為同形的單字。

□ 我已經練習使用這些語塊。

□ 我學到了 5 個關於這個主題的慣用語，且知道如何運用。

□ 我已經理解在運用慣用語時需要特別注意的一些問題。

□ 關於這個主題，我已經能確實掌握一些易混淆字詞的用法。

PART
2

附錄 語庫索引 ❶

彙整本書各單元所有學過的字串以方便複習。

	5 V/N	10 chunks	
Unit 1 **The Environment**	〈P.048〉 aim cause focus help result	〈P.043〉 be a part of be capable of be concerned about be eager to be necessary to	be responsible for be suitable for have an opportunity to pay attention to take responsibility for
Unit 2 **Technology**	〈P.100〉 decrease increase impact access lack	〈P.095〉 be capable of be optimistic about the advantage of the benefit of the consequences of	the disadvantage of the effect of X on Y the problem with the risks of the solution to
Unit 3 **New Media**	〈P.150〉 post blog like livestream visit	〈P.145〉 make s/o V make s/o adj let s/o V keep Ving be difficult/easy/hard	listen to information about share s/th with s/o be/become addicted to block s/o
Unit 4 **Inequality**	〈P.203〉 value need change question start	〈P.197〉 be/put s/o at a disadvantage be better (for s/o) to V be better if v.p. be (un)fair that v.p. be (un)fair to V	give s/o s/th give s/th to s/o provide (s/o with) s/th the elderly the young
Unit 5 **Gender Issues**	〈P.255〉 balance challenge demand function respect	〈P.250〉 be acceptable (for s/o) to V(s/o) be familiar to be familiar with be in charge of be qualified to	be related to fight/go/be against have the right to V intention of Ving discriminate against

5 phrasal verbs	5 idioms	confused words
〈P.055〉 cut down on break out stamp out throw away chuck out	〈P.060〉 be caught between a rock and a hard place cut no ice a drop in the ocean light a fire under make waves	〈P.064〉 scenery/scene hard/hardly less/few method/way ___ing /___ed
〈P.107〉 break down turn off charge up sort out bring about	〈P.111〉 bells and whistles all singing, all dancing at the crossroads climb on the bandwagon fifth wheel	〈P.115〉 technique/technology supply/provide shortage/deficiency resolution/solution question/problem
〈P.157〉 put s/th up take s/th down scroll up scroll down hack into s/th	〈P.161〉 be cutting edge be light years ahead of be right on the button hit a roadblock move up a gear	〈P.164〉 apply for/apply s/th to s/th avoid/prevent spend/take worth/worthwhile raise/rise
〈P.211〉 cut back on come up with draw up bring about trickle down	〈P.215〉 be economical with the truth toe the line the body politic big bucks earn a living	〈P.219〉 cost/price worker/staff/labor wage/salary financial/economic work/job
〈P.263〉 rule out phase s/th in run up against spring from come out	〈P.267〉 a break with the past glass ceiling the status quo a man's man a new man	〈P.271〉 worsen/deteriorate expand/spread popular/common chance/opportunity solve/resolve

	5 V/N	10 chunks	
Unit 6 **Euthanasia** **and Medical** **Ethics**	〈P.311〉 burden cure practice pressure request	〈P.305〉 be ethical for s/o to care about care for take care of deal with	get rid of quality of life manage to v suffer from treat s/th with s/th
Unit 7 **GM Food and** **Science**	〈P.365〉 study test research use risk	〈P.358〉 be allergic to be good for be bad for be damaging to be made of	compared with pass s/th on to s/o worry about be worried about be resistant to
Unit 8 **Democracy and** **Government**	〈P.420〉 control limit measure protest support	〈P.415〉 be well-established be supposed to v be (im)possible to v be (un)willing to lead to	mean that reason for reason why relate to in general
Unit 9 **Individualism**	〈P.472〉 exchange hope influence offer sacrifice	〈P.467〉 an obstacle to be inspired by take s/th into account be the same as equate to	give priority to be united be successful be content with be content to
Unit 10 **Morality**	〈P.529〉 act blame claim form guide	〈P.524〉 be controversial be derived from be opposed to be relative to be unprincipled	be widespread in compared with consists of devote s/th to s/o explain s/th to s/o

5 phrasal verbs	5 idioms	confused words
〈P.319〉 pass out pass away come down with pull through get over	〈P.323〉 bitter pill to swallow just what the doctor ordered go/be under the knife behind s/o's back be up in arms about	〈P.327〉 be ill/be sick diagnosis/prognosis treatment/therapy prescribe/proscribe heal/recover
〈P.373〉 go off eat out turn out that live on look into	〈P.377〉 I wouldn't do it for all the tea in china put all your eggs in one basket best thing since sliced bread different kettle of fish food for thought	〈P.381〉 prediction/forecast view/perspective correct/appropriate amount/number most/most of the
〈P.427〉 stand by stand for carry out stand up for do away with	〈P.431〉 game plan have their work cut out between the devil and the deep blue sea play devil's advocate against s/o's better judgement	〈P.434〉 trend/tendency reduce/decrease aspect/side prohibit/inhibit function/cause
〈P.481〉 point out pull s/th off build on stay ahead of fall through	〈P.485〉 an/the average Joe be a high flier movers and shakers pull rank work the system	〈P.489〉 expand/spread rise/arise notion/theory affect/effect person/people
〈P.536〉 hit back lay into measure up to take s/th out on s/o let s/o off	〈P.541〉 all hell breaks loose devil may care as cold as ice as hard as nails as bold as brass	〈P.548〉 child/children/childhood convention/rule/law almost/mostly consider/regard forbid/prohibit

附錄 語庫索引 ❷

彙整本書各單元所有學過的關鍵名詞以方便複習。

Unit 1 Environment	Unit 2 Technology	Unit 3 New Media	Unit 4 Inequality	Unit 5 Gender Issues
biodiversity 029	accident 081	account 130	distribution 181	attitude 234
climate 030	appliance 081	bandwidth 130	economics 181	culture 235
conservation 030	battery 082	blogosphere 131	economy 182	discrimination 236
consumption 031	breakthrough 083	content 132	equality 183	dominance 237
deforestation 031	device 083	debate 133	government 184	gender 238
destruction 033	electricity 085	follower 135	investment 186	injustice 240
drought 033	electronics 086	hashtag 135	issue 187	law 240
ecosystem 034	engineer 086	influencer 136	legislation 188	marriage 241
emissions 034	functionality 087	information 137	market 189	parenthood 242
environment 035	innovation 088	journalism 138	poverty 190	reform 243
nature 037	machine 089	media 139	society 191	rights 245
pollution 038	machinery 090	news 140	tax 192	role 246
recycling 039	robot 091	opinion 141	taxation 193	sexism 246
resource 039	robotics 092	profile 142	wealth 194	stereotype 247
waste 040	transformation 092	site 142	welfare 195	tradition 248

Unit 6 Euthanasia and Medical Ethics	Unit 7 GM Food and Science	Unit 8 Democracy and Government	Unit 9 Individualism	Unit 10 Morality
advice *289*	advance *342*	authority *397*	ambition *450*	behaviour *505*
choice *290*	calories *343*	candidate *398*	argument *451*	code *506*
condition *291*	danger *344*	democracy *399*	aspect *452*	compromise *507*
consideration *291*	diet *344*	election *400*	aspiration *453*	conduct *508*
death *292*	food *345*	government *401*	civilization *454*	development *509*
decision *294*	evidence *347*	history *403*	disappointment *456*	evil *511*
ethics *295*	growth *348*	majority *404*	fulfilment *456*	good *512*
illness *295*	harm *349*	party *405*	group *457*	ideal *513*
opponent *296*	health *350*	policy *406*	happiness *458*	morality *514*
pain *297*	modification *350*	politician *407*	individual *459*	philosophy *515*
profession *299*	nutrition *352*	politics *408*	life *461*	principle *517*
recovery *300*	organism *353*	power *409*	potential *462*	standard *518*
suffering *301*	product *353*	revolution *410*	responsibility *463*	tradition *519*
support *301*	safety *354*	system *411*	selfishness *464*	values *520*
surgery *302*	science *355*	voter *412*	spectrum *464*	virtue *521*

國家圖書館出版品預行編目(CIP)資料

IELTS 高點：雅思制霸 7.0⁺ 字彙通 / Quentin Brand 作：
戴至中譯. -- 初版. -- 臺北市：波斯納出版有限公司, 2021.08
　　面：　　公分

　ISBN: 978-986-06066-5-2（平裝）

　1. 國際英語語文測試系統　　2. 考試指南

805.189　　　　　　　　　　　　　　　　110008611

IELTS 高點：雅思制霸 7.0⁺ 字彙通

作　　者 / Quentin Brand
譯　　者 / 戴至中
執行編輯 / 朱曉瑩

出　　版 / 波斯納出版有限公司
地　　址 / 台北市 100 館前路 26 號 6 樓
電　　話 / (02) 2314-2525
傳　　真 / (02) 2312-3535
客服專線 / (02) 2314-3535
客服信箱 / btservice@betamedia.com.tw
郵撥帳號 / 19493777
帳戶名稱 / 波斯納出版有限公司

總 經 銷 / 時報文化出版企業股份有限公司
地　　址 / 桃園市龜山區萬壽路二段 351 號
電　　話 / (02) 2306-6842

出版日期 / 2021 年 8 月初版一刷
定　　價 / 600 元
I S B N / 978-986-06066-5-2

貝塔網址：www.betamedia.com.tw

喚醒你的英文語感！

Get a Feel for English!

喚醒你的英文語感！

Get a Feel for English !

喚醒你的英文語感！

Get a Feel for English !